DREAMS
OF
SIN

A Devil's Trials Novel

Stephanie Gluck

Cover art and illustrations: Etheric Tales & Edits
www.etherictales.com

Editing: Krystal Nicol
https://www.krystalnicol-editing.com/

ISBN Paperback: 978-0-6459347-1-7
ISBN Electronic: 978-0-6459347-0-0

Oh, hey, AJ…
This one's for you!
Shut up and accept it.
You deserve it.
You deserve all the good things.

&

Ira & Mr. Puff, always

In memoriam Heather Mitchell.

Also, by Stephanie Gluck:

THE DEVIL'S TRIALS

Feast of Samael

Heist of Haures

Ire of War

Tower of Hubris

Dreams of Sin

THE FOUR REALMS

Death's Stalker

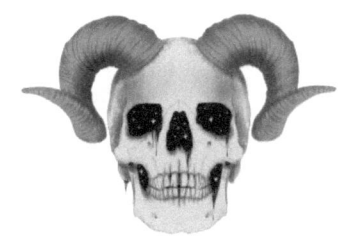

Chapter One

The acrid, jarring scent of smoke and charred human flesh pulled me from the depths of a dreamless sleep. With a gasp, I bolted upright on a small pallet bed in search of bright, flickering flames. My heart thundered against my ribcage. My head spun with the threat of oblivion. The explosion, I could hear it. Fear clotted in my throat, but not a single scream passed my lips.

I'd been dreaming of fire. I needed to escape. The memory of my skin burning haunted me. I tasted ash and burning feathers, phantom on the edge of my tongue. It still felt like I was there, crushed beneath an angel. Flames licking at my vulnerable skin.

The agony that seared through my left side was no mere memory. My skin felt too tight and sore for comfort. I wanted to rake my nails across it, open my skin and free my discomfort. When I pressed my palm against the pain, I could feel thick bandages. They hid the damage. Wrapped around so much of my body that I couldn't tell what lay beneath them. Only feel the itchy, crawling sensations of my skin.

The pain intensified and I cried out. My head spun, making me breathless. Unable to hold my weight, I slumped against the wall. My hair stuck to my throat. Sweat beading across my skin. Breathing in sharp, panicked bursts. The smell of smoke caught in my nose.

Despite the pain, I kicked at the sheets. They tangled around my thighs, trapping me. The heat was unbearable. I was suffocating beneath the flames — and the danger they represented — the fire had to be close.

Tears rolled down my cheeks, falling thick and fast. I struggled to pull myself together. I needed to get free. The last thing I remembered was Pride peeling his burnt body from atop me. Any fire that could burn an angel of sin could destroy me. I was fragile and only human. I didn't know where I was, but I needed to get somewhere safe. The world rocked with the next explosion, and this time the flames burned me through.

"Octavia?"

He was quiet, but the sound made me flinch. A wild shriek poured from my throat and I curled into a tight ball. I couldn't stay upright without the world spinning on its axis. The dark spots in my vision grew, making it hard to focus. Bile crept, acidic and unwelcome, up the back of my throat.

"Fire," I whispered, my bone-dry lips cracking on the word. A tendril of smoke danced in front of my eyes and my entire body jerked. My throat seared with pain as I repeated, "Fire!"

"There's no fire."

The stranger stepped forward, blocking the flash of light beyond the doorway. The entirety of his body struggled to fit within my vision. Stocky and imposing, he had a sharp chin, covered in a wiry orange beard. A smoke dangled from between his full lips, the end of it burning with an orange glow. The source of smoke that set my heart racing.

He inhaled, glancing at the open door behind him. When he exhaled, a cloud of soft, pink smoke poured out, seeping into the space between us. Different from the explosion, where it had been the black and grey of death and decay.

The man took a step closer to me. I cringed as far away as my broken body would allow. He was a stranger, and he was a threat. Every time I moved, though, it felt like I was going to pass out.

I recognized his simple black uniform, marked with a chalky white handprint. It stood for the murderers who had brought down a palace while I stood within it. The rebels that had killed and caused pain.

"Don't," I croaked. The word felt like a blade running down my dry throat. My half-numb fingers clawed at the threadbare sheet. He was here to kill me. I was certain of it. He had no other motivation to come for me. I was burning up from the inside out. "No!"

The man sighed. His eyes rolled as he crouched beside the pallet. His forearms rested on his knees while he studied me. Long, reddish-brown hair spilled over his shoulders, one side of his head shaved close to his scalp. He was in no hurry. Taking another drag of the smoke and rubbing at his chin.

When he plucked the smoke from his lips to exhale, he held it out to me. The too-sweet smell of the pale smoke flowed over my face. Tiny freckles were scattered all over his face, as well as across his neck and arms. He had more freckles than there were stars in the sky, I thought, but they didn't make him pretty. Especially not as his eyes narrowed and he scowled in my direction.

"Chuckleweed?" he offered. He jerked the smoke in my direction.

My fear stole my ability to speak, no matter how badly I wanted to scream. I couldn't move. With the pallet tucked into the corner of the room, there was no escape. It trapped me in, with the bulk of his body barricading my only exit. Pain stabbed through my chest every time I breathed too deep, let alone moved. I wasn't going anywhere.

"I assume that's a no." He set the smoke between his thick lips again. "Shame. It'd probably help with everything you're feeling."

My lips moved, testing my ability to form words before I dared try to speak. My voice still felt wrong. It sounded husky. As damaged as the rest of me. When I whispered beneath my breath, he didn't seem to hear.

The man picked up the pillow I'd knocked to the floor, and he held it between both hands. His brow creased and he studied it as if he were considering the best way to smother me.

"Who are you?" I asked, louder now.

His head jerked up, and he regarded me carefully. He took two more drags before dropping the smoke and stomping it out. "Nobody."

He shifted, and I flinched. The movement caused the nerves along my left side to zap with unimaginable pain. I cried out in half a scream.

The man and the rest of the world slipped out of focus for a moment. His face was a blurry mix of reds and browns, and I couldn't regain stability.

"Devils, Tate!" A familiar voice thundered from the doorway, too loud for such a small space. "What the fuck are you doing in here?!" The man disappeared from view, as the intruder jerked him back. "Get out!"

I struggled to breathe through the pain as it seared through my body. I took ragged breaths. Each exhale dragged with it a whine of pure agony.

The pallet creaked when Niklaus kneeled upon it, but there was no way for me to move away. I couldn't do anything but feel. His tattooed fingers delicately pushed strands of sweat-dampened hair from my tear-stained cheeks. The blurriness faded, and his familiar jewel-green eyes sharpened in my vision. It was comforting to see a familiar face.

"Octavia, love…" Niklaus stroked the side of my face. He clucked his tongue, reaching for a small glass bottle beside the bed.

I tried to reply but could only cry in pain.

"You shouldn't be awake yet. Drink this," he coaxed. He pressed the bottle to my dry lips. A disgustingly bitter tonic slid over my tongue. Thick and earthy, it tasted like mud. I recoiled, but Niklaus grasped my chin and held me in place. He made me drink mouthfuls of the tincture. Until it dribbled down my chin.

The pain in my limbs numbed, and a blissful haze swept through me. It started at my feet and rose through my body until everything felt deliciously numb. Somehow, I was floating, drifting away.

Niklaus slid his arm around my shoulders and gently lowered me back onto the pallet, cradling my head to place the pillow beneath me as I fought against the growing heaviness in my limbs.

His bright, haunting green eyes were the last thing I saw before I succumbed to the darkness again.

When I woke again, the sound of boisterous laughter echoed in the distance. The air was uncomfortably still, the room filled with the smell of sweat. I blinked at the roof, covered in peeling paint and a water stain, attempting to identify my location. This place was a far cry from Pride Palace.

Niklaus sat in a chair at the end of my bed, eyes closed and chin tucked to his chest. His chest rose and fell as he slept. He looked so peaceful that I decided I wouldn't wake him.

Wriggling my toes, I took a moment to get my bearings, cautiously testing the movement in my limbs. My muscles were stiff and unused, causing a dull ache. My skin had a definite tightness that I couldn't ignore.

Carefully sitting up, the thin sheet pooling around my waist. I pushed my greasy hair off my face, feeling overwhelmed. I could feel the uneven ends where it had burned away.

Niklaus snored loudly but didn't stir. I slowly climbed out of the bed. Standing wasn't as easy as I'd expected. Fatigue hit me hard, making my legs tremble. Bracing myself, I pushed up off the bed, hands outstretched to steady myself as the spinning sensation faded. Until I found the courage to step forward.

Every step took effort. I staggered forward, off-kilter, towards the door. I walked with the grace of a toddler, stumbling twice.

Pausing with my hand on the knob, I glanced back, watching Niklaus sleep. I didn't want him to wake. The thought of facing everything that had happened was overwhelming. The thought of asking him for help felt shameful. I sneaked out into the eerie dark halls of the house when I was certain he was still fast asleep.

It took me a long time to find the bathroom. Longer still to find the front door, fumble with the latch and find relative freedom. Where I was didn't really matter because it wasn't where I was supposed to be. I had to find my way back to the palace, or wherever the surviving competitors had gone.

Staggering outside, I inhaled deeply for the first time. The chill of the night shocked my lungs. I dropped to my knees on the soft grass. I gasped for air, realising I hadn't been outside in a long time. The chill seeped into my bones, but it kept me alert, forcing me to stay awake.

Slowly, I straightened, battling dizziness to get my bearings. The tiny village before me was unfamiliar. Small log cottages were arranged in a half circle. I could smell roasting meat, could hear the spit of dripping fat as it sizzled against the fire. My mouth watered and my stomach rumbled. I clenched my fist against my stomach, hoping it would stay silent if Niklaus came searching for me. The smoke merging with the clouds made me uneasy, and I felt the urge to flee from the fire.

Standing a second time was difficult. The echoing sound of laughter in the distance gave me enough motivation to get moving. I didn't need to face the rebellion while struggling to find my feet. I edged my way around each of the buildings. Nearby, a man yelled, and I flinched, pressing myself up against a house.

My heart pounded. I assumed they had taken me from the aftermath of battle, but nobody had demanded I stay. Nobody even knew I was awake.

The rough panelling on the side of the house caught against my thin shirt and scraped my arm. Tiny splinters embedded beneath my skin.

Unsteady, I circled the next house and collided with the hard body of a man who had been moving silently in the shadows.

"Fuck!" he cried.

His strong hands grasped my shoulders and he tried to steady us both. Not quickly enough, though, as I tripped over his feet and the added momentum forced us both to the ground. Crashing into him left me dazed.

"Get off me!" he snapped. I rolled through the grass with a pathetic cry, landing just near the dying embers of his crudely rolled smoke.

The man climbed to his feet. His fingers raked through the long length of his coppery hair, pushing it from his face. I blinked blearily up at him. He appeared familiar, as if he had come from one of my dreams, but I couldn't remember who he was or how I knew him.

"Wait," he muttered. "Octavia?"

Sitting up, I squeezed my eyes closed, bracing myself for the possibility of passing out. My head throbbed, and the world narrowed to a pinpoint. After five deep breaths, everything settled. "How do you know my name?"

He scrubbed his palms across his face, looking distressed. He didn't answer my question, even as I gazed up at him, struggling to piece everything together.

"Fuck me," he groaned. "Heira is going to kill me."

"Probably not," I said. He didn't offer to help me stand. I forced myself to my hands and knees, praying to Samael that I wouldn't pass out as I stood. My balance was shot. I swayed on the spot but somehow stayed upright. Bits of grass clung to my body.

The man glared at me, his amber gaze fierce. "Not if I return you to him."

"What?" I asked.

"You heard me." He barrelled towards me before I could protest. He quickly grabbed my waist and threw me over his shoulder, causing pain to sear down my side. The wind was knocked right out of me. "Back you go."

"No!" I shrieked. Finding a burst of energy, I slammed my fists against his back. Not that it did much good. He kept walking. "No! Put me down!"

He ignored me, of course. I let out a bloodcurdling scream. It drew attention as I wanted, but the villagers didn't offer any help. They openly snickered at me, dangling down the brute's back. I didn't know why I bothered. They weren't my friends or allies. I was sure they were my enemy.

"You stole Heira's woman?" one man laughed. "That's a death wish and a half, mate!"

"I'm not his—" The man carrying me shifted, cutting off my protest.

"You don't talk to them," he warned in a low voice. "Just shut up, or you'll get us all in the shit. The last thing we need is Heira with his pants in a knot."

"You're a grumpy bastard," I muttered into the small of his back. "I hope you fall in a hole and die."

"I hope I'm still carrying you when that happens," he snapped back.

He jostled me again, and I cried out. He set me on the ground, making me stumble into another person. The man behind me smelled familiar, with soft hints of tobacco and oranges. He forcefully pulled me against him, holding me upright.

The man with copper hair wiped his hands on his shirt as if I had made them dirty. I glared at his theatrics, but he paid me no attention now. He stared at the man behind me. "Keep your bitch in your own yard, Heira. I don't need her skulking around my place looking to hide because she can't stand the sight of you."

Niklaus' grip on my arms tightened, his nails biting at my skin. He roughly shoved me behind him. It blocked my view of the freckled man as he got in his face. "Have we got a problem, Maksymilian?"

"Don't call me that!" The man snapped. "I'm the one doing *you* a favour. I caught your little prisoner running away. I could have just let her piss off into the night."

Niklaus shoved the man backwards. forcing him down the front steps. "Get the fuck out of here! For all I know, you were creeping into her room again, looking to steal her!"

"You want to go, Heira?" He clenched his fists and raised them at Niklaus. "I'll fucking annihilate you, pretty boy. It's two against one, after all." He wiggled his fingers mockingly. I couldn't help but stare at Niklaus' scarred stump. The hand I cut off.

Niklaus swung first, and they tumbled to the ground. A mess of flying fists and bone slamming into flesh. Losing a hand hadn't made Nik any less brutal in his attack, his rage shining through.

They rolled through the grass, hissing insults with so much venom that I knew their issues went far deeper than my adventure in the night. It had nothing to do with me. I was just an excuse.

A deafening whistle scattered the crowd, and a somewhat familiar man entered the yard. He held a half-gnawed drumstick tight in his fist. It was the stocky man we had met before the Wrath trials, Chester. His presence proved that I was in the heart of the Wastelands Rebellion.

He wiped his greasy fingers on his shirt and waved the drumstick at the fighting men before attacking them. Three harsh kicks. He didn't seem to aim at either in particular, but caught them both at least once. Each strike was hard enough that I could hear the sickening crunch of bone. The impact of the blows forced the brawling men apart.

They rolled to the side, panting hard and glaring daggers at one another.

"Stop that," he growled. He spat on the grass beside them. "Fighting between yourselves like sin-possessed madmen. Pathetic! As bad as those devil-damned angels."

Chester brandished the roasted meat at the crowd. It was a sweeping gesture that caused them to turn and wander away until only the four of us remained. "Maksymilian, piss off home. Niklaus, you better lock her the fuck back up."

Niklaus rose to his knees, a muscle in his jaw thrumming. He gave both men a dark look before storming towards me. As he approached me, I reflexively stepped back, flinching away from the wrath in his eyes.

"Come on," he barked. He pulled me behind him into the house. Flinging the door closed, so hard that the small glass pane rattled and cracked. It felt like an ominous sign that his patience was fracturing, too. Nervously, I watched him.

"Nik," I said, using his name as a warning. "You need to calm down."

It was possibly the worst thing I could have said. His expression turned blank, his lips pressed into a thin line. A storm raged in his eyes, the anger he couldn't suppress. That same impulsive, burning emotion had him failing before Wrath.

"Calm. Down," He repeated, tone glacial. He stepped towards me. "You want me to calm-the-fuck-down?"

He moved towards me, and I tried to keep my distance, but the door blocked me. Niklaus quickly cornered me against the cracked glass, making me anxious. A muscle twitched in his jaw.

"It would be an improvement," I said. He braced his scarred arm on the door over my head, caging me in with his body. He used his weight to keep me pinned. His arm slipped past my waist, and Niklaus deliberately locked the door.

The click suggested I wouldn't be leaving anytime soon. I stared at him, and he stared back unflinchingly.

"Why did you go to Maksymilian?" he asked, finally, in a deceptively calm tone. "Tell me the truth."

"Is that his name?" I asked, avoiding eye contact by looking at the ink on his throat. Niklaus had always been difficult to look in the eye.

"Answer the question."

"You want the truth?" I asked. I had faced Pride without fear, but Niklaus' icy demeanour was worse.

His lips thinned, his jaw tightening. The pressure of his body against mine ignited pain. I pressed my palm against the thick bandages secured around my abdomen, taking slow, deep breaths.

"That's what I asked for, yes," Niklaus said, brow raising.

"Huh," I shrugged as he waited for his answer. "Tough shit. You don't always get what you want."

His hand slammed against the door, and the glass rattled again. I could almost imagine that crack growing wider. Despite all my bravado, I cringed. Niklaus' expression flattened, tightening with fury. "Tell me."

"I didn't go to him," I said, finally. "I didn't go to anyone. I was just trying to get the hell out of here. Where am I, Niklaus?"

He ignored the question, countering with one of his own, "Why would you want to leave? I got you out of there. I got you away from Pride." He leaned close. "You're free, Octavia."

My throat felt constricted; the truth of the matter was that I would never be free. Pride ensnared me with commands, waiting

19

for my failure. Samael also owned a piece of my soul. The iridescent cuff on my wrist was dented but still firmly intact.

"Nik, no. I'm not!" I said, in a tone so sharp that he flinched. "You just locked me in here."

His nostrils flared. He took me by the arm and dragged me forward, spinning to switch our positions. Niklaus leaned back, folding his arms across his chest, staring down at me.

"You can go anywhere you want," Niklaus said.

"Oh, really?"

"Anywhere inside the house," he amended.

My hands dropped to my sides, the reality of my prison sinking in. Closing my eyes, I wished upon the devil that when I opened them, I'd be back in Pride Palace. No such luck. There was only the man from my childhood, and his stubborn, angry stare. "Okay, Nik."

Turning away, I slunk back into the house. The sound of the door unlocking was loud, opening and closing before it clicked a third time. Niklaus had left me in this house alone. I slid to the floor, back against the wall, knees pulled to my chest.

Another day, another cage. I hadn't been free for a very long time.

The overwhelming itchiness of my skin pulled me from my near-catatonic contemplation. It was enough that I found my feet and headed for the bathroom. It had a tarnished mirror but still good enough to see my reflection. I'd purposefully avoided it.

I stood in front of it, unable to look up and take myself in. It reminded me of the maze of mirrors Pride had forced me through. Of telling Helina I would beat her through the trials — only to step over her broken, burnt body days later. It had been a threat that came true.

My reflection had appeared on every polished surface of Pride's grand palace. Even after the great stained-glass windows had shattered into tiny fragments. They'd still reflected my image back to me.

I concentrated on peeling off the tape from the bandages. They wrapped around my left upper arm, shoulder, chest, breasts, abdomen, hips, and left thigh. My nails had grown since the night of the attack. I could tell I had been asleep for a while based on the long, rough edges which helped to pick the tape free. I held my breath as I ripped it off in shreds, the sticky underside pinching against my tender skin.

I unbound the cotton bandages, closing my eyes at the sight of my discoloured skin peeking out. I quickly pulled each bandage, panic increasing my heartbeat.

I was all too aware of the change of texture beneath my fingertips, even though I refused to look. My skin itched again, and it was hard not to rake my nails along the length of my thigh. I ignored everything else and focused on the cloth on my jaw and neck.

I stood naked and alone in the bathroom. My scars bared for an audience of one. Unshed tears stung in my eyes but still I refused to look and see the truth in the mirror.

These were the consequences that the attack on Pride Palace had wrought, not for those who attacked him. But for people like me — who had been standing too close to the angel. Niklaus and his band of wretched men might have damaged me more than the angels ever had.

'*Octavia Nox,*' Samael purred in my ear. The sound of his voice filled me with violent relief. He was here, and maybe that meant everything would be okay. '*Open your eyes.*'

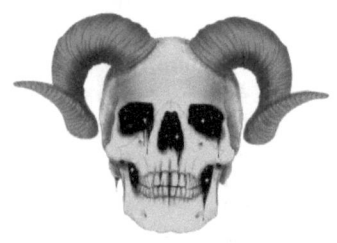

Chapter Two

It was easy to obey. Simple to do exactly what Samael wanted of me. Not because Pride had coaxed me unwillingly into obedience through his never-ending demands, but because I wanted to please the devil. I was eager to hear him praise me. I had missed him in a way that felt dangerous to admit.

Relinquishing the comfort of refusing to look, I opened my eyes and stared into the mirror. The distorted image of myself shifted. Her eyes widened and her lips parted as I studied my body. Or more specifically, my skin.

It was a mottled mix of pink, purple and reddened scars with raised ridges and knotted edges that covered my body. They spanned across my collarbone, spilling down the front of my upper arm and curving around my waist, hip and most of my left thigh. They collared my throat and wrapped the left side of my cheek and jaw with shiny discolouration.

They didn't hurt, but I still flinched when I dared touch the textured skin. I traced my fingers over the thickened tissue, a reminder of pain and misfortune. My heart sank at the sight of myself, of the discoloured patches that the kiss of flames had left behind.

I'd lost weight, and muscle, hard-earned in the Wrathlands war. I could see the outline of my ribs and my skin had an unhealthy pale sheen. Beyond my marred body, I looked unwell.

"I'm ruined," I whispered. I shrank from the sight of myself as tears welled in my eyes, emotion burning the back of my throat.

Samael growled softly. A reprimand. *'I didn't think you would be so vain. Did you not pass the Trial of Pride?'*

"I'm not!" I protested, voice rough with emotion. Quickly, I reached for the oversized shirt and tugged it back over my head. A shield between me and my reflection. "I just... I don't want the reminder. Every time I look at it, I'll remember Pride crushed against me, suffocating me. The way the tiny pieces of glass sliced into my skin, and the smell of burning feathers. I'll remember the ruin and torment and murder. The pain... Samael."

He let out a chilling hiss. A shiver rolled from my scalp and down the back of my neck at the devil's displeasure. *'Every time you look at it, you'll be grateful that you survived, that these markings on your skin are the worst of it. You could be dead, like many others.'*

I turned my back on the mirror and Samael.

"You don't understand," I told him, irritated by his insistence that I was fine. I was not fine. My body may have crudely stitched itself together, but my mind was fractured. This, of everything I'd endured, felt like it could be my breaking point.

Samael was quiet. Crawling back into bed, with my knees drawn to my chest, I stared at the wall. Stroking my fingers along the ridges of my fresh scars.

'What I understand,' Samael said, quietly. *'Is that humanity is incredibly adaptable and foolishly tenacious. I have seen men*

and women learn to survive the presence of sin on earth. Your people learned to walk again after we literally severed their legs from their bodies. They persevered when things were difficult. Humans rise again after grief to continue on for their loved ones, their hearts keep beating despite their insistence that they shattered. I have seen them breathe in spite of the magic in the air, and the way it settles heavy and suffocating in their lungs...'

Sniffling, I squeeze my eyes closed, trying to shove him from my mind. I wanted nothing more than the quiet of my own thoughts, despite being relieved to have him back. I needed space to process everything. "Well, I have seen people die, over and over again, just because life is too hard!" I cried. "We're not all the strong sort of human."

'Which type of human do you want to be, Octavia?' He asked.

I pulled the sheet over my head. As if that would block him out. As if he were more than a voice inside my head. "I can't be like those people. I can't! Just leave me alone, Samael."

'Why not?' The devil pressed, an edge of urgency in his tone, as if he truly wanted me to understand but I was missing his point. He always sounded like that though, always so sure that he was right. *'You are no more or less magical than them. You all breathe the same air. Face the same challenges.'*

As I sobbed, Samael finally let me be. His presence slipped away, leaving me alone in the echo chamber of my mind.

I missed him the moment he was gone, regretting ever wishing him away. Niklaus didn't come back that night, and I spent hours choking on my loneliness.

Amid my self-pity, Niklaus woke me by shaking my shoulder.

Sleepily, I blinked up at him. My head was pounding, and my mouth felt bone dry. I licked at my lips. "What do you want?"

Niklaus frowned and looked at me as if I'd grown two heads. "I thought you'd be hungry."

He'd been delivering food twice a day for the past week. Every time he tried to strike up a conversation, but I didn't want to talk. I barely wanted to exist.

He seemed angrier and more prone to temper since we parted ways. It was as if Wrath's influence was implanted deeply within him. I wondered if, as her forfeit, he fully embodied Lady Wrath.

We'd never been friends. Our brief encounters in Ilrea were purely sexual, with no room for conversation. Through the trials, we'd been antagonistic. Niklaus and I struggled with simple conversation. We had nothing in common.

He often left me locked away in his house. Loneliness had become a festering wound inside my soul.

Irritation rippled down my spine, and I glared at him. I pulled the sheet up to my chin like a shield. "What? Now you care?" I asked. "Why not drop it and run like every other time?"

His throat bobbed as he swallowed down his initial reaction. His lips moved slowly, and I realised he was counting to three, calming himself. It appeared to take an extreme amount of effort.

"You think I don't care, Octavia?" he asked. "I pulled shards of glass from your body for hours. I bandaged your wounds even when you screamed and scratched at me. I devils-damned nursed you back to health and you have the balls to act like I don't care."

The overwhelming anger within me ebbed away, replaced with a soft thread of guilt. I didn't know he'd done any of those things. I'd never even thought about who must have tended to my wounds. "I don't remember any of that."

"Well..." From the way Niklaus swallowed and glanced away, I wasn't the only one feeling guilty. "We had to drug you. A lot. You kept screaming and you just wouldn't stop. Chester said it'd be the best way to let you rest and heal properly."

Slowly, I sat up, staring at him as I tried to correlate the dark void in my memory with what he'd claimed had happened. No wonder I'd felt like death when I'd woke up. "Chester said what…" Chester looked like he barely knew the sum of one and one. Let alone what was best for healing. "Devils, Nik, how long did you drug me for?"

Niklaus bit the metal ring pierced through his full lower lip, toying with it, until I couldn't look anywhere else. It was new and distracting. I wished he'd stop playing with it so I could focus.

"Seven weeks," he admitted.

My back hit the wall as I flinched. Pure shock wrenched hoarse words from my throat. "Seven weeks?!" I hissed. "Nik! Tell me you're lying!"

"I'm not," he said, unabashedly. He sat back, arms folded, daring me to argue. "You needed that time to get better. I won't apologise for it."

"I should be at the next trial by now." I pressed my hands to my flushed cheeks and licked my lips again. They were flaky and cracked beneath my tongue. An acrid horror was pooling in my veins. "I might never catch up."

Niklaus watched me lick at my lips. He picked up a mug from beside his chair, holding it out in offering. I was almost tempted to ask him if he drugged it.

"You're not going to the next trial," he told me, calmly. "You're going to stay here and help us win this war on the devil. Bigger things are going on than some competition, Octavia."

My thirst won out. Clutching the mug, I drank deeply. The bitter tang of old, cold tea burned down my throat. It didn't matter, greedily, I drained it dry. "You don't tell me what to do. I don't want to stay here."

'Yes, you do,' Samael corrected, surprising me as he intruded on the conversation. I should have known he'd be listening. He rarely wasn't. *'You want to stay just a little longer and be my eyes in this camp. I'm curious about this supposed rebellion. I want to know what they have planned.'*

"Octavia," Niklaus spoke over the murmurings of the devil in my head. He said my name in a pained manner, wishing I would just agree. Maybe he'd been expecting me to argue. "You don't have to continue with the trials. You can stay here and join the rebellion, I promise. Chester and I have discussed it. We'll keep you safe here."

Loosening a breath, I stared at the door across the room to stop my head from spinning. It was difficult to work out what I wanted, despite the demands of both Niklaus and the devil.

My stomach added its own thoughts about the situation, grumbling loudly enough to make Niklaus' brows rise. He shook his head, hair falling across his eyes, obscuring their dazzling green. I pressed my hand against my stomach, blushing. "Don't look at me like that. I'm hungry!"

He rose, holding out one tattooed hand. When I hesitated to take it, he cocked his head to one side and narrowed his eyes. "Chester says if you want to eat, you need to do it with the rest of us. No more private dining."

Somehow, I thought Chester had said as much in a less polite way. I wanted to point out that I hadn't asked to eat in the privacy of this room. They had locked me in here. My rumbling stomach couldn't be denied, though. So, I took his hand.

Niklaus pulled me out of the bed. His eyes flicked down to my naked legs, and warmth spread through my cheeks. Automatically, I tugged the hem of the shirt, pulling it down to hide the burns on my thigh. The only saving grace to being locked inside was hiding away amidst my self-consciousness.

"I'll find you something to wear," Nik said, gruffly. He disappeared down the hall and reappeared a moment later with a soft grey pair of pants. I held onto his shoulder for balance while pulling the drawstring tight. They were his size, and I'd barely put any weight back on in the past week.

"They're a bit big," I commented, needlessly. Bending to roll them up at the ankles so I didn't trip over the hem. "Warm, though."

Niklaus said nothing but stared at me, bright-eyed and expectant.

It took me a beat to realise he was waiting for me to thank him. With a sense of selfish pleasure, I denied him, staring blandly right back. The silence became awkward, but he looked away first.

I knew he wasn't averting his eyes from my scars, but the cruel whisper of self-consciousness that lived in my soul told me he was. I shifted awkwardly, wrapping my arms around my middle in a tight hug.

"Let's get you fed," Niklaus prompted, holding out a hand and waiting until I took it. I couldn't win by refusing to take his hand, given his stubborn expression. His fingers slid between mine as he held my hand tightly, looking for a moment like the teenager he'd once been. Back when my life had revolved around my infatuation with him, when my desires and problems had been so simple.

He tugged me down the hall, through the door and off the patio. Effortlessly leading me through the rough gravel pathways of the little town as if he had lived here his entire life. People smiled at him while I tried to hide behind his body.

We stopped at a campfire. Our late approach drew attention, and I cringed beneath the scrutiny. It was painfully reminiscent of the Wrath camps. There were logs set out around the fire and bodies perched lazily atop them, chewing and chatting all at once. The sound of sizzling fat and the smell of roasting meat made my stomach growl.

"She lives," Chester crowed through a mouthful of food. Half of his dinner was spilled down his front. "Lucky that, since Heira went to such lengths to steal you away from Pride." He sucked droplets of fat from each of his stubby fingers. When I didn't respond he waved them haphazardly in our direction. "Go. Sit. Eat."

Once he gave permission, the group shuffled to make room for us. None of them spoke to me, but they passed along tin bowls filled with meat.

I sat cross-legged behind Niklaus, where he perched on the log, keeping my distance from the flames. The memories of blistering pain and excruciating heat were too hard to ignore if I went close. I couldn't risk a floating ember setting me alight. I couldn't go through that pain again.

Clutching my tin bowl like a lifeline, I peered at the food dubiously. After dining with Pride, night after night, it looked like something that had been chewed up and spat back out. No better or worse than the other meals Niklaus had delivered.

"What is it?" I asked.

A woman on Niklaus' left sniffed, tossing her long, dark hair over her shoulder and narrowing her eyes at me. "Why? I don't suppose you're in any position to be picky."

"Verona, chill out." Niklaus nudged her, flashing a smirk. "It's just forest pig. We eat a lot of pig out here, and snakes. Birds, if we can catch them. Chester likes the symbolism of eating the mark of the sins."

My nose wrinkled, but the woman — Verona — had been right. I had no room to be picky, especially not as my stomach rumbled in loud demand again. It seemed like a bad omen, inviting trouble, to eat the symbols of the seven sins so blatantly. If that were true, I could only hope all the misfortune went directly to Chester.

I scooped the hot meat from the bowl and ate it. It was fatty, chewy, but it didn't taste any worse than roasted toad or half-cooked potatoes. I'd eaten much worse. Only after the first swallow did I realise just how ravenous I actually felt, swallowing the rest down as quickly as I could.

Until Niklaus tugged sharply at a lock of my hair, reaching over my shoulder to pluck the bowl from my grip with two or three mouthfuls left in it.

"Hey!" I protested. I went to snatch it back, but he held it out of my reach. In order to get it, I'd have to cross the log and move closer to the fire, which I was completely unwilling to do. "Give that back!"

"You need to slow down," he said. He ate the rest of my food, and my jaw dropped at his audacity. "All you've had is tea and soup for weeks. You're going to make yourself sick."

He wasn't wrong. My stomach was already roiling, twisting and turning in protest. My nose wrinkled, and I clenched my teeth tightly. Unwilling to admit out loud that he was right.

"Whatever," I muttered, fisting my greasy hands in my lap. Now that I'd eaten, all I wanted to do was retreat to the house and get away from curious stares. No matter how hard I tried to ignore them, these people kept glancing over at me.

'Stay,' Samael coaxed as Chester wiped his hands down his front and stood. 'I want to watch them.'

It was on the tip of my tongue to make a crack about the devil being a perve, but I swallowed it down. It wasn't the right time, and I wasn't sure if Samael would appreciate the cheeky barb when everything else felt so rocky. If I didn't get out of here, I might lose him altogether.

Chester cleared his throat, flicking something at the fire that caused it to pop and sizzle in response. I flinched back. He'd proved once before that he wasn't against setting things on fire to make a point. What a point the destruction of Pride Palace had been.

"Well, lads," he said. "We've got news from the border of the Greedlands. Our men set off one nice little bang and a whole mine has collapsed in. According to our sources, it'll damage an entire section of the Greed economy. Hit the bastard where it hurts!"

The group cheered, and suddenly, my heart squeezed tight in my chest, searing with enough pain that I choked on it. My hand pressed to my heart, rubbing in slow circles.

Niklaus turned to glance back at me. "What is it?" he asked, sounding impatient.

"Nothing," I muttered, ducking my head.

It wasn't entirely true. My blood was turning hot and cold as I remembered Boyd saying my brother had a job in the Greedlands. Most people who went there mined for the treasures Lord Greed was so desperate to possess, but what if Mason had been squashed beneath Chester's ambition to destroy? If this man had taken the rest of my family from me, I'd... Well, I'd never even know. I didn't know where the rest of the Nox family had ended up, or if they were alive.

"My sources also tell me," Chester continued, pacing around the fire. The light of the flames cast shadows across his face, accentuating his features in a way that spoke of darkness and deceit. "That Pride still hasn't resurrected his famed glass tower. It's still in pieces across his city, a representation that we humans fought back. Everyone who sees it will know that we took down, Pride. We're making progress, lads!"

"Burn the sins!" The group cheered again, a loud symphony of noise. They beat their hands against their thighs and tossed their bowls against the ground to create even more noise.

"Now," Chester continued, not missing a beat. A wide and ugly smile stretched across his face. "We move on to the next phase. You should all be ready for this one, lads. The half of you that I spoke to earlier today are on recruitment. You need to intercept the trial mongrels once they leave Desidia and convert them to our cause — by any means necessary!" He lifted a hand, pointing a gnarled finger at me. "Kidnap them, if you have to, she's proof that it's worked once before."

He stared at me, making an example, and his followers turned to look, making me blush. I'd rather have the ground swallow me up than have them stare. I wouldn't have said I was converted to their cause, just damaged by the process. I was wise enough to recognise it was the safer choice not to argue. To let Chester use me for his little performance.

Chester was unfazed by my lack of a reaction. "The rest of you will be with me. We march on Eternis in a season's time. We'll slay the devil himself. Humanity will take back what's owed to them! We'll reclaim our power and bury their magic! The sins will bow before us!"

Their cheers turned into wild screams, and Chester beamed.

'Hmm,' Samael mused. He'd been so quiet that I'd forgotten he was listening in. *'I do wonder how that man expects he'll slay me. You should get yourself allocated to the "Kill the Devil army" and learn all their nefarious plans.'*

I wondered if the freckled man wasn't the only person smoking chuckleweed. I didn't want to be part of the rebellion with their emotions and tactics, so joining the group to kill Samael was a terrible idea. I didn't know what nefarious meant and didn't have enough courage to ask. Something told me it would only confuse me more to have the devil expanding my vocabulary.

My head pounded, my stomach still rolling uncomfortably. I grimaced and watched Niklaus and Verona talk, their faces lit with excitement, heads tilted close. The sight of it stirred something ugly in me. A bitter emotion I thought I'd been guaranteed to master by besting the Envy trial. But mastering the sins wasn't as easy as playing their games, and I hadn't truly learned enough to gain full control of my unwanted emotions.

Leaning forward, I tapped Niklaus on the arm, breaking their conversation. I ignored the dark look Verona sent my way, a look that promised revenge. "Which group are you in?"

"The second one," Verona answered for him, her tone dripping with derision. She twisted back to face the fire, muttering beneath her breath, "Obviously."

It hadn't seemed obvious to me. Not when Niklaus would be the ideal candidate to sway the competitors from the trials into their cause. As someone who had been one of them and known what it was like to tremble before one of the deadly sins. Someone who knew how it felt to survive them.

There was a determined glint in his eye, though, which mirrored the movement of the flames, and told me he wouldn't have missed out on facing the devil for anything in the world. Especially after he'd failed the trials, tormented by his inability to control his anger. Niklaus had expected to win.

'Go on,' whispered the devil in my ear.

I swallowed roughly, still unsure. Could I really spy on these people for the devil? I was torn between betraying Samael and betraying my people. He chuckled, a low and sensual sound that made me shiver. I enjoyed making him laugh, but not like this. This was different.

'Do it for me, Little One,' Samael coaxed.

"What's in it for me?" I whispered, as softly as I could, so as not to draw any more unwanted attention.

Samael didn't hesitate. *'I'll make it worth your while in Eternis. I promise.'*

Two deadly words.

Even a fool knew not to trust the promises of a devil, not after he'd ravaged us all so completely. It was the words of tall tales and the cautions we were given before bed. Even Samael himself had told me not to trust him. "No, you won't."

'Of course, I will,' Samael said with a surprising, offended bite to his tone. *'I'm waiting for you, Octavia.'*

It was those words, more than the promise of reward, which pushed against my resolve and cracked it as easily as the glass pane in Niklaus' front door. The idea that he wanted me, waited for me, filled my heart with an unexpected longing — as if Eternis could be the one place I actually belonged. A place where the jagged edges of my soul fit together.

I reached forward, wrapping my hand around Niklaus' wrist and tugging hard to get his attention. He turned, breaking off mid-sentence to glance in my direction. The fire sent light and shadows dancing across his face, his emerald eyes both bright and haunting.

"Can I help?" I asked.

"What?" His brows sunk, knitting together with confusion.

"With hunting down the devil," I explained. "I want to help."

A smile bloomed across his face as the confusion cleared, blindingly victorious. Less than an hour ago I'd said I didn't want to be here, and now I was trying to get involved. I'd thought he'd see right through me, but the idea of getting what he wanted blinded Niklaus.

"Of course!" he said, quickly. "I knew you'd change your mind once we got you out of that city."

He spoke those words with such conviction that my stomach twisted uncomfortably.

"Yeah," I said, for lack of a better answer.

"Hey Chess," he called a moment later, capturing the attention of their leader. "She's in!"

The portly man raised one stubby thumb in answer, grinning like I'd been a foregone conclusion. They invested in my healing, so joining them or dying was the only option in Chester's eyes. Neither of them offered any more details, though, on their plan against the devil. Or how they ever expected to win. The conversation, instead, turned to mundane matters like cooking duty.

I didn't last much longer in the crowd when I felt so uncomfortable. Along with the deep-seated self-conscious feelings that were eating me from the inside out. Restless, I shifted in my seat, startled by every pop and crackle of the fire.

When I jumped to my feet, Niklaus followed suit, reaching to grab at me. "Where are you going?"

I stared at him, not realising I'd needed his permission to even move. "Back to the house? I'm tired."

"You slept for seven weeks…" He shrugged. "I thought you'd be excited to be socialising."

His face fell when he realised I wanted to leave, irritating me. This wasn't socialisation, not when I sat mute by his side. His gaze flicked to where Verona sat, and I rolled my eyes. "Because I've always been the life of a party? You drugged me for seven weeks Nik, I wasn't having a nap for fun."

He heaved a sigh. "I'll walk you back."

"Don't leave for me." I gestured at the dark-haired woman who scrunched her nose in my direction. "I can find my way back."

I couldn't. Not when all the little wooden homes looked identical, but that was beyond the point. I didn't want Niklaus following me around like an angry cloud of emotion. I didn't want to have to process his stress on top of my own.

"Don't be stupid," he said, repeating, "I'll walk you."

It was a tense, silent walk down the gravel pathways, and the stairs creaked underfoot as we walked up them. Niklaus followed so closely behind me that I could feel the wash of his breath against my neck. He wrenched the door open, and I staggered inside, suddenly even more exhausted.

This time, he didn't follow, pulling the door closed between us. The click of the lock echoed around me, before that squeaky stair announced his departure. I leaned back against the door, sliding down to sit on the ground and closing my eyes.

'Good girl,' Samael murmured, and I wondered if he had been waiting until I was alone to praise me. Or if he hadn't cared to check in since I did what he asked. 'You did well.'

Forcing myself to my feet, I staggered down the hall and towards the bedroom. Darkness crept in at the edges of my vision, my exhaustion unable to be denied. With my face pressed into the pillow, I sighed heavily.

"You owe me," I told the devil, deciding it was one debt I'd be sure to collect. "You owe me big time."

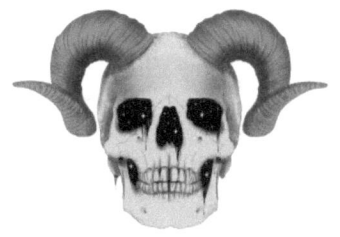

Chapter Three

Several days later, I sat inside Chester's house. He'd drawn a giant map of Kaida across his walls. Each of the sins' territories were marked out in their respective colours. If nothing else, it told me that the leader of the Wastelands Rebellion was no artist.

Chester had confidently explained its meaning, even though I had stared at it for a solid ten minutes, attempting to understand his decision to draw it. He outlined each of the territories, along with each of their camps, proud to show me they had people everywhere. Deep in the recesses of my mind, Samael hummed, interested.

Big, red Xs were scattered across the map. It didn't take a literate person to realise these represented the places they had already attacked. My heart sunk to my stomach as I counted them. There were more than I'd ever expected. Despite Glorae's attack showing their power, I imagined the rebellion as small. Unable to do too much harm.

The devil brushed against my mind. A featherlight stroke that had the hair on the back of my arms standing on end. A purposeful reminder that he was listening in. That he was paying attention, even when I was not.

The room filled with people, who packed in tight before Chester called for some order. I found myself shuffled to the back of the room, too unimportant to stand up front, barely able to see over someone else's head. Purposefully, I tuned out the grandiose lecture from the front of the room. Samael could pay attention. I didn't want to hear Chester boast his way through all their achievements, again.

The red-headed man from the other day was pressed against my side. His body was warm, and he smelled faintly of smoke and liquor. His long hair had been braided out of his face. I asked if he was stalking me, but the man rolled his eyes. He absentmindedly stroked his beard, occasionally glancing to the front of the room.

"You'd have to be interesting for me to do that. Otherwise, it's a colossal waste of my time and I never do anything that's not worth it. There are not enough minutes in my life to spend wasting them."

"I bet that's a lie," I muttered. A hot flush of mortification climbed my throat at the idea that I wasn't worth his time. It was likely the case for many people, those who looked down their noses at me. Nobody had ever had the balls to imply it out loud, to my face, before.

He blinked, pushing at his sleeves until they rested by his elbows. It revealed a stack of thin, braided brown bands around his left wrist. He snapped at one, and it bounced back against his arm with a sharp 'thwack!' A red mark appeared on his skin.

"Why would I lie to you?" he asked me, still without looking in my direction. "I have absolutely nothing to gain by doing that. Unlike some people, I value my integrity."

Narrowing my eyes at him, I asked, "Who are you?"

A boyish grin stretched across his face. A dimple flashed beneath his bushy beard, and he held out his hand. "Maksymilian Tate, born of the Greedlands. Member of this here rebellion."

When I took his hand, it was warm and slightly sweaty, his grip strong. He gave my hand an exaggerated shake and let go quickly. His fingers drifted to his throat, reaching to toy at a coin on a leather strap around his neck.

"What are you doing here?" I asked him, my curiosity piqued by the man who couldn't stop fidgeting. It didn't feel like he fit, not with the rest of the power-hungry men and women around us.

"Same thing as you," he replied.

I sincerely doubted that. If he had the devil whispering in his ear, then I was the daughter of an angel of sin. "What?!" I gasped dramatically. "You were kidnapped and knocked out for weeks, as well? I can't believe it."

He laughed, amusement reflecting in a wide grin. He dropped the coin and tucked his hands behind his back, rocking onto his toes. "Not exactly the same experience, then. But I am in this room to hear Chester's plan for getting into Eternis." He paused, and when I glanced behind his back, I could see him worrying at the bands around his wrist. "I don't think it'll be as easy as he thinks."

I tilted my head, taking in their almost manic leader. Chester's beady eyes warred between squinting and flashing open, and spittle flew in every which direction his arms were thrown. He had passion and confidence for what he preached.

My attention returned to Max. "Oh yeah?"

"Yeah." He shrugged. "I once lived on the border of the Greedlands and Eternis. You can't just walk right in and sit down to dinner with the overlord. We'd have to get through the dead forest first."

His comment didn't match the stories I'd been told by the cursed triplets. "But ..."

"Shh," Maksymilian cut me off, waving a hand in my direction. "I'm listening."

He definitely wasn't paying attention to Chester's lecture. Especially, since he's started playing with the coin at his neck again. I silenced my protest and refocused on the front of the room.

Chester had stabbed his finger at the black centre of the map. Which I guessed was his ultimate goal, Eternis. He spoke rapidly about dividing into teams and which points of entrance would be the best for them to get into the city and strike Samael down.

"Through the Slothlands!" Verona yelled out confidently. She pushed her dark hair out of her face and elbowed her way to the front of the room. "Nobody would expect an attack from their side. It'll be the best cover. If we can take them unawares, we'll have the upper hand."

Chester tipped his chin, giving the idea some thought.

Maksymilian, however, scoffed loudly. "That's the dumbest thing I've ever heard."

His words carried even over the murmurs that swept through the room. People turned in our direction and narrowed their eyes at him. The flush marring my skin deepened at the attention. Quickly, I loosened locks of hair from behind my ear to fall across my face and obscure my scars. The thought of them staring at my flaws, scrutinizing me... It left my chest tight with anxiety.

"Have you got a better idea, Tate?" Verona challenged him. She folded her arms across her chest and looked down her nose as if that might intimidate him. Rather than cower, Maksymilian laughed in her face.

"Yeah," he said. "We go through the Greedlands, instead. When the Greed trial finishes, we can slip in with the competitors and walk right up to the devil's door. He might even think we're with them. It's the perfect disguise. He's welcoming humans into his city, so why not take the invitation?"

Chester's entire face screwed up in thought.

'He looks like he's in pain when he thinks that hard,' Samael said.

It was hard to stifle my laugh.

Finally, he grunted and shook his head, planting his hands on his hips. "I'm not waiting that long to make our move. The trials could take years to finish," Chester said. "The time to act is now!"

That was the end of that. Around here Chester's word was law. Everyone turned away from Maksymilian, as if his suggestion had been useless and it was a waste to consider it any longer. They moved on to discussions about whether the Slothlands or Pridelands were a better entry point.

Niklaus argued that sneaking back through the Pridelands would be easy. He, like others, was confidently opinionated.

"How many places border Eternis?" I asked, peering up at the splashes of colour behind Chester.

'Five lands of sin,' Samael replied.

Maksymilian had heard me. He nudged me and pointed at the map. "Is it too far away for you to see it? You must be blind as a harpy, Octavia. He couldn't have written it any bigger."

I said nothing, not wanting to voice my flaws. Especially, when I didn't know him well. More and more often, I wished I could read.

Maksymilian, to his credit, accepted my agreement with no further comment. "Eternis is the bit in the middle, the black splotch. The big yellow bit bordering it is Greedlands. If you work your way around Eternis, it's Gluttony, Sloth, Pride and then Wrath."

"If black is for the devil and Eternis, then what's the other two black bits?" I asked, curious now. I hadn't realised that Samael might have more than one territory. Painted on the wall,

Kaida appeared a lot bigger than I'd ever imagined. But it had been easy to pretend the world was a small place from the confines of a small village.

"Those are considered Wastelands. Same as those little razed villages inside the territories, those places where nobody lives 'cause it's too dead to inhabit. Or there's just not enough humans left to fill the space." Maksymilian said. "It's what we're named after, 'The Wastelands Rebellion', 'cause most of our numbers started from within those areas."

He lifted a hand and pointed out one of the larger black territories. "The Northern Wastelands, that's the one that borders Greed, Envy, and Wrath and it's unclaimed because all three wanted it. So, the devil, the conniving bastard that he is, gave it to none of them. The Southern Wastelands are the same thing but fought for by Envy and Pride." He waited for me to nod, to show I was following his story. "Chester says they alternate claiming it, but it's still known as a wasteland."

'That boy is a wealth of information. I wonder where he learned it all,' Samael mused. *'Ask him more questions.'*

"How long have you been part of the rebellion?" I asked, doing as I was told. I didn't think Maksymilian was a boy. In fact, he looked to be all man, but to an ancient being like Samael, he might seem young.

'I meant for you to ask useful questions,' Samael snarked. *'About their plans, or where he learned about the sins fighting for land, just as a suggestion.'*

"Since near the beginning," Maksymilian answered, toying with that coin, again. "I got sick of Greed taxing us to the end of our lives and decided to up and leave. I didn't have anyone keeping me at home, if you know what I mean."

"Taxing you?" I asked. I didn't know what that meant.

"Yeah." He gave me a strange look, rubbing his fingers through his long auburn hair. It loosened strands from the braid, and he pushed it over his shoulder. "What? The evil sin overlord from where you're from doesn't make you pay your dues? Greed takes a giant cut of any wealth we discover. By giant, I mean nearly all of it." He snorted. "We mine at his instruction and can only afford to live off his mercy. Avarita thrives off our efforts."

I frowned, biting my lip as I struggled to understand his bitter words. "He makes you pay him money? What are you paying for?"

"For existing on his land, or just because he wants..." Maksymilian shrugged. "Or because he's a Greedy bastard. He always wants more."

Samael chuckled, and I wondered if he agreed with the sentiment. He rarely shared his thoughts on the seven deadly sins, but I knew he had strong opinions.

"Are you paying attention or flirting, Max?!" Chester barked from the front of the room.

For the second time in only a few minutes, the attention of the crowd turned in our direction. Their gazes seared through me. I swallowed and dropped my chin.

"Yes," he replied bluntly, nonplussed by their stares. "I am."

Chester didn't look impressed. "Which one are you admitting to?"

"Both," Maksymilian grinned widely, nudging me in the ribs, and I choked on my laugh. Not for the first time, I wished he'd fall in a hole. Maybe the one he was digging for both of us, because Chester looked entirely unimpressed with his attitude.

Chester sneered at us, his face clouding over with anger. "You're both on border watch tonight!"

I blinked, not sure what that meant. I glanced up at Maksymilian, who rolled his eyes. It couldn't be anything good, not if it was handed out as a punishment. The last time I'd received that sort of penance, I'd been mucking out lavatories and quite literally burying shit in the desert. I'd had to put up with Niklaus' tormenting on top of it. Compared to that, border watch couldn't be too bad.

"Octavia can't do that," Niklaus cut in sharply.

I looked to him, frowning.

He abandoned me near Chester without considering my discomfort. He'd not bothered to check in with me since the meeting started. This sudden demand of what I could and couldn't do set my blood on fire. Niklaus constantly showed he didn't have time for me, yet still wanted to control me. It was hard not to wonder if he'd changed since the Wrath trial, or if he had always been this way, and it was me who had grown.

"Why not?" I argued.

I had no idea what Chester was punishing us with, but I didn't want Niklaus to rescue me. As much as he liked to claim otherwise, I wasn't his responsibility. I could look after myself.

He flicked his gaze to Maksymilian and his expression shuttered, a muscle thrumming in his right cheek. "You're *tired*, remember?" Those three words dripped with sarcasm, and I clenched my fists. "You were drugged for seven weeks. You were healing. It's not a good time for you to be walking the borders."

He had turned to look at Chester as spoke. The rugged man started nodding in agreement, his hands planted solidly on his hips. "You're right, boy," he said. "She doesn't know her place yet. So, you make sure she's locked up tonight."

Niklaus smirked, and my heart sank. Across the room, people whispered. Their gazes slid to me and then back to Nik, again. Verona chose that moment to press against his side. The noise around us rose and everyone easily forgot about me, not finding me nearly as interesting as I might like to imagine.

"Get out of here," Chester snapped a moment later. He bristled now that he had lost their focus. "The lot of you. This meetin's over. We'll discuss the best way to kill the devil next time we meet."

On my way out, I asked Samael beneath my breath, "What *is* the best way to kill you?"

'Wouldn't you like to know?'

44

"You need to stay away from him!" Niklaus yelled from across the room. He had herded me inside the house the moment the meeting ended. His hand clamped down on my shoulder to pull me through the streets, looking like he regretted ever letting me out. "He's bad news."

"You could say the same about you!" I threw my hands up in the air, exasperated. "You were Ilrea's bad influence. Everyone said you ruined people, and you did. You blackmailed a favour out of me just for somewhere to sleep!"

The comment bounced right off him. A vein in his forehead was throbbing as he glared at me. Maksymilian became more enticing when I saw his ability to provoke Niklaus. The more stifling Nik became, the more I wanted to antagonise him. Getting under his skin was the only win I could manage at this point.

"I mean it, Octavia!" he roared. "Devils, why don't you ever listen?!"

He took a menacing step forward, looking like he wanted to throttle me. Then, growled with frustration and turned to storm out the door. It slammed hard against the frame, the glass windows rattling. Racing after him, I desperately tugged on the handle, but he'd locked it.

Trapping me inside the house, again.

Niklaus had become my jailer. He obediently followed Chester's commands like a good little soldier and proved that there was no trust between us. We weren't allies. I was just a tool he thought he could use in his fanciful little war against Samael.

The next day, we fought again.

Niklaus could not let the issue of Maksymilian go, and every conversation circled back to the man. He hounded me for a promise to stay away from him. He worked himself into such a rage that he'd driven his fist into the wall. The boards cracked and splintered beneath the force of his attack, leaving a large dent behind. It showed that severing his dominant hand hadn't affected his strength, it showed that he was on the cusp of becoming truly violent.

My throat tightened as I studied the hole his fist made, unsure if I could dodge Niklaus if he directed his anger towards me. Once, when we were training for war, I'd learned how to evade an attack, and how to fight back. It should have been second nature, but since I'd woken here, I always felt tired. My energy was wasted on the simple task of keeping myself alive. Fighting would be impossible.

"Why do you care if I talk to him?" I asked, wary of inciting violence. "You said you didn't love me."

Niklaus scoffed. "What? You think you love him?"

"I never said that. I don't even know him." I rubbed my hands over my face, tired of going round and round in circles with him. "But you have no place to be telling me I can't talk to anyone. You're not my… anything, Nik. It shouldn't matter to you what I do."

His lips pressed into a thin line. He tilted his head, gaze narrowing on me. "Would you do what I asked, *if* I told you I loved you?"

"No."

"Of course not," he huffed. His fist was still clenched so hard that his knuckles blanched. "I may not love you, Octavia but I care about you. You need to understand that. I care enough that I hunted you down and pulled you from Pride's broken palace. When I tell you not to talk to him, it's for your own good. You need to trust that I'm just looking out for you."

"You don't get to decide what's in my best interest, Nik."

"Why not?"

"You don't love me," I repeated, as if love made all the difference in the world. It didn't, but I thought it was at least a concept he'd understand. "You just feel you owe me. I've said it before, and I'll say it again. You don't get a say in what I do with my life."

He threw up his hand, stalking closer to me. "Do we have to be in love to be good together, Octavia? I could make you feel good. I can keep you safe. Isn't that enough for you?"

My tongue darted across my lips. He took a step forward another, standing too close now, and I wavered on the spot. It could be so easy to overlook his flaws, overlook my own bubbling frustration, and give in to what he offered. Especially when he'd once been all that I wanted.

I couldn't do it though.

The time for me to give in to other people's desires was long gone. If I couldn't hold my ground in front of Niklaus, how would I ever stand tall in front of the devil? He could offer me a thousand mind-blowing orgasms and it still wouldn't be worth my freedom.

I opened my mouth to tell him to fuck off, but Samael cut through my thoughts.

'Don't be so hasty, Little One,' he whispered. *'Don't anger him too much. You need to play his game. We may want their information, Octavia, but most importantly, we want a way for you to come to me. If he keeps you locked inside his home forever, you won't make it to the Slothlands for the next trial. Remember that Pride won't let you go if you cannot make it to Eternis.'*

My throat tightened, misery welling in my gut. Overwhelming emotions weighed down my shoulders and tingled on the bridge of my nose. It felt like I was forever under someone else's control, no matter the day. There was a man, angel, or devil waiting to tell me what I should do next. I was constantly tempering the bright parts of myself to appease others, dulling gold edges to become malleable for their plans and my survival.

It was exhausting to shape constantly into something new and lose key parts of myself along the way.

"If you want me to stay here, Nik," I said, meeting his eye. Carefully weighing up how to do as Samael asked without angering the man further. "You need to relax. Stop locking me in. I don't want to be your prisoner. I thought you wanted me here, but you just keep me trapped."

"I want you here, Octavia." He groaned, fisting his hair with frustration. "Why can't you see that? That's what I've been saying for the last twenty minutes."

He took another step closer, and I wanted to step back, so badly. It took all my willpower to stay in place, to lift my chin and continue, "Then, you need to give a little. I'm not your enemy Nik, or your property, but you treat me like both. It's not fair!"

He stared right through me, his green eyes flickering with light as he processed my request. The tense hold of his jaw didn't give me much hope. Niklaus had claimed me as his spoil of war, and now I didn't think he wanted to let me go. Even if he didn't really want me. I represented a memory, the last pieces of his old life.

"I'll talk to Chester about not locking the doors," he said, "but you have to promise not to run away."

"I won't!" I said, quickly, too quickly.

Niklaus looked dubious, his eyes narrowing with suspicion. "Octavia…"

"I mean it." Raising my hands in supplication, I looked at him. "I have nowhere to go, Nik. I want to settle into a better life like you couldn't believe. But I can't do that if you escort me everywhere and lock me in this house. I promise I'm not going to run if you leave the door unlocked tonight."

Making these promises felt as dangerous as those from the devil — it was a way to damn me. One day soon, I would need to run from this place, but not yet, so I'd need to be careful with exactly what I offered him. With the way I tied myself up in pledges.

He sighed. "You'll stay away from Tate, then?"

I flashed Niklaus a toothy smile, feeling victorious, but unwilling to give him everything he wanted. "I'm not making any promises there."

For the next few days, Niklaus was on his best behaviour. He'd turned back into the son of a gentlemen instead of a brute of war. True to his word, he'd left the door unlocked that first night, and every night thereafter. I tested it by turning the handle while he slept, only relaxing when I could open the door. I stood on the cusp of freedom, breathed in the chilled night air, and closed the door again.

He began asking for my opinions and preferences for our day-to-day activities. He invited me to dinner instead of ordering me out the door. Much to Verona's displeasure, he also tried to draw me into conversations each night. Although I often refused. I was still too wary of the crackling fire, and curious why Maksymilian never turned up to chat.

Niklaus had relaxed. Just enough that the vein in his forehead didn't throb as hard. Just enough that my anxiety loosened its tight, restricting hold on my body, and I slowly felt rested again. It wasn't enough, it wouldn't ever be enough, but it was a start.

Sometimes he gave me hope, a glimmer of the man he'd been before his anger had bested him. Before his focus had become so singular. Until I sat on the front porch, mourning the loss of the little hellhound. Until the attack had taken her away from me. Always eager to see me, and full of energy. Ira had been the one being to lift my spirits. Now, I stared at the members of the rebellion who had callously taken from me and tried to temper my rage and stave off the threat of tears.

"What's wrong with you, now?" Nik sighed. I flinched.

It was difficult to face these people and smile, knowing the death and destruction they'd caused. Pretending to be thankful for my life, which they believed they had saved. "I miss Ira," I admitted.

His face scrunched up. "The hellhound runt?"

"She wasn't a runt," I muttered, determinedly staring straight ahead. "She was in the palace during the attack, Nik."

He sighed again, the sound weighted and pointed. "Octavia."

I hated the nuances in the sound of my name when he said it like that. Like I was a child who hadn't been paying attention. Like he was sick of correcting me. Like everything I did was wrong.

"What?" I snapped.

"There are worse, and more important things happening," he said. "You need to get over it and focus."

I wished I could set him on fire for the seething disappointment I felt for him. He jumped down the stairs and left me behind. "Thanks so much for that amazing advice, Nik. Really."

He was too far gone to hear it.

One evening, we sat in the woods behind the village. We watched as the sun dropped below the tree line, marring the horizon with streaks of orange. The temperature had dropped quickly, and each of my breaths appeared in front of my face in a puff of white. Niklaus, assigned to border patrol, asked if I wanted to join him. Although it felt too cold to venture out, my curiosity had won out. The offer felt like another step forward.

Skilfully, he played with a small knife, effortlessly tossing and catching it. "It feels a bit like the forest in Gula, doesn't it?"

I shivered. Those forests had been the start of an exhaustive trauma. I'd had no idea what I was getting myself into, and what my life would become. "Don't tell me that's where we are…"

He chuckled. "No. Don't worry, love. We're definitely not back there."

"Where are we then?" I asked when he didn't elaborate. I wasn't sure how I felt about the fact that Niklaus still called me 'love'. Half the time it felt teasing, and the rest of the time it felt mocking.

"We're still in the Pridelands." He threw and caught the knife again. "Not that far from home, really."

A shiver wracked my body, my throat sticking on my next words. "Y-You mean… We didn't actually leave?"

"It's one of our many bases. We have one in every territory, but Pride is too arrogant to think we'd stay on his lands," Niklaus said. "I bet he thinks we fled as far as the Northern Wasteland just to avoid him."

The shadows felt like they'd grown as he spoke, flickering in the corners of my vision. They taunted me, as they twisted into different shapes and I asked, "Are there Erlkangs here?"

The shadowy creatures haunted my nightmares, leaving me sweaty and tangled in sheets. The scars on my back were a constant reminder of the monsters I endured. Erklangs had been the monster in the night during my childhood, and my fear of those shadows would never dull.

Niklaus blinked, his head whipping around to stare into the dark trees on our other side. He stared into the trees, as if daring one of them to come out and face us. The knife sailed towards the ground, dropping past his hand, in his distraction, and it clattered to the ground.

"Not that we've seen," he said after a beat. "But they could be out there. I've only ever seen them in the Pridelands, and if they were near Ilrea they could be here, too."

"Oh," I said, but I was distracted now. I couldn't look away from that small blade. Battling the rising need to dart forward and pick it up, to hold it close. To keep a weapon in case I needed to defend myself.

My entire body swayed towards the knife, but Niklaus turned his attention back to me too quickly, he reached down to pluck it off the ground, his knuckles blanching with his tight hold.

"Nik?" I called to capture his attention.

"Hmm?" The full force of his green gaze locked on me, as he gave me his undivided attention. I swallowed, feeling inexplicably nervous. Gathering my courage, I finally asked the question that had been on my mind.

"Where's my knife?" I asked.

"Your knife?" he repeated, the corner of his mouth twitching up into a smirk. He didn't pretend that he didn't know what I was talking about. "It's somewhere safe."

Relief mixed with a new anxiety, and I leaned closer to him. He had no idea what that blade was intended for, and part of me thought he would never let it go if I told him the truth. If he was keeping it somewhere safe, that meant it hadn't been lost in the explosions. It meant I could get it back. "But where, Nik? I need it."

He laughed, the sound bouncing through the trees until wildlife rustled in the distance. Niklaus was quick to shut me down. "No, you don't. Why would you need that here?"

I frowned. "For my protection?"

"From what, exactly?" he asked, his face still bright with laughter. I hated that he found amusement in my need to defend myself. That it was funny that I might feel like I was in danger, even though every person in the camp had likely killed more than once. Niklaus scoffed. "Nobody's going to attack you in my house."

"I won't always be with you," I said.

"Yes," He replied, his tone firm as he clenched his jaw. "You will. There's no need for you to carry around a knife, Octavia."

"Nik!" It was my turn to laugh, half-hysterical, that he thought he could keep me nearby at all times. He may have unlocked the doors to the house, but he still had delusions of keeping me as his prisoner. "Don't be stupid. I know my way around a weapon, you were there when I learned. You can't be naive enough to think that nobody in this camp attacks each other? You expect me just to stand there when I get attacked?"

Emotion rolled across his features like a storm cloud. He climbed to his feet, his body rigid with building tension. "I'm not discussing this, Octavia."

Jumping to my feet after him, I frowned at his back, he'd already started striding away.

"But it's mine!" I cried. I knew it wouldn't win me what I wanted, a petulant outburst of emotion and nothing more. I wanted to punch him. How dare he steal my blade and not give it back.

Niklaus gave me a sharp look, his green eyes filled with intensity. "Not anymore, it's not!"

"Son-of-the-devil!" I swore, but he was already striding away, flipping me the finger over his shoulder. That blade was dangerous. It held magic that I didn't understand, and I needed it back. "You're a bastard, Niklaus Heira!"

Hesitating, I glanced back over my shoulder at the thick woods and the shadows that lie beyond. It would be all too easy to turn and run. I could flee into the darkness of the woods and disappear, but I knew I'd likely die cold and alone. My days in the rebellion camp would be a waste if a beast devoured me.

No, there had to be a better way to survive, and I planned to find it. Survival, and my blade.

53

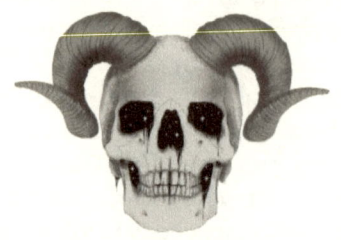

Chapter Four

Progress was slow in the rebellion camps. Mirroring other aspects of life, trapped in a cycle of discussions and plans without action. Until, after days of having nothing concrete, there was suddenly a plan in place, and everything moved forward at a surefire pace.

I felt as if I'd heard every option Chester's small mind could consider to kill Samael: poison him and watch from afar as he fell, or fire at him with every weapon and ounce of manpower they could find. Niklaus argued fiercely for the standpoint of poison, relaying everything he had learned in the Wrathlands about waging a war. Neither felt like a good choice to me.

His top choice was to burn the devil within Eternis. Chester liked fire, often mesmerised by the flicker of the flame. The sinister look in his eye when he watched things burn left my mouth dry and my skin prickling uncomfortably. Almost as if I could feel the flames burning me again. He was the man behind my scars, and I couldn't afford to forget it. Rough, messy and belligerent as he might be, he was a dangerous man.

It was no surprise that firepower was the plan they settled on. They used Maksymilian's ideas of entering through the twisting underground network of tunnels in the Greedlands. They wanted to burst into Eternis and catch the devil unawares.

Only the devil knew every detail of their plans. He watched from behind my dull, disinterested gaze as they plotted to end him. Samael laughed as their ideas grew. They thought they were ready for him. In reality, the devil was beckoning them forward, daring them to attack. He was prepared to show them who truly reigned across Kaida. The more they plotted, and the more he commented on their ideas, the less I wanted to be caught in the middle of it all.

My initial guilt of letting Samael listen to their meetings had faded in the past two weeks. Chester's blatant disregard for the human lives caught in the crossfire of his war ignited my anger. No matter how often I tried to argue it with Niklaus at night, he, too, saw their lives as easily expendable.

I had never pretended to be a hero. Or to care so much about other people, but I'd grown tired of needless deaths. The bodies that I left in my wake. I didn't want to be part of a movement that thought killing thousands was worth it to annihilate the bigger threat. I didn't want to be associated with the people who didn't stop to mourn their sacrifices.

Finally, the day came when everything changed. Samael brushed against my mind with an urgent burst of magic, the nauseating feel of it startled me from the depths of sleep so quickly that my palms grew clammy, and my heart pounded with fear.

"What is it?" I croaked into the darkness, struggling to re-orientate myself. The sound of Niklaus's deep snoring drowned out my whispered words. "Samael?"

'It's time to go, Little One,' Samael said gently. *'You need to find your blade and leave this camp within three days if you want any hope of finishing the next trial. The Sloth trial takes a great deal of time, and I imagine you will need every minute of it to pass.'*

The time to leave had arrived quickly. The night before, I'd thought I'd be stuck in these camps forever. Lost in a complex web of terror that I wanted no part in. Waiting for an angel to come and feast on my soul, to claim my debt to him.

With each passing day, I resented ever finding myself here. Hating that Niklaus had dared steal me away for the future he thought I wanted, instead of the one I desired. I deserved more than this violent existence. I hated the people around me, the way they whispered, and the way they stared. I knew they would always glance at the cuff on my wrist and see me only as a player in the devil's game — a woman whose life was owed to the sins.

The rasping growl of Samael's voice motivated me to move. I hadn't been able to find my blade anywhere in the house. Over the past week, I'd systematically turned it upside down. Taking everything apart and putting it back together to avoid Niklaus' suspicion. The only positive aspect of his leaving me alone so often was that I had time to search.

So far, all I'd found was an overwhelming accumulation of dust and grime. Niklaus was not a tidy man by any means, and I stubbornly refused to clean. I was not here as his housekeeper, he could live with a menagerie of dust bunnies for all I cared. But there were still more places to search, and Samael had told me that my time was limited. I needed to get a move on, I couldn't leave without Pride's blade, it was a key part of his orders. The devil had to be stabbed with that blade, and nothing else.

As I crept from the room, half-dressed and moving quickly, the floorboards let out a deep groan. Hesitating mid-step, I cocked my head, listening for the next rumbling snore from Niklaus' room. My chest ached until I heard his snores and soft mumble down the hall. He'd often talked in his sleep, mostly mumbled nonsense, and often the cries of his twin's name.

There were two more kitchen cupboards to search, although all the others were mostly bare. If I couldn't find the blade in Niklaus' room, I had to accept that he'd lied to me. Maybe he'd given the blade to Chester, and it wouldn't be as easy to get back as I'd expected.

Sneaking into Niklaus' personal space to retrieve my belongings was one thing, but being near Chester made me uncomfortable. There'd be no mercy if he caught me.

The kitchen was quiet, dusty and undisturbed. Niklaus rarely used the area since the rebellion mostly cooked and ate by the fireside each night.

A gauzy curtain hung over the partially opened window, and it did nothing to block the light of the moon, which spilled across the floor. It offered just enough light for me to creep around the counters and reach for the last of the cupboards.

The smaller of the cupboards was bare beyond dust and crumbs. My fingers pushed and probed against the back walls to make sure there wasn't anything I missed. Niklaus had to have at least one secret hiding place within this devils-damned house. I found nothing valuable, suggesting the once-rich boy had hidden his wealth. Leaving the small cupboard, I wiped the dust off my fingers and continued my search, smearing it on my shirt.

The final cupboard rose from floor to ceiling, tucked into the corner of the room. When I pulled open the doors my dimming hope reignited. Brown sacks sat beneath the bottom shelf. Dusty tins forgotten at eye height and the shadow of something more lingered beyond my reach.

Dropping to my knees with a thud, I pulled at the edge of the first sack. The rough material felt scratchy as I hauled it towards myself. I pried at the knotted rope. I struggled to untie the knot, and it took longer than I would have liked. Panic welled in my veins, and I glanced over my shoulder, certain that the longer I took, the more likely it was that Niklaus would find me.

The sack fell to the side as it opened, dried grain spilling like a river across the floor. Huffing with frustration, I kicked at it when I rose, pain lacing through my toes on impact. I used the bag as a step to see further along the shelves. It wasn't something I'd be able to clean before sunrise, so I'd have to leave it there.

The tins were difficult to get into as well. My fingers ached by the time I'd prised the lids free and shaken out the contents across the shelf. Some were filled with dried food and tea leaves. Another held a strange sticky substance that ended up smeared across the shelf.

The last rattled with an all too familiar sound. The unmistakable bounce of coins against metal brought a victorious smile to my face. I tipped out five golden devil's coins. It wasn't my angel-cursed blade, but it was still a win. The heavy weight of them soothed my soul. My life felt less helpless when I had coins in hand.

Tucking them into my sock, I climbed the shelves, desperate to find what else was hidden in there. Only, when I reached the top of the cupboard it was empty. The shadows had been just that. I tested the ceiling, but it was solid. Disappointed, I rested my forehead on the shelf.

It would have been easier if all his treasure had been here. The search was growing difficult. But, as Nash had once said to me, nothing worth doing was ever easy.

"What are you doing up there, love?" Niklaus asked.

His body blocked the only source of light in the room. My grip on the shelves slipped and I fell to the floor. Grains of rice pressed into my knees, feeling more like torture than anything I experienced in the Wrathlands. The feeling was so sharp after the painful impact that tears burned in my eyes.

"Ow," I wheezed.

Looking at Niklaus, I saw a smirk on his lips before his brows furrowed. He crossed his arms, tattoos shifting, and waited for my response.

"Well?"

"Well, what?" I asked, too innocently, as I struggled to my feet.

Niklaus sighed, then gently pulled me up by my arm. My knee twinged in protest of my weight as I found my balance. I grimaced. He began brushing small grains of rice off my thigh, leaving tiny little red marks behind.

"What were you doing up there?" he asked, again.

"I was hungry," I said. It was a stupid excuse, and I knew it. But desperate times called for desperate measures, and sometimes that meant utilising the first lie I could come up with. Niklaus and I were once physically close, but he couldn't tell when I was being honest. It might be my only saving grace. I had lied so much that trivial lies felt like facts.

"Hungry?" Niklaus repeated.

"Yeah…" I agreed slowly. Suddenly sure that the lie I'd latched onto was as transparent as Pride's palace had been. Imaging that he knew exactly what I had been doing and was waiting for me to confess the truth. I didn't. If I'd learned anything in life it was that simple falsities were easier to remember, and when in doubt I needed to double down instead of backpedalling. "I was looking for some food. That's all."

He looked dubious but didn't protest. His hand brushed along my arm to grasp my wrist, holding tight. Turning on his heel led me through the house, his hand becoming another manacle. I followed wordlessly, looking down at the way he held my arm and the new shackle he'd created around my skin and bones.

I wondered if anyone would want to hold my hand and walk with me instead of controlling me. Very few stood by me as equals, instead of dragging me around or using me as a game piece.

In Niklaus' room, I heard my pulse thumping in my ears as

59

he stopped by the bed. A precursor to the nerves that knotted in my stomach. Over the past few weeks since I'd woken, he hadn't let me in this room. Shutting the door behind him, a firm barrier between us.

It was the last place I needed to check, and I'd been imagining all the ways I would need to convince him to let me inside. Most of all I'd been envisioning the awkward consequences that would follow if I tried to seduce him. I would have needed all the power of the Sin of Lust to succeed because, although I'd wanted Nik intensely once before, I'd grown out of the desire. He was a memory, a past moment, but he no longer lit a fire within me. It wasn't his gaze, attention, and approval I sought, anymore.

We shuffled into the low-lit room. It smelled musky, like sweaty sheets and unwashed man. I wrinkled my nose, despite trying to keep a straight face. I tried to inspect the room without being too obvious about it. The room had sparse furnishings, with a bed set against the far wall. He had hastily discarded his clothes, leaving them wrinkled and scattered across the room, from one corner to the next.

There was a stack of bags in the far corner, along with a pile of discarded weapons but at first glance, I couldn't see my blade amongst them. Another sweep of the room and I got distracted by the man himself. By the deep pink scars that ran down Niklaus's back. Rough, raised ridges that formed two matching lines. My mouth dried out when I realised they were from our time in Invidia, when I'd pulled him free of the gates. It almost looked like someone had torn wings from his back.

I wondered how many scars I'd left on him that couldn't be seen on the surface. If his mind felt as fractured as mine, or if Niklaus was surviving better than I ever could.

"I've got some dried fruit around here, somewhere." Niklaus had turned to the basket in the corner, rifling through it. He tossed a wax-paper-wrapped package through the air, not looking to see if it made its mark. "Midnight snack."

A solid year of training helped me catch it with ease. Running my fingers across the small piece of brown string that kept it secure, I said, "Thanks." I wasn't hungry, but I needed to back up my lie, so I tugged it open.

"You can sit down," Nik offered, gesturing at the rumpled bed. "It won't bite you."

I sank down onto the edge of the mattress, the sheets still warm from where his body had been. I tasted a piece of dried apple from the open pack on my lap. It had a tough texture and a foul taste, and I wanted to spit it out.

Niklaus leaned against the wall, arms folded across his bare chest. He watched me closely, so I forced myself to chew, chew, chew, and swallow. "No snappy comebacks or glib remarks for me today?" he asked. If I didn't know any better, I would have said he sounded amused.

I folded the wrapping over the apple, sighing heavily, not wanting to eat more. "I don't really know what to say, Nik."

He grimaced. "Things have changed between us, haven't they, love?"

"It would actually be impossible for them to stay the same," I told him gently. Unsure how we got ourselves to the point of facing hard truths in the middle of the night. "We've been through so many terrible things, Nik, together and apart. We're nothing like the kids we once were."

"Do you hate me for bringing you here?" he asked, fidgeting with the ring hooked through his lip again.

My throat constricted, but I forced myself to meet his eye and shook my head.

"I…" It was hard to get the words out for fear of expressing myself wrong. "No, I don't hate you, Niklaus. I don't think I've ever hated you. At one point in my life, you were the only thing I could think about. My days started and ended with getting you to notice me, even if only for a single moment. Devils, the number of back-alley parties I attended just to see if you'd give me the time of day. But… I'm not that girl anymore. I haven't been for a long time."

"No, you're not," he admitted, sounding reluctant. Niklaus pushed himself off the wall and closed the space between us. The bed squeaked as he settled next to me, close enough to feel his warmth. "You're a lot stronger now, Octavia."

A bitter laugh rose up my throat. "That means you can calm down now, Nik. I'm strong enough to hold my own."

He pulled a face, half pained and half teasing before he nudged me in the ribs with his elbow.

"Can you blame me? It's hard not to remember you struggling so much at the start, you know. Floundering around Gluttony's challenge like you wanted to die."

I flinched. "I never wanted to die!"

The words came out sharp, a bite I couldn't take back. Niklaus' green eyes flared with interest, a smirk pulling at the corner of his lips. "Are you sure about that? You were making stupid choices even before we left."

"Even at home, I didn't want to die. Not even on the days when it felt like my stomach had turned into a void and it was sucking me inside out. Or when I'd cried so much that I couldn't form any more tears. I always wanted to survive," I said. I stared down at my legs, at the raised scars marring my skin. "That's what I've done. Survived."

Niklaus wrapped his arm around my shoulder. I tried not to look at the knotted scars that formed the stump of his wrist. He pulled me backwards, flopped onto his back, and stared at the white ceiling. The mattress shifted beneath our weight. We lay in silence, and I didn't know how to break it.

Niklaus pulled one of the apple pieces from the packet and popped it in his mouth. He gagged, reaching for a canteen of water. "That's feral. How did you eat that?"

"I've eaten worse," I commented, shrugging awkwardly.

"And so have you. Those glowing mushrooms in Gula tasted like foot slime, and candied or not, the butterflies still tasted like bugs."

"And how would you know what slimy feet tasted like?" he asked. He pushed the apples off the bed, adding to the mess on the floor.

Out of sight, out of mind.

"It's not hard to imagine… Is it?" I snorted.

He flopped back. The silence fell between us again, soft and easy this time, instead of strained. It was the most comfortable I'd felt in his presence for a long time, and I couldn't help but wish it would stay that way. Niklaus shifted, and I curled against his side, hooking one leg over his thigh, seeking the warmth of his body. His hand rubbed circles along my back, a comfort that I didn't deserve.

"What did you think you were going to be when you grew up?" he asked.

I startled back into consciousness. My eyelids had grown heavy, and I'd been on the cusp of sleep. Fighting a yawn, I lifted my head and stared at the side of his face. His expression was serious, and I wondered where the question had come from. It took a moment to pull my wits together, and I relaxed against him.

"I wanted to be anything except like my mother," I said, then snorted. "No, that's cruel. My mum wasn't that bad, really. Honestly, I hoped I'd be rich."

"Yeah?" There was a thread of amusement in his tone. As if he knew as well as everyone else that it wouldn't have happened. My reputation as a desperate gambler preceded me in our village. Noticing his amusement, I decided to keep my fleeting desire to marry him for his money a secret.

Niklaus wasn't thinking about my long-dead aspirations any more though. "I was going to ask Cyn to teach me how to tattoo," he commented. "Maybe set up my own parlour in Glorae. I can't draw for shit, but I could learn."

I bit down on my lower lip, the mention of Cyn making my chest squeeze tight. My wrist burned with a phantom pain for the mark of completion that I was missing. I pushed the feeling away long enough to ask, "You didn't want to stay in Ilrea?"

"Devils, no!" Niklaus laughed. His grip around my waist tightened and he held me closer to his side. There was no affection in the squeeze, mostly it felt like he was holding onto a memory. "Mikhael is insufferable when he's in charge. You've seen it for yourself. There wouldn't have been enough room for both of us in Ilrea." He paused, his throat working as he swallowed. "Besides, I didn't want to stick around as the second son. Existing as a backup in case anything happened to him. Or. Worse, attending boring summits at Eternis on his behalf. I wasn't cut out to be a Chancellor, and I definitely didn't want to be my brother's lackey."

I scoffed. "You'll break your mother's heart if she hears you saying that."

"Yeah, well…" He shrugged awkwardly beneath my weight. "A little hardship wouldn't hurt my mother. She's had a very easy life, always got exactly what she wanted, when she wanted it."

Regret filled me as soon as I mentioned his mother. Nik didn't know she had hung herself. Turned herself into a spectacle for the entire town and Pride himself. He didn't know she'd rather die than outlive him by too long. Lying by his side, I couldn't bring myself to tell him, either. It wouldn't do anything but hurt him to know she was gone, and there was no reason to add to his pain.

Unaware of my emotional conflict, Niklaus kept chattering about his family. I tried hard to pay attention, but beyond his connections to the devil, Chancellor Heira didn't interest me at all.

"Then, when we entered the trials. I thought I'd be walking through the gates to Eternis with you and Mikhael in tow." He turned his head, flashing me a triumphant grin. "I thought we'd reign supreme in the devil's lands. Victors above everything else." His expression darkened, turning serious. "We still will, you know. After we win this war, I'll find Mik and the three of us can settle in the devil's lands. We can take what was once our ultimate prize."

"Why me?" I asked. There was nothing I wanted less than to remain anchored by his side throughout their mission, and then beyond that at all. The idea of betraying Samael left me nauseous.

It was a selfish question, but despite passing my first trial, I was still a glutton for some things, and that included validation. I'd always been desperate for validation.

Feeling desperately alone was the worst possible feeling. Wondering if anyone would remember you if you disappeared in the middle of the night. I sought reassurance that Nik had considered me, enough to imagine winning The Devil's Trials together.

"Why not, love?" he said it flippantly, cheekily.

I thumped the back of my hand against his chest. Causing him to exhale sharply.

"Seriously, Niklaus!" I huffed. "You must have a reason?"

He twisted, reaching towards the stand beside the bed for a small round tin and a pack of matches. He plucked at one of the three roughly rolled smokes inside, and when the end of it burned bright, the too-sweet smell of chuckleweed permeated the air. Soft tendrils of pink smoke drifted above us. At home, he'd always smoked tobacco, the scent sharp and acrid. This sweeter scent reminded me of the red-headed man, more than him.

"Now?" he asked. He puffed out a lung full of smoke which lingered in a haze above us. "You remind me of home, Octavia. But back during the Gluttony trial? I don't know. We'd hooked up...What? Once? Twice? We were just one quick moment in an infinite stream of consciousness. Nothing that memorable. If I'm honest, I barely thought about you again until you popped up in front of me. On that bus, right before the ceremony? You were just fun to toy with. But sitting across my dining table… You looked at your stack of devil's coins like they had answered all your sin-forsaken prayers — that's when you became interesting."

It hurt to hear that I was a forgettable, fleeting moment to him. But I should have known not to ask a question when I might not like the answer. Swallowing past the lump that formed in my throat, I forced a bitter laugh, trying to put space between us. "Well, shit, Nik. Don't sugarcoat it for me or anything."

"You'd hate it if I did," he said, tightening his grip and not letting me go. It was amazing that he could hold on so tightly when he didn't have a hand. He waved the smoke at me. "Want some?"

"No!" I snapped. "Devils, you're an asshole. Nobody wants to hear they weren't memorable."

He inhaled again, offering a single comment on the edge of his next cloud of smoke. "Sorry, love."

"No, you're not."

"You're right. I'm not," he agreed, twisting and stubbing out the smoke on the side of the tin. When he rolled back, he offered me a slightly lopsided grin, having relaxed from the chuckleweed. "We could still be good together now, though, love. We'd be a post-revolution power couple."

"Oh, shut up, Niklaus!" I laughed as if it was the worst idea I'd ever heard. However, if I hadn't been trapped by Pride's impossible tasks, and if the thought of disappointing the devil didn't create a cavernous hole in my chest, I might have considered it. "We'll never be a couple."

He did as I asked, falling asleep not long after. I stared up at the roof and half wished I'd taken him up on his offer to indulge in the smoke. The weed could have loosened the tension in my bones and let sleep come a little easier. I wondered why the nights dragged on while the days flew by.

After he started snoring, I counted the tiles on the ceiling to pass the time, eventually noticing that one of them was askew. Excitement flooded through me, hot and fast, and sleeping became the furthest thing from my mind.

"Hey, Nik?" I rolled back towards him, rubbing my hand over his chest until his eyes opened. "Nik?"

"Yeah, Octavia?" he mumbled, still half asleep.

"Can I stay here tonight?" I asked.

He yawned sensually as he asked, "To sleep with me or *to sleep with me*?"

Before I could think better of it, I punched him in the ribs, dulling the hopeful glint in his eye. "Nik!"

"Ow!" Niklaus complained, turning to bury his face in my hair. "You didn't need to hit me. Course you can. Just go to sleep, I've got patrol early in the morning. I'll try not to wake you."

Sleep reclaimed him with an ease that seemed to only belong to men. He relaxed against me, snoring before I could say another word. I glanced up at that misplaced tile, convinced I needed to get into his roof. If I were going to hide anything, it would be somewhere just that difficult to reach. It felt like there was no way to sleep now, though, not with plans to make, but somehow, I did, lulled by the warmth of Niklaus' body and the rhythm of his breathing.

I woke up alone.

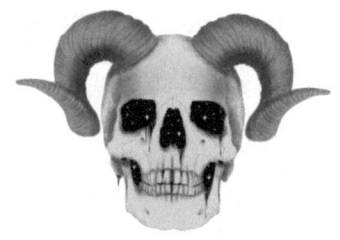

Chapter Five

After two days and new bruises, I climbed into the hole in Niklaus' bedroom ceiling. I felt trapped between the ceiling and the roof after successfully squeezing through the narrow opening. Inhaling a dust bunny, I realised a little treasure trove surrounded me.

Random junk cluttered the area around me, with some of it making no sense. At least in my opinion. They obviously meant enough to Niklaus that'd taken great lengths to hide them away and keep them safe. The small roof opening was hard for me to get through, let alone him. It must have been a struggle.

Niklaus's Heira family ring lay wrapped in a piece of dark cloth. Dried blood tarnished the metal. He had worn on it on the hand I'd severed. He must have plucked off his lost limb before he fled. My heart ached with torment at the thought. That it had meant so much to him, he would pull it free of his own discarded flesh.

I found a black notebook, the cover worn with age and use, the inked words beginning to fade. I flicked through the illegible pages. The notebook contained his brother's smooth, flowing handwriting. I burned with curiosity to know what it said, wondering what secret lay between the pages. Mikhael Heira had been an enigma to me, a man in a suit, poised to take over our village. It was a struggle to understand his willingness to sacrifice everything for love. Or to believe he even loved Margot.

Finally, I found Pride's cursed blade wrapped in a square of dirtied cloth.

Still tucked into the thigh holster I'd been wearing when the rebellion attacked Glorae. Blood flecked the blade. I rubbed at it with the pad of my thumb, wondering how many had come from my body. Gingerly I unbuckled it from the holster, the protective barrier that stopped it from slicing through my skin, and pulled the blade free. Sucking in a sharp breath when I caught sight of the weapon.

It kept its dangerous allure, the dark edge shimmering and captivating. The blade felt inherently deadly, its purpose too great for a human like me, designed for inhuman creatures. It amazed me that Niklaus didn't notice the magic coming from the weapon. My hands trembled as I touched its flat side, feeling a sudden nervousness.

The devil whispered soft, encouraging praise in my ear as I bundled the blade back up. Muffled noises in the distance were enough to set me on high alert. I had to leave, tidy up and continue with my plan before Niklaus noticed. If he found me here, he'd never trust me again.

I had three things to do, and I'd achieved one of them. There was a light shining at the end of the tunnel, but if I didn't get moving that tunnel would collapse on me. I ran through my plan in my head and crawled back to the hole I'd come through.

Step one, find the blade. Done.

Step two, find a means of getting out of the rebellion camp. Easier said than done.

The last step? Flee for Desidia and try to survive the journey. Possibly the hardest of them all.

From the ceiling, the floor looked a lot further away than it had when I'd climbed up here. Determination led to a false sense of success, and the furniture I used to climb fell on my way up. The thought of simply dropping to the floor left me dizzy, and I glanced towards Niklaus' bed. The unmade sheets and dirty clothes wouldn't soften my fall.

Without hesitation, I threw the blade through the hole, aiming for the bed. It bounced on the mattress once and then thumped to the floor. I prayed to Samael and then lowered myself out of the ceiling. Hanging by my fingertips, my arms burning with the strain of holding my weight. Clumsily, I tried to balance holding myself with one hand and edging the tile back in place with the other. When it was nearly there, I swung my legs, pulling my body back and forth until I hopefully had enough momentum to make it as far as the bed.

With my eyes squeezed closed, I let go. Telling myself it was just like the bars above the river in the Wrathlands, that I needed to find my momentum and throw my body forward to make the last leap to safety. I'd done it once; I could do it again.

For a moment I was nothing but a speck of dust in the air, weightless, limitless, free. Time suspended along with gravity. I was infinite. Then I slammed into the wall, having thrown myself too far. The force knocked the wind from my body, and I crumpled down onto the bed. My lungs spasmed as I wheezed, struggling to catch my breath.

"This was a bad idea," I groaned aloud.

'Many of your ideas are,' Samael mused. *'In fact, your track record for good ideas is rather grim.'*

I flipped off the ceiling, imagining that the devil was there to see it. "Thank you, for being ever so helpful."

'I live to serve,' the devil snarked. *'Now get moving, Octavia.'*

It felt like it took another hour to pull myself off the bed, and the entire time I was sure Niklaus would burst through the door and catch me red-handed, stealing something that was already technically mine. I stuffed the blade between my mattress and the bed frame for the time being. It was the most unoriginal of hiding places, but it only needed to last another day. I wasn't planning to stay any longer than that.

I had just returned the furniture back where it belonged, righting his room to its usual messy state, and hoped his own bad habits hid any differences, when the front door burst open.

Guilt flooded me as I turned to face Niklaus. He barely noticed how frazzled I was, raking his fingers through his cropped hair and beckoning me forward. "Come here."

Eager to prove I'd done nothing wrong, I hurried towards him, taking advantage of his distraction.

"Chester called another meeting," Niklaus said, holding the door open and gesturing me forward. I glanced over my shoulder to make sure the doors to both of our rooms were closed. To reassure myself that I had left no evidence in plain sight.

"What for?" I asked from the front porch, as he locked up, ushering me down the stairs.

A wide grin spread across Niklaus' face, and he stood a little taller, his chest puffing out with pride. His hand pressed to the small of my back to direct me down the gravel road. "He wants to send a team ahead to scout out the devil's lands. Gathering information so we know what to expect."

"Oh, really?" I blinked, shocked by this sudden turn in their plans. The last meeting had been all about learning the routes of the Greedlands tunnels. I shouldn't have been surprised. Chester jumped from topic to topic with the wavering attention of a child.

"Really!" Niklaus increased the pressure on my lower back, forcing me to walk faster.

"Wouldn't that be dangerous?" I asked. "The devil could capture and torture information out of someone and ruin all his — I mean, *our*, plans."

It was difficult to use the right language, to include myself as part of their group, but correcting myself was necessary. My mistake made Niklaus clench his jaw. He looked me over, his expression serious, and his lips pursed. When I blinked at him, schooling my face to hide any of my concern, he relaxed.

"No." He was quick to shoot down my concerns. "It'll be completely safe. It was my idea, actually. We need to know what we're dealing with. It's the perfect way to make sure we're not going in blind."

"I don't think…"

"Trust me, Octavia. You don't need to think." Niklaus cut me off, pulling me to a halt and stepping in front of me. He glanced behind him at the people entering Chester's house, then lifted my chin to meet his gaze.

"I don't need to think?" I asked, offended. "I'm perfectly capable of reasonable thoughts."

"There are other people. Smarter people, developing these plans, Octavia. Just trust them," he said in earnest. "You need to come with me on this mission."

"W-What?" I stammered, taken aback, and upset that he'd implied I was stupid.

"You heard me," he said confidently. His thumb stroked against my scarred skin, and I sucked in a breath, trying not to flinch back. "March on Eternis with me, love. Let's do it. Let's be the key to bringing down the devil. You and me. It'll be poetic, the two of us, from the devil's trials, being the reason he dies."

"Niklaus…" I whispered, and his shoulders tensed. The rejection in my voice was clear.

He sighed, a long-suffering sound. "Come on, Octavia. Things are getting better between us, right? You slept in my bed last night!"

"It's not that," I protested quickly. I pulled away, hating how his fingers still traced the flame-marked patterns in my skin. "It's just that I'm not sure it's a good idea…"

"I know it's dangerous, but I believe you can do this," he said encouragingly. As if Nik knew that what I wanted most in the world was to have someone in my corner. He thought that by expressing his belief in me, he could change my convictions. "But you need to decide quickly, Chester's putting together the team today to leave in a few days' time. You need to raise your hand in the meeting to commit to it. Show Chester that this is what you want."

Samael offered no advice on how to get out of this one. I was floundering for the right thing to say. Anything I could think to say would break the peace we'd created. "I'll think about it," I said. Niklaus's expression flattened, showing just how impressed he was by my answer.

"Think quickly," Niklaus urged with a sharp nod. He confidently smiled at me before disappearing into the house. Apparently, confident that I would follow along.

I heaved a sigh, feeling shaky and pressured. Stuck between two conflicting desires, his and my own. Hurt that Niklaus had dismissed me, and my intelligence, in his eagerness. Feeling Samael's touch against my mind, my loneliness subsided. The feeling worsened when Niklaus spoke over me, and demanded things of me, without knowing what I thought or wanted. He didn't care for my opinion.

'He's pushy today, isn't he?' Samael said. *'Perhaps he knows, deep down, that you're planning to leave. He's trying harder to tether you to him.'*

"Or he's just caught up in the excitement of invading your city." I sniffed. Niklaus's excitement hinted at the intense energy in Chester's house.

Samael scoffed. *'As if he could get in. Niklaus Heira would find death before he found my front door.'*

I frowned. Edging towards the steps, I muttered, "You mean if I went with him, you wouldn't welcome me with open arms?"

'You, Octavia?' Samael chuckled darkly, and an icy shiver worked down my spine. *'I'd cut down a path through the dead forest to greet you at the gate myself. But the rest of this ragtag rebellion can hang for the carrion to feast on, for all I care.'*

It felt like fireflies took flight in my stomach. I could feel their fluttering wings through every nerve I possessed. There was no stopping my smile. "Aww, Samael," I whispered. "You do have a heart."

'Don't be fanciful. My black, poisoned heart beats for no one,' the devil chuckled. *'Now, focus, Octavia, you need a way out of there by tomorrow.'*

"Samael?" I asked, hesitating. Finding the courage to voice one of my fears.

'Yes, Little One.'

"Will Pride come for me the moment I leave here?" I asked. "I don't have his mark. All he has to do is change his mind and he could drag me back to his city. He could claim me as a forfeit, for breaking the rules of your trials."

'You make it to Suain, safely, and I will take care of Pride's mark.'

"You promise?" I whispered, feeling needy for his reassurance.

'I swear it on the devil himself.'

"I don't think it counts when you swear on your own soul."

Samael just laughed.

"Are you going to actually go in?" someone asked, from behind me. They stood so close that I could feel their breath tickling the back of my neck. I startled, almost tripping over the step and I twisted to see Maksymilian standing at my back. There was no one in sight except for him.

They all entered the meeting without caring if I turned up. I'd been so wrapped up in my mental conversation with the devil that I'd barely noticed them.

"Are you?" I asked, turning the question back on him.

"Nope." His lips popped the 'p' sound as he answered. A lazy smile curved across his face, brightening his entire expression. He stood back from the house with his hands tucked into his pockets, fiery hair left loose over one shoulder.

"Why not?" I asked, prepared for him to dismiss the question. Because nobody in the rebellion camp trusted me enough to answer my questions, I had more left unanswered than not.

Maksymilian surprised me by shrugging. "I have no interest in heading to The Devil's Lands. It's a fool's errand. Logic says if I don't go to the meeting, then Chess can't allocate me to the team. Then I don't have to deal with it."

"You mean he wouldn't ask you if you wanted to go?" I frowned. Surely a team with willing participants would be more successful than ones who dragged their feet because they were unmotivated.

Maksymilian laughed. "Does this really seem like the type of movement where everyone gets a say?"

"Good point, well made," I said, sighing.

"You'll be going along, I expect," He added. He stepped a few paces away, grinning like he expected I would follow. I did. He was the first person to talk to me openly, and I wasn't giving that up for the world.

"I never said I would go!" I called, lagging a few steps behind him.

"Oh, but Heira will nominate you. I would put money on it." Maksymilian sounded smug. "There's no way he'll leave you here on your own for three months. What if you started talking to someone else more than you did to him? What if you started thinking of your own ideas? He wouldn't be able to cope."

A cool breeze floated between the houses, and I shivered, stupidly protesting again, because there was a part of me that clung to the easy peace that had developed between Niklaus and me. The same part that didn't want to shatter it and ignored that Maksymilian had also realised Niklaus thought I was dumb. "He just asked me to think about it," I said. "I haven't agreed to go."

"When's he ever really given you a choice, Octavia?" Maksymilian's gaze was bright as he crowed the question. He paused by one of the old trees in the middle of the courtyard, leaning against the trunk. "When's the last time he asked what you wanted?"

My mouth dried out, and I tried to think about the last time I had truly been included in a decision bigger than whether I wanted to go to dinner before sunset or after it. I couldn't think of anything, even before he brought me here, Niklaus never valued my thoughts or opinions. My heart sank into my stomach as I realised the truth. Niklaus had only ever included me in inconsequential decisions, just enough to appease and include me. The things that would make me feel like I'd contributed but not affect anyone else, or the world around me.

My bitter pain reflected in my tone: "Never, I guess."

Maksymilian looked so smug that I itched to slap the expression right off his face. He bounced on the balls of his feet, leaned close to me and asked, "What do you want, Octavia?"

"I want to go to Desidia," I said.

"You want to finish the trials, right?" He nodded as if he'd known the answer all along.

Denying it would be pointless. "Actually, yes, I do. I committed to the trials, I committed to completing them if I could. I'm not really a woman of my word, but I'd like to see them through."

"To what end?" he asked, rubbing his chin through his beard. "Are you going to enter Eternis and slay the devil in the rebellion's name?"

"Uhh," I hedged, unable to tell what the right answer was in this situation. "Well…"

Discomfort swept through me. He couldn't possibly comprehend that I had to confront the devil solely due to the unreasonable trial rules, not out of any misguided notion that humanity could triumph over the devil, sins, and magic.

"Don't answer that," Maksymilian cut me off before I could elaborate. "I'd rather you say nothing at all than listen to you tell me a lie."

Pressing my lips together, accepting his challenge, I said nothing.

It didn't take him long to break the silence. He moved close enough for me to feel his body heat through his shirt. I could smell the bitter tea and chuckleweed that lingered on his breath. When he turned his head, his wiry beard tickled my skin. "What if I knew how to get you to the Slothlands?"

"What if you did?" I asked, keeping my tone neutral, although my heart raced. I swallowed, unsure of whether he was just toying with me.

If Niklaus looked outside and saw me so close to Maksymilian, all pretences of peace would shatter whether I wanted it or not. These days it felt like the only thing Nik hated more than Maksymilian was the devil. I couldn't step back, though. The red-headed man had effectively enticed me to stay longer and keep giving him my wholehearted attention.

His smile widened. He reminded me of a hellhound, of a predator who knew he'd caught the attention of his prey. "I could take you there…If you wanted."

"What's in it for you?" I asked, suspicion creeping through me. For all I knew, Chester had put him up to this to test my loyalty. If I failed, they would secure me behind locked doors before I could say a word to defend myself. "I'm sure you don't do anything for free."

"Well…" Maksymilian clucked his tongue, glancing over my shoulder at the house before he continued. "Chester's plan is pure devil-shite, if you ask me. I like my plan. It's solid, and I'll act on it myself if he's too scared to see it through. If I want to walk into his city with the victors of the trials, I need to literally be with them. Let me tag along while you finish the trials, and I'll make sure you make it to each of them."

I took a moment to decide whether I believed him. It was exactly what I needed and also too good to be true. My luck rarely ran that way. Maksymilian was hiding something, but I hesitated to press him further.

"You just want to tag along, just so you can take your shot at the devil whenever we get there? Even though it could literally be years from now. And you're going to attack him all on your own?" I asked quickly. I was equally worried our conversation would get cut short or he'd bore of entertaining my curiosity.

"Sure." Maksymilian nodded, patting his pockets as if he were searching for something. "You don't think I can do it? If we knew each other, your lack of confidence in me would be wounding."

"I don't believe you," I told him. He pulled a slim silver box from his pocket and turned it between his fingers. I'd seen one of them before, Niklaus had had one in Ilrea. A lighter, a substitute for matches that only the rich could have afforded. "You're not going to take on the devil alone."

"I never asked you to believe me," he said. He acted like he didn't care if I believed him or not. As if he didn't care what anyone thought of him. "I asked you if you wanted to go with me to the Slothlands."

"No, you didn't."

"Well, I implied it." He shook his head, stroking his beard with his free hand. "In just as many words. Can't you read between the lines?"

"I can't read at all," I said, flippantly. "You'll have to say it."

"Come again?" The freckled-faced man narrowed his eyes at me, fingers falling still around the lighter. He tucked it in his fist, holding it tight. Surprise had flared in his eyes. I knew he was trying to work out whether I'd told him the truth. I didn't know why I had. The words had burst from my chest before I could give them proper thought. I was sick of carrying my secrets around like burdens, especially when the worst of creatures — Pride — already used them as weapons.

"You don't like lies, Maksymilian," I said, refusing to repeat myself for him. Refusing to confirm or deny. "So, tell me what you want. Tell me the truth."

Voices rose inside Chester's house. Cheers echoed out the half-open door. Someone pounded against the window, making it rattle. Maksymilian glanced towards the house and then held out his hand. After a beat, I took it, and he led me out of view of Chester's home and its occupants, leaning against the thick trunk of a tree. He let go of me quickly, rubbing at the shaved side of his head, and nodding to himself.

"I'll take you safely to the Slothlands, the Lustlands and through the Greedlands, *if* you'll lead me into the heart of Eternis, Octavia. I won't force you in on my attack on the devil unless it's what you actually want. I'm not Chester, or Heira."

"I don't know what to say," I admitted, shocked that he'd actually said it aloud. The earnest look in his eye convinced me that this wasn't a test.

'Say yes, Octavia.' Samael prompted.

"Say yes," Maksymilian unknowingly repeated the words of the devil. He held out a hand, offering to shake on the deal. "You can call me Max."

Maksymilian Tate either had a very good understanding of the inner workings of the rebellion, or he was a fortune teller, imbued with gifts that allowed him to see the future. I was willing to bet it was the former, but still questioned if he didn't have a premonition. Niklaus confronted me in the main square, reprimanding me for not attending the meeting. He then revealed that he had nominated me for their expedition. Whether I liked it or not.

"What?" I threw my hands in the air. I was more exasperated at the fact that Max had been right than Niklaus's now predictable anger. "I said I'd think about it. I didn't say I was going with you."

"I told you that you didn't have long to think!"

"You didn't tell me I only had five minutes!" I spluttered, fisting my hands in my hair. "You can't just make these decisions for me, Nik. What if I wanted to stay? What if I'd be more useful here?"

"Doing what?" he snapped, face pinched with displeasure. He paced back and forward in front of me, a trapped lion of a man. "You've been as much help as a dead fish the last two weeks. There is literally nothing you could do of use here."

"I don't know." I reared back, resenting the comparison. If anyone was a dead fish, it was him. "Cooking? Stomping down the grass? Fixing the windows. Just about anything would be more useful than traipsing across the country, getting in your way, and potentially dying."

He rolled his eyes. "You weren't there to nominate yourself or decline. So, I decided for you. Get over it."

"I wouldn't have nominated myself, even if I was there." I huffed. "What are you not understanding about this, Niklaus? Nobody said you could make choices for my life."

He scrubbed his hand down his face, aggravation turning his tone rough. "It's too late to back out now. I already told Chester you were going, and it's final."

"Nik…" I sighed his name and wanted to wrap my hands around his neck and throttle him. I wanted to shake him until he actually heard what I was saying. "Just listen to me, won't you? This isn't something I want to do!"

"We're leaving in two night's time, Octavia," he said, stiffly, speaking over the top of me. Ignoring my protests. "I need to get things ready. There's a lot to do. But I tell you what, if you think you'd be good at cooking, you can help with it tonight. Cook dinner to learn for the trip, and that can be your job while we're out there."

He walked away before I could protest. Leaving me open-mouthed and fuming at his back in the middle of the square. Storming back towards the house, I envision several ways that I'd like to see Niklaus die. Most of them involved choking on his own audacity.

After the regular cooks had collectively decided that I was going to be completely useless in their kitchens, I'd been put on potato duty. I sat in front of a bucket, washing and peeling misshaped vegetables. It wasn't the worst job in the world. The vegetables were familiar. My father had worked as a potato farmer, and I'd eaten them all my life, but that didn't mean I'd cooked with them before. That had been my mother's job.

My fingers had turned wrinkly from the water, and red from the awkward way I held the knife. The tips of my fingers pinched with pain. Each minute reminded me of my dad tirelessly digging up vegetables to feed us. The way the dirt had stained his skin, never completely washing from the creases in his knuckles.

Misery welled in my gut the entire time until it felt like my mood was poisoning everyone around me. My grunted answers to their questions became aggressive, and they slowly left me to my own devices, chattering among each other instead — sealing my position as an unwelcome outsider.

"You're really butchering those potatoes, aren't you?" Max asked with a laugh.

He crouched in front of my bucket of dirty water. He'd pulled his long auburn hair into a knot at the back of his head. Spilled flour covered his shirt, it was on his arms, and there was a smudge on his cheek. He spent a significant amount of time kneading dough, and I tried not to stare at his strong arms. More than once, he'd caught me looking.

I ignored him, focused on peeling. He dipped his fingers into the bucket, swirling them around and flicked droplets of water at me.

I jerked backwards, causing the vegetable to slip and plunge into the bucket, dousing me in cold water. My shoulders slumped.

"What do you want?!" I snapped, waving the small knife at him. "Are you here to tell me what to do, as well? Because you're shit out of luck, I'm done taking orders today. The next person who commands me to do something is getting stabbed."

"Never!" he exclaimed. "I don't care what you do enough to order you around."

He sounded so sincere about it that I faltered in my anger, some of the irritation ebbing from my muscles. It was strange to be comforted because someone didn't care about me. The tap of his flour-covered fingers against my nose recaptured my attention, and I jerked back. "Came over to ask if you're ready to leave?"

My heart seemed to slow in my chest, every beat a hard thump against my ribcage.

"Right now?" I whispered, absolutely certain I wasn't ready. I was aware I had limited time before Niklaus took me away on his grand plan. I just thought it would be longer than a few hours.

"No, not right now. I haven't had dinner yet, and I'm not leaving on an empty stomach." He grinned, as if he thought himself hilarious for that comment, and I responded with a dry look. Everyone thought they were funny when I wasn't in the mood for banter. The corner of his smile slipped as he studied my expression, and Max nodded, looking serious for once. "Just name the time. The sooner, the better."

Sighing, I realised I had to commit to the idea of going with him, of escorting him to Eternis. It was my only true chance of getting out of here and if it didn't work, at least I could say I'd tried. Plunging my hand into the bucket of water, I grasped for the potato and held the knife firmly in my hand, scraping at the next piece of the peel. I made him wait until I finished before answering him. But Max didn't seem aggravated by my silence. He just settled on his heels, content to wait me out.

"Tonight," I said, deciding I was angry enough at Niklaus that I wouldn't stay another day. Not even to give myself the chance to say goodbye. "Meet me when the moon is in the middle of the sky. By the tree where we spoke this morning."

Max flicked two fingers off his forehead in a mock salute. As his shirt rode up, he flashed a patch of skin which hinted that he had freckles everywhere.

"It's a date," he said, whistling to himself as he went back to work.

I groaned, tossing the potato into the next bucket. "It's definitely not a date!"

He was downright delusional.

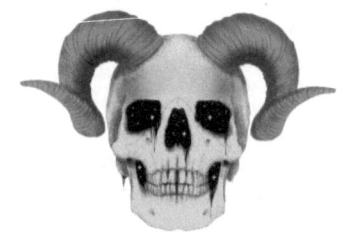

Chapter Six

I tightened the leather strap on my thigh to secure Pride's dagger. It was looser now that I'd lost some of the muscle in my legs, yet somehow, with the glittering black blade strapped against me, I felt balanced. I was more confident with a weapon in hand.

The trauma of my experiences etched everything I'd learned in these trials into my soul. I had to trust myself and believe that I would continue to survive.

I took a final look in the mirror, grabbed my supplies, and rushed out the door.

Since the night we slept in the same bed, Niklaus had stopped locking the front door, trusting me a little more. The night that he claimed had improved our relationship. Despite the rise and fall of his anger, and his ever-controlling nature, he seemed willing to show I wasn't his prisoner. Still, I hesitated in the front room to listen for the soft sound of his snoring. He slept heavily, a luxury afforded to those who had always had a warm bed at night.

Flinging the door open, and before I could second guess my plans, I escaped into the cold night.

Maksymilian waited for me in the darkness, perched by the gnarled old tree.

Just as he'd promised.

Despite his dark clothes blending in with the shadows, his rolled-up sleeves and unbuttoned shirt still made him noticeable. His pack sat at his feet, three times the size of my own, and stuffed full. He had his hands tucked into his pockets, his copper hair unsecured and tumbling over one shoulder. His pale skin almost glowed under the light of a complete moon.

With his chin lifted and head tilted, he stared at the star-filled sky. I wondered if he was making wishes. His distraction was enchanting, making me watch him, hesitant to disturb him. I'd have felt more nervous if he'd been stoic or worried, staring in the direction I'd come. Worse yet, if he'd been tense in his wait for our escape. Instead, somehow, his peace was reassuring. If he wasn't worried, I wouldn't stress myself out either.

"Octavia!" My name rolled through the night, sharp and demanding.

I looked back over my shoulder at Niklaus. He stood framed in the doorway of his house. His pants slung low across his hips, tattoos on full display and his hair rumpled from sleep. He must have heard the door open. I quickly glanced away from him and hurried towards Maksymilian.

Max nodded at me and immediately led the way without waiting. It was time to go, and I'd promised myself I wouldn't stay for a difficult goodbye. Even if they followed me into the night.

'Quickly now, Little One.' The devil crooned in my ear, encouraging me to move faster. I held tight to the pack I'd stolen and ducked my head to march forward.

"This way," Maksymilian grunted, not slowing at all for

Niklaus' appearance. In fact, he walked away like the man hadn't interrupted a thing. "We need to be out of here before Chester wakes. He won't like this one bit, and I'm not in the mood for a fight with him tonight."

"Octavia!" Niklaus called again, louder now. My name had become a sharp beckoning demand. As if he could stop me with a single word. But Niklaus didn't possess the powers of an angel, demanding my pliant obedience with nothing but his voice. So, I kept my eyes on Max in the distance, determined to follow him.

Gravel crunched beneath Nik's boots when he jumped down from his porch and onto the path. He was away from the house, across the green and gaining on me fast. Seven weeks of drug-induced sleep had wasted away my strength, and I'd become slow.

Nik caught my left arm and wrenched me back. Stones dislodged beneath my shoes and I almost stumbled. His grip tightened, bruising against my skin, ensuring I didn't fall.

"Niklaus! Let go!" I snapped, fighting my arm free of his grip and for my balance. My hand moved to the blade at my thigh, grasping the handle, and I stopped just short of pulling it on him. The threat remained though. "I swear on the devil, I'll splice you from throat to cock, if you don't let me go right now!"

"Get your hands off her," Maksymilian had stopped walking, standing a few paces ahead of us. Although before he'd pretended the other man didn't exist, now he didn't hesitate to turn and glare at Niklaus. Max may not have been in the mood to fight with Chester, but his demeanour showed that he was prepared to fight with Niklaus. He prowled back to us.

He stalked back to get between us, pulling his hands free of his pockets and fisting them by his sides. Their feud went deeper than me and my attempts to escape. The tension of their mutual hatred grew thick in the air as Max drew closer. His approach had Niklaus's grip loosening, granting my freedom. "She doesn't want to go with you, Heira. Go back to bed."

"Piss off, Tate!" Nik barked, chest puffed out. When I met

his green eyes, I could see a flash of hurt within. Hinting at the betrayal he felt because I'd fled in the night to meet this man. "I'm not talking to you. This has nothing to do with you."

Max scoffed at the demand. His gaze flicked in my direction, deferring to me, waiting for my order to move. Nobody had ever let me lead before, but it seemed he would only walk away if it was what I wanted. My heart stuttered over its next beat.

"It's okay," I said, after giving it a moment of thought. Although I was weaker than I had been, I had some faith that Niklaus wouldn't truly hurt me. If he tried, I still had the knife, and he only had hand one hand to fight me off. "Go have a smoke, Max, I'll be with you soon."

A slow grin tugged at the corners of Maksymilian's lips, and he stroked at his copper-tinted beard. There was a moment as he studied me, as if deciding whether I meant it, but his shoulders relaxed when he accepted my request.

"Don't mind if I do," he said, nodding firmly. He glared at Niklaus before heading towards the shadows near his house, brushing against my arm. A few paces away from us, he added, "Yell if you need me."

With him at my back, I felt confident and less alone.

"Where the fuck do you think you're going?" Niklaus asked, not waiting for Max to move away before he hissed at me. He sounded more like my jailer than a friend and lover. Anger and pain were clear in his voice. "And with *him*."

"I'm leaving," I said, told the obvious. Maksymilian had disappeared down across the green, lighting a flame with a metal cylinder in the shadows. It cast a soft glow across his freckle-smattered face, enhancing the shadows beneath his eyes. I licked my lips, feeling the need to explain it to Niklaus. Though I owed him nothing. "I need to make it to the Slothlands before the next trial is over. Just because Wrath won't claim your forfeit, doesn't mean Pride or Sloth won't come for me when I fail. I'm not prepared to sit here and let them hunt me down."

"Pride?" he asked.

A muscle in his jaw twitched. He said the angel's name with a mocking edge, oozing clear derision. They'd burned the angel, wounded him, and he no longer seemed like such a threat. Even sins could burn. But to me, Pride was still the biggest threat in my life, the biggest danger of them all.

Niklaus scoffed as if I were stupid. "You passed that trial before we attacked Glorae. There's no reason for him to come looking for you. If anything, he's too busy hunting us for the slight. He's got his sights set on the rebellion. We're the ones that angered him."

Niklaus would be the sort to think that hunting him was more important than hunting me. He didn't understand the Pride's true nature. He didn't know the value the angel had placed in me by trapping me within the carefully articulated rules of the trial by weaponising my fears of death, life, and failure. It felt like I was afraid of everything big, and that discomfort kept me alive.

Nik was clueless because he'd already failed.

A phantom pain seared along my wrist, just below the iridescent cuff that kept me chained to the devil. The vividly inked markings of the pig, snake, and lion sat stark against my skin, and I swept my fingers over them. I trusted Samael's promise to solve the missing mark of Pride.

"I don't have a mark of completion, Nik, and it's in the rules that I have to get them all." I twisted my wrist for him to see. "If I don't get it, I'm still forfeit to Pride."

His expression fell, and I wondered if he'd expected his weak reassurances to work. If he'd thought that making himself out as the ultimate target would help me feel safe. Shifting his weight, he grimaced and tried another tactic. "They won't come for you," he said bluntly.

"You don't know that."

"Stay, love," he whispered then, moving closer, the scent of him washing over me. His attempt to manipulate me was cruel, leaving cracks in the stubborn part of my heart that wanted him to love me. He knew of the cruelty too, taking my hand, stroking my knuckles, and asked, "Won't you do it for me?"

There were many, many things I would have done for Niklaus in the past, but losing myself wasn't one of them. I'd never do that for the sake of another person again. I deserved more.

"I need to go, Nik," I told him, loathing the pleading edge to my tone that sounded like I was asking his permission. Amongst the underlying fear that Pride would come for me — even here, tucked away from the seven sins, in the heart of brewing human hatred — was the fear that I'd lose myself. I hated the part of me that wanted to ease his pain at the expense of myself. "I need to see these trials through *and win*. This is the life I chose for myself, Nik."

He pursed his lips, a vein throbbing in his temple. His jaw tensed, indicating Niklaus's shift away from gentle persuasion. He changed tact so quickly that it left my head spinning. His nostrils flared and he tilted his chin, sneering at me.

"What use is winning and immortality if the rest of humanity are still oppressed?" he seethed, advancing on me. His fists clenched by his side, and wrath lighting his gaze. When he stepped forward, I stepped back. He still carried that sin, and always would. Violence pushed him forward. "You want to finish the trials and leave the rest of us to rot? What about me? Or everyone else? What about your family, Octavia?"

I flinched. He was one to talk about family. His own brother was halfway across the continent, struggling to survive in the face of his sins. His mother was dead. His father? Well, that man would likely never change, too preoccupied with himself to think of anyone else. Niklaus couldn't preach about family. Not when he sat amid the Pridelands and had never once thought of visiting them — where he would learn the truth.

I bit my tongue, holding back the news of Prudence Heira,

not wanting to reveal it in anger. It wasn't how I would have wanted to find out I'd lost my mother.

"Immortality is more time for change!" I argued hotly, unwilling to back down in the face of his ire. This was why I hadn't wanted to see him before I left, because he asked the impossible of me. I wouldn't be able to back down and agree, I wouldn't be able to let it go.

Meeting Niklaus halfway, I lifted my chin. My entire body trembled with overwhelm, emotions running rampant with each steady beat of my heart. Ebbing through me like a poison that threatened to cut me off at the knees. Beneath the bright light of the moon, I felt exposed and judged. "You can't honestly believe that change happens in a single day! Winning immortality would be like gaining an eternity to help humanity. It wouldn't be abandonment!"

"We don't need an eternity!" Niklaus screamed in my face. "We need here and now! Don't be selfish, Octavia!"

Incredulous laughter bubbled over my lips, high-pitched and filled with my anger. "We need longer than a human lifespan. What's fifty years, Nik? Enough time for a single step forward and three steps back?"

He was trembling with the force of his rage. His muscles locked as he held himself in place. He raked his gaze over my body and hissed, "You just want more time as the devil's whore!"

My hand cracked against the side of his face, the force of it snapped his head to the side. The sound of the slap echoed between us. My palm smarted and burned from the impact. He had a fucking hard head.

Niklaus panted, his chest rising and falling sharply, but my assault only intensified his burning eyes. His jaw tensed and the muscles in his neck corded. He sneered at me. When his hand twitched by his side, I braced myself for an attack.

"I am not the devil's whore!" I said. "Find a better insult."

"Do you think I'm that stupid, Octavia? You think I haven't

worked out who '*Sam*' is?" he spat the name, literally. A glob of spit landed on the toe of my boot. Bile crept up my throat, and I scowled, disgusted. "We've all heard you talking to yourself. Whispering your hopeless prayers to the devil beneath your breath. You taunted me for months in the Wrathlands with the idea of Sam. It was all fake, this fictional love you have for the devil. Where is he, Octavia? He's not helping you. He's a fantasy at the end of a quest that's designed to kill you. He's the one leaving you to rot. You're stupid for giving him your loyalty and your soul, and when you get there. If you make it to Eternis, he'll never let you go. He'll ruin you." Niklaus was panting, seething. "Will it be worth it then? All this pretending? You need to grow up."

My heart was thumping in my chest, heavy beats full of agony. There was no good way to tell him I'd rather be ruined by the devil than suffocate beneath his heavy-handed grip. I was painfully aware of Maksymilian standing only a short way away, listening to every word we said. Listening to Niklaus condemn me as delusional, or stupid. Worry slithered through me — if Maksymilian decided I wasn't worth the risk, I'd be on my own.

As our argument escalated, I worried the others would wake up, and it wouldn't just be the three of us. That I'd have to escape them all. With every person we woke, my chances of leaving would diminish.

Thrumming with anxiety, I said, "You mean, the same way you won't let me go, right now? I don't belong to the devil, and I don't belong to you either, Nik. This is my choice to make, and you can't make me stay. If you do, then you're no better than Samael. Is that what you want? To be as bad as the devil, the being you're so desperate to annihilate?"

'*Excuse you...*' Samael protested, although he sounded more amused than offended by my claim.

Niklaus visibly flinched and deflated despite the way his fingers curled into his palm, hand fisted and ready for a fight. I

91

could almost hear the way his teeth ground together as he weighed up his next words. When he looked up again, he narrowed his gaze and glared past me, through me, to fixate on Maksymilian instead. A look that dismissed me.

Frustration bubbled within me, and I wanted to slap him again.

"Tate!" Niklaus barked, the name echoing through the nearly empty village. He didn't care who he woke.

Max turned and loped towards us. His hands buried in his pockets and the lit smoke dangled from his lips. He regarded the two of us cautiously, eyes narrowed, and the tip of his ears turned pink, as if he'd rather be anywhere than in the middle of our spat. Or maybe he was just aggrieved to have come to Niklaus' call.

"You called? I answered. I live to serve, dickhead," he said with a dramatic bow. The pinch of his lips around a smoke muffled his words. He addressed Niklaus with all of his usual mocking derision. Although he'd offered to come if I called, he looked pissed to have been beckoned by Nik instead.

Niklaus' eyes gleamed with undisguised hatred.

"Why are you taking her out there?" he asked, folding his arms across his chest. "What did she offer you? She has nothing of worth, Tate. You're an idiot if you think this is a good idea."

"Why not?" Maksymilian shrugged. Unfazed by Niklaus's tumultuous emotions, he stepped in front of me. Ensuring that Niklaus' full attention remained on him. "It's been getting boring around here. Especially since you turned up. At least she has the balls to go do something exciting."

"You're spineless," Nik snarled, undeterred by the insult. "You're just running away from a challenge because Chester didn't like your weak plans. Revolution isn't supposed to be simple, Tate, you aren't supposed to be comfortable. You aren't the smartest man in the room anymore, and you can't handle it."

Maksymilian tilted his head, a slow, purposeful move. The tension in the courtyard increased, and I realised Max was giving

Nik a chance to take back his words. Exhaling, he let the smoke fall from his lips. The embers bounced on gravel, and then he crushed them with his boot.

The two men stared each other down.

"You'd know all about things being easy, wouldn't you, Heira?" Max asked. There was a wolfish sharpness to his expression that left me uneasy. As if he didn't have blades or fists to fight. Niklaus had redirected his aggression towards Maksymilian. But this man had little to no affection for Niklaus, and no reason to hold back. "Didn't you have a nice cushy life back in your shit hole little town? You're the son of a chancellor, I heard, scrubbed up with soap made of gold. I bet you had the peasants folding your underwear and their spit shining your shoes. What would you know about discomfort?"

A flush fused across Niklaus' chest, rising along the column of his neck and burning around his ears. A vein in his temple throbbed, as if warning that his head could explode. I took a purposeful step back, unwilling to put myself between these two men as they worked out their egos.

The moon retreated as they continued their argument, anticipating the sunrise. With the rising dawn came the village waking, came Chester, and the threat of being locked up, again. We had to leave soon.

"Are you serious?" Nik hissed. "Says the man who bakes bread with the women instead of protecting our camp. You spend more time high than functional, Tate. I'd say you're the one living an easy life. Chester doesn't even trust you with a blade."

"I'm always serious, and I always tell the truth." Maksymilian countered. "Your shiny life must have come with a chronic case of stupidity, too, if you can't see that having Octavia inside Eternis is our best way in. I'm not surprised you're too thick to understand, though. You are just here as muscle, after all."

Niklaus growled, shoulders tensing in preparation to swing,

and I rolled my eyes.

Samael urged me to leave, and I decided he was right. With Niklaus focused on Max, I could escape and meet up with the redhead later.

"Have fun comparing the size of your trauma, boys," I muttered, unable to leave Niklaus with the last word. Loosening strands of hair from behind my ear to hide my face, I turned away from them. "I'm sure it'll solve all your many problems!"

I didn't need to sit through their argument or linger to face Chester. Not every uncomfortable moment had to be endured for the sake of growth. I'd done enough growing for a lifetime.

While I didn't know which way to go, I didn't think it would be a problem. Something told me one, or both, of the men would catch up to me soon enough. I headed for the thicket of tall, dark trees behind Maksymilian's house. Unsure what I'd do if Niklaus decided he was coming along, too.

The trees loomed ahead of me, the shadows shifting in my vision. Fear clutched at me like a vice. Chester could be avoided, but I needed to confront the possibility of facing Erlkangs. If they were out there, I'd have to face them.

"Go on then, coward! Run away with her. I won't stop you." I heard Niklaus hiss from the distance. I glanced over my shoulder, watching him shove at Max's chest. "But you better keep her safe and bring her back, Tate, or I swear on the devil himself I'll make you suffer."

Maksymilian snorted. "Looking at your face makes me suffer, Heira. Nothing else you do could be worse."

"Piss off!" Niklaus snarled. "Get moving. She's already gone!"

Their voices carried, and I peeked around the house, hesitant to enter the forest. I saw Max flip Niklaus off, pick up his pack, and spin on his heel to race after me. Quickly, I turned away, edging closer to the trees and pretending I hadn't been watching them. Waiting for him to catch up.

"Hey! Octavia!" Max called, only moments later, his husky voice loud as he gained on me. His hand clamped around my arm to wrench me back a step. I was sick and tired of men wrenching me around like a rag doll. With a huff, I pulled myself free, and surprisingly, Max didn't even try to resist, letting me go the moment I moved.

"You're going the wrong way, dumb-ass," he grumbled. He backed off and raised their hands in supplication. "If you go too far that way you'll walk right off a cliff."

"Call me a dumb-ass again, I dare you," I grumbled. Allowing him to shepherd me around to the other side of the house, further from the tree line.

"Better than being called a Devil's Wh — *Ow!*"

My fist slammed into his shoulder. "Don't you dare say it!"

"You let Heira call you that," he cried. "What a devils-damned double standard!"

"Don't feel so special," I growled. "I hit him, too."

His answering chuckle eased the tension in my shoulders. He shrugged, as if that were apology enough. A smile crept across his freckled face. "Of course you did. You're a bit violent tonight."

"Why are you being so nice to me when you're so rude to Nik?" I asked. We turned towards the south side of the little village. "You're always ready to fight him. But here you are offering to help me, making sure I don't walk off cliffs."

"For one thing," Max said. "You've got a bigger knife than him, which makes you a bigger threat. Secondly, I like you more. Thirdly, I'm not helping you, we're helping each other."

"You don't even know me," I said, trying to tamp down my nerves as we finally entered the thick trees. The sun was rising, and with sunshine came shadows. With the morning came the threat of demons. I didn't know why I was almost trying to convince Max he shouldn't be nice to me. It would be a long journey if I secured a spot on his shit list, right below Niklaus.

"That doesn't change my point," he said. "Now, we're going

to the Slothlands, right?"

"Yeah," I confirmed. Twigs and leaves crunched underfoot. Anxiety flooded me out of nowhere, overwhelming me as the village disappeared behind us. There was no going back now. I'd expected to breathe easier when we left, not harder.

"You know the way?" I asked. "Right."

"Not at all," Max said, grinning.

I paused mid-step, stunned. "You said you did!"

"I implied I did," he said, correcting me. "I said I'd get you there. Which I will, we'll just ask for the directions at the next village."

"Oh, my devil." I scrubbed my hand across my face and suppressed a groan. "That won't work. We're doomed! I can't believe I trusted you were telling the truth. You always preach about being honest and you've devils-damned lied to me in the first minute of the trip."

"Have you tried?" he asked, shifting the weight of his giant pack. He reached into his pocket for a piece of dried meat and offered it to me wordlessly.

"What? Trusting you?" I rolled my eyes, waving off the food. "Obviously. I'm here, aren't I? Even if it was a giant mistake."

"That's not what I mean." He took a bite of the meat, chewing before he asked. "Have you ever just tried asking for help?"

I stopped walking and stared at him like he'd grown two heads.

"It'll work," Max said, and he said it so confidently that I wanted to believe him. His freckled face didn't betray any signs of lying, but I didn't know his tells. He may have been deceiving me from the beginning, making me believe his lies as the truth. "I promise."

"Don't!" I protested. "I'm sick of people making promises they can't keep."

"Oh, I keep all my promises. Just you wait and find out."

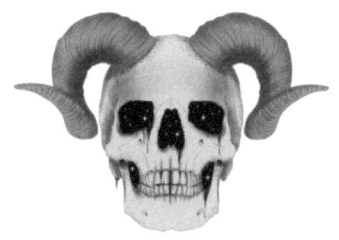

Chapter Seven

Max couldn't keep himself from making noise. He started with humming tunes, then transitioned to whistling a single jingle that stuck in my head.

I buried my face in my hands, wondering if a nicer delivery would help. "Will you shut up, *please*?"

He shook his head. "Still a no."

"Devils, you're infuriating!" I told him after enduring three more verses and hearing Samael hum the tune in my mind. Between the two of them I was going to lose my mind. "Just stop it."

Max was quiet for all of two minutes, which I realised was a huge feat for him. "Tell me a story, Octavia."

"Do I look like someone's grandmother?" I huffed. He slowed down his pace, falling into step behind me. "I don't tell stories."

"Come on," Max said, jabbing me in the ribs with his elbow.

Sharp pain lanced through my side. "You must know something."

My eyes narrowed and I wondered if he was subtly calling me stupid. It wouldn't surprise me if he was. "I know a lot of things. Just not any I want to tell you."

"Why'd you join the trials?" he asked.

"Because I wanted to," I replied.

It wasn't a lie, per se, but there was no reason to get into the nitty, gritty details of my pathetic life. I barely knew Max and I wasn't sure if I trusted him. Giving him an insight into my weaknesses was the last thing I wanted.

"That's a stupid answer," Max said, grinning widely. He freed the tie from his wrist and secured his long hair in a bun.

"Ask a stupid question, get a stupid answer."

"Who's the most interesting person you met in the trials?" he asked.

It was on the tip of my tongue to ask him why he wanted to know, but honestly, I thought he just couldn't handle the sound of silence. I took a moment to mull it over, thinking of all the people I'd met and the impact they had on me — for better or worse.

"Ngaire," I said.

"Who's that?" His face lit up with genuine curiosity. "Tell me more."

Irritation washed through me. It was my fault for bringing her up in the first place, but I didn't want to turn Ngaire, or any of the other people who had ensured I survived, into gossip on a long walk. Truth be told, I also didn't know enough about her to fill the journey. All I really had was the impression she left on me. The way she haunted my memories.

"It's none of your business," I said.

"Has anyone ever told you that you suck at making conversation."

"Yeah, you." I huffed. "Just now."

Maksymilian sighed, but he didn't look pissed off. He kept moving at my pace, his arms swinging by his side. "This is going to be a really long walk if you won't talk to me."

Within minutes he'd started whistling again. The tune was so annoying that I spent the rest of the day debating the best way to gag him.

When the sun disappeared in the trees, darkness flooded in around us. Maksymilian grandly announced that we'd stop for the night. It stunned me, because naively, I'd thought we'd skip out on their rebellion village and reach the next town the same day. I hadn't thought about how far away it might be or the risks of spending another night in the forests.

Max dropped his pack and stretched, letting out a soft groan as he massaged his shoulder.

"How long until we get there?" I asked, staring around the small clearing.

He crouched down, brushing a patch of dirt clear of sticks and leaves, bundling them all to one side. He marked a circle with his boot and packed sticks and leaves in the middle. Wide-eyed, I watched him, unsure if he was ignoring me or just hadn't heard me.

Finally, he spoke. "We'll have to camp out at least two nights before we get to see another person. Unless there are some other hopeless sods roaming the forest to join us."

"Oh."

"Oh, what?" He paused with a fist full of leaves and glanced up at me. His face creased with a frown. "What's wrong?"

"I don't have a sleeping bag," I admitted. "I thought we'd be going from town to town."

"Ah." He clucked his tongue. "How about a tent? Did you bring one of those? Heira would have had one in the house from our trip to Glorae."

"Nope." I bit my lip.

A chill seeped into the falling night, and I shivered, realising I'd packed badly in my panic. I'd stowed away any food I could find in the house, and one of Niklaus' spare shirts. A pair of socks, and the devil's coins that I'd stolen. Beyond that, I only had my knife strapped tight to my thigh, pulsing with an unsettling energy.

Max sat back on his heels, still in a squat and rested his forearms on his knees. He cocked his head and studied me. "Did you bring food?"

"Of course," I said, half indignant, although my supply was pitiful. "Who doesn't pack food?"

"Water?"

"Not a lot," I admitted. "I'd thought we'd be able to refill at the village or a river."

"What did you bring with you, Octavia?" he asked, and although I expected to hear a thread of frustration in his tone, he simply looked curious. He sprinkled the fistful of leaves over the pile of sticks.

"A really big knife and a good attitude. I honestly thought it would be enough." I said, although my attitude didn't feel fantastic right then. My temper grew short, influenced by Niklaus' mood swings the past few weeks. My fuse had become a live wire instead of a string. "Why? What did you bring?"

He ticked each item off on his fingers. "Camping gear, food, water, change of clothes, about a month's worth of weed and a lighter, or two."

"Why do you smoke so much?" I asked.

While I watched on, he pulled the lighter out of his pocket, his thumb stroking down the metal barrel. When he activated it, a small flame appeared. He leaned over the pile of sticks, his free hand cupped as a barrier against the breeze. The leaves caught alight, creating a thick, white smoke that felt like it stuck in my lungs until I coughed. Turning away, I shuddered. The memory of flames licking my flesh was so blatant that for a split second, I couldn't breathe.

"Everyone has a vice," he said, finally answering the question. He waited for me to regain my breath, not commenting on my distress. "Don't they?"

"Right," I scoffed, feeling distinctly like he was fobbing me off.

The stick caught alight, the flames growing, and I flinched at the crackling sound. Max's face creased with concern, and he straightened, shifting between me and the small flames. The tension in my shoulders eased with his stocky body as a barrier.

"They do," he insisted. "What's yours, Octavia? What's the one thing you just can't give up? I bet there's something that lights the fire in your blood, too."

I knew he was trying to distract me from the nightmares that pulled me from the here and now. The ghost of fiery flames climbed the length of my body, searing with their phantom movements. I took a step back from him, my chest tight. My mouth had dried out, but I swallowed, forcing an answer: "…Cards."

"There we go." He raised his hand like he was going to touch my arm, but I darted away from him. I needed space. Looking away, I couldn't face the shame of my feelings, or risk seeing pity in his expression. Too many people looked at me that way. "Octavia…"

"Don't!" I breathed deeply, shaking my head.

"I've got a pack of cards in my bag," he said, ignoring my plea. "Play a round with me after I get us some more firewood?"

He didn't push for an answer, remaining as a solid barrier between me and the flames as they grew.

"What are we betting for?" I asked, only after I felt I could catch my breath and realised cards might be the distraction I needed. "It's no good without a gamble."

"Information." He shrugged. "It's the best currency in the world. Sins would die for it."

"You don't believe that." I didn't think the seven deadly sins would die for anything. They would ruin the world forever.

"No, I don't," Max admitted. "Blue diamonds are actually the most valuable currency in the world. Even Greed would sell his soul to the devil for a good amount of those."

My curiosity piqued, and I glanced at him. "Are they better than the stones Envy has?"

"What stones are they?" His head tilted and Max rubbed at his chin through his beard, his eyes wide with open curiosity. "I've never heard of Envy having a gem that Greed didn't keep in his collection. Greed has nearly everything, it's in the name."

"I... think they're called akelda," I said, screwing up my face as I tried to remember. I had lived and breathed to obtain one of these stones for a solid month during the Envy trial. They used to be important and were now just a foggy memory. The second trial could have been a lifetime ago. "They're green, and black, I guess. He said they were bits of the old world that he brought with him. Before the sins came here."

Max shrugged, his expression blank. "I haven't heard of them. It's probably a scam. Like black dirt in a jar being marketed as a piece of a night sky."

"They're not a scam!" I protested, exasperated at this flippant dismissal. "We had to hunt them down for his task. He adored them, gave them to the best in his city."

"Envy wanting them doesn't make them valuable," Max pointed out. He fidgeted with the coin that hung around his neck, shifting it back and forth along the leather strap. "No matter what the sod of an angel thinks, his desires aren't what the world rotates around."

I frowned at him, folding my arms across my chest. A breathy scoff caught in my throat. He had a lot of big opinions about the sins. "I'm thinking you've never stood toe to toe with an angel before."

Max grinned and it transformed his freckled face. He looked

boyish when he smiled. Instantly, he felt like less of a danger and more of a true ally.

"Ah! See, you're smarter than Heira gives you credit for, you know. Now go find the cards in my pack while I get some more sticks for the fire." He waved me off. "If you win, I'll answer anything you want to know, honestly. But you need to do the same for me."

Having something to do was a relief. It was better than staring into the flames and getting lost in the past. Half an hour later, we sat a good distance from the fire — far enough that the tension ebbed from my spine — and Max split his hunk of bread with me as I dealt out the first round of cards. He didn't know any of the popular games, so I picked one and explained the rules.

His furrowed brow and full attention captivated me. He tried in earnest to follow along, and his questions made me laugh. It was the closest thing I'd felt to peace in weeks.

"I win!" I crowed, lifted by the win.

Max's face fell and he tossed his remaining cards into the dirt. I reached forward to scoop them up, shuffling them back into the deck. Max pulled a smoke out of his pocket, lighting it and inhaling. The tight lines around his eyes relaxed as he exhaled. The space around us filled with the sweet, pink smoke. "Devils-damned."

I couldn't help but laugh. "You're actually terrible at this game. The worst I've ever seen."

"Terrible is a matter of opinion. I'm just warming up," he said, taking another drag. "Ask your question."

I'd already worked out what I wanted to ask. The very question that had been bugging me for weeks. "Why do you and Nik hate each other so much?"

"Hmm." Max blinked. He didn't answer straight away but

cocked his head to glance up at the night sky. "Not holding back for the first question, are you? Brutal. Honestly, I don't know why he hates me, maybe because I don't fawn over him? I don't like him because I think he's fake. He doesn't care about anyone but himself. He's used to having power and can't imagine working for it. He charmed Chester, promising his knowledge of the devil and the trials, assuring us of victory. He fooled that man into changing his plans on his faulty advice. We weren't supposed to attack Glorae, not yet. It was too big and too fast for our little faction of the rebellion. But when you try to deny Heira, he gets angry, and his anger makes him strong. Chester wants to harness it. I think it's going to kill us all."

"Why did you attack Glorae, then?" I asked.

I hadn't realised until right that moment that I wanted a reason, an explanation, for the terror they'd caused. For the loss of lives and the damage that came with it. I didn't know if Nash and Finley were still alive. Or if Peridot's home had been one building to crumble in the distance. The damage was unfathomable.

Nobody had apologised for the harm that came to me, and the death that befell others. Nobody had even bothered to rationalise why it had to be done — why Pride, and why right at that moment? Those questions had been haunting me for weeks, and I hadn't even realised it.

"Because Heira wanted to find you," Max answered. "He was obsessed with getting to you, because you got him out of the trials. All he could talk about was clearing that debt."

My mouth turned dry at the implication that I was to blame for it all. That it never would have happened if I'd let Niklaus die, or if he hadn't wanted to find me.

"That's the truth of why we blew up the good part of a city and stormed the palace. Do you know how many people died trying to kill that angel? Not just in the city, but in our numbers, too. We failed, by the way. Pride's still alive."

"He is?" I clutched at the cards, wondering which outcome I would have preferred. The fire popped and I cringed.

"We lost valuable men and women. They were people I'd been working alongside for years, friends. Their bodies couldn't be recovered, or we'd have lost more people." His chin tilted and he held my gaze. "We lost them to gain you."

Max didn't sound bitter — although it was obvious that he felt it was an unfair exchange — he sounded miserable as if the deaths had taken a toll on his heart, draining his love for life.

"Shouldn't you hate me, then, not Niklaus…" I dared to ask.

"You didn't ask to be kidnapped," Max said, shrugging. "Why would I blame you for that?"

A lump formed in my throat. The bridge of my nose prickled. "You're the first person who's called it kidnapped and not rescued. Everyone seemed to think I should be thankful."

"That would imply you were better off in the rebellion." Max pulled a face, his voice as flat as his blue gaze. He had strange opinions on the Wastelands Rebellion. He encouraged it but condemned it all at once. Almost as if he liked the idea but hated the practice. "Few people are."

"What about you?"

Max turned his head and puffed out another lung full of smoke. He didn't answer my question. "Deal another round, Octavia. It's my turn to win."

It wasn't. I pummelled him, which did amazing things for my mood.

"Loser," I teased him, grinning. "Tell me why you smoke so much? I want the truth this time."

Max didn't hesitate. His smile widened with a lazy edge. The smoke hung from his lips, and he spoke around it. "Life is less painful when the edge is numbed."

It felt like too sharp of an answer to probe any further. I picked up his discarded cards and shuffled them back into the pack, dealing out another round. Moving on.

"A third question for me," I said, smugly. I'd expected him to have a little beginner's luck at some point, so I hadn't anticipated another question. My attention snagged at his hand, which hovered by his throat. "What's the coin around your neck?"

"Ah." He glanced down, pulling at the leather strap around his neck and touching the edge of the coin. "This is the last coin I ever earned before I fled the Greedlands. Nothing more than a little piece of home."

"Why not spend it?" I asked. It looked like it was solid gold. Roughly shaped, and I couldn't see the imprint of the devil on either side when he twisted it. It didn't look like any coin I'd ever seen before.

"That's two questions, Octavia," he said, miming buttoning his lips closed. "You only won one. Deal if you want more."

"Wow, you are getting better," I said. I was slightly stunned that he had actually beaten me — although, everyone was due some luck, every now and again. Even Maksymilian. "Go on, then, ask your question."

"The weed helps. Stops me overthinking my moves." Max nodded. He tossed the butt of the smoke into the fire. "Was Heira right? I mean, when he accused you of talking to the devil? I've heard you talking to yourself but…"

I bit down on my lip, wondering if I should lie. If Samael wanted me to lie and keep our secret. It was tempting to tell him what was happening. I didn't want to make up another story, or flippantly explain it away. I wanted someone to know the truth, or at least part of it, so I nodded. I wanted to share the heavy burden, because for all that I adored Samael. It was hard to keep him hidden. "…Yes."

Max's eyes widened. He licked his lips and leaned towards me. "Does he ever talk back?"

106

"One question only, remember," I told him, amusement widening my smile. An affirmation was bubbling up through me, and I desperately wanted to tell him. If I made him work for it though, our night wouldn't end too soon.

When we set our cards down, I lost again. Realising he'd want a follow-up on the question I'd denied him. This, I imagined, would be the moment he lost any faith he had in me. When I admitted that Samael talked to me, whispering in my ear, offering advice and commentary. It would take him all of a heartbeat to deem me a fool and want to leave me behind. Maksymilian was smart enough to put two and two together and realise I'd been funnelling information to his enemy. It would take him the second heartbeat to hate me.

"Oh, go on. Ask me," I said. It would be a relief to share my secret and cut the burden in half. But still I mourned the easy conversation between us, worried about the conflict that would follow. Pinching at the hem of my shirt, I twisted it around my fingers.

He surprised me by changing directions. Max leaned forward to snag a piece of dried meat from the open pack between us. He bit into it. "Can I trust you?"

"No," I replied without missing a beat. I was confident in my answer. "If there's anything I've learned in these trials, it's that it's a bad idea to trust anyone but yourself."

"That sounds pretty cynical to me," he spoke around the mouth full of food, jaw working as he chewed through the tough meat.

Tapping my fingers against the deck of cards, I admitted, "I don't know what that means. Cynical?"

Max nodded. He didn't seem to judge my lack of understanding. "Hmm. It sort of means... Only motivated by thinking of yourself."

"Is that what you think I'm like, Max?" I asked. Sharp hurt pierced through me. His opinion shouldn't matter, but it still bothered me. "That I only think about myself?"

"It would only be human nature if you did. I'm surprised there isn't a sin named selfishness," he commented. When Max glanced up again, he stilled, studying my face. His thick brows creased with confusion. "Are you upset, Octavia? Have I offended you?"

"No," I said. My denial was too quick, the hurt too obvious in my tone. "It's not like your opinion matters, anyway."

He was fighting a smile. It twitched at the corner of his lips, his dimples flashing even as he tried to tamp it down. "Try saying that again, without sounding like someone broke your heart."

"Hearts can't break, Max." I scoffed. "They're not made of bone."

"Tell me that again after we visit the Lustlands." He laughed. "I hear they specialise in shattering them."

Leaves rustled in the distance, followed by the sharp snap of a twig. I reached for my blade, sliding it from the sheath. Max pulled a dagger from his boot and launched to his feet. His grip around the handle was so tight his knuckles blanched. He stalked around the fire, peering into the darkness of the trees. His shoulders tensed and he stared down at the darkness, as if he were silently daring the threat to come and find us. I followed, standing a step behind him, comforted by the feel of the weapon in my grip.

When the forest fell silent, Max glanced over his shoulder at me again. "One of us should sleep. The winner of the last round goes first."

It turned out we only needed one sleeping bag because only one of us would sleep at a time, placing their trust in the other to watch their back. Suddenly, his question felt a lot more important than it had before. I lay on my side, my knees curled to my chest and my blade hidden beneath the pillow. I couldn't bear to turn my back on the flames and instead watched the fire as it burned. They couldn't hurt me if I could see them coming.

"Goodnight, Max," I called as he paced along the trees.

He chuckled, a sound that soothed me. I heard the flick of his lighter. "Sleep well, Octavia."

"What?" I asked, groggy.

Max shook my shoulder, forcing me from the deep recesses of sleep. My head pounded in protest, a sharp ache banding around my skull. Clumsily, I moved to sit upright, groping beneath the pillow for the handle of my knife. My heart was racing, and fear flooded through me, certain he'd woken me for a threat.

"You turn to keep a lookout," Max said. He yawned so widely that I could see right down his throat. "I need some beauty sleep. It takes work to look like this."

My tired body ached, but I nodded. Only after raking my gaze over his messed red braid, and the dark circles beneath his eyes. He looked beat. I gulped water from a nearby canteen to wake myself up. "You do need it, but it won't help," I told him as I stretched. "You can't fix ugly."

Max flipped me off, his grin making it a light-hearted gesture. Once I moved, he pulled the bed closer to the fire and laid down on his stomach. He was asleep in under a minute, snoring under the heat of the fire. I watched him for a moment, rubbing at the crust at the corner of my eyes. It was difficult not to envy the ease with which he slept, the peace that transformed his speckled face.

"What pain are you running from, Max?" I asked, instinctively feeling like this man could be an unexpected danger but I didn't know why. Something about him unsettled me, as if my body sensed he had the power to destroy me. "What secrets are you hiding?"

The second night followed a similar pattern to the first, and the more information I got from Max, the more I believed he was telling the truth. He had a deep-seated scorn for liars, and it encouraged me to match his honesty. I wanted to live up to his expectations. I wanted to show that I appreciated his honesty, by offering it in return.

The days passed quickly as our conversation grew easier, and by the third day, I had no problem teasing him for his clumsiness or off-key singing. He was no tavern bard.

"Sweet, devil above." Maksymilian cried, from a few paces ahead of me. My chin lifted and I narrowed my eyes on his back, reaching for my blade. "I think that's the village up ahead! We're finally at Cardend."

"Good to know you weren't leading us in complete circles," I laughed. Although I was just as relieved to see the small buildings through the thinning trees. Two nights of half-sleep hadn't been enough, and our progress had slowed because of it. It felt like my feet were made of stone.

"Have a little faith in me, Octavia." Max paused and waited for me to catch up. His arm slung around my shoulder, and I staggered beneath his weight. "I've been here once or twice before."

"So, they'll recognise you?"

"Devils, I hope not." He sighed, looking guilty as he glanced at the village ahead. "I was six drinks and two smokes into the wind last time I was here. Pretty sure I danced around a fire pit."

"You know the more I learn about you…" I shook my head, trying not to grin.

"The more you think I'm the most amazing man you've ever met." He let go of me. His elbow jammed against my ribs, and I shoved him sideways a step. "Right?"

"Amazing isn't the word I'd choose for you."

"That's a shame," Max said, clucking his tongue, but grinning widely. "Anyway, the best part of this village is there's an inn. You know what that means? A cold glass of brew *and* we can both sleep at the same time."

"Thank the devil for small wins," I said, walking a little faster at this news. I sauntered ahead of him,

'Don't thank me too soon, Little One.' Samael purred. At the sound of his husky voice, I relaxed, unaware I'd been tense and waiting for him to reappear. The absence of his commentary had me worried. Samael never left me alone for too long. I was curious to know what kept him busy in Eternis. Too busy to listen in.

With the devil's reappearance, and the promise of the soft comfort of an actual bed, I practically skipped into Cardend.

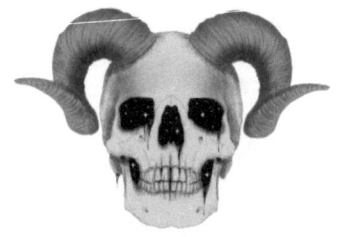

Chapter Eight

We stood by the bar of the inn. The smell of soap, stale ale and wine drifted through the room. It was a lot warmer in here than it had been outside. A handful of patrons sat at a long table, tucking into food. It smelled so good I could have cried. It would be amazing to have a hot meal after three days of bread and chewy, dried meat. I'd die happy if I never had to eat snake jerky, again.

"What do you mean there's only one room?" I asked Max, staring at the single key he had clutched in his hand. The wooden tag swung from the end. "I thought you said it was an inn. As in travellers stay here when they come through. As in you'd stayed here before."

"I have!" he protested, frowning. "It says *'Inn'* in the name. I haven't lied to you."

"An inn with only one room, though?" I asked. I suspected he was trying to provoke me, and he had another key in his pocket.

That he was trying to get me to squirm.

"So, it's a small inn." He shrugged so flippantly that my hopes fell.

Max had proved over the past few days that he liked to bait me for an emotional reaction. I'd proved that I often rose to the occasion. But he never kept it going too long and never did it maliciously. "Max…"

He shook his head. "We can handle one room. It's better than sleeping in the dirt and I'm betting it's not the worst place you've ever slept, is it?"

I followed him to the narrow staircase, staying on his heels. "If there's one room, I want the bed."

"Uh, no," he said firmly. The stairs creaked as he climbed them, precarious beneath his weight.

"We're not sharing, Max!" I cried. I almost ran face-first into his pack when he paused. Two stairs ahead, he loomed over me.

"Well, you're not getting the bed," he said. When I tried to push past him, he blocked the stairs with his body. "I'm the one with a stiff back from camping on the ground. Besides I'm older than you, so I need it."

"I'm the one who got burned alive ten weeks ago!" I countered, folding my arms across my chest and refusing to back down. "I need the rest more than you! I'm properly injured. Your bad back is probably from carrying the weight of your ego."

"You can't use that excuse forever!"

"It hasn't expired yet. You need to fold to it. Since you were the idiot that lit me on fire," I told him, gripping the banister. "You broke it, you fix it."

"I was not!" he spluttered. He turned away and almost knocked me over with his pack.

"Excuse you!" I screeched, my nails digging into the wooden rails. "I'm standing right here!"

He turned back to me again, his expression fierce. His blue eyes narrowed. "I was in the outer city as a scout that day. I wasn't anywhere near you when they blew up the palace. I didn't light the match or set you on fire, Octavia. I didn't try to blow you up, that was all Heira. You can't blame me for what you went through."

"You were still involved," I argued and his face fell.

He looked distressed. He ran his fingers over the shaved side of his scalp before yanking at the long strands of his hair.

I added, "You caused me pain and suffering, so I get the bed, and you get the floor. End of story."

Max tipped his head to stare at the ceiling. I could see his lips moving as he counted to three just below his breath. Then he turned back and stomped his way up to the third level, leading the way to the room. At first, I thought he was going without protest, but his next words bounced right down the staircase. "I'm not giving up the bed, Octavia! You snooze, you lose."

"Get off me!" I cried.

I beat him to the bed, feeling smug. Max was no gentleman, however, and didn't hesitate to throw the entirety of his weight over the top of me. His chest pressed to my back like a human blanket. I could feel the solid beat of his heart against my shoulder. Devils. He was heavy. Sometimes he didn't look big, but he had enough muscle that he pinned me down. It felt like his weight was suffocating me, my lungs unable to expand fully, and I turned my head to the side, gasping for a full breath. His long hair sucked into my mouth as I inhaled. Spluttering, I pushed at him with every bit of strength I could find.

"No! Budge over!" he demanded, poking me in the ribs with his fingers. "I swear I'll spend all night lying on top of you. Or I'll do this…" He started tickling me.

It was so jarring and unexpected that I let out a loud shriek that bounced off the walls. I shuddered beneath his tough, flailing against the sensation. Max laughed evilly and kept going. He sat up and straddled my hips, blocking my access to my knife as he tickled me. Not that I would have stabbed him for it. He was unaffected by the way I shrieked, squirmed and lashed out at him.

"Okay! Okay!" I nearly screamed the words so loud that half the inn would have heard them. "Stop it! I'll move."

He laughed. His weight shifted, and Max dropped to the bed beside me when I squirmed to one side. He rested a hand behind his head, and we stared at the ceiling, Max chuckling while I caught my breath.

"If you do that again, I'll kill you," I threatened. "In a really slow, painful way."

"No, you won't," he said. He sounded so self-assured that I considered punching him in the balls to make us even. That would be just as distressing for him as this whole experience had been for me. "Who knew you were so ticklish?"

He was thrilled by the new information, and I expected him to leverage it against me.

"Devils, you suck," I sighed. He didn't reply.

When I looked at him, he was already fast asleep.

After a short nap, the growling of our stomachs led us back downstairs into the warmth of the inn. We sat at a small, rickety table and I ordered the same thing as Max since I couldn't read the menu. I hoped he had a decent taste in food, but also worried, since he'd been the one to pack the jerky.

The meal turned out to be some sort of meat-laden sandwich doused in a tangy gravy. It dripped down my wrists as I ate. It was messy, but devils, it was delicious.

We ended up wearing more sauce than we ate, and Max struggled to clean it off his beard. When I teased him about it, he grumbled he was saving some for later.

"So, who do we ask for directions?" I asked him.

A quick look around the dining area didn't reveal the most knowledgeable person in the inn or town. I didn't want to search for a devil's chancellor for directions. I had no memory of getting to the rebellion camp. No actual idea of where it sat in the Pridelands. Chester had never marked it on his map. Everyone else knew where they were and how they came to be there.

"Anyone you want," Max said. He slurped at his mug of spiced brew. "Just pick someone."

I clutched at my cup and shook my head. The drink was unpleasantly spicy, but it warmed me up from the inside out. "Ask, Max. You're the one that promised this would work."

"Are you scared to ask?" he teased, his eyes crinkling at the edges. "The woman who's faced an angel is scared of a couple of villagers… That's hilarious."

I scoffed. "I'm scared of a lot of things, but asking whether we need to walk left, or right isn't one of them."

His eyes flickered to the roaring fireplace in the corner. I'd deliberately picked seats as far away as possible from it. He hummed an agreement under his breath but didn't comment on that fear.

"I'll do it," he said, setting down his mug.

It took him an age to pick someone. I drained the horrible drink dry, one tiny sip at a time, while he people watched. Saying nothing but listening to everything. He waited for the crowd of locals to thin. Until, finally, he caught the attention of one woman working in the bar, waving his hand in her direction. "Hey! Yeah. Sorry. have you got a second?"

The young woman paused. She set down the glasses, tossed a towel over her shoulder, smoothed her skirt, and approached. She smiled at Max and spared me only a passing glance. She looked young. Tiny and bright-eyed, unburdened by too many hardships. Suddenly, I'd never felt so old and worn out. Amidst the trials, I'd forgotten to celebrate my birthdays.

"Can I help you?" The woman asked, perfectly polite. "Another round of drinks, maybe?"

"Definitely." Max grinned.

"Water for me," I cut in, grimacing at the idea of forcing my way through another mug. "Or something sweet."

"But," Max added quickly as the woman reached to clear our cups. "We also wanted to ask your expertise about something."

She hesitated, glancing at him nervously, leaving me to wonder what unfamiliar patrons usually assumed she was the expert on. "Yes?"

Max offered her a wide smile, looking at the picture of innocence. I wanted to laugh, knowing that he was anything but innocent. There was blood on his hands. They were as red as mine.

"Which way and how far is it to reach the Slothlands from here?" he asked.

The woman stacked the two cups together, gripping them tight, and frowned at him. "Why would you want to go there? It's nothing special. You'd be better off staying in the Pridelands."

Max didn't miss a beat, nodding his head in my direction. "We're following The Devil's Trials. She knows a few people who are competing, but we lost our way a little while back and I'm afraid we might not catch up. We're going to miss all the best bits if we don't get there fast."

Despite not lying, he frequently twisted the truth to suit his agenda. Everything he'd said was true enough, after all. She noticed the cuff on my wrist. I was too slow to hide it.

Understanding flickered in her eyes, followed by a look of startling compassion — the last thing I'd expected. Most people treated trial competitors like they were beneath them, nothing more than a waste of human life. Or at least that had been my experience so far. It took a beat too long to realise her gaze lingered on my neck, and it wasn't the cuff that gained her sympathy but my wounds.

I swallowed, dropping my head and untucking the hair from

behind my ear. My dark locks swung in front of my face to hide the scars from her scrutiny.

"I expect you'll want to go to the city, then?" she asked, returning her attention to Max.

"Yeah," he said eagerly, head tilting as he flashed her a charming smile. "Straight to Desidia."

After Samael's prompting, I suggested, "We need to go to a place called Suain."

"Suain," Max repeated the name of the town. His smile didn't falter. "I completely forgot we needed to stop there. Traveller's brain, you know?"

"Hmm." The woman nodded. "Well, Suain is just past the border, so it's not really out of the way. It's a long walk, though. Much shorter if you have horses."

"We don't..." Max grimaced. "Just our feet and a lot of energy."

"Old man Hazel is selling some older horses if you're interested," the woman said. Max's head tilted as he gave her a second look. Under his scrutiny, she pushed a lock of her hair out of her face and smiled. The action was enough to make me self-conscious, and I checked that my hair obscured my face. Unable to stop the comparison between her smooth skin and my scars.

"Are you playing us?" he asked her bluntly, his palms laid flat on the table.

"No," she said, sounding as innocent as could be. "But it wouldn't hurt our village if you spent some coin before you went. We don't get many visitors outside of that damned rebellion these days. They just spend their money on drinks and ruin things every time they come through. It costs us to repair it, so we're at a loss every time. It's why half our rooms are out, at the moment."

"Ah." Guilt flickered across Max's features for the second time that day. He looked haunted. "That sounds unfortunate."

I pressed my hand to my mouth to stifle a snicker.

"Besides," the bartender continued, not noticing his

discomfort. "You're not exactly dressed for the Slothlands. You'd need to prepare, anyway."

"What do you mean?" I asked, drawing her attention again.

"I mean, you're going to get very, *very* cold. You think the night feels cold here? It's bitter down there. I heard it snows all the time, even in the summer. You're going to need better clothes than those to survive it." Her gaze dropped to Max's worn shoes. "Some good boots wouldn't hurt, either."

"Noted, thank you." Max relaxed and grinned, leaning closer to her again. He laid his palm on top of her hand, stroking his thumb along her soft skin. "So, tell me, which way do we go?"

I sat on the bed the next morning, tossing and catching a coin. Max stood at the mirror, his face creased with concentration. Using a knife, he trimmed his beard to his jawline. He'd already shaved the side of his head.

Whenever his gaze flicked up in the mirror, I looked away, pretending that I wasn't watching him. It was a strange sight, and I couldn't help my fascination, but I didn't want him commenting on it.

"Did you know…" he said, suddenly. "That you snore! Worse than my dad ever did."

"Um…" I choked on an unexpected laugh. "I hate to break it to you, but…That was you, Max."

"No, your snoring woke me up," he insisted, catching my eye in the mirror. "At least thrice."

"You woke yourself up," I protested. "You're louder than a harpy."

"At least I didn't hog the bed," he said. He set down the knife and inspected his beard in the mirror, running his hand over his chin.

"If that's what you think, then you're more of an idiot than I

119

first thought," I said. I flung the coin at the back of his head. It missed him by a mile, bouncing off the wall, but his reflection in the mirror grinned at me. He stowed his knife, shoved his dirty clothes into his pack, and hauled it onto his shoulders.

"Never have I ever claimed to be smart," he said.

I laughed.

"Come on, Octavia. Let's go shopping."

"This is going to be expensive," Max muttered under his breath as we stood in the small markets. They were bustling, villagers meandering through the market, chattering between themselves and unfazed by our presence. "I hope you brought some coin with you."

"Not much. Just what I found in Niklaus' pantry," I said, testing the weight of the coins in my pocket. It seemed to be my way in life to gain some coin, lose it, and find a little more later. Just enough to keep me going. Niklaus' coins would last a few days if I'm careful.

"Heira's coin. That's even better! That'll buy us a horse or three."

I snorted. "He's not as rich as you think."

"That's a shame." Max laughed as he led me towards the first stall. Filled with thick, padded clothing.

"These jackets are heavy," I said. Wearing a thick woollen coat, I felt uncomfortable and sweaty in front of him. The sun was too harsh to be wearing it. "And hot, I think I'm going to sweat to death."

"Stop complaining. If she's right and it snows that much out there, we'll need them," Max said. He studied me and then reached forward to roll the sleeves. "Have you ever seen snow, Octavia?"

"I don't even know what snow is…" I admitted.

Max's entire face lit up, blue eyes glittering with bright anticipation. "You're in for a treat when we get there. It's beautiful."

The way his face had brightened tempered my desire to tease him about whether he knew what beautiful meant. I didn't know what it meant to Max, or what it was that filled his face with such unrestricted joy, and I realised I wanted to see the snow and find out. If the mere mention of my seeing it for the first time filled him with such joy, it must have been something spectacular.

"You'll need some thicker socks, too," the shopkeeper said, cutting through my thoughts. "People freeze to the end of their life in the Slothlands all the time. Many go in without coming back out. It's a dangerous trek."

"Sounds creepy, if you ask me," Max commented, adding two pairs of socks to our pile.

I laughed, the sound tainted with a bitter edge. "It sounds like a normal day in the devil's trials."

"Excuse me?" Max sounded strangled, choking on his own shock. He twisted to glance back at me, as if he wanted to check if I shared his outrage. "Can you repeat that number for me?"

The old man smiled, the sagging, loose skin of his face crinkling with the movement, and repeated himself without shame. He took seeds from his tin and chewed on them. Each glimpse of his yellowed teeth showed pieces stuck between them. Every now and again, he spat kernels on the ground by our feet. It felt like he was trying to provoke us rather than make a sale.

"Is that for both the horses?" Max asked, glancing over at the two big beasts tied to a nearby post. "Or just one?"

"Just the one," Old Man Hazel replied. He leaned heavily on the roughly carved stick that seemed to help him stay upright. From beneath his bushy brows, he watched Max.

Max spluttered, "This is robbery!"

Old Man Hazel's brows rose, and he nodded in confirmation. His wide grin betrayed the fact that he was not at all unashamed of stripping us of our coins. We needed the horses, according to almost everyone we'd spoken to, and this old man knew it. Max studied the directions that night and calculated the days we would walk. It was a long journey. Samael had then chided me for being too slow.

The old man spat at our feet again. "I suppose you could rent her, but I don't trust you'll be bringing her back to me in one piece. She's a good mare, but I don't know if you're good folk."

"That's probably a fair assessment," Max sighed. He walked around the horse, inspecting her carefully while I kept my distance, not really sure about the animal. The horses in the Wrathlands camp had had a penchant for biting. "Can't say when we'll be back here again, either."

Old man Hazel nodded. "Most people don't come along here twice, boy."

Max glanced back at me and held out his hand. He gestured for a devil's coin from my pocket. I had enough money for both horses but didn't want Max to know. Mostly because he had decided it was fun spending Nik's money.

I tossed a coin in his direction, and he caught it easily. His wide smile never faltered. "Looks like we're sharing again, Octavia."

Oh, joy. Sharing a bed with Max had been a jostling, somewhat uncomfortable experience that I had little desire to repeat. He tossed, muttered, and snored in his sleep, trapping me with his body. Only to shove me away a few minutes later, grumbling that I was the one taking up all the space. When half asleep, Max was delusional.

I wasn't sure I wanted to ride it at all, let alone share it with him. There was even less space for the two of us on its back than in the bed.

"I've never been on a horse before," I admitted. I thought of the sleek, black horses that Wrath's senior ranks had ridden. They had snapped their teeth at passersby, and I'd seen one deliver a powerful kick that had taken a life. The woman had crumpled on impact, and her limp body dragged away.

"That doesn't surprise me," Max said. "But there's a first time for everything."

"It's not going to bite me, is it?" I asked, biting my lip.

The old man snatched the coin from Max's hand and slapped the horses' reins into his palm. As if worried, I'd talk him out of the purchase. They both gestured me closer, and I edged forward a single step. When I didn't move again, the old man laughed and shuffled back towards his house.

"What's the horse's name?" Max called to Old Man Hazel before he could disappear through his front door.

The man paused, tapped his cane, and named the beast.

"Honey," he announced, offering a smile that flashed the seeds stuck between his teeth.

When he disappeared, Max gestured me forward. And after what felt like an age of trial and error, he got me on top of the horse. I sat, trembling, unsure of how to steady myself, while my unhelpful new instructor watched. If I pulled on its hair, would it toss me right off? There was nothing to steady me.

When Max took the reins and led the horse forward a few steps. The jolt of movement was so unexpected that I lost all balance and toppled right off the horse. Landing on the ground, next to a pile of chewed and spat-out seed husks, I groaned. All the while Max stood above me, his brows lifted at the sight of me. His lips pursed, holding in a laugh. I glared at him. Daring him to do it.

"That's… absolutely fantastic," he said, sarcasm dripping from every word. He hauled me back onto my feet. "You're going to hate riding a horse. I'd put money on it."

He was right. I did.

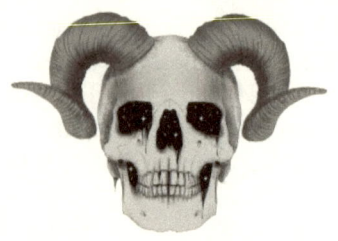

Chapter Nine

"I hate you," I growled, wobbling across the grass clearing as if I'd never walked on solid ground before. From behind me, where he tied the horse to a nearby tree, Maksymilian snickered. He'd been laughing since he had to help me down off the horse.

"I mean it!" I shouted into the evening sky, wincing as I took another step. "I despise you more than all seven sins together."

His husky, rolling snicker turned into full belly laughs. When I spun on him, he was holding his ribs, his red-faced from amusement.

"Stop laughing, Max!" I stamped my foot on the ground.

He shook his head, wheezing as his laughter prevented a full breath, "You're walking like Pride crawled up your—"

"Don't even say it!" I cut him off, scrubbing my hand down my face with exasperation and glaring at him. "How are you not sore?! My muscles are wobbly and rock-hard at once. Ugh. This is worse than training for Wrath!"

I'd felt pain before, but horseback riding was still more painful than I expected. The unrelenting jolting movements that had thrown me forward, and then back against Max. Until he'd finally turned cranky and threatened to tie me in place. Urging the horse to go faster didn't help. I struggled to keep my balance, gripping his shirt tightly. I couldn't focus on anything except holding myself upright, with nothing more than the power of my thighs. My sore, sore thighs.

When Max could finally composed himself — after he'd walked across the field, mimicking my wide-legged and wobbly stance — he shrugged. "I've ridden horses a time or two before. You get used to it."

"Will I be used to it by morning?" I asked, more than a little hopeful that tomorrow would be a brighter and better day. Experience told me that muscle pain wouldn't ease quickly.

He shook his head, unwilling to tell me a little white lie. "No. You'll probably be so sore you wished you were dead by morning."

I stared at him, horrified. My gaze flicked to the horse, which grazed without a care in the world. I couldn't imagine climbing back on top of it.

"That's... so perfect," I said, the word high and squeaky and so obviously a lie. "I can't wait."

Max's amusement finally faded, and a look of sympathy flashed across his face. "Go down to the river and wash up. The cool water might help your muscles," he said. "I'll start a fire, and you can sleep first. You need the rest more than me."

The river was refreshing. Although I couldn't float, I enjoyed the sensation of touching the rocks in the shallow water. There was less risk of drowning here, no dark depths to swallow me up.

After removing my pants, I carefully entered the water and winced at the iciness of it against my skin. I forced myself to sit down. With my back against the grassy riverbank, and the water flowing over my aching legs, I could have relaxed, but the quiet peace did nothing but give me more time to worry about what was coming. My thoughts buzzed in my head like an angry swarm of bees, deafening me, demanding attention.

When night fell, the temperature dropped with it. A soft, grey mist crawled across the riverbank, creeping towards me. It forced me into action, quickly putting on my wet pants and seeking refuge by the fire with Max.

True to his word, Maksymilian let me sleep first. Or try, at least.

Cuddled by the fire, I fought for warmth beneath our bundled jackets. The chill of the air felt like it sucked the life from my bones. My teeth chattered.

"Go to sleep, Octavia," Max said. I heard the now-familiar flick of his lighter, and the sweet smell of chuckleweed drifted through the air. "You need the rest."

"I can't," I sighed, my breath appearing in front of me as a puff of white. The flames crackled before me, but I couldn't react, exhausted yet alert. My thoughts never stopped turning. "Sleep feels impossible."

"You better not be fishing for a bedtime story…"

If I had anything to throw at him, I would have aimed for his head. I rolled onto my back and looked at him across the fire. "You wouldn't know any good ones, anyway."

Max looked up, brown eyes reflecting the flames. He raised both his brows and jerked his head pointedly. "Sleep."

"I'm trying!"

"No, you're not. Your eyes are open. Try harder, Octavia," He stretched and rose from the log he'd been sitting on. "I'll be back in a minute."

"Where are you going?" I asked, sitting up. Haunted by the

sudden strange idea of Max walking into that slow-rolling fog and never returning. I feared being left alone on a cold night with a horse I couldn't ride and directions I couldn't read. Left to find my way to the trial or death alone.

He shook his head. "I'm going to take a leak, and no, I don't need company."

"I wasn't offering!" I called after him as he disappeared into the trees. I had been, without so many words.

I lay on my back, looking at the stars, attempting to relax and sleep, but my mind was restless. It took me through conversations and embarrassing moments from the past, searching for something, anything, to raise my anxiety.

"Samael?" I whispered to the devil, checking that he was still there.

His presence brushed against my mind. *'Yes, Little One?'*

I debated asking him to possess me again, commanding my body for the rest of the journey. But his magic always had consequences. So much so that he hadn't saved me from Pride's impossible demands. Now, I was trapped in a magical demand that I couldn't escape. I latched onto that thought and obsessed about it in the dead of night.

"Will immortality destroy me?" I asked, fidgeting with the collar of the coat. "You said once that humanity wasn't built to hold magic. That it poisons us. So, what will the cost be if you give me enough magic to live forever."

'The cost of magic, Octavia, is not worth you worrying about right now.'

"Why not?"

'Because you have bigger problems coming your way,' the devil answered, sounding unhappy. *'And you need every bit of mental strength and willpower you have to pass the Trial of Sloth. It won't be easy, Octavia.'*

I didn't like the sound of that. "None of the trials have been easy, Samael."

'None of them have been like this,' he answered. *'Do as your friend says and sleep now.'*

Even though Samael demanded it of me too, it took an age for sleep to come.

The closer we drew to the border between sins, the further the temperature dropped. My breaths were visible, misting in the air, and my jaw ached from chattering teeth. Even the warmth of the thick clothing we'd bought did nothing to help. I ended up bundled against Max, stealing his body heat, with bedding covering my legs.

"Does the Slothlands have any sun?" I asked, rubbing my hands together. My fingers had turned pale and stiff, and I now wished I'd paid for gloves, too. Anything to stave off the cold. "It's colder than the devil's balls out here."

"You complain about everything." Max huffed out a laugh and his breath warmed the tip of my ear. He was right. I had spent the previous day lamenting the ache in my legs and spine. Cursing the fact that it would be worse by the time we stopped. "It's not even that cold yet."

Fisting my hands into his shirt, I struggled to stay upright when he shifted. "What do you mean, *yet*?"

"I mean, look up there…" Max pointed ahead of us, and I squinted into the distance. Every tree and hill looked the same, but ahead the sky looked darker. The clouds hung low over the mountains, the silence of the terrain ominous.

Ahead of us, the world looked as miserable as I felt.

"It's a grey cloud on a mountain," I told him, scoffing. "Am I supposed to be impressed by that?"

Max snorted. "Octavia…That's snow."

Studying the low-hanging cloud in the distance, I felt like he was mocking me. For days, he'd been telling me stories of what it felt like to stand in the snow. I was certain he did it only to build up my expectations so that I would be disappointed.

"It doesn't look that special," I said.

He reached back to flick my nose in response. It smarted with a prick of pain. I jammed my fist against his side, and he laughed.

"You'll see…" Max told me, sounding smug. "Then you'll eat those words like a Gluttony fanatic."

He was right, infuriatingly so.

Snow started as a muddy dusting on the ground and settled in the taller branches of the trees. When the temperature dropped again, it thickened. Mounds of soft powder surrounded us and turned the bland green and brown scenery into a winter wonderland. The world became white.

"Oh… Wow." I breathed when suddenly it covered everything. I twisted on the spot for a better look, holding tight to Max to make sure I didn't fall.

Even the birds had hushed their chirping as snowflakes fell. They glistened in the soft daylight, landing in my hair and lap with nothing more than a feather touch. Reaching out, I cupped one in my hand, and it melted against my skin.

A laugh bubbled up in my throat, and I reached for another.

"Told you so," said Max, sounding smug. "Gorgeous, isn't it?"

I longed for him to compliment me instead of the ice flakes surrounding us. I swallowed. "It's…"

I couldn't speak, my eyes welling up with emotion. Peace settled through me as I felt snowflakes on my cheeks.

The world had gone quiet, and with it, so had my worries.

"Come back to me when you can form a proper sentence," Max laughed, shattering the silence. "See if you can catch one long enough to get a proper look at it. Apparently, every single one of them is different."

I watched the flakes land against my skin, melting away before I managed a good look. It felt like the horse was moving too fast, and I worried we would leave it behind before I could truly appreciate it.

"Can we stop?" I asked.

Max pulled on the reins and brought us to a halt. "Of course. I'm not in a hurry to get to Suain."

I scrambled off the horse, kicking away the heavy blankets. Max grinned, barely able to keep a hold of me as I slid down onto the ground.

Suddenly, I was standing knee-deep in the powdered snow and my pants felt too thin. A shriek burst from my throat. "Devils! It's cold!"

"What did you expect?!" Max swung himself down off the horse and stood behind me. He urged me to move further into the snow. We staggered forward, leaving deep footprints behind us.

I turned and spun in a slow circle, my hands outstretched to catch more of the flakes. They were a featherlight touch and as close to magic as I thought nature could produce.

"What do you think, Octavia?" Max asked, and I turned to the sound of his voice, seeking him out.

A cry of delight pulled from my throat at the sight of him. His auburn hair was loose over his shoulders and smattered with white flakes of snow. It clung to his beard. I could see the ice forming on his lashes as I trudged forward.

"It's beautiful," I admitted.

He reached out, brushing his fingers against the curve of my jaw. He stared at me, unashamed, and smiled. His eyes filled with unsuppressed joy. "Yeah, it is."

The way he stared at me took my breath away. Heat crawled up my neck, but I said nothing. Instead, I smiled and stared into the falling snow, hoping he wasn't only talking about the snow.

Max crouched down, scooping his hands through the snow. It drew my attention, and I frowned at him, certain that his fingers were going to freeze right off. He clumped it together, compacting it in his hand until it formed a tight ball.

I glanced up to see his mischievous expression, but it was already too late. He had already smashed the snowball over my head. It crumbled, pieces of snow covering me, slipping down the back collar of my jacket and melting against my spine.

I shrieked so loudly that it unsettled the birds in a nearby tree, and blindly shoved at him to distance myself from his attack and the icy confrontation of the snow.

The force of my push sent Max stumbling backwards, tripping over his own feet. He reached for me as he fell, holding tight to my forearms and pulling me down with him. We tumbled into the snow, and I landed with a thump against his chest.

If I thought I'd been cold before, it had nothing on how it felt to be soaked through. My wet clothes clung to my body. The chill did nothing to stop Max, though; he hooked a leg over my thigh so I couldn't escape and buried his fingers beneath my coat, tickling me mercilessly.

He was a bastard, and I shrieked the sentiment. Max laughed and covered my mouth to stop the noise.

"Stop! Stop!" I cried, the words muffled against his skin.

He let me go, pushing me off him and I rolled into the snow. Lying on my back and shivering as I stared up into the pale sky. Even though he had essentially just tortured me, I still felt at peace. Mesmerised by my first interaction with the snow.

"Have you been through here before?" I asked him. "Is that how you knew about the snow falling?"

Max was silent for a beat, and I twisted to look at him.

"No, it snows in the north back home." For a moment I thought that was all he'd say, but a moment later he continued. "I grew up in the Kyanite mines. I don't think you would have heard of it. It's this sort of blue stone. Everyone says it's beautiful and it's worth a lot of coin. I'll show it to you someday. When we have time. If we have time."

I found it surprising that he could effortlessly anticipate a future event, like showing me a stone from his hometown. Even more that he did it without wallowing in the curious dread of whether we'd survive that long. He lived as if he assumed we would. Predicting nothing but a thriving future for us. His implied optimism was sweet.

The cold was too intense. My skin froze and my teeth chattered. Max's lips turned blue. He didn't seem fazed though, clambering to his feet and holding out a hand to help me up.

He hoisted me onto the horse, smoothly mounting behind me and pulling me back against his chest again. But where he'd been a source of heat before, he felt frigid behind me. Two icicles continuing on a journey.

He consulted the now-smudged map from his pocket. His brows pulling together, his face crumpling, as he tried to decipher it. Then bundling the heavy blankets around us both, building a ward against the world, or at least the still-falling snow. Which was losing the edge of its beauty as I stopped being able to feel my fingers.

"We're going to ride through the night," Max said softly against my hair. "Hold on tight."

All I had was a thread of faith that he would keep me on the horse or get us to our destination before freezing to death.

The endless white of winter had not ended, but our refuge appeared as low, twinkling lights in the distance. One small home on the outskirts of a village with smoke chuffing from the pipe in their roof. It led to more and more homes until we came to a halt in front of a big sign.

Max tilted his head, glancing up at it and releasing a weary sigh. His body slumped forward against my own, his weight making my back ache.

"Welcome to Suain," he said. His voice was low and raspy, likely from the rawness of his throat. He coughed for hours, hacking up greenish phlegm and spitting it off the horse. I wasn't much better. My eyes watered and my nose dripped relentlessly, my throat aching as if someone had skinned it with a knife. The cold was taking its revenge on our bodies.

"Thank the devil," I gasped. Despite dozing on and off throughout the night, I kept my chin tucked to brace against the wind. "Get me off this horse."

'This time I had nothing to do with it,' Samael said.

Max was unaware that the devil had saved us during the journey. Whenever Max fell asleep because of his sickness, the devil urged me to wake him. Preventing us from falling off the horse.

"Where should we go?" I asked, peering into a house, envious of the flickering light and presumed warmth inside their walls. I'd stopped being cold some time ago, and now just felt numb.

"I don't know..." Max said, and he didn't sound like his usual, optimistic self. "A tavern, maybe?"

'Find Chancellor Elodie Wylles.' Samael said, guiding us again. *'She'll be expecting you.'*

Nodding, I sucked in a deep breath of cold air. I didn't know what we would do without him. "We need to find the chancellor's house, Max."

"How do we do that?" he asked. Max coughed again, his entire body jerking with the deep, hacking sensations.

"Didn't your home have a devil's chancellor?" I asked, sure that he had to be joking. Among all the villages and cities I had visited, only Wrath's war camps had lacked a chancellor. I couldn't imagine he didn't know the wealth and privilege that came with being one of the devil's favoured humans. "It'll be the biggest house in the village. Believe me, it's going to be really hard to miss."

He shifted behind me, shuffling the heavy blanket. "The Greedlands are a little different to everywhere else, Octavia.

Greed is paranoid. I'll take your word for it, though." His hands clenched the reins, his knuckles blanching. "Hold tight, the biggest house in the village coming right up."

It hadn't been hard to find. Chancellor Elodie Wylles' black, stone home spanned two storeys, and soft lights twinkled in almost every window. A small awning covered the front door, protecting the path from the falling snow.

Max had tied Honey to one of the front posts. It took a while to find my footing and walk down the path. We stood in front of the door in a moment of silence, leaning against each other. It'd taken everything out of me to get there. I wanted nothing more than to sleep.

"You should knock. You're the one in the trials," Max said. I wanted to protest, but his valid point and exhausted appearance changed my mind.

"Scaredy-Cat!" I teased, the jibe half-hearted and lacking its usual punch.

"Pfft!" he scoffed, swaying on the spot. His fingers curled into the back of my coat, as if I could hold him upright. I turned to look at him, feeling a pinch of worry at the dark shadows marring his pale face. His pallor made his freckles jump out, too prominent, as if they were taking over his skin.

Those freckles gave me the courage to knock, but before my knuckles hit the door, it swung wide open. I stood like a fool, with one hand raised, blinking at the frail woman filling the doorway. With sharp features and an even sharper gaze, she had soft brown hair pulled back into a smart bun. She pressed her thin lips together and took a moment to look us over.

"Oh," I said, surprised by her sudden presence. "Hello."

A tight smile pulled at her pink-painted lips. "Good evening. You're both spectacularly late, but somehow right on time for dinner."

Stepping aside, she held the door so that we could see inside the home. When we didn't move, she clicked her tongue. "Please, come inside. You're letting the cold in."

"Are you Chancellor Wylles?" I asked.

She nodded, correcting me, a sweeping hand motion directing us forward. "I go by Chancellor Elodie. Now come inside, it's freezing out, and you both look like you've had enough of the cold."

Our boots brought the snow inside with us, leaving a trail of water and mud that stained her wooden floors. Another woman approached, bustling in from another room. She dressed much like my mother when she cleaned the Heira house. Quickly, she helped us out of our heavy wet jackets, throwing them over her arm and disappearing again. The house was deliciously warm, but still I stood in my wet clothes and shivered, sure that my body would never return to its normal temperature.

"How did you know her name?" Max whispered in my ear, reaching for my hand and holding me tight.

"It's a secret," I said. "If I told you that, Max, I'd have to kill you."

"Ha ha." He rolled his eyes. "You're so funny."

"Call it a lucky guess, if you like," I said. I looked up at his frowning face and questioned if he already knew. Or if he thought I was lying by omission.

"This way, please!" Chancellor Elodie called. She led us through the halls of her home, her shoes clicking against the floorboards.

I suppressed a groan. Despite her announcement of dinner, I had no desire to eat or engage in small talk with the chancellor. All I wanted was to rest and let the pain and sickness take over.

Max led the way, standing just in front of me as we turned into the dining room. Only when I peered around his body did I see a familiar face.

Their bald head shone under the lights, accentuating the glittering ink on their skin. Their design has changed since I last saw them, now more floral and complex.

Sharp features lit up as we entered the room, and the demoness flashed a smile full of pointed teeth.

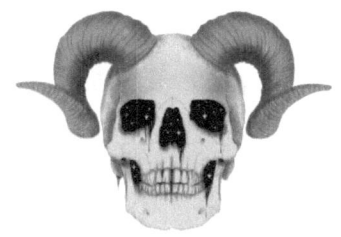

Chapter Ten

"Cyn!" I cried, filled with overwhelming relief at the sight of them. Samael promised my Pride mark, but I hadn't wanted to be too hopeful. Seeing the demoness in front of me was proof that he held true to his word.

"Octavia of Ilrea," they greeted me in familiar growly tones. Cyn nodded their head at Max. Their forehead wrinkled and I imagined if Cyn had any brows, they'd be rising in question. "I see you've made a new friend. It's no surprise you're travelling in different company since you left Niklaus with Wrath."

"Oh. Max, this is Cyn. They're a tattooist out of Gula, and they give out the marks for the trials." I shifted, in case they couldn't see one another above my head. I waved a hand half-heartedly between us. "Cyn, this is Maksymilian Tate of…"

"The Kyanite Mines. Greedlands," Max interjected. He appeared tense, with clenched fists and narrowed eyes.

"Ah." Cyn's lips pressed into a thin, thoughtful line, their face shuttering. "That's fascinating."

"What's fascinating?" I asked, frowning. I looked between them both. The tension in the room thickened until even the chancellor looked uncomfortable. "Is there something wrong?"

"Nothing at all." Cyn raised their glass, swirling the deep red contents and gestured to the chair on their left. "Take a seat, Octavia. Chancellor Elodie was just serving dinner."

After I'd dropped into the chair on their left. Max sat to my left, facing Cyn, and they locked eyes with lingering tension.

The chancellor pulled out her own chair, flashed a smile and called for the food to be brought in. The housekeeper entered the room with a large platter. "It's roasted boar with crackled skin, honeyed vegetables, and some sleep-aged wine," Chancellor Elodie said, proudly.

Max rubbed his chin through his wiry beard, leaning back heavily in his chair. "You have an entire boar for just the two of you?" He glanced around the table. "Wow, I thought we were in the Slothlands, not the Gluttonlands."

The chancellor blushed, making me question Samael's selection process for his favoured. The town seemed less grand than others and Elodie Wylles often appeared flustered.

"Oh, of course not." Her reply was a sharp snap. "We roast some, then dry it so it will last the next cycle and be distributed throughout the village."

"The next cycle?" I asked. "What's that?"

"Yes, when—"

"Elodie," Cyn cut her off, turning the chancellor's name into a sharp word of warning. "Enough."

The chancellor smiled tightly, the shine of her eyes dulling at the rebuke. "A conversation for another time, perhaps. Let's eat before it gets cold."

The chancellor served three courses during the lengthy dinner, and the bright lights worsened my headache. My patience thinned for small talk and recounting the trials so far. Max fidgeted, sliding the coin at his neck back and forth on its strap, turning his spoon over and over. It had been well over a day since he'd had a smoke, and the strain showed in his face. Cyn never ate, sipping at the blood-red brew until their lips stained.

Finally, Cyn set their goblet down and cleared their throat, drawing the attention of the three of us. They reached forward, pressing their warm hand atop my still-freezing fingers. "What would you like first, Octavia, your mark, or your clue?"

"I want the mark," I said, without a beat of hesitation.

I wanted to ease the weight of worry on my shoulders and know that Pride had one less way of getting to me. Although I was still trapped in the web of his demands, I refused to let him figuratively have me by the throat any longer. I wanted to be well and truly done with the trial of Pride and leave the trauma of Glorae behind me. Easier said than done, but this would be a moment of progress.

"I thought you might say that." Cyn smiled, flashing their pointed teeth, and rose from their chair. "Give me a minute."

"What's the mark for?" Max asked.

Blinking away my confusion, I realised Max had been embedded in the rebellion for longer than I'd thought. He may have missed the speeches recruiting humans for the trial. That day, in Ilrea's town square, felt like a lifetime ago.

I'd died and been reborn four times over by now. Forcibly shaped into a new version of myself with every trial I'd passed.

"It's for completion of the pride trial," I told him. Turning my cuffed hand over, I flashed him a look at the tiny tattoos on the inside of my wrist. The purple piglet, the red lion, and the green snake. Tiny reminders of what I'd achieved, and how I had survived, despite every hardship thrown my way. "Without it, I'm still technically forfeit to Pride. He could turn and claim me at any time."

"What?" The colour drained from Max's cheeks and fear flickered in his gaze. "Pride could just know where you are and come and get you because you're forfeit to him? The fuck. Did Heira know about this?"

I winced. "Yeah, he did."

Max's hand slammed against the table. The glasses rattled and the chancellor startled. "That prick!"

I reached for his hand, lacing my fingers through his and holding it still against the table. Lifting my chin, I held his eye. "It doesn't matter now. I'll get the mark and it's over."

That wasn't completely true. Pride's intricate demands for my future and the need to obey them meant I was still tied to the angel; there were some things that Max didn't need to know. Ignorance was safe.

He huffed an angry sigh, but before he could protest further, Cyn returned to the table. They carried a tiny bottle of glistening, milky white ink and the needled machine they used to tattoo.

Although they had stamped Wrath's lion into my wrist at the previous trial and dismissed me just as quickly, this time they seemed content to take the slower route. As if they, ironically, took pride in this insignia.

"Ready?" Cyn asked. "This one will bite."

"Can't be worse than enduring Pride himself," I muttered. They uncorked the bottle of ink and dipped the pointed end of their tool into it. A soft and familiar buzzing sound filled the room. I relaxed my fingers, closing my eyes and trying not to move. I'd learned that if I didn't look, I wouldn't be tempted to pull away from the pain.

Cyn pulled my arm closer to their body, holding my hand firm to the table, and began.

It hurt enough that I bit my lip until it split. The white peacock had too many tiny details, and Cyn was sure to capture each tiny feather.

When they finished, I tugged my hand back and stared at the tiny reminder of Pride. If I won these trials, it would be inked on my skin for an eternity. My body ached for rest, and I didn't know how much energy I had left. Not when my skin had become a patchwork of scars, the brutal aftermath of pain and suffering.

Chancellor Elodie cleared her throat. It was a surprisingly soft and dainty sound. "I have something for you, too, actually."

"What is it?" I asked.

My neck cricked as I turned to look at her, focused on the small wooden box on the table.

"You sound suspicious." She laughed. "I suppose that's a nasty side effect of The Devil's Trials. It's just a little concoction that the devil said you'd need by the time you arrived."

"What does it do?" I asked. Her laughter didn't calm my nerves, so I impulsively asked another question. "What's he like? The devil?"

Max nudged me in the ribs with his elbow, his brows raised, but I ignored him. I hadn't intended to ask the chancellor about the devil, but I'd take any information I could get. If Max gave me a hard time about it, I'd play it off as needing to know our enemy. Not a lie, but a manipulation of the truth. It was too easy to forget that Max and I had different agendas. Where I wanted so desperately to find and meet Samael, he wanted to end him.

"It'll help you recover that cold well enough to see the Sloth trial through." Chancellor Elodie opened the box and pulled out two small vials filled with a pale blue liquid. Small, unidentifiable chunks floated within them. "Don't worry I'm not showing you any special favour. I offered these to every entrant that passed through Suain before you."

"Oh." I whispered. I wished I could ask her about Nash and Finley and whether they had passed through. "Did you make it?"

"Devils, no!" If anything, the chancellor laughed harder now, and it was becoming offensive. "The Chancellor of Kyama ordered it before her cycle began. Well, before the trial began. We find many newcomers to the Slothlands don't acclimatise to the cold weather well. If we leave you to rot, you'll die before Sloth can test you."

"What about people who come from here?" Max asked, sounding mildly curious. "Surely they have an advantage."

Chancellor Elodie shook her head. A strand of hair fell from her perfectly smoothed bun, swinging in front of her face. "Nobody from the Slothlands takes part in The Devil's Trials."

"Why?" he asked.

"It would be impossible," she said. Her entire face was alight, but it gave nothing away. "They—"

"Elodie!" Cyn snapped. The woman fell quiet, but her smile never faded. I bet she was enjoying teasing us with half-answers. "You need to stop indulging his curiosity. There are some things that cannot be revealed. Do you understand me?"

"Right. Can't spoil the trial." The chancellor spoke through her teeth, the muscles in her neck cording tightly. "As for the devil…"

"Yes?" I leaned forward, eager for an answer about the devil. More than I wanted clues for the trial ahead.

The chancellor smiled, her blue eyes glimmering with amusement. "Maybe one day you'll find out for yourself."

It was a devilshit answer. Silence descended between us until Max picked up one of the small vials. Given her past success in healing, I had confidence in the crone's ability to make helpful tonics. So, I reached for my own and tipped it to my lips, swallowing quickly.

Bitter and thick, it burned the entire way down my throat, until I hacked a cough and my ears popped. I hadn't realised how dull my hearing had been until it happened. Suddenly, everything was louder.

Max's intense gaze made me feel like he expected me to die from the potion. When I breathed in deeply, my exhale was absent of the soft, rattling wheeze I'd developed. He nodded. Swiftly, he tossed back his own dose with a lot more grace than I had.

Cyn sighed heavily. "Elodie, I think it's time these travellers went to bed."

"Agreed." Max said, pushing his chair back and clambering to his feet. "I'm beat."

"Before you go, Octavia." Cyn pulled a gold-foiled envelope from their pocket and held it out to me. My stomach twisted into a complicated knot at the sight of it. "This is for you."

"Thanks, Cyn." I took the envelope but didn't open it, toying with the corner instead. It marked the beginning of a new adventure and the start of new struggles. Some part of me wanted to delay that for as long as possible. "Will you still be here in the morning?"

They shook their head. "No. I refuse to stay in these lands too long. I won't let Sloth lay claim to me."

"What do you mean?" I asked.

Their swirling, narrowed eyes were otherworldly that I couldn't imagine how I'd once thought they were human. "I mean be careful, Octavia. Once Sloth has you in her grips, she rarely lets us go."

The housekeeper showed us two doors set opposite one another in the hall. They looked identical. One was for me, and one for Max. There'd be no sharing a bed in this household. It had more rooms than the village seemed to have inhabitants. An excessive amount.

"Would you read me the clue, Max?" I asked.

He was leaning against his door, his head bowed forward.

"Right now?" he asked. "Octavia, I'm dead tired. Can't we read it in the morning?"

"Oh." A wave of disappointment felt acidic in my gut. I'd wanted to delay it, but not that long. Max's tiredness was visible through his drooping eyelids and slumped shoulders. "Yeah. Sure."

He turned, reaching for me. He gently kissed my forehead,

leaving me stunned. "Sweet dreams, Octavia."

Max had already closed the door before my brain rebooted. Safely hidden away where I couldn't question him why he'd done such a thing. I blinked at the door, whispering belatedly, "Goodnight."

My room was large and painted in varying shades of pale blue. There was a bathroom off to one side. I was grateful for my time in Glorae for teaching me how to use the taps. I quickly filled the tub with warm water, antsy to climb inside.

I dunked myself in the steamy water, feeling the burn of the heat on my cold muscles. The nerves in my hands and feet prickled. I couldn't stand the feeling and immediately jumped out, wrapping myself in a towel.

By the time I slid beneath the heavy blankets on the bed, Samael made himself known, stroking my nerves as if he were running a finger gently up the length of my spine. I shivered. Blinking into the darkness, barely able to keep myself awake now that I'd relaxed.

'Not going to wish me a goodnight, too, Little One?'

"Would you wish me sweet dreams?" I asked. "Be honest."

'Not here.' Samael sounded grave. *'Be careful of your dreams tonight. Trust nothing.'*

The aching weight of my body won out, and I was asleep within minutes.

When I finally woke again, my head spun and my lips had dried out, cracking when I opened my mouth. A heavy, imaginary sand filled my limbs, keeping me weighed down onto the mattress for the first few minutes. I blinked up at the ceiling and tried to piece together the fractured memories of a dream. It hadn't been good. A cold sweat had gathered at the back of my neck and across my brow. My heart still hadn't settled into its normal rhythm.

'Rise and shine, Little One.' Samael crowed in my ear. *'It's time to get moving. You wouldn't want to be late for Sloth.'* He laughed at the joke I didn't understand.

I wanted nothing more than to slip back into a deep sleep. I felt better than in days, but my bones ached to stay put.

Flinging open the door to Maksymilian's bedroom without knocking or announcing myself, I found it empty. The room smelled of sweaty man and I wrinkled my nose. Backing into the hall, I noted his things were still there, and reasoned that he hadn't abandoned me yet.

He smoked in the back garden, which didn't surprise me.

The melting snow and ice revealed a swing made from a rickety plank and fraying rope. It looked like someone had made it for a child years ago and then completely forgot about it, leaving it to rot.

Max didn't mind, rocking back and forth, squinting through the leaves. The rays of soft sunlight filtered down on him. It wasn't enough to warm us up, just to brighten the day.

When he dropped his chin and caught sight of me, his face brightened. I exhaled, relaxing at his positive reaction. "I thought you'd never wake up," he said with a chuckle.

"Me either," I admitted. "I had the weirdest dreams…"

"Yeah? What about?"

"I…" Closing my eyes, I tried to piece together the feeling of running but getting nowhere. I recalled flashes of various beasts that hunted me but couldn't tell if they were dreams or memories. "I don't remember. I felt so shaken when I woke up. Now that I'm awake properly, I can't tell you a single thing that happened. Stupid, isn't it?"

"Typical." He shook his head. "Hate when that happens."

"What's the plan for today?" I asked, glancing around the small garden. It seemed as if we were all alone in the quiet, but I could never be sure.

Max grinned, taking another puff. Pink smoke clouded

145

around my head. "Figured I'd read your little clue, if you wanted?"

He took his time, turning the envelope between his fingers. He broke the seal, pulled the card free, handed me back the envelope, and flipped over the card. I clutched the gold foil to my chest, wishing for a clue I could easily decipher.

Max didn't review it before reading it aloud. I asked him to repeat it quietly.

"There is a weight to the world.
Does life not fatigue you?
In the realm of dreams and nightmares,
The impossible becomes true.
But be warned,
if you cannot persevere once you meet her,
Sloth will beguile you."

He flipped the card over, showing me the indecipherable handwritten words. Each letter dragged into one another, and there were smudges across the card. I wondered if the angel had written them but doubted it. That was not the way of the sins, at least not in my experience.

"What do you think it means?" I asked Max.

He snorted, holding the card out for me to take. "Do I look like the devil's adviser on cryptic riddles?"

I took a moment to look him over, slow enough that he knew I was doing it. Sleep had transformed Max into a new person, with a brighter complexion and a half-braided, knotted hairstyle.

"Hmm," I said. "You could be."

He kicked out at the slushy snow, sending droplets flying at me. "Pffft."

"One line is clear enough, I guess." Forcing the card back into its envelope to keep it safe. "We have to meet Sloth. So, we need to go to Desidia."

A lazy smile tugged at the edge of his lips. "That sounds like a fantastic one-step plan. Did your clue come with directions?"

Glaring at him, I shook my head. "Has anyone told you today that you're an idiot? Let's go ask the chancellor. She'll know where the city is. You're the one that said it's as easy as asking for help."

"Only you, Octavia," he said, jumping off the swing and following me. "Always you."

With some sleep and perspective, I could see that the village of Suain wasn't as big as I'd first thought. The houses were few and far between, many of them lay quiet and abandoned. The Chancellor, in pressed clothes and a bun, was found boarding up windows in an old house.

"Chancellor Elodie?" I asked, approaching slowly.

She turned once the board was secure, but upon seeing us again, she recognised us and smiled. "Oh! Octavia, Maksymilian! I didn't expect you'd wake for another day or so. You both seemed so exhausted." She brushed her hands together, wiping them clean. "How are you feeling?"

"Fine, thanks," Max said. He nudged me forward. "Octavia had some questions for you about the Sloth trial."

The chancellor approached us, giving her full attention. "Yes, Octavia?"

Heat crawled up my neck. The idea of asking her for help was easy, in theory. But standing in front of her, my tongue refused to connect to my brain. The words wouldn't flow.

"Well…" I said, buying myself a second to think. "It seems like we have to go to Desidia. I was hoping you'd tell us how to get there? We're not familiar with the Slothlands."

"No. I don't imagine you are." Her face had brightened with understanding. She glanced over her shoulder at the house, raising a single finger in a signal to wait. "Give me one moment and I can help you."

The chancellor briefly disappeared into the house, visible through the open door. Her hand rested on the arm of another woman. She leaned close as she spoke in earnest. The other woman was crying, her face red and splotchy. She nodded and turned away. Shifting from my view.

When the chancellor returned to us, I was dying to ask what had happened. I wanted to know why the woman cried and why they had boarded up the windows. I kept the questions to myself, though. It felt like an inappropriate time. Then again, there was never a good time to ask sensitive questions.

Chancellor Elodie smiled at us stiffly. "Now, I feel like I must forewarn you…It's difficult to travel the Slothlands."

"We don't have much of a choice," I said, fidgeting with the end of my sleeve. "I made a choice. It feels like a lifetime ago, but now I need to see it through."

"No, I suppose you're right," she agreed, heaving a small sigh. "I'll tell you what I told everyone before you. It's best to remember the following key places. While they don't make the most direct path to the city, it is the safest way to proceed. Head to Kyama first, then Cottle Creek, Nuriv, the Danby Woods and finally onto Desidia. A river of ice surrounds the city. You won't be able to miss it. It's one of the most spectacular, but quiet places in the lands."

Max repeated the names of the towns back to her, and the chancellor nodded. She beamed as if she were proud of him for memorising something so simple. He grinned back, a dimple flashing beneath his closely cropped beard.

"How long have you been the chancellor here?" I asked, suddenly curious. There was something about her…Something fresh. While the other chancellors were arrogant, this woman was cheerful and positive.

"Me?" Elodie blinked. "Well, only nine months now."

"Wow," I said. "So, you're new to this?"

Her smile dimmed. "Yes, my father was the last chancellor. But he didn't wake for this cycle, so I assumed his position."

Again, I didn't know what she meant by this cycle. The town gave away nothing of the customs and cultures of the Slothlands. I glanced at Max, who pulled a face. Proving that he had less of a clue than I did. Not that it surprised me.

From within the house, someone called the chancellor's name. She turned, in response, to glance over her shoulder again.

"I need to go," Chancellor Elodie said. "Please let the household staff know if you intend to leave after lunch or dinner. They'll pack a basket of food for you to take on your way. Can't have you leaving empty-handed."

"Wait," Max called out, causing the chancellor to pause halfway up the steps. "We can't stay one more night? You said you didn't even expect us to be awake yet."

"You've been asleep for four days," Chancellor Elodie replied, barely glancing back at us. "I imagine it's high time you were on your way. You have a big adventure ahead of you yet."

She disappeared into the house and Max let out a low, rumbling laugh. "Well, Octavia, I believe we've overstayed our welcome and been officially kicked out of Suain. Let's get our things together."

By the time dusk fell, we were back on the road. The chancellor didn't see us off, but the household staff gave us food and wine.

We rode into the dark of the night. My growing nerves stopped any jokes about whether the harpies or hounds might come out to feast on us. Instead, I kept my eyes on the road ahead, listening to the bawdy tune Max hummed beneath his breath.

The longer we rode, the thicker the air seemed to become. It pulled at my limbs like an invisible weight until I was battling to keep myself upright. My eyes felt heavy and a yawn pulled from deep in my chest. Even though I'd just slept for days, I'd never felt so tired.

A thick, rolling mist shrouded the path head. It obscured my view, and the heavy fog rolled across the path, it hurled around the horse's legs. Honey snorted, jerking her head.

"I feel strange," I mumbled softly to Max, expecting him to tease me about it. Instead, his weight slumped heavily against my back, his head nestling into the crook of my shoulder. His breath warmed my skin.

I tensed, not sure how I'd move him, or if he was okay. "Max…"

The dead weight of his body held me pinned against the horse, and only the tickle of his slow breaths and faint rumble of a snore reminded me he was alive. "Max…"

He didn't wake, didn't respond. He snored softly again.

Before long, the pull of fatigue became too hard to resist. The air felt heavy, making it hard for me to stay alert. My head nodded forward, the drop of my chin to my chest waking me with a startle.

Before long, I succumbed to sleep.

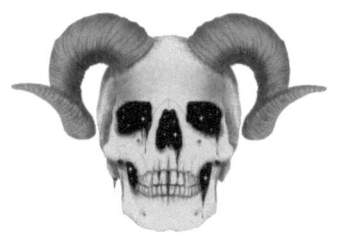

Chapter Eleven

"Hello, Little One," his voice whispered through the air, piercing through the foggy veil over my subconscious. Samael was always present, whispering in my ear, but now he sounded louder. Closer than he had ever been before. "I've been waiting for you."

I struggled to open my gritty and swollen eyes. My body felt strange and heavy, and my brain was disconnected from my limbs — the same way I felt when I slept too heavily, waking up thinking days had passed when it had only been an hour or two.

"What?" I mumbled, wriggling my fingers. Fighting for the energy to move.

"Open your eyes, Octavia," he said.

I felt his breath against the shell of my ear like he was right here with me. A shiver rolled through my body, and I shifted onto my side.

"Go on. You know you want to…"

Sitting up slowly, I did as he said. I'd learned that it was never a wise idea to ignore Samael's advice. He was — frustratingly — usually right.

Pressing my palms against my eyes, bright lights danced in the darkness, giving me a moment to centre myself. When I dropped my hands away, it was difficult to adjust to the glaring light of the day. I blinked at the unfamiliar lands in front of me. A forest full of bare, spindly trees. Their bark was an almost sickly grey colour and peeling away at the trunk. At first, I thought they'd dropped all their leaves, but there were none littering the ground. Only rotting, black apples that had fallen from their branches.

The first true day of summer had a blue sky with white clouds. It was a far cry from the overcast, grey skies of the Slothlands.

A man — no, an angel — stood only a few paces away from where I sat.

He leaned against one of the thick tree trunks. His muscular arms folded across his chest, booted feet crossed at the ankles as he watched me carefully. He had dark skin, and an even darker gaze, which stayed narrowed unwaveringly on where I sat and openly stared at him.

A three-day-old shadow lined his sharp jaw, his face angular, with high cheekbones and a narrow nose. His tongue darted across his full lips, and I jolted when I realised it was forked. My brain finally put two and two together and came up with a reasonable answer. I tried to suppress the hope blooming within me, feeling my heart quicken.

The angel tilted his head. He narrowed his dark-lashed almond-eyes, as if wanting to be in my mind instead of in front of me. As if he wanted nothing more than to know my innermost thoughts.

His head full of wavy, dark hair curled around his ears and

swept effortlessly across his forehead. Thick, dark horns rose from the crown of his head and curled towards his temple. Reminding me — as I continued to stare and assess him — that he was not a man. He was a demon, or an angel. He might've even been both.

Behind him, his stunning white wings rustled, but remained folded close to his body. He didn't look at all uncomfortable about having them pinned between his body and the tree. He unfolded his arms, and I watched as he unbuttoned his shirtsleeves, slowly rolling them up to his elbows.

Instead of racing, my heart now thumped with slow, pointed beats, as if reminding me I was only human. That I could die a very human death. I studied him from head to toe, a mix of exhilaration and fear swirling in my gut in equal measure.

"Who are you?" I whispered, almost choking on the words.

A smile teased at the edge of those full lips. "You know who I am, Little One."

"Samael?" I breathed his name, barely daring to hope it was true.

His chin dropped, a silent acknowledgment, and the angel pushed himself off the tree, stalking towards me. Sticks cracked underfoot, with each step forward, my heart thumped, thumped, thumped.

The angel crouched in front of me. His wings blocked out the sun as it peeked from behind the clouds. He reached forward, not offering his hand, but taking my own, his fingers stroking against my skin. "Hello, Octavia."

My breath caught in my throat. I reached for him, desperate to know whether he was real, or whether I was imagining the feel of his fingers wrapped securely around my hand. The callous on the pad of his thumb tracing the ridges of my knuckles.

Samael's grip tightened, and as he stood, he pulled me with him. I shot to my feet with no grace, and lost my balance, crashed against his chest. He was so close that I couldn't deny his reality.

He was here. *My Samael.* The voice inside my head had a body and a face.

Devils. He was the most intimidating, otherworldly being I had ever seen.

His fingers traced my scarred skin, lifting my chin to face him.

Breathless, I followed his lead. Standing this close, I could see the way his irises shifted. They were an inky pool of darkness, but utterly dynamic as they flickered full of starlight and flames. Shifting, swirling colour. All seven of the sins reflected in his gaze. A scar ran through his right brow, paling his skin and slicing through the dark hair.

A smile pulled at my lips. He was right here in front of me, *finally.* It felt like I'd waited an entire lifetime to meet him.

The devil grinned down at me, a wicked sight. His eyes glittered, as if he knew — although he was no longer invading my mind — exactly what I was thinking. As if he'd always known how much I'd wanted to see him.

Everything about him drew me in, and despite any misgivings I'd had about who he was, I felt myself relaxing against his chest, inhaling deeply. His laugh rumbled through his chest, and he snaked an arm around my waist, holding me close.

There was no escaping the devil now.

I tried to piece together how I'd come to be with him. The last thing I remembered was riding out of Suain with our sights set on the next town. There was a ghost feeling, of Max's weight pressed against my back, his breath against my neck. I shivered at the feeling.

"Where's Max gone?" I asked him, twisting to look over my shoulder in search of my companion. Thoughts of him filled me with worry, paralysing me. Had I abandoned him? Or had he abandoned me?

Samael captured my chin again. When I faced him, I could see the discontent that clouded his features. The pinch of his full lips, and the darkening of the flickering colours in his irises. "You need not think of him while you're here, Little One."

Biting down on my lip, I debated whether to push for information. Wondering if Max might not be lying dead somewhere, struck down when Samael came to collect me. Only I couldn't remember Samael coming for me. I couldn't remember travelling to this place of spindly trees and black apples.

Quietly, I asked, "Where's here, Samael?"

He chuckled, a deliciously dark but soothingly familiar sound. When Samael laughed, I was sure that it proved it was him, that he was here, with the same low, husky sound I'd heard in the back of my mind — the same sound I wanted to draw from him. I couldn't help but beam when I heard it.

"Full of questions today, aren't we?" He brushed his thumb along the curve of my jaw.

His grip remained tight on my jaw. Unrelenting and since he wouldn't let me look away, I didn't back down, raising one brow pointedly. "Honestly, it'd be nice if you answered a few of them. Even Pride gave more away than you."

"Which one would you like me to answer, then?" Samael asked. He smiled widely, as if indulging my curiosity amused him. His white wings rustled and stretched, drawing my attention. I stared at them, mesmerised by the opalescent sheen of the glossy feathers. Surely, they couldn't be as soft as they looked. I didn't like that he had wings, not really, as it aligned him closer to the seven sins. His horns shattered my illusion of him as a human man. I couldn't deny the raw power of him when he looked like he did.

"Are you real?" I asked. Settling on one of a hundred questions that begged to be answered. One of a few of a thousand things I wanted to know. There were so many things I wished he would tell me it was hard to know where to start.

"Define real…" He smirked, and a teasing glint flickered in his gaze.

"That's another non-answer," I said. Tapping two of my fingers against my forehead, I asked, "Am I hallucinating you? I could be still sick from the cold."

If there was anything I couldn't forget, it was the bone-deep cold of the Slothlands.

"No, Octavia." Samael shook his head. A curl of dark hair fell across his forehead. My heart raced as I dared to touch his skin, brushing it away. Samael's gaze flared with heat. "You're simply dreaming."

Recoiling, I drew my hand back from the path it had been tracing along his stubble-lined jaw. I blinked, studying his face for any sign of amusement or trickery.

"Sure." It was my turn to laugh. "As if I'm going to believe that. Tell the truth."

"I am." Samael sounded offended at my accusation. He turned his head, his stubble rough chin grazing the side of my hand. The casual touch sent tingles running down my arm. "Haven't you heard the tales of Sloth? I thought every village would scare their children with stories of the monsters of sleep."

Drawing my arm back, I swallowed roughly. I couldn't work out how to give myself enough distance to breathe without feeling dazzled by him. Not when I wanted to stay so close that he couldn't disappear. I couldn't risk him leaving, not before I had answers. Or at the very least, enough time to appreciate the dangerous intoxication of his presence.

Who were the monsters of sleep? Were there more demons at his beck and call? The thought turned my stomach, my hair on my arms standing on end as my skin prickled.

"Obviously not." It felt like my wit split and shattered, so I responded with blatant suspicion. "Care to share, Samael?"

His eyes glowed, flashes of green, pink, and purple making my breath catch in my throat. His grin widened, and Samael slid his arm around my waist, his fingertips brushing against the scars on my hip. A gentle caress.

Simultaneously cringing and wanting to melt against the small comfort, I reached for his wrist to stop him from touching any more of my scars. Opting to shy away from his attention.

The devil flicked his forked tongue at me, a silent rebuke, before holding on tighter.

"Sloth is both an angel and one of the seven sins... But she is a little different to the rest of her brethren," he said. "The closest thing I could liken her to in this world and the next is an incubus." He paused, glancing at me, but I didn't know what that was. I stared blankly at him. "Maybe you've heard the old tales of those? Or not? It is a creature who walks through the dreams of others and steals their coveted moments of rest. Their victims wake fatigued and troubled until one day they do not wake at all. The complexities of the experiences and worlds inside her dreamscape empower Sloth."

He gave me a meaningful look, and I frowned. "I still don't understand."

Samael didn't seem surprised, and much to my relief, he didn't get upset at my lack of understanding. He only nodded. "Sloth encourages a deep slumber. She controls dreams and nightmares. She pulls strength from her citizens' emotions in their dreams." He reached out, tapping his finger against the end of my nose. "Slothians spend more of their lives asleep than awake."

That sounded impossible. Except I'd slept in Suain for days on end. Until then, I'd never spent more hours sleeping than awake. Four to five hours of rest and the sweet buzz of fear fuelled adrenaline had become my best friend.

Besides, the tight shackles of my relentless anxiety would never have allowed it. There were far too many things to lie awake and think about in the middle of the night.

"So...I'm asleep," I confirmed, stupidly.

Samael nodded. "Yes."

"I can remember that we were riding and then... Sloth forced me to go to sleep."

"That sounds right." His smile was tight this time, wary. "It's hard to stay awake when traversing the Slothlands. Even the strongest of people struggle to resist the call of Sloth."

Disappointment flooded through me, and I shrank back from him.

This time, Samael let me go. His hand skimmed my waist as I pulled from his hold. My throat turned tight, the bridge of my nose prickling with emotion. I looked away from him, glaring at the peeling bark of a nearby tree. "That means I'm just dreaming you up."

Samael stepped forward. He swiftly closed the gap between us before I could even think of moving again. "You've manifested me," he said, and although he didn't reach for me, he kept invading my space. Moving until he was all I could see, until his proximity overwhelmed me. "You brought me here."

"You just said Sloth created this whole thing!"

"The Angel of Sloth fulfils desires, dreams and nightmares, but it is sometimes nothing more than a game of roulette. You never know where in the dreamscape you might land."

Stubbornly, I shook my head, leaning into the kernel of bitterness that burned in my chest. I should have known it was too good to be true. That Samael couldn't possibly be standing in front of me as the solution to all of my problems. "But it isn't the real you…"

He leaned close to me. His breath washed over my face. Then the angel shifted, spreading his arms and his wings wide. "Are you disappointed, Octavia?"

The truth stuck in my throat, but I forced it out. If days of riding with Max had taught me anything, it was that there was something noble about telling the truth. That it was a relief to be honest, instead of hiding behind a wall of lies. "Yes. I am."

He pressed his lips together. I expected him to fall into a fiery show of rage, like Niklaus might have, or like nearly any other man who had been rejected. But Samael was no mere man. I could see the amusement crinkling at the corner of his eyes. I huffed, certain he was laughing at me.

"What if I told you that you've done a remarkable job of conjuring my likeness…"

I tipped my head back, suddenly frustrated. I didn't want to be placated. I didn't want to be soothed. I wanted the devil, right here and right now. Not a facade, but the otherworldly being that haunted me. In the flesh. "I've never seen you before," I snapped, tempted to reach forward and shove him back. Tamping down the bold desire, I fisted my hands by my sides. "Maybe I'm dumb, Samael, but I'm not stupid enough to believe I could conjure something I've never seen."

As the wind whistled around us, he reached out and stopped a strand of my hair from blowing across my face. It was strange the way the forest rustled, even with no leaves on the trees. "Consider that I left you clues, Octavia. I've been inside your mind, remember? Into every deep recess of your subconscious."

"What a mess that must be…" I muttered.

"You're not as broken as you think you are, Octavia," he said, his expression turning thoughtful. He reached out and touched me, his icy fingers sliding and cupping my neck. His black nails scratched lightly against my skin. "There was an old human custom once, before I came to the earth. Humans used to have a practice where they repaired fragile things with gold after they shattered. They found a new beauty in the now-glittering cracks. They valued them for their trauma. Your mind is no different."

Mulling his words over, I decided I didn't know what to make of that. There was no assurance that Samael told me the truth and not just pretty words to make me more compliant. He could make up customs and claim that they had existed before him, and I would never know the truth. There wasn't a human soul on earth who had been alive before the devil. He had reigned over us for so many generations that anything before was kindling for myth.

I studied the slope of his nose, the scar through his brow and the texture of his horns, waiting for his tell. I wanted to believe him so badly. I wanted to accept the compliment that my fractured self was beautiful. The distrust in my heart — the part of me that believed I couldn't succeed, no matter how hard I tried — rejected his words.

"Tell me something, Samael…" It sounded like I was begging for more information, or a fraction more of his time.

"What sort of something?" he asked.

"*Anything*." I glanced at the too-blue sky, and the naked trees surrounding us. I shivered, feeling as if I shouldn't have been aware that I was dreaming. Now that I knew I was, even the air felt unnatural. "This feels wrong."

"I've been preparing you for the Sloth trials for quite a while." His tongue flicked across his lower lip, distracting me. "I've been leaving hints in your subconscious and waiting to meet you in your dreams, Octavia. Do you know what this scape is based on?"

Glancing around, I shrugged. "I wouldn't have a clue."

"A forest of dead trees surrounds my land. These trees, despite their thin and prickly nature, bear fruit."

He turned, stalking to one tree and reached into the branches to pluck a piece of said fruit. When he turned back, he held it out in an offering. It was plump and inviting, and my mouth salivated at the sight of it. "The black apple."

"We're in your lands?" I gaped at him. He threw the fruit at me and I caught it. My nails dug into the flesh and juice dripped down my wrist. It wasn't truly black. On closer inspection, the flesh was a dark purple. I raised it to my lips, biting into the flesh with a sharp, crisp crunch. The inside of the fruit was pale, filled with dark seeds. A beat later, as I chewed on it, the juice dripping down my chin, I realised I couldn't taste it. At all. There was no sweetness, and no flavour.

It turned my stomach. The sharp and dizzying reminder that it was all just a dream made it hard to breathe. I dropped the apple. It bounced across the ground. Samael kicked out, catching the apple with the toe of his boot and sending it flying through the trees.

"Not literally, Little One." Holding my waist, he turned me on the spot. Allowing me to soak in a little more of the surrounding forest. "But this is as close as I could get to bringing you home early."

"Home?" I echoed the word, feeling uncomfortable. I didn't have a home, not anymore.

"That's what it will be, someday. When you meet me in Eternis," Samael told me. The heat of his body pressed against my back. He was a looming presence, filling the space, but I didn't feel intimidated by him. Instead, it comforted me. "It will be your home, too."

My body flushed hot and cold, my anxiety spiking unexpectedly. I wanted nothing more than to belong somewhere, but the devil calling this place home jarred against the knowledge that this wasn't real. It put me off-kilter, and suddenly I didn't know what I was supposed to do. Or how I was supposed to act.

"What do we do?" I asked him, tilting my head to look up at him, and realising just how tall Samael was. Taller than Nash, even, whose lanky frame had always towered over me.

"Whatever we want," the devil replied. It sounded like the simplest answer in the universe, but what did I really want? At that moment, I didn't know.

Samael tugged me down the path. "Come, Octavia. We'll visit one of the nearby cities."

Travelling was strange in the dreamscape. Once Samael determined our destination, the trees vanished into fog and transformed into houses. My boots moved to land on a polished cobblestone path instead of sticks and dirt.

"Oh." I blinked, stunned stupid by the quick transition.

Quaint little buildings surrounded us. A mixture of polished stone and wide glass windows. It gleamed beneath the daylight, everything carefully maintained. Greenery grew over the archways and fell from second storeys; soft leaves fluttered towards the earth, creating an overwhelming feeling of life. Everything here was vibrant, even the glimpses of people through the windows.

"Where are we?" I asked him.

"Rathyn City," Samael answered, as if I should have already known. But I'd need two more hands to count the things I didn't know about the devil and his lands.

"Is that near Eternis?"

"No, Eternis is my residence. It's home to the garden of souls, and a chosen few that I can tolerate." Samael said, leading me over a small stone bridge. I could see the clear running water beneath it, along with devil's coins that had been tossed into its depths. There they sat, snug on the base of the river, almost taunting me. The need for another coin. The symbol of success in our pitiful lives.

"Rathyn City is on the southern border of my lands. It's home to any demon-born soul who wishes to live here."

My head tilted at the stipulation of demon-born souls. "Like Cyn?"

"Exactly." Samael smiled, praising me with nothing more than a look. My body warmed at the sight of it, craving more. "For many years, Cyn lived on my lands. They flourish in the indulgence of Gula, and I won't restrain my demons from pursuing their desires in this world."

I couldn't blame Cyn for the choice, not really. There was something about Rathyn that was setting me on edge. A trickling anxiety crept up like cold water dripping over my scalp and sliding down my spine. Every one of my instincts screamed that there was something wrong. That perfection hid a sinister shadow.

Samael led me through the city with the confidence of

someone who had explored every street. A marketplace webbed through one corner, lining the spindly alleyways. It smelled of pungent spices, and my throat burned with the bitter tang of magic. My stomach rumbled for food as we passed eateries with tables and chairs set out. Most of it appeared completely normal, just like every other city I'd visited. Yet something still felt wrong, and I couldn't quite put my finger on it.

We wove through a thick crowd of people. Someone brushed past me, and I stumbled, tripping over my own feet. The devil was quick to catch me. His fingers stroked across my knuckles. He gripped my hand tightly, anchoring me to his side.

Samael set me right and we moved on as if nothing had happened. I allowed him to carve a path along the riverbank. The riverbed sparkled with coins while black swans swam nearby.

Another man bumped into me. He slammed so hard into my shoulder that my breath caught in my chest. I spun to confront him, my free fist raised, but only when I lifted my chin to ask him what his problem was, did I realise what was wrong.

Fear and panic shot through me, hot and fast. I looked at the devil for reassurance, but he was focused on the path ahead of us. Using our interlinked hands, I tugged against his hold, forcing a moment of his attention. "Samael?"

"Yes?" the devil murmured. He turned, tucking his wings tightly, but wasn't fast enough to slide between me and the next person. They bumped into my shoulder painfully.

I staggered to the side and Samael caught me before I plunged into the river. Sudden fear of the icy water rushed through me, and I shuddered. He crushed me hard against his hard body, rubbing his palm across my shoulder blades in big, soothing circles.

"They don't have any faces," I said. My panic grew, making my voice squeaky and my words rushed. "The people don't have faces. What's going on?"

"Ah." His forked tongue flicked. "You noticed that."

163

Samael didn't sound bothered, but I couldn't get my heart to settle. It had taken me too long to pinpoint what was wrong. Their faces shifted out of focus, lacking human features.

"Samael?" I asked. "Why…"

"It's a dream, Octavia," Samael reminded me, hand pausing mid-rotation. He cupped the back of my head, pressing me against his chest. "Does everyone usually have a detailed face in your dreams?"

"I… No? I don't remember," I admitted. I'd never paid attention in my dreams before, never noticed if the people within them had faces and features. I'd easily known who they were. The same way I'd known who Samael was when I'd woken up here, pure instinct. "Why do they keep slamming into me? They feel angry."

"Because you're aware that you're dreaming! A big part of you knows this isn't real, and you're not immersed." His grip on me tightened as he spoke, and Samael reached for my chin. Tilting my head and holding my eye, he continued. "Sloth can't feed on you, if you remember that it's a dream."

"Is that important?" The intensity that burned through his gaze told me it might be. A power swirled behind those luminescent irises.

"Try to remember it, Octavia," Samael said, earnestly.

His white wings flared before they curled around us. They blocked out the city for a moment. My throat felt like it was closing over. For a sudden moment, a memory of Pride doing something similar came to mind. Entrapping me in a demand from behind the feathered shield of his wings. My heart felt like it was clamouring up my throat, and I curled my fingers into Samael's shirt. Anchoring myself to him while I tried to remember that this wasn't Pride. That maybe the devil was the lesser of two evils.

"Why are you saying that like you're going somewhere?" I asked him.

He gestured towards our feet, drawing my attention to

164

another thing I'd failed to notice. A white mist rolled off the river — not unlike the mist that had slipped over the road as I'd been riding with Max — and curled around our ankles, tendrils breaking free to climb up our legs, threatening to consume us.

"That mist. It's called Sloth's miasma," He explained gently, reaching for my hands. His thumbs brushed over my knuckles as he uncurled my fingers from his shirt. "It means you're about to leave. Remember that, if you can."

"But, Samael, I don't want to go…" It sounded like I was begging, pleading with him to let me stay. In a way, I was — I'd only just met Samael in this way. There were so many things I still wanted to ask him, so many things I still needed to say. I couldn't let this opportunity slip through my fingers like sand and stardust.

With a sad and regretful expression, he tousled his dark hair. He looked like he wanted me to stay, too.

"Next time, Octavia." the devil promised, giving my hand a gentle squeeze. "Next time, we'll inspect the stars together, every single one. Next time, I'll show you the secrets and possibilities of eternal life."

"But what about right now?" I clutched at him, winding my grip back into the fabric of his shirt. Determined to stay close. It didn't work, though. I felt suddenly weightless. When I looked down, my legs were disappearing, as if I'd never existed to begin with.

"For now, Octavia…" Samael leaned close, and his cold lips grazed against mine. It was a soft ghost of a kiss. Another promise, before the mist claimed me.

Between one breath and the next, I disappeared.

His voice echoed in my ears, nothing more than the same whisper in my mind that he'd always been. "Remember that you need to wake up. *Every time*. Wake up. Keep going, Octavia."

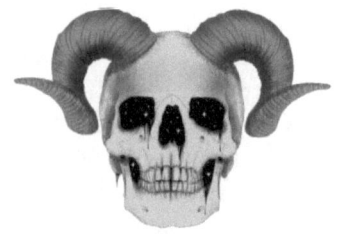

Chapter Twelve

The feeling of desolation and loss never left me. Even as the world faded away and reformed around where I stood. Lingering tendrils of mist swirled around my feet. This new world was darker than the last, and it took a moment for my eyes to adjust. Fear raced through my heart as I tried to work out where I had been taken. I longed to go back to my place in the devil's arms.

It almost felt like being at home in Ilrea. I stood amid broken concrete and kicked up dirt. Half-destroyed houses crumbled all around me, a picture of devastation. My skin prickled, but there was nobody watching me. I was alone. There was a distinct vastness to the world around me, and I felt insignificant within it. A reminder that I was, in the grand scheme of things, insignificant.

"Samael?" I called his name on the thin thread of hope that he had followed me here.

He was the devil, and by my thinking, should be able to achieve the impossible. He should be able to walk through my dreams and nightmares to hunt me down. He should have been able to follow me anywhere.

My voice echoed through the air. Nobody answered, the silence just as much of an answer. My heart clenched, my stomach doing flips, but I refused to accept it, yelling his name, "Samael! Samael! Where are you?!"

Still, nothing. While I'd known from his soft goodbye that the devil wouldn't be joining me, I still felt the cold disappointment of his absence. He'd been guiding me for so long, I was afraid that I couldn't find my way without him.

Unsure of what to do next, I stumbled forward. It was difficult to find my bearings when everything looked the same — there was nothing key to this broken little village, no life to be seen. Except me.

The smell of smoke drifted towards me, acrid and unpleasant. The back of my throat tickled. No flames were visible, but I broke out in a cold sweat and my hands became clammy. The scars that wrapped around my body tingled and itched. I scratched my hips, my lungs seizing against the memory of flames burning their imprint against my skin.

I couldn't remember exactly where I had been when sleep claimed me. The sudden idea struck me that this could be my reality. I could have woken up and not even realised it.

My teeth sunk sharply into my lower lip, igniting a kiss of pain that would surely wake me if I was in fact sleeping. Nothing changed, and the next beat of my heart felt heavy with dread.

"Max?" I whispered his name. It carried on the wind like a haunting melody, but still nobody replied.

I shivered when the breeze carried back to me without an answer, whipping pieces of my hair around my face. For all the heavy silence and empty space, I couldn't shake the feeling that I wasn't actually alone.

The back of my neck prickled, and my palms itched, again. As if someone were watching me, and my body knew it, even though I couldn't see them.

My hand drifted to the leather straps that wrapped tight around my left thigh. Reaching for the angel's blade. It had been there when we left Suain. Now I felt nothing but the brush of my skin. I couldn't believe I hadn't noticed the missing weight of the dagger immediately. It should have felt like losing a limb. Wrath had trained me to become one with my weapon, and now I had lost my only means of protection. Angel-forsaken or not.

My heart raced, and panic flared through every one of my nerves until suddenly I couldn't stand still. Or at least that's how it felt, the acute knowledge that I could be in lethal danger. That, finally, I had failed to outrun my death.

I realised I must be dreaming, since my blade was missing. Still, uncertainty crept in. I felt untethered and unsure of whether I could trust myself or my beliefs. Especially when something about these crumbling, wrecked buildings felt so familiar. The gravel beneath my feet felt real, crunching beneath my boots, as the wind howled.

I wrapped my arms around my middle and squeezed tight. I pinched my waist to regain focus and stop my thoughts from spiralling. But it was useless. Nothing changed.

The longer I stood still, there more the temperature dropped around me. The disappearing mist gave way to a chill that left my teeth chattering. I couldn't remember where my heavy coat had gone, much like my blade. Someone might have stolen it from me while I was sleeping. Instinctively, I reached for my pockets to see what else was missing, before remembering that I owned nothing of good value.

When the consequence of standing still was wasting away in an infinite loop of passing time, I kept moving. Unwilling to lose myself to the chill of the Slothlands. The darkened clouds rolled across the horizon and blocked the sun. They left me suspended in a world of gloomy grey.

I staggered forward and decided I would find Maksymilian or Samael for myself. I wasn't a damsel in distress that needed to wait for them to come and save me.

The broken buildings and sprouting weeds seemed to extend forever. No matter how long I walked, everything stayed the same. I could have sworn that although I didn't turn a single corner, I'd walked the same path repeatedly. But as soon as I lamented the surrounding monotony, the landscape both smoothed and roughened simultaneously. The remnants of structure and evidence of destruction fell away. Building smoothing into rocks, and then those disappearing behind me.

The path shifted from stone to dirt, overpowered by loose foliage. Trees surrounded me, and not for the first time, a forest swallowed me whole. I could have sworn they hadn't been there a minute ago. That I'd barely breathed before everything had shifted from buildings to forest. Only... Maybe I hadn't been paying enough attention. The cold made it hard to focus, and I couldn't recall if I had been in a crumbling village before.

Perhaps I'd always been here, lost in the soft silence of nature.

There was something comforting about the rustle of the leaves and the call of the beasts beyond. It felt less eerie than open, empty space. With the creatures inhabiting it, deadly or not, I wasn't alone. The very thought filled me with such relief that my body sagged forward, my limbs heavy.

I wasn't alone. I would find my way.

Too soon, though, my throat dried. My head throbbed with a painful, demanding thirst.

Traipsing through the forest alone, I was completely unprepared. There was nothing to help me survive. Thick branches and dark leaves shielded me from rain. There'd be no catching droplets on the end of my tongue. I moved faster. Stumbling over tangled roots, climbing over falling trees, and listening hard past the chirp of birds for a noise I so desperately wanted to hear.

The whirring flick of Max's lighter as he created a flame. Or the rough rasp of Samael's deep laugh. Neither of them echoed through the forest. I could only hear the soft trickle of water rushing across the land.

By the time I recognised it, I was so tired and so achingly thirsty that I thought I was hallucinating. Dreaming of what I wanted instead of what I had. But I found my way to the edge of the river. Collapsing to my knees and leaning over the riverbank. The cool flow of water against my skin nearly pulled a sob from my arid throat.

I couldn't be dreaming. I drank greedily from the river, savouring its cool and sweet taste. Relief, the way I felt it, as if all my hopes had lifted, couldn't be replicated in a dream. It had to be real.

Thirst quenched, I rocked back onto my heels and stared at the way the river moved. I caught sight of my reflection, my hair hanging around my jaw. Reaching for the ends of it, my reflection frowned back at me. I tried to remember when it'd grown back in. I'd had uneven burned lengths after Glorae. My reflection still showed the dark purple scars marring my face and neck. The new texture of my skin that would never fade.

Sucking in a sharp breath and cringing away from the sight of it, I pulled myself to my feet. As I moved forward, my dress dropped a bead that got flattened in the mud.

"Octavia…" My name floated on the river, calling me from upstream. Turning, I stared upstream, towards a mountain. Familiarity tugged at the knot that had twisted in my stomach. I'd been here before. The climb ahead suddenly looked steeper and darker. I shook my head, raking my fingers through my hair and twisting it from my face. Telling myself that I was hearing things. That the forest hadn't sung my name and carried it across the water.

But when I turned away, my name drifted out again. "Octavia…"

My skin rippled with discomfort, my heartbeat slowing to a dull thud, thud, thud. I changed my path and started climbing along the riverbank. Following the siren call of my name like a woman possessed. Desperate to find myself company in this lonely place, because suddenly the signs of life weren't enough. I needed to see someone else. I needed to truly know that I wasn't on my own.

The ground slipped beneath my feet. Mud sucked at my ankles and clung to my skin. It didn't slow me down. With single-minded determination, I climbed until the trees thinned. The call of my name led me away from the water. The Feast of Samael had been held in these Gulan forests.

I recognised them now.

Surrounded by thick, old trees, their gnarled trunks rose high above me. Crowding me in. As the landscape had turned rocky, a cave sat not too far from where I stood. The entrance was marked by a flickering torch on either side, their dancing flames tossed shadows onto the rocks. They brightened and then disappeared with nothing more than a curl of smoke.

Turning, I almost expected to see the Heira twins standing by my side. They had been my only hope the last time I had stood in the mouth of a cave like this one — *just like this one*. Hesitation gripped me tightly, like a demon's hand around my neck, holding me in place as bile rose in my throat.

"Octavia…" that voice called again. All at once, I both relaxed and tensed up, unsure of what to do and who to trust. It didn't sound like Gluttony calling me forward. An old demon, a sin that I thought I'd conquered the hard way, hadn't called me here. But still my scalp prickled with the warning of familiarity.

"Come in…" the voice invited.

The world spun around me, even though I hadn't moved. Everything darkened at the edges of my vision, and my hesitation finally let me go. It freed my limbs so I could stagger forward to the mouth of the cave, where I stood on a precipice, unsure of how I got there. Torn between the safety of the woods and burning curiosity about what lay within the cave. It felt like the most important decision of my life.

Bigger, even, than the moment I'd trusted the devil.

"Come on, Tav…" the familiar voice coaxed me forward. Recognition sparked within me, like the single bolt of lightning that ignites a forest fire. Setting everything around it ablaze.

One moment I was unsure, wavering in my choice, and the next I was running straight into the cave. My movements were so frenzied that my mud-caked feet slipped beneath me, and I slammed into the ground. Rocks and sticks scraped against my limbs, grazing my knees, tearing at my arms. Desperate to follow that voice, I pulled forward and up, forcing myself to my feet. Blood dripped free of my body, soaking into the dirty material of my dress and sliding down my wrists. I wiped my hands against my thighs, wincing at the sting of pain, but dismissing it. Just another scar for my collection — by the end of these trials I'd be nothing more than thick, ridged scars connecting the shreds of my humanity. More of a mess than I'd ever been before, but what was one more wound when I knew that voice?

The cave darkened and my approach slowed, only because I couldn't see where I was going anymore. I threw my hands forward and grazed the sides of the tunnel for guidance.

"Phee?" I called into the darkness, wishing she would speak again and give me direction. "Ophelia, are you there?"

As I staggered forward, the edges of the cave glowed. The presence of the soft blue luminescent mushrooms offered some light. I knew, this time, not to eat them. Even though my stomach suddenly rumbled with demand. No amount of hunger could coax me into experiencing that level of fear again.

There was a soft flutter ahead of me, and butterflies with gently glowing wings rose from the sides of the cave. They swirling around me, their tiny legs brushing my skin until I shrieked. The sound bounced off the walls and echoed further into the cave. Blindly I struck out at the little insects, but when I caught them in my grip, they crackled and crumbled, turning sticky beneath the heat of my palms. Nothing more than a candied delight.

"Octavia..." Ophelia called back to me. Her thin voice was like a ghost in the night, but I knew better than to dream of non-existent horrors. If she was speaking to me, then she was real, just like Samael had been. The devil, who had been devastatingly quiet since I'd left him, who must be so angry that I'd disappeared.

With my hands outstretched to prevent another fall, I turned and twisted down a precariously narrow tunnel. Descending into the heart of the mountain. It sloped downward, taking me deeper and deeper beneath Gula. The path narrowed until the rocks scraped against my arms and hips. The mushrooms crushed against my body, leaving me dusted in their dazzling glow. Fear gripped my heart as I thought about not fitting through and reaching Ophelia.

The walls gave way and I fell into the larger cavern, landing on my hands and knees in the mud. A single, fluttering butterfly came to rest on my hand. My body glowed, the luminescent residue of the mushrooms painting my skin. When I rubbed at it, it smeared and spread, leaving my fingerprints behind.

Ahead of me, sitting primly on a rock in the middle of the cavern, was Ophelia Bell. She had her back to me, wearing a familiar pink dress. Neon butterflies fluttered around her head. She had tied her blonde hair in a thick but loose plait. It hung down the length of her back, with little pink blooms threaded through it.

The crown of flowers she wore had wilted and withered. The roses turned brown and the petals fell free as I watched. They drifted to mud around, but the girl barely appeared to notice. She was humming to herself, a bright tune, completely undisturbed by my entrance. She looked okay, and for the first time in years, the grief-laden ache in my chest eased just a fraction.

"Is that you…" I asked, my voice trembling. I felt stupid the moment I asked, not when it was so obviously Ophelia Bell. She was unmistakable. I pulled myself upright and edged closer. With each step I took, the rocks turned slick beneath my feet. The slimy feel of it was so familiar that my stomach clenched and turned. The rocks weren't coated in mud because the sharp, distinct smell of blood was unmistakable. "Phee? Look at me? Phee?"

She didn't turn to look. Now that I stood closer, I just saw the pink stain on her golden locks. The way the pool of blood weighed her down her skirts. The flimsy layers soaked through.

I couldn't help but move closer, extending my arm towards her shoulder. My breath caught in my throat, as something within urged me not to touch the girl. Something deep in my chest warned me to flee. Desperate for my friend, I ignored it.

When I touched Ophelia, finding the courage to make that contact, it felt like a shock ran through me. A zap travelled up my arm and left every nerve in my body tingling. I flinched back, instantly regretting my choices.

Then she turned to face me. A wide smile split across her face, horrifying as blood coated her soft lips and discoloured her teeth. It dripped down her chin, and I couldn't help but watch the drops fall.

"Ohmidevil!" she cried. She sounded so much like the girl I remembered that my heart cracked in my chest, breaking all over again. "Tav, you've come to visit!"

Filled with morbid curiosity, and not trusting my memory of the first trial, I looked down at her chest. I saw a gaping hole where her heart had been ripped free, blood, bone, and sinew on display, no heart buried inside. The front of her dress was stained with blood, just as it had been that day.

The back of my hand slapped against my lips to hold in my

shocked, pained gasp. Her warm brown eyes were devoid of light when I looked at her, ignoring her bloody lips and the piece of flesh between her teeth. While she sounded eager, there was no spark of life to be found within. The creature in front of me had a dead gaze and a creepy smile.

Ophelia tilted her head. For all the world looking concerned about me.

"Were you looking for this?" she asked. Her right hand rose, unveiling the tightly clutched organ. A heart. *Her heart* throbbed pitifully in her palm, twitching with slow, shuddering beats that should have been impossible. It was beating outside of her chest. The sight of it. My stomach lurched, twisted. I was going to vomit. My trembling fingers pressed harder against my mouth, willing my stomach to settle.

My heart thumped, thumped, thumped in response to the beat of hers and tears prickled in my eyes. "Phee…" I mumbled, at a loss for anything else to say.

She clutched the organ tight again and raised it to her lips. Her dead eyes closed, and her nostrils flared when she inhaled deeply. She chewed through a ravenous bite, bloodstained lips, and sharp teeth at work.

"It's delicious," Ophelia assured me. She had the same confidence she had had during the ridiculous dinner with her family. The naïve belief that this was how things should be. Ophelia leaned close to me, and I could smell the blood and decay on her breath.

My stomach flipped and I retched.

"Try some," she urged.

"No!" I took a step back, but Ophelia moved too quickly. She kept herself in my space, unavoidable. A giggle rose from her open chest. I retched again. "Phee, I don't want any."

The girl, once like a fairy, now a mistress of the dead, twirled around me. She dragged her finger against my back, marking my skin with her blood. Her bright laugh had become chilling. "The trial's over, Octavia. You can try some now, promise. It won't hurt you."

I was very sure that it would. Trying not to gag, I twisted to look behind me. There was no way to pinpoint the tunnel I'd come from. All the rocks looked the same and I couldn't see any entrance or exit. I had no way to flee.

"I just don't want any, Phee. I'm not hungry." Begging was not beneath me. Not right then. "Please."

She had come to a stop in front of me, her face falling with unmistakable disappointment. Her lower lip rolled into an over-exaggerated, trembling pout. "Don't you trust me, Tav?"

It felt like the sort of question that could kill me. I was fairly certain I didn't even trust myself. I didn't know how I could get myself out of this predicament. Something dark flickered in her dead eyes, and I took it as a warning. I smiled tightly, breathing through my mouth to avoid the scent of old blood.

"It's not that, Phee..." I shook my head, raising my hands placatingly. "It's just... How long have you been down here?"

Ophelia reached up and pressed that impossibly still-beating heart against my mouth. My lips pursed, denying myself a taste, but I could feel it pulsating against my lips. My stomach flipped and my nausea crested. Bile rose, trapped by my pursed lips, searing my nose. I choked on it, spluttering, but still refusing to open my mouth. Unwilling to risk it, in case she shoved that heart between my lips and doomed me, too. Wrapping my arms around my middle, I turned my head to the side, hesitant to push her away or strike her down. Blood smeared against my cheek and Ophelia huffed.

She sniffled, and after a moment, she backed away. Blood-stained tears filled her eyes, rolling down her face and dripping from her chin, adding to the gory mess. I struggled to reconcile this image with the woman I once knew. They were not one and the same.

"I thought you had come to have dinner with me, Tav." She

sounded completely miserable and despite my growing fear, she struck a chord of guilt. Especially as she continued, glancing at me mournfully, "I've been so lonely, especially since you left me. It's rude not to eat when invited, you know."

"But Phee, you failed the trial, and I didn't." It felt hopeless to remind her, as her fragile body flinched. "I couldn't stay with you."

My left wrist seared with pain, and I glanced down at it. The small tattoos had transformed; now a purple human heart replaced the tiny purple piglet. It beat, shifting on my skin, throbbing to the same rate as my pulse. It quickened the longer I watched it. My fear doubled, palms turning sweaty, before I realised I'd taken my attention off the real threat.

When I looked up again, Ophelia's tears had stopped flowing, but her pout remained. Her face clouded over, and her hand tightened around the remnants of the heart. White-knuckled around the organ, as she stormed towards me, raising it, shaking in her fist.

Fear made me scramble backwards, slipping in the blood, until I hit the rocks. Ophelia didn't stop until she was so close to me I could feel her rotting breath again. There was nowhere for me to go in this cave, and I had no way to escape her.

She gripped my chin with her free hand, surprisingly strong, as she forced my face to turn to one side. She brushed my hair from my jaw with her knuckles, clucking disapprovingly beneath her breath as she inspected me.

"What have you done to yourself, Tav?" she asked. With bloody fingers, she traced my scarred skin, frowning and wrinkling her nose. I swore I could see the edge of her heart between her fingers. "This never would have happened if you'd stayed with me. I would have looked after you."

"Don't touch me!" My demands melted into begging. "Please, Ophelia. Don't touch me."

"Phee," she corrected, sounding cross. Her once beautiful

face crumpled with anger. "You need to call me Phee. We're friends. Friends use nicknames, Tav."

I nodded, my attention flickering around the cavern for any sort of escape. I'd dig my way to the core of the world if I needed to. I couldn't stay here with her, especially not as the blonde took another bite of her heart, chewing slowly beside me. I could hear the way her teeth smashed against the muscle, her lips smacking together. When she ate it all, inherently, I knew she would come for mine next.

The butterflies had abandoned us. The mushrooms dimmed in the distance. There was nothing more than an old mirror in the far corner of the cave taunting me with our reflections. Set in a tarnished bronze frame, the glass cracked, but the mirror still resembled something from Pride's palace. Despite the darkness, our reflected image against the wall was clear.

A flicker of white within the frame distracted me from Ophelia. Snowflakes drifted lazily past us, even though it wasn't snowing within the cave. My chest ached, and Ophelia turned to glance over her shoulder at what had captured my attention. An aggravated sigh rolled from her lips.

While we watched, a soft white mist poured from the mirror. It drifted onto the floor of the cave and edged towards us. It rolled and lifted, almost alive. When it licked around her ankles, Ophelia let out a second heavy and miserable sigh.

"You're leaving me again, Octavia," she said. I didn't understand. She had me trapped here. There was no way for me to leave.

Ophelia stood on her tiptoes, and her cold, bloody lips pressed to the corner of mine. A gentle kiss, which tasted metallic. Her dead eyes lit with rare emotion — it took me a moment to name it as regret. She didn't want me to go anywhere; I didn't want to stay and become her next meal.

The mist swirled around our waists as she sniffled. Another blood-tainted tear slid across her skin, and she whispered, "I'll miss you."

The feeling wasn't mutual. Not anymore. Ophelia Bell had become a figment of my nightmares.

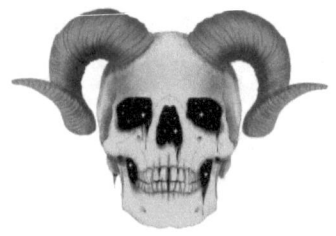

Chapter Thirteen

Awareness slammed into me with such brute force, that I thought I'd been stabbed. One moment I was dreaming and the next I was lying in the snow, staring up at the grey morning. My entire body throbbed with a bone-deep fatigue. I'd never felt so tired in my entire life. The edges of the dream slipped away, along with the haunting image of Ophelia's bloody face. I questioned how I'd ever thought it could be my reality. I gently pressed my fingers to my mouth, half expecting blood to coat them.

'Good. You're finally awake,' Samael said scathingly, as if he'd lost his patience for me. The world spun violently when I attempted to move, leaving no time to process his disgruntled tone. The sky twisted as if it might fall down atop me, and I sucked in a sharp breath. *'You need to get moving, Octavia.'*

Flinching at his steely tone, I slowly dragged myself upright. I wanted to rest on the grass and close my eyes. I tried to ground myself by rubbing my coat fabric. Deep breaths helped balance the world but couldn't relieve the heaviness in my eyes or the pounding in my head. I would have given anything for a nap.

"Where have you been, Samael?" I asked, one hand lifting to cup my throat at the sound of my croaky voice. The memory of the woman faded, but the feeling of abandonment from Samael remained. I grumbled, "You weren't there. Where were you?"

'Me?!' Samael snarled, his rage so potent that I trembled. *'You dare think I abandoned you?! I have been screaming at you to wake for days, Octavia. I told you to remember to wake.'*

Frowning, I slid my hands back up to my face and pressed my palms against my eyes. Pressing hard into my lids until light and colour flashed in the darkness. "I don't remember that," I admitted. It felt like there was a hole in my memory. I trembled, as if I'd experienced a trauma, but I swore could have only been asleep for a minute. Nowhere near long enough to get any rest. "It couldn't have been days. I'm so tired."

'You will be tired for a long time, Octavia. Get used to it.'

"Stop calling me that." I sniffed, rolling my shoulders, and trying to gather the energy to stand up. "I don't like it."

'It's your name,' Samael said. *'Is it not?'*

I pursed my lips and dragged myself to my feet, staggering as my balance slipped. He was deliberately antagonising me, but still it managed to get under my skin. "It's not what you call me."

Slipping on the grass, I fell on my hands and knees, a memory flashing through me. Almost as if I'd fallen like this before, and could feel rocks and musd beneath my body, but when I looked down, it was only grass and small stones. Bowing my head, I closed my eyes and tried to fight the next wave of exhaustion. I just wanted to go back to sleep, and the grass wasn't entirely uncomfortable. Just a small nap.

'Little One,' Samael said gravely. His frustration rolled through me, warring against the tired ache I felt. *'You must stay awake, just a little longer. Go and find your friend.'*

"Who?" I rasped, trying to think past my pulsing headache. He didn't need to answer my question, as a shudder ran down my spine and I remembered who he meant.

I gasped. "Max!"

Craning my neck, I couldn't see him anywhere. Snow had settled on the ground around, but Max was no small man and should have been easy to spot. Especially with his long, flaming red hair. Worry sparked within me, and as it stoked into a burning fire, it was enough to force me onto my feet. I wobbled my way into the middle of the road to search for him, squinting against the blinding white snow.

"Where are you?" I whispered more to myself than Samael or Max. My heart turned solid, sinking into my stomach as I moved forward. My worry doubled as I looked for any sight of him.

A good way up the road, I found the horse. It lay on its side on the ground, so cold and still that I thought it had died. However, when I placed my hand tentatively on its flank, I could feel the slow but steady rise and fall of each breath. I knelt down and inspected the beast, even though I had no idea how to care for it. Beside one of its hooves, I found the first clue that Max had to be nearby. The shiny, cylindrical lighter that he never let out of his sight lay half-buried in the mushy, melting snow.

Reaching out, I snatched at it, holding it tight as I stood, and kept moving.

He lay face down in the grass. His skin was pale as the snow that surrounded him, and his bright hair was knotted around his scalp. For a heart-stopping moment, just like with Honey, I thought he wasn't breathing. But when I drew closer, he let out a soft, solid snore, and the heavy tension melted from my shoulders.

"Hey, you," I called as I dropped to my knees beside him. Reaching for his shoulder, I was struck with an uncomfortable feeling, like I was repeating a moment in time. I hesitated, my breath catching in my throat. Desperation forced me to act, as it always did. I needed to see his eyes open, and life come back to his freckled face.

"Wake up, sleepy." I shook him, gently at first, and then harder when he didn't rouse. "Max! Wake up!"

With the last of my energy, I pushed his shoulders and turned him onto his back. He was too still and pale, barely breathing. His beard had grown. As I leaned over him, the hair felt bristly.

"Max!" I called his name again, one last plea for him to wake. "I'm sorry."

The truth of it was that I was sorry for what I was about to do. Although I'd never admit it if he was conscious. Letting his head loll to this side, I slapped him as hard as I could. My icy hand stung from the impact against his face, though it wasn't my best slap. Nothing like the punches thrown in the war.

His bright blue eyes snapped open. Max moved startlingly fast. He bolted upright. Our heads collided with a crack. Yelping, I fell backwards, clutching my throbbing head.

He blinked at me, his gaze unfocused. Then he shook himself, scraping strands of hair from his face. A red mark formed against his freckled cheek. The imprint of my fingers darkening. I decided not to mention it.

"What happened?" Max asked, his voice husky with the remnants of sleep. He rubbed his eyes. "Why were you on top of me?"

"I wasn't on top of you!" I objected quickly. "You were asleep, and I was trying to wake you."

His eyes narrowed in disbelief. I tried not to take offense. He had no reason to have faith in my word.

"I don't remember going to sleep…" he said. He rose to his feet, swaying as he tried to find his balance, his voice thick with suspicion. He looked as disoriented as I'd felt.

"Me either," I said. "But I remember you going to sleep behind me on the horse."

Max screwed up his face, lips pursed like he was sucking on sour berries. "I wouldn't sleep on the horse. Everyone knows that's a good way to die."

He glanced around us, carefully absorbing our surroundings, from the imprint in the snow and grass where his body had been, to the horse lying in the distance. "Are you sure we weren't attacked by someone?"

"Are you hurt?" I asked him.

"No," he admitted, after finding his chuckleweed smokes in his pocket. He touched the coin at his neck, checking it next. "Looks like I lost my lighter, though."

The lighter was biting into my palm. I was still holding onto it for dear life. I sighed, tossing it in his direction. "Here."

Without hesitation, Max caught it and lit up, inhaling deeply. I wondered how he could be bothered, or if he didn't feel as sluggish as me. Every movement felt like wading through mud, but with a smoke between his lips he looked completely relaxed.

"Is the horse dead?" Max asked, breaking the silence.

Shrugging awkwardly, I admitted, "I think she's sleeping, too. But I'm not an expert on horses, so who knows."

He sighed heavily, shoulders slumping, soft pink smoke rolling between us. Finally, he nodded, pausing as he slipped past me, turning to tap one finger against the end of my nose gently.

Startled by his touch, I looked at his concerned face and took a sharp breath. His brows were drawn together, emotion flickering in his gaze.

"Are you hurt, Octavia?" he asked.

My attention shifted to his reddening cheek. The impact he hadn't mentioned or didn't remember. I was no more hurt than him. My forced smile was brittle and fragile, threatening to break me. Although not physically hurt, I felt inexplicably broken inside. Recalling my dream was like capturing smoke in the palm of my hand. So, I didn't know why I felt this way. "I'm fine," I murmured the two words that always meant the opposite of what they were.

Max didn't argue with me, turning back to the matter at hand. He knelt by the horse, his hand pressed to her flank and head bowed low. I stayed back, just in case he declared it dead, but thankfully, the beast woke and stood.

The deep knot of tension in my chest relaxed. Easing the worry that we would have had to walk, when I already felt so exhausted. Max brushed the snow off the horse's mane and re-secured our supplies.

"Thank the devil," I murmured softly.

Samael snorted. *'Always a pleasure to receive praise for things I had no hand in.'*

Max grinned at me. The wind whipped his hair around his face. Snow began falling. He beckoned me forward with a lazy curl of his fingers. "Let's get our asses to Kyama."

It took longer than expected to get to the next village. Whenever I started drifting off, Samael would shout in my mind. A primal, reverberating sound that jerked me back into consciousness.

'Do not fall asleep,' he growled. His determination kept me alert and awake. I elbowed Maksymilian whenever he began to snore. If I wasn't allowed to sleep, then neither was he. We would share in the punishment of having to stay awake.

"I'm not sleeping," Max snapped, after the fifth time I'd jabbed him. He twisted and poked me back.

I scoffed. "You were about to! I swear that was a pre-snore."

"What's a pre-snore!?" Max threw his hands in the air and scoffed. "You're making things up now, Octavia. I didn't fall asleep on the horse last time, and I won't do it now." He was stubbornly sure it would never happen. His voice slurred, heavy with fatigue.

We both needed some rest. Badly.

Kyama appeared ahead of us. Shrouded in fog and snow.

"We're here!" I cried.

"Don't do that!" Max snapped, unusually caustic.

I frowned. "Do what?"

"Wriggle around against me," he grouched. "You're going to knock us both off this horse. Besides, you don't know if this is Kyama, so hold still, will you."

Sighing, I squinted out into the snow. The houses and the village gave me an uneasy feeling, but I couldn't explain why.

Max agreed we could get off the horse and continue on foot. Knee-deep in the snow, I stared at the closest house. The windows had been boarded over, and the front steps were covered in a thick layer of snow. This village had been undisturbed for a long time.

"It feels like there's nobody home," I said. The wind carried my words away, and I had to repeat myself before Max heard.

He stomped up the front steps, fist raised to knock on the door. It rattled on its hinges, but nobody answered. He rattled the handle, but it was locked. Returning to my side, he looked up at the roof, shielding his eyes from the snow.

"Maybe you're right," he said. "There's no smoke coming from the chimney, and they'd be freezing in there without a fire."

"What was that?" I asked, the corner of my mouth lifting into a smile. I nudged him.

"I said they'd be freezing without a fire."

"Not that." I groaned. "The first bit. You said I was right."

Max snorted. "Don't let it get to your head, Octavia. It's big enough already."

"Oi!" I went to shove him, but he twisted out of the way quickly. A laugh bubbled up from his throat, the first joyful sound I'd heard in hours. Max quickly made a snowball and threw it at my face.

"Ha!" I cried, as it sailed over my shoulder. "You missed!"

He didn't miss the next three times. Wet and chilled, I still managed to hit him once. The simple achievement carried me through discomfort. We walked down the street, bright-eyed and snickering.

Each house we passed was the same as the first. Nobody answered the door. There were no signs of life. Max's impatience grew as he fidgeted.

"She could have told us the town was abandoned!" he huffed. "I really need to use the bathroom. I've been holding since I woke."

I blinked at him, confused. "So? Go pee on a tree."

Max glared at me. "I'm not risking freezing my family jewels off."

I burst into a loud laugh and hastily covered my mouth. "You call your nuts 'jewels'?"

He blushed. "Shut up!"

Samael sighed heavily in my mind. *'Are you two finished wasting precious time?'*

"I don't know," I said, shivering at the chill in his voice and the wind. "Are you going to tell us what we're supposed to be doing here?"

'You're supposed to be going to Desidia. Focus on the city. This village means nothing.'

"Huh?" Max spun around and frowned at me, talking over Samael's commentary. "How am I supposed to know what we're doing?"

A flush heated my cheeks. I'd forgotten to whisper and hide my conversation with Samael. I blinked at Max, hoping he would let it drop.

Max studied me with a worried expression before shrugging. Deciding he didn't need an answer. "Let's just find the chancellors' house."

He took hold of the reins, leading Honey the horse ahead of me. Suppressing the urge to slap myself, I trailed behind him.

"Don't forget, biggest house in town," I called after Max.

He waved his hand at me, finding the chancellor's house with ease. It looked exactly like the one we had left behind. A looming building, with multiple floors and big front windows. A soft light spilled onto the snow-covered porch, the first sign of life in this town.

Peering through the window, I saw no one inside. "Anyone there?" he asked. I startled, not hearing him approach.

"Not that I can see." My hope was draining away, increasing my exhaustion. Doubting my ability to continue travelling, I rubbed my eyes.

Max knocked on the door. Again, nobody answered. Despite the light inside, we were still very alone. He growled with frustration. "Stand back, Octavia."

"What?" I asked.

Max pushed me back and out of his way. When I glared at him, he shrugged. "I said stand back. Learn to listen."

It didn't take long to realise why. Climbing the porch, he took a deep breath and kicked the door. The loud crash of the impact shook me. It would have drawn attention if anyone was close by.

The door splintered, denting with his footprint. Teeth grit, fists clenched, he kicked it twice more. The door didn't burst open as expected, but the wood gave out beneath his boot. Falling forward, he cried out in surprise.

"Shit!" I ran up the stairs, hands outstretched to steady him. "Max!"

He shook his head, waving me off. Bracing against the door, he pulled his leg out. He winced when he put weight on the limb. He spoke through grit teeth, "I'm okay."

"Thought you didn't lie…" I frowned at him.

If looks could kill, I'd be dead and buried beneath the snow. Max pushed his arm through the splintered hole. I heard the soft snick of the lock, and he pulled the door open. Offering a glimpse of the cold, sterile interior of the house.

White marble floors and pillars supported the second story. A thin layer of dust covered the floors.

Max threaded his fingers through mine, holding tight as he pulled me inside. The slamming door cut off the howl of the wind.

Despite the lack of life, the house was much warmer than outside. Struggling out of my wet coat, I abandoned it on the floor. Max did the same, pushing his sleeves up to his elbows.

"Let's have a look around." He took charge, pressing his palm to his stomach. "Food first."

"Then somewhere to sleep," I added, fighting a yawn. Away from the harsh elements, I felt worn out and ready for bed. "I'm completely beat."

Samael's snarl of objection was chilling. *'Do not sleep, Little One. Hold out as long as you can.'*

I didn't have the energy to argue. Instead, I huffed and ignored him. The devil hadn't steered me wrong in four other trials, but I had human needs he couldn't possibly understand. The devil wasn't like me, and I needed to remember that. I had to put myself first and rest.

The lower level had undisturbed rooms, with furniture covered in white sheets. In the kitchen, we found a small pack of dried meat. We devoured it quickly. We eagerly licked the salty residue off our fingers.

"Not exactly Gulan food, is it?" I commented with a laugh, and Max shrugged lazily. There were crumbs of meat littered in his wiry beard.

"I've never been to Gula, so I wouldn't know," he said. "What's it like?"

"Um..." If I closed my eyes, I could almost imagine the wild forests of Gula again. The ravenous hunger and decadent food. The struggles of my exacerbated gluttonous desire. I could almost smell the fresh pine forest and taste the candied butterflies. "It was like... Like I'd never eaten food before. Or that I'd never known flavour. They were sweet, tart, earthy... All of it, but so much more than regular food. Almost like you could taste the emotion that went into creating it. It made everything I'd ever eaten before it seem dull."

Max glanced down at the crumpled wrapper. "Wow. This must be pretty disappointing for you."

He sounded dejected, and I didn't understand why. He didn't cook the meal, just scavenged the cupboards for it. "I didn't say this was bad. It's just different," I said. The defensive edge to my voice was all too clear.

He shrugged. It was infuriating. I wanted to confront him, but he left before I could. "You coming, or what?" he called out.

Frustrated, I knocked the wrapper onto the floor and hurried after him. Max ignored me until we reached the top of the stairs, and then he suddenly turned and yawned in my face. "I'm ready for bed."

We stopped at two rooms opposite each other. Max pushed through his door, but I hesitated. I didn't understand how I offended him. Or how to fix it.

He disappeared into the room. A complicated knot twisted in my stomach. But I was too tired to confront him.

"Octavia!" he called urgently. "Come in here! Right now!"

I hurried to his side. "What's wrong?"

Max stood by the bed, horrified. My jaw dropped as I followed his gaze. Three people were already in the bed. Two women with a small child tucked between them. A thick white web covered their bodies. Spun into a spider's trap.

"Are they dead?" I asked. Speaking too loudly felt like it would disturb them. "What if all the other houses are filled with bodies, too?"

"I dunno," Max admitted. "Go check if they're breathing."

"Me?" I spluttered. "You want me to check?"

"Yes, you. You're smaller and faster than me. You can get away if anything attacks us." He pushed me forward. "I'll watch the door."

How helpful.

I had no desire to press my hand to the pulse point of these bodies, searching for the thrumming beat of their hearts. Especially when they were wrapped so tightly in the web.

When I'd gathered the scraps of my courage, I touched it. It was soft and fragile beneath my fingers. I grasped at a fistful and ripped it open. It peeled away from the closest woman's face. Beneath it, her skin greyed. Her thick hair was braided and stuck beneath her shoulder. It was the same soft wheat colour as the little girl pressed against her side. Mother and daughter, I guessed, from the near identical soft bow shapes of their mouths. Their lashes pressed against their cheeks, eyelids shuddering. Watching it left me queasy.

"I think they're sleeping," I said to Max. Their chests rose and fell slowly, with long pauses between breaths. I hoped my quick visual assessment would be enough.

"Check for a pulse, Octavia." Max sounded disturbed. He wasn't watching the door. In fact, his attention hadn't strayed from the bodies. "I don't see them breathing. I think your brain is playing tricks on you. You just want them to be alive."

Cringing, I hesitated to touch their greying flesh. I'd endured worse for less, so I went for it. Her neck was freezing, and my heart sank.

It took a minute to find her pulse. But sure enough, it beat slowly beneath her skin.

Flinching, I wiped my hand against my thigh. "Alive and sleeping," I rasped.

Max pulled me back out of the room. We hurried into the one across the hall. The next room had different people in the bed. Covered in the gossamer web, presumably asleep.

We checked the next room, and the next. Every bedroom was occupied, filled with lifeless, sleeping people.

"We need to get out of here," Max said urgently. He dragged me down the stairs. When he stopped, I crashed against his chest.

I could feel the rapid beat of his heart. "I don't like it here. Something feels wrong."

On our way to the door, a wave of aching fatigue struck me. I felt drained of adrenaline, like my bones turning to sludge. I doubled over, bracing against the heaviness in my limbs.

"Maksymilian," I called. He stopped in the doorway. "We can't go yet. I need some sleep."

He grimaced and scratched his chin. "Not here. I won't sleep with them."

"Where else are we going to do it, Max?" I asked, holding my ground. "I don't like them either, but at least it's warm here."

"We can stay in one of the other houses!" he argued. "Anywhere but here…"

"What if the rest of the houses are the same? Filled with creepy bodies." I asked. Max stared at me. I stayed stubbornly in place, too tired to go back in the snow. I could wait him out.

He tilted his chin, looked up at the roof, and sighed. He strode into the sitting room and swiftly removed the white sheets from the couches.

"Fine, but we're staying down here together," he muttered something beneath his breath that I didn't catch. He pointed a freckled finger at me menacingly. "If any of them so much as move a muscle, we're out of here faster than the devil claims a soul. Agreed?"

I swayed on my feet, completely exhausted, eyes already half closed. "It's a deal."

Max's powerful arms enveloped me and I fell asleep instantly.

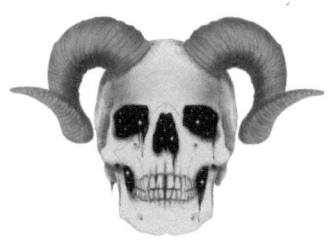

Chapter Fourteen

Birds cried in the distance. They were black-feathered predators with sharp claws, circling in the sky, waiting to pick the meat from my bones. They snatched a fishy reward from the ship's wooden deck and swiftly fled. I waited nervously for one of them to swoop and attack me next.

The world rocked beneath my feet. Shifting with a rhythmic sway that left my legs unsteady and my stomach rolling. I couldn't catch my breath or tamp down on the nausea. When I dragged my tongue across my lips, they were dry, cracking and salty. Standing on a polished wooden ship's bow, I gazed at the endless expanse of glittering sea.

Strangely, I couldn't recall having ever seen the ocean before. The coast was too far and dangerous to visit for a casual look. It had always been nothing more than a whisper in a story, the thing of fables and dreams. The ocean was a luxury for the Lustlanders, not for someone like me.

There was something spectacular about the ocean, though. Now that I could see the vast expanse. So wide and unforgiving, in a constant motion that made it feel alive. Pushing and pulling at the boat, as if it were trying to tip me free. The water drew me in, strange and alluring, as I stood by the railing, listening for the whisper in the waves.

The passage of time felt strange on the ship. The days passed quickly but simultaneously seemed to drag when I had nothing to do. Which was often. The boat had been my home for days, the soothing waves lulling me to sleep. I woke up in a bunk bed in the cabin, confused about how I got there.

I didn't complain, though. Standing with my face tilted to the sun, I wondered if I'd ever felt so at peace. Despite the flurry of activity on board, there was no trial stress here. No angels hunting me down. I wasn't worried about Pride appearing in the corner of my vision, demanding something more of me. He was a constant threat looming over my shoulder. I longed to know if Ira had survived. She was the missing piece for true peace.

Struggling to find my sea legs, I shuffled around busy men who hurried through their daily duties. Max had to be around here somewhere. No doubt he'd be down below, with his sleeves pushed to his elbows and flour dusted on his face. Just like he had been in the rebellion camp. I felt guilty for disrupting Maksymilian Tate's life. Knowing that I'd left Niklaus to go on a journey that almost certainly would end in his death. When it came down to Nik versus the devil, I didn't think the former would win.

A cry pierced across the deck. A man screeched they'd seen a creature off the side of the boat, and I ran for the edge. Gripping the rail, I peered down to see what had captured their attention. Desperate to know what lived below.

There was nothing there, at least nothing that I could see. The ocean was a mix of bright blues and muted greens, glittering back at the sky. I knew there were depths I couldn't see, deep shadows where monsters had to exist. Or it could be the world below, a place free of sin, and filled only with peace. I fantasised about diving into the depths and discovering hidden truths.

Except that was just a dream, and I was only human.

Twisting away from the edge, I turned to look back at the hustle and bustle of the ship. Everyone seemed to have something to do except me — and mostly the men pretended I wasn't around. They muttered under their breath that they didn't enjoy having a woman on board. Whispered predictions I would bring them bad fortune, and I never disagreed. I was no lady luck.

A young boy scrubbed fish guts off the deck nearby. His cheeks puffed with a held breath, and intermittently he turned to the side, retching against the smell. His fingers were pinched and red-raw as he worked the brush back and forth, scrubbing with all his might. His brows furrowed and his lips pouting with sheer concentration, a youthful determination that I wished I could capture.

"Hello," I said. He paused mid-scrub, looking up at me through his sweaty hair. He was squinting as if I were as harsh to look at as the sun. "Can you tell me where we're going?"

The boy sat back, dunking the brush into the water bucket and wiping his hands on his thighs. He huffed a breath to push his hair from his eyes. "You mean you don't know?" he asked, sounding suspicious. "How'd you get on here, anyway? The captain doesn't like women."

"No, I—" I faltered. There were a lot of things I didn't know lately.

Where we were going eluded me. I didn't know how I got on the ship to begin with, or where Max had disappeared to. They felt like inconsequential questions, though, and I barely noticed when the boy didn't answer. The desire to know slipped out of my mind as fast as it had entered it.

The boy bit his lip and peered up at the sky. I craned my neck to follow his gaze towards the shifting grey clouds.

"There's going to be rain tonight," he said. "Big rain. Dangerous."

A moment ago, the sky had been a clear blue. Barely a cloud around and the sun had prickled against my skin, glistening off the water. The day darkened quickly, the sun disappearing, and the men around us began to grumble again about bad luck. "How dangerous?" I asked the boy.

He gave me a nervous look, a small half-smile. "Well, it's bad luck to have a woman on a ship. That's what I've been told. If you're the supersish? Superstish…"

"Superstitious?" I interjected, tilting my head and frowning at him.

The boy flushed a deep shade of red and nodded. He gestured at me as if everything was my fault.

"Oh." I bit down on my lip and looked down at the freshly scrubbed deck. He could be right. "Does that mean…"

When I glanced back at him, the boy had disappeared completely. Him, his bucket and the brush. As if they'd never been there to begin with. I questioned if fresh air was affecting me as I rubbed my eyes.

I stood slowly and pulled my sleeves down to my wrists. The warmth of the sun was well and truly gone. The wind picked up from across the sea, causing the ship's sails to snap and billow.

The ship's rocking motions intensified, reaching a point where I couldn't maintain my balance. Rough, darkened waves lashed against the ship, pulling the vessel this way and that. The tides had turned too quickly. Now I understood why the gnarled old deckhand called the ocean an unforgiving mistress. She was relentless, battering us without remorse.

As I stumbled across the deck, my footing slipped out from beneath me more than once. I landed hard on my knees, pain lancing up my legs. The deck became slicker once the rain fell. It drenched me through, and my teeth chattered, my fingers shaking from the cold. Escaping into the cabins, I started searching for someone, anyone, who could tell me what to do. The ship had been filled with people, but now I couldn't find any of them anywhere. As per usual, I was alone.

"Samael?" I murmured beneath my breath, because if nobody else could direct me, I could always rely on him. The devil remained silent, and my chest twinged with worry that he was angry at me. My pity transformed as quickly as it had arrived, though, and I fisted my hands. Fury rippled through me, along with a pang of betrayal. I wished he would stop leaving me to learn important lessons on my own. I was sick of important life lessons.

"Well, fuck you and the demons you rode in on, Samael."

The ship jerked. The ship rocked so hard to the side that it lifted my entire body into the air. I was suspended for a moment and then crashed into a nearby wall. It knocked the wind out of me. I slid to the floor, wheezing to catch my breath. I felt sharp chest pain and rubbed it to relieve the tightness. Sitting there indefinitely wasn't helping me. Nobody was looking for me or coming to my rescue. I had to get up.

Gritting my teeth and deciding that I had to keep moving, I pushed myself upright. I crawled on the cabin floor, feeling splinters beneath my nails. If the sea was battering the ship this hard, I couldn't be the only one it had tossed around. There had to be others struggling just as hard. Life was unfair, but never exclusively for me.

"Hello? Is anyone there?" I called down the hall. Climbing to my feet, I shoved at the door to one room. The room was empty, with mussed bunks and a pair of boots kicked into the corner, but there was no sign that anyone had been there recently.

It was hard to shake the feeling that there had been others

here before — I could have sworn I hadn't been alone on the ship. But when I found another empty room, and another, it was hard not to doubt myself. Too late, I realised they might be on the deck, trying to control the ship in the storm.

Emboldened by the idea, and despite the shiver of warning that crept down my spine, I fought my way back onto the deck. Bursting out onto the slippery wooden surface. My boots lost their traction, and I landed hard on my arse. Pain shot through my tailbone, and I groaned. The rain poured around me, splattering against my face as I tried to gather my wits.

"Hello!?" I called again. It came out like a plea, a desperate scream, from the very depths of my lungs. "Where is everyone?! You can't have just left me here!"

The storm had worsened. Lightning cracked through the sky, splitting it open with a blinding flash. A moment later, the clouds roared. A rumbling cry of dissent left me trembling. It reminded me of the Angel of Gluttony, and his barbaric, earthly roar for more. The sea was hungry and ready to devour me.

The rain fell so heavily that I could barely see further than the end of my nose. I slipped across the deck, grappling for something to hold on to as another wave crashed into the ship. The waves were growing bigger and angrier, each one slamming against the ship violently. They doused the deck with a wash of cold, salty water.

I shivered, colder than I had been in just the rain.

Suddenly, the ship careened to one side. I snatched at a nearby rope, willing it to hold me as gravity tried to pull me down. It slid beneath my hands, tearing at the skin of my palms. They burned as I fought to keep a hold of it. A scream of pain peeled from my throat, and I squeezed my eyes closed against the relentless rain. Gritting my teeth, I reminded myself that I'd survived worse. That pain was the least of my problems. Especially as the thunder rumbled overhead.

The ship levelled out, and I heaved in a relieved breath. I released my grip on the rope and took deep breaths to calm myself. Venturing onto the deck had been a bad idea. I needed to go back below, barricade myself within and wait out the storm.

The next wave covered me with water and rushed up my nose and down my throat. I choked on it. Coughing, spluttering. My lungs burned and tears prickled in my eyes. When the ship levelled, there was a slimy piece of dark green seaweed caught around my wrist. My hands were bleeding and my lungs ached as I gasped for air.

I curled over and gagged, trying to hack up the water I'd just taken in. Just like I had in the third trial, after I'd dragged myself out of that sin-forsaken river. Pushing my fingers past my tongue to scrape the back of my throat, I forced myself to vomit. Not once, but twice. Spilling salty water from my gut and over the deck. When I finished, my body trembled and ached, but I felt slightly better.

The ship rocked dangerously. It sent me sliding towards the edge.

Scrambling onto my knees, I moved in a panicked frenzy, my discomfort forgotten to save myself. I searched for something to hold onto, to prevent falling into the water during the ship's dangerous tilt.

It was an endless, torturous cycle. The ship rocked as the waves lashed over me. Over and over again. All while I clung to the mast for dear life, praying to the devil that the weather would settle. Wondering if I really had caused this misfortune, if I shouldn't have climbed aboard the ship at all.

With the next wave, something washed up onto the deck. A heavy shape slammed into me. My shoulder twinged as it took the force of the impact. Surprise loosened my death grip on the wooden pole and sent me sliding to the side.

The waves settled slightly, and the rain eased. I retched salt water on all fours. My throat was raw, snot dripped from my nose, and I pushed sopping wet strands of hair from my face. Glancing up, intending to find the mast and tie myself to it, I realised I was no longer alone.

For all my praying to find someone else, I hadn't expected them to rise from the depths of the sea.

The person who had slammed into me remained on deck. Drenched dark hair fell to her shoulders, and even darker eyes pinned me in place. Her soft, full lips were blue from the cold. And her clothes... Those black fighting leathers were all-too-familiar. The sleek, dark uniform of Wrath's army.

It took a moment, a shameful too-long moment, to recognise who I saw, to place her delicate features.

"Ngaire?" I choked on her name, forcing it over my lips. Drowning in unwanted emotions. "Is that you?"

I should have remembered her easily. She was on my list of people who shouldn't have died before me. Of people who had given their lives and pushed me a step closer to winning.

She'd been spat up by the ocean and deposited in front of me, waterlogged and entwined with seaweed.

A woman I'd thought I would never see again. I'd seen her eyes above that mask, daring me to push harder and achieve more, carrying me through most of the trial.

The woman dragged herself to her knees, staying silent as she shivered from the cold. Just like me. Her sodden dark hair pushed across her face.

"What are you doing here?" I whispered, my blood turning cold as a sudden feeling flooded through my body. There was no good reason for this woman to rise from the dead, and even less of a reason for her to visit me.

When Ngaire sat up, my stomach soured with dread. Worsening as I noted the tight, red binding wrapped around her wrists and ankles. My breath caught in my throat, emotional pain lancing through me, as acute as any physical injury. She had not left the Wrathlands and her brutal death behind.

She heaved a breath, gulping down air, before she parted her lips to speak. "Octa—"

A wave slammed into us, cutting off whatever she wanted to say and sending me sliding off balance again. Because I was distracted, I was unprepared and the force of the wave easily knocked me aside, washing me to the edge of the ship. My body hit the railing, and I reached for it, clinging to it for dear life.

When the sea settled again. I coughed and coughed, trying to catch my breath. My muscles strained as I hung from the edge of the ship. Gritting my teeth, I tried to pull myself up. My muscles burned and I wished I was still the same person I had been when I'd left the Wrathlands. Fit and confident in my ability to undertake physical challenges. Weeks of sleeping as I'd healed after the Pride trial had stripped away my muscle, and with it my confidence. Despite the searing pain in my shoulders, I caught the corner of my boot on the deck.

My body squeezed through the taffrail, and I rolled onto the deck. Wheezing as I lay on my back and squinted at the sky. It felt like the salt from the ocean was eroding me from the inside out. The waves had left me waterlogged. My ears were blocked, and my body felt battered.

I refused to stay still and let the ocean consume me, so I crawled across the deck, slipping and sliding. Ngaire lay on her side close to me, her skin pale and body jerking as she vomited up the ocean. She floundered like a caught fish, her bound limbs allowing her no leverage to save herself.

When I reached her, my fingers hooked around the red rope, and I tried not to flinch. It felt exactly as I remembered it. Difficult to manage, the knots bound just as tight. Exactly like the bindings she'd died within. I didn't bother picking at the tight knots, and instead I held tight to her wrists. Clambering to my feet, I tried to drag her back towards the middle of the ship. She was heavier than she looked, all lean muscle and weighed down with water.

Ngaire's gaze burned a hole in the back of my head. Or at least that's how it felt. The back of my neck prickled as she stared right through me. She offered no resistance as I moved her body towards the cabins.

The ship tilted sharply, and the next wave sent me skidding backwards. By some miracle, I kept my feet and my hold on to my friend. Or the ghost of her, whomever it was that has risen from the depths to greet me.

With slow determination, I made it to the mast before losing energy. My arms ached and my head spun. Every time I licked my salty lips, I wished I had fresh water to drink. Suddenly, I was deliriously thirsty.

Wrapping my legs around the mast, hooking them at the ankles, and squeezing the wooden pole tight with my thighs. I let go with my hands and clung to Ngaire as the next wave crashed. The water lifted and pulled her, making it hard for me to hold on.

The dead weight of her body trying to drag us backwards and out towards the sea. I kept hold of her, but only just. My rope-burned, stinging hands seared with pain. It crossed my mind to just let her go. Give her up. But I'd failed Ngaire once before, and I couldn't bring myself to do it again.

A brief reprieve from the waves had me gasping for air. Each cough was thick and wet, as if her lungs held an ocean.

"Devils," I croaked, the words rough and gravelly from my parched throat. I slapped her on the back, trying to help her get the water up. Her breaths were laced with the telltale rattle of death. "Close your mouth when the wave hits."

My hands were useless at untying the knot. My skin had softened and wrinkled from the constant wet, and the rope pinched my fingers. It refused to budge. Just like last time.

Ngaire stared at me through wet strands of her hair, watching on as I failed.

"I can't get it undone," I admitted. My body burned with a flush of shame, my heart pounding rapidly in my chest. I scrabbled at the red rope again, a hiss of frustration rolling from behind my clenched teeth. "I'm sorry Ngaire, I…"

Her cracked, pale lips parted to release a blood-curdling scream.

My ears rang, and my head spun. Her hands released mine as a wave carried her across the deck. Salt water burned my vision as I tried to monitor where she went. I prayed she didn't go over the edge, but simultaneously, deep down, wished that she would. Lady Luck had no interest in me, though, because when the ship balanced again, she was still there.

Still screaming.

I cringed as she inhaled more water, imagining her submerged in the river. Ngaire didn't stop looking at me, her dark eyes piercing through my very soul.

Stupidly letting go of the mast, I crawled along the deck towards her, unsure if I wanted to comfort her or press my hand over her mouth until she couldn't breathe, scream, or live. She had died once, I'd seen it, and she could do so again.

Each movement sapped my energy. I'd been holding on for so long, I didn't think I had the strength to save her again.

"Stop screaming, Ngaire," I said. Soft and soothing, as if she were a child. She didn't obey. She held my eye and shrieked wildly. Instead of grabbing at the red bindings around her wrists and ankles, I reached for her face. Cupping my hands against her cheeks and trying not to flinch at how icy her skin felt. Her lips were still blue, and her eyes lacked the spark of livelihood, clouded with the unseeing fog of death. "Please. Stop. Screaming."

My fingers inched towards her nose and mouth, halfway intent on suffocating her.

She stopped screaming, a sinister smile pulling at her cracked lips. "Die, Octavia," she croaked — a threat, an omen, and a promise.

Her eyes brightened with a knowing look. A wave slammed into my back, pressing our bodies together. With nothing to hold on to, we skidded towards the edge of the ship.

I could barely breathe. I wasn't prepared. Water rushed in my open mouth and through my nose, into my stomach and lungs. Ngaire tangled me up, making it impossible to find my grip and get free. We were entangled in a mess of limbs; she was suddenly everywhere, too close, holding tight to me.

She lifted her hands and looped her arms over my head. The red knot that kept her bound pressed against the back of my neck as a hard lump. It roughly scraped my skin, pulling at strands of my hair, and my entire body prickled with ominous warning.

The ship levelled, but still she clung to me. Her body plastered against my own, and where the mast had anchored me before, Ngaire anchored me now. We were already at the edge of the ship, her body slipping through the rail. The knot around my neck, a red noose, pulled me forward.

Lashing out, I pushed at her body, my nails scratching along her skin as I struggled to get free. Panic settling in my lungs heavier than the water had ever been.

"No!" I cried. "Please. No."

Ngaire slipped off the side of the ship, laughing, and dragged me down, too.

The cold water shocked me as we plunged below. I barely had time to gulp down a breath before we went under. The cold weight of Ngaire's body dragged me down, down, down.

I instinctively started to struggle and kick, but her arms remained looped around my neck. Her bindings kept me secure. I could swim, but not enough to get us both free. I couldn't swim with her weight. History was repeating itself in the worst way.

I kicked out at her, screaming for her to let me go. All that came out were bubbles, a waste of my last breath of precious air. Water rushed down my throat, and my body spasmed.

Grasping her face, I clawed at her, my nails gouging into her skin, but I'd lost my energy. She still held me close. Blood flowed around us. There was nothing in her eyes, as she stared at me beneath the depths of water, dragging me deeper and deeper, her mouth stretched wide into another scream — one that this time I couldn't hear.

She was a harpy of the seas, and she had come to take my life.

My head spun, darkness creeping in at the edges of my vision, and I sagged against her body. My lungs burned, desperate for air, and if could cry beneath the depths of the sea, I would have sobbed. The salt burned my eyes, and I couldn't keep them open long.

Ngaire's blue lips, stretched into a wicked smirk, were the last thing I saw before being swallowed by the dark ocean. She was the mistress of the sea, and she had claimed me.

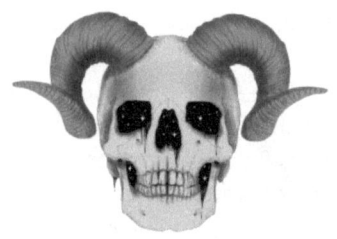

Chapter Fifteen

"Shhh, *shhhh*. Easy now. It's okay."

Soft, crooning reassurances coaxed me to wake, but it was the brush of cold fingertips along the scarred side of my jaw that jolted me from the depths of unconsciousness.

Bolting upright, my stomach churned, bitter as if it were still filled with salt water. Shuddering, I pressed my hand to my mouth. I was going to retch. My entire body jerked as it revolted, trying to force me to expel seawater that would not come up. I moved my palm to my abdomen, letting out a distressed whimper.

A firm hand settled on my back, rubbing in wide, soothing circles. When I tensed, lifting my chin to give him a sharp look, his hand fell away. The angel offered me a crooked grin. The same lopsided smile that I imagined had coaxed the sins to come to this world.

"You're safe now, Little One," he said.

"Samael?" I croaked, and my body finally relaxed. I sat back on my heels. Lifting my chin, I sought him out, sucking in a sharp breath at the sight of his troubled expression.

His nostrils flared, his eyes narrowed, and his full lips pressed into a thin line. The devil was unimpressed.

I refrained from begging him to rub my back some more. I missed the contact now. "Sam! Oh, my devil, I was… I was *drowning*. There was water everywhere. I couldn't breathe. I was dying…"

"I know." He sounded grim. "You weren't dying, though. You need to remember that."

"You know?" I repeated, turning still with shock. My voice rose in pitch. "You knew I was drowning, and you didn't help me?!"

"I couldn't help you," Samael corrected. The panes of his face smoothed with apathy as he controlled his expression. One of his shoulders lifted in a nonchalant shrug, but his jaw still clenched sharply with tension. His stubble had grown, a darker shadow across his chin. "I have no more power in this realm than you do. I am only here because Sloth desires it."

"Why would Sloth want that?" I asked, pressing the heel of my palms to my eyes and rubbing hard. It still felt like tiny grains of salt sat beneath my eyelids. Rough and irritating. "I thought the sins didn't like to share."

More importantly, why would he do what Sloth wanted? I thought the sins obeyed Samael.

I was completely dry, almost like I'd never plunged to the depths of the ocean, but somehow, I still felt gritty, wishing I could brush the residue of my trauma from my skin.

The devil's mouth quirked. Widening into the full, deceptive smile of someone who knew secrets I didn't. Someone who would never share. "Because she believes it's what you want."

"Pfft," I scoffed, glancing away and screwing up my face. "An angel has never cared about what I wanted before."

Unmuted fury flashed across his features, the dark depths of his gaze turning from liquid oil to coals and fire. "I care, Octavia. You have a frustrating tendency to underestimate me."

Biting my lip, I turned away, floundering for the right thing to say. There was no right thing to say to a statement like that. I couldn't call the devil a liar, but I didn't believe the words he said, either. It took a minute to force an apology over my lips, just in case that was what he wanted. "…Yeah. I know. I'm sorry."

"Don't apologise for lashing out after trauma," he snapped. His wings rustled, and Samael stood, towering over me. He offered me his hand, and when I took it, his grip was strong, pulling me easily to my feet, where I swayed on the spot. "Your coping mechanisms are what they are… and apologies won't change them."

He was right, and somehow, I imagined that he often was. But it didn't make me feel any better, either. Despite the devil's reputation, he only guided me towards making good choices and seeing the truth. Yet here I was, snapping at him. Treating him like he was any of the seven sins, determined to ruin me.

The devil dropped his hands to his sides and tilted his head. He assessed me with narrowed eyes, and his dark brows pulled together. I wished I could dive into his head, the same way he so often invaded mine. I wished I knew what he was thinking.

"Come," he said. "Shake it off, Octavia. I don't know how much time we have right now, and I'm hoping for your sake that it's not long. If so, we must make the most of it."

"What do you mean?" I pulled a face at him. I was sick and tired of being the last one to know everything. It hurt to hear him wish our time away, as if I was inconvenient and he didn't want me here. "I don't understand."

"I don't expect you do," he agreed, laughing.

A flush of white, hot fury fused through me. I lashed out, jabbing him in the ribs with my clenched fist. His torso was all lean muscle. Pain laced through my knuckles. I regretted my actions instantly. Especially when he dragged those otherworldly eyes to meet mine. He stared, and colour moved through the depths of his dark irises like an ink spill on stone. Chillingly, I thought I could wither beneath his gaze. A lazy smirk eased my fears.

Samael chuckled, darkly, an all too familiar sound. "Was that supposed to hurt?"

"Did it?" I asked, before I could stop myself.

He flicked his forked tongue at me, a move so unexpected that I flinched. I couldn't tell if it was cheeky or threatening. There was something dangerous glimmering in his eye, but I couldn't put my finger on what exactly bothered me. Samael laughed again. "I'm the devil, Octavia. Your pathetic human attempts at violence won't hurt me."

He was so arrogant.

"They would if I really tried," I told him, raising my chin with faux-confidence.

The devil's lazy smirk widened. He looked strangely delighted that I'd snapped back at him, that I'd challenged him. "That's doubtful, but you get points for spirit, Little One."

Samael pressed his palm against my lower back, and he urged me to turn around. The world shifted and shaped around us as I spun. We suddenly transitioned from a field to a stone bridge. Right at the cusp of a bustling little city.

The quick change stole my breath from my chest. The discomforting knowledge that this couldn't be reality prickled against my skin. I rubbed at my sternum, swallowing roughly as I tried to orientate myself.

"Where are we?" I asked, feeling distinctly dizzy. The world transformed quickly, with the angel by my side as its biggest flaw. I had never met the devil, but now he stood before me. His icy fingers traced a pattern against my shoulder. A cheeky smirk settled on his full lips.

"I've told you before…" Samael urged me forward. "You're dreaming. You can go anywhere you want."

It took a massive effort not to roll my eyes at him. "But where am I dreaming about? I'm sure I've never been here before."

I would have remembered a town like this one. Filled with tall, grand, dark stone houses. Each had stone stairs and wide front windows, offering a glimpse inside. Twisting plants wrapped around the doorways, nearly all of them dried and turned brown.

Narrowing my eyes at him, I realised what had been bothering me. What was different about the devil today? "Where did your horns go?" I asked, folding my arms across my chest. His windswept dark locks looked soft, but his thick, curling horns were nowhere to be seen.

"Not entirely unobservant today, are we?" he laughed, a dimple flashing on his cheek. "I'm not as polymorphic as Lust, but I can hide away a few more of my demonic features. It helps me appear more human."

My head throbbed as I tried to process that information. Trying to work out what polymorphic means, but also completely unwilling to ask and appear stupid in front of him.

"I thought you were only here because Sloth wanted it," I said. "Shouldn't they be the one making you look one way or another? If it's their dream."

Samael looked affronted. His entire face froze in a nasty expression, oil-spill eyes narrowing to slits. The devil's tone sharpened with an edge of reprimand. "I control all forms of myself, Octavia. Regardless of how they came to be. You continue to underestimate my power, and frankly, it's becoming insulting."

This time, I rolled my eyes.

He constantly inferred that he had unlimited power, but apart from the few times that he'd taken over my body, I'd seen no actual evidence of it. I was wondering if most of Samael's power stemmed from the stories woven about him, and the fear they created. If he wasn't powerful, only because of humanity's fear of him.

"Right." I glanced away, jaw set. Picking up my pace so that his hand no longer rested on my back. "And what about my other question?"

Samael's sultry laugh set my teeth on edge. "Are you angry with me, Octavia? Oh, Sloth will love that."

"Do you always have to talk to me like I'm stupid?" I snapped, spinning to face him. I dared lift my chin and meet his eye.

An ugly expression flickered across his face, like he wanted to argue to the contrary. A heartbeat later, Samael's face smoothed into a perfected look of bored nonchalance. His scarred brow rose, and he waited me out.

"I'm not angry. I'm *fine,*" I said through my teeth. "Now answer my question, where in the devils-damned eight lands are we?"

Samael regarded me carefully. He shifted and reached for my hand. I wasn't fast enough to pull out of reach. He captured me quickly. His hands were cold and strong, his fingers twining through mine. With one rough tug, he swiftly anchored me by his side again. His white wings rustled behind us.

"We're not. In the eight lands of Kaida, I mean." I walked through the town with the devil. "We're in the old world. Or an image of it. The world I came from could never truly be recreated solely within the expanse of human imagination."

"…The old world?" I could hear my disbelief ringing in my ears, the scoff in my words. Samael had to be fucking with me. All the stories had started with the same premise, that someone had expelled the devil from a world before our own. That he had existed and ruled a lifetime elsewhere before he'd ruled here. I stared at him, but he didn't relent.

"There were nine realms of the old world. The earlier forms of the sins, back when they were more... Virtuous beings. Before they fell. Plus, two realms of my own. A realm of death and decay, and a realm of... pure possibility."

Samael paused. His thick brows drew together, and my attention caught on the scar that ran through one of them. A desperate urge to ask how he got it bubbled up inside me. Samael spoke before I could act on the impulse. "There's something tempting about infinite possibilities. In your fables, this realm has a name. I think in your old human stories they named it... Purgatory."

He glanced back at me, as if I could confirm, but the word meant nothing. The only stories I'd heard had come from my mother's mouth. Weary tales of caution with a tiny glimmer of hope. Nothing of the realms the devil had ruled before ours. I shrugged. "I've never heard of it."

Samael shook his head. A lock of dark hair fell across his forehead. He sighed, not expecting anything more, but still disappointed in me. It turned my stomach sour, emotion prickling along the bridge of my nose. A threat of tears. I didn't want to disappoint him. I didn't want him to look at me that way.

His forked tongue flickered. "It's a realm where people can become better or worse. They struggle through challenges. Battle grief and experience joy, all that decide how they might reform in the next life."

"You're saying we have more than one life?" I asked, gasping. My scalp prickled uncomfortably. I thought I had only one shot and I messed it up. "A second chance to do better?"

"Not everyone," he corrected. Samael led me down a stone path in the middle of the town. The sun set, dropping on the horizon, and lights flickered to life within the houses.

The devil walked with the confidence of someone who knew

the streets intimately and knew exactly where he wanted to go. He barely paused at corners and intersections, sauntering onwards as if the world would move out of his way.

"In fact, not most people," Samael continued. "Many move straight into the realm of the dead. Not everyone has the gall to try again."

But I wasn't listening. I'd become distracted by a woman. With a heartbroken look, she stood by her window, staring into the house opposite hers. Her face was angular, teeth sharp, ears pointed, and eyes cat-like. She was surely a demon of some sort. A thick, opalescent tear rolled down her cheek.

Turning to follow her gaze, I saw a man in the home across the way. He was holding a small child, their heads tucked together, faces bright with laughter. They had paid no mind to the woman watching them, consumed by their own joy.

"Octavia!" Samael said. "Are you listening to me?"

I startled, glancing at him. He stood ahead of me, his arms folded across his broad chest. I hurried to catch back up to him. Samael barely waited for me to fall into step before he kept moving.

"How long do they stay here before they get their next life?" I asked, unable to keep the bite of curiosity at bay. I was lucky that nosiness wasn't one of the seven deadly sins, or I'd have failed Samael's trials long ago.

"Sometimes forever. Some are too stubborn to admit defeat. They would rather suffer. Even if it meant they could stop living a life of punishment. Others just need a long time to learn their lessons." He paused, letting go of me as he stood on the corner. The houses' lights threw across the cobblestone, casting shadows across his face. Samael tucked his hands into his pockets, taking the time to study me. "It's not all bad here. I assure you there are some causes for joy."

"Like what?" I asked. Challenging him because he'd just said the word punishment, and I couldn't reconcile that with any form of happiness. Surely nobody liked to be punished by the devil. "You let them drink wine and dance in the rain once a year?"

He snorted. "No, but there is the All Souls Carnival."

"The what?" I asked, confused. Like before, I had no clue what he meant. He was speaking in forked tongues.

His face fell, as the impact missed its mark. Then his full lips split into a grin that flashed white teeth wickedly. "That's where I'm taking you, dear Octavia." He coaxed me forward with a crook of his fingers. "Come see for yourself…"

My suspicions arose as Samael walked around the corner, unconcerned if I followed. It was only after two heartbeats of silence, left on my own, that I realised I wanted to follow. I wanted to see what surprises he had in store for me. I'm curious to know what the devil had in mind to make me forget my irritation with him. That I could even forget to be scared.

"Samael!" I called after him. "Wait for me!"

He laughed, a husky and infectious sound, like he knew I would choose him all along. When I rounded the corner, turning into the main square, I faltered. Nothing had readied me for this sight.

The setting sun cast the sky in dusky pinks and soft shades of violet. The sort of colours that Nash Wickham would have adored. At the thought of him, my chest ached. I hoped he was okay, wished that he could see this, too. Giant, colourful balloons bobbed in the sky, drifting lazily through fluffy white clouds.

The square sprawled out in front of me, filled with laughter — the secret pulsing heart of his purgatory. Twinkling, bright lights decorated it, along with an assortment of paper lanterns. Vines that bloomed with tiny white flowers crawled from the surrounding buildings to vibrant, striped tents. Petals drifted to the ground. There were people everywhere. Nobody looked entirely human, but they all looked thrilled to be alive. They thrummed with joy, wonder, excitement, and it was positively contagious. Watching them, I caught myself mesmerised.

Samael led me into the thick of the crowd. He walked leisurely as the people slipped out of his way, giving him space to move. The King of the Damned. They nodded their heads and murmured greetings in languages I couldn't understand. Meanwhile, I fell behind, looking at everything.

The woman showed me small jars of blackness and sparkling objects, claiming they were the night's stars. She said they brought luck, for the price of a secret never shared. My heart thumped in my chest and my mouth dried out. What I wouldn't give for a little extra luck.

A little girl with deep purple skin and aquamarine hair distracted me. Her tiny hand reached into one stall as she pocketed a fist full of sweets. The wrapper of one drifted to the ground, before she popped it in her mouth, and chewed loudly.

Her lips smacked. She tilted her head and blew an enormous bubble. Growing larger, it lifted the girl off the ground as the wind caught it. The child let go with a joyous shriek. I startled as she dropped to the cobblestone street. The impact should have knocked the fun right out of her. She quickly bounced back up and raced into the crowd, giggling.

The temptation to chase after her and discover what moment of joy she would experience next overwhelmed me.

A bark-textured man tugged on my arm as I tried to move forward. He pulled me towards his wagon and placed a crown of wilting flowers on my head.

"There. Baptisia and witch hazel," he said, voice raspy. His serious expression and flickering oak-eyes warned me further. "You'll need a protection crown to be around death."

"I don't have any money," I said.

He waved his long fingers dismissively. "Consider it a gift."

An icy dread twisted in my stomach at the seriousness of the man's expression. At the idea that even these souls thought I needed protection from the devil, and from death. I turned and realised Samael was watching me with barely contained devilish glee. He held a black apple tightly, the same jewelled fruit from the first dream I'd met him in. He lifted it to his full lips. Sharp fangs pierced right through it, the juices dripping down his chin.

I swallowed roughly, catching myself as I stared at his full, glistening lips.

Again, Samael crooked his fingers and beckoned me forward. It was almost like he'd hooked me behind the navel and reeled me in. I couldn't stop myself from moving towards him, even if I wanted it. I felt my pulse flutter as I took another bite, imagining tasting the sweet apple juice on his skin.

By the time I stopped in front of him, I could barely breathe. The desire had wrapped itself so tightly around my chest. Unable to tear my attention from his lips. I rocked on my heels, convincing myself that I could do it. Samael smirked, as if he knew what ran through my mind.

"Enjoying yourself?" he asked.

"Yes," I said, emboldened, but the word half choked. I closed the space between us, so close that I could smell the apple on his breath. It would take nothing to kiss him, to taste him, and find out if those fangs were so sharp beneath my tongue. I swallowed roughly, raising myself to my toes, leaning close, breathing his name, "Samael…"

He cocked his head to one side, and his opalescent eyes narrowed. He pulled the flower crown from my head, stepped back, and tossed the apple onto the street. It rolled into the crowd, instantly forgotten. The crown dangled from one of his long fingertips as Samael stared at it. His upper lip curled, and a deep growl rumbled in his chest. "Who gave this to you?"

The space he put between us was the equivalent of dousing me in water. I gasped and shivered. I struggled to stay composed as the fog lifted from my mind. I'd been so close to kissing him, and now I didn't know if I was angry or disappointed by it.

"What?" I asked, stupidly.

"Who gave this to you?" he repeated.

I twisted, glancing over my shoulder for the man. But he was gone, swallowed by the crowd. "I don't know. Why? What happened?" A hot flush of shame rolled through, burning up my neck and across my cheeks. "Did I do something wrong?"

"Never you mind." Samael dropped the crown, crushing it beneath his shoe. "We're here to enjoy the carnival, but not all of its spoils are meant for you, Octavia." He cleared his throat, reaching for my hand, and tugging me forward. I stumbled, hesitant to get close to him. "You have, hopefully, limited time here. You should enjoy it while you can. It'll be the only way you ever see the glory of the Old World."

There was heaviness in the way he held himself as he pulled me through the crowds. I so badly wanted to ask why he'd been thrown out of this world and sent to Kaida. It was easier than pushing him for an explanation of what had just happened.

I wet my lips, feeling brave enough to question him, but surprising myself with a needier query instead. "Why do you want me to leave? You keep saying that you hope I'm not here long. Don't you want me around, Samael?"

He blinked, colour swirling in his eyes. "Do you not understand why you need to go, yet?"

I frowned at him. Alarm shot through me, and I squeezed his hand tight. So that he couldn't pull away or disappear on me. He stroked his thumb absently over the back of my hand. The movement was so gentle that I shivered, whispering, "No. I don't want to go!"

"You need to go," he said, calm as ever.

I looked around us, at light and the wonder, at the strange contraption behind him, filled with brightly coloured hellhounds that children sat on as they rode in circles. Suddenly the bright wonder had dulled slightly. There was less joy when he was wishing me away. "But I feel safe here… with you."

The music behind him, the chattering of demons, and the shrieks of joy should have drowned out the words, but I knew he heard me. Fire flashed in his eyes. He looked simultaneously pleased and utterly disappointed. I squeezed his hand, reassuring myself that he was here, right in front of me. That I could feel him, and that Samael was more than just a whisper in my ear.

"What should we do first?" I asked, forcing myself to sound happier than I felt.

His forked tongue flicked over his lower lip, and Samael scratched at his chin absently. His expression warring, as if he didn't know what he wanted more. I offered a tentative, encouraging smile. He sighed and with it the tension eased from his shoulders. His ruffled wings pulled tighter against his back.

The devil nodded firmly, and we moved further into the depths of the carnival. Tiny women with iridescent wings fluttered around his head. He swatted at them cruelly, hissing with such sudden malice that they screamed and scattered — a brutal contrast to the softer side he showed me. I tensed, but when he glanced at me, all the anger had faded. His smooth mask of nonchalance set firmly back in place.

"We could visit the hall of demons to see their show. There are many vendors to peruse, or I could take you up in the balloon…" He gestured towards the darkening sky. Huge, brightly coloured balloons bobbed and swayed.

Uncertain and overwhelmed, I let the devil choose. We ate our weight in strange, sweet foods and ended up in what he called a tormented house. As soon as we slipped through the doors, Samael let go of my hand. I lost my anchor, and almost instantly, terror slithered through my veins.

When the door shut behind me, pitch-black darkness

engulfed us. My breath caught in my throat. Now I couldn't see him, either. The seeds of loneliness swelled within me.

"Samael?" I whispered, reaching in the direction he'd been, but my fingers falling only through the air. "Sam. Where'd you go?"

His husky laugh bounced off the walls, and he coaxed me forward with nothing more than his voice. "Come find me, Little One. Catch me if you can..."

Stumbling into the dark, I followed the sound of him. Hunting the whisper of his bemusement the soft hiss of his tongue in the air.

"Where are you?" I called. My voice bounced off the walls, echoing back to me.

"Not that way!" he teased. I spun around, moving in the opposite direction. My heart pounding in my ears. He continued to tease, "Your other left, Octavia."

Lights flashed through the room, briefly illuminating the corridors. A man with a face full of beady black eyes appeared in front of me and snarled. The light reflected off his many irises. Fangs glowed in the dark.

I screamed. My heart rate doubled as I skittered backwards and slammed into a wall. "Stay away from me!" I hissed, reaching for my thigh, and realising I was, once again, missing my blade.

"Hello my pretty..." a voice cackled in my ear, and icy fingers brushed against the back of my neck. I nearly jumped out of my skin. Swinging my fist hard, I caught them, and they let out a soft grunt of pain. I bolted forward, trying to put as much space between us as I could.

"Look out!" someone cried. The next person appeared from nowhere. Formed out of mist in a strobe of light and disappearing again with a soft warning. "You're going the wrong way," they cackled.

Heeding the demon's advice, I took a sharp turn. Throwing

my hands out to brace myself and staggering in the opposite direction. Something cold and wet dripped from overhead, slipping down my back. It pulled a hiss from behind my teeth.

I jolted, there was a touch to my elbow, and I lurched the other way, scrambling until I hit a wall. My body ached. For a moment, everything was blessedly silent, except for the way my pulse raced in my ears. The candied pink mandarins I'd eaten soured in my stomach.

Until a soft breath tickled my cheek. I let out a blood-curdling scream, unaware anyone had been next to me.

"Boo!" Samael whispered when my scream died down. His amusement only frazzled nerves further. Clenching my fists, I lashed, feeling like my heart was climbing up my throat.

His icy fingers wrapped around my wrists, and he crushed me against his chest. He held me tight, waiting out my panic. Despite his close grip, my breathing continued to hitch with every flash of lights.

Samael's fingers pressed against my neck, feeling the flutter of my pulse. "You need to calm down, Little One."

"If only," I wheezed through my panic, "it were that easy."

He picked me up, securing his arm around my waist and beneath my legs. Before I could blink, he'd whisked me out the door and into the cool night air. I gulped it down, my hands trembling, my face buried against his chest.

"Hmm," Samael looked down at me as my panic slowed further but didn't let me go. He didn't set me down. I could still smell the sweetness of the apple juice staining his skin. "Perhaps demon rides aren't made for human hearts to withstand. Do you feel alive yet, Octavia?"

With my eyes squeezed closed, and mortification reddening my cheeks, I tried not to be bitter about my utterly human emotions.

"Honestly," I mumbled against his chest. "Right now, I feel

half dead."

His gentle touch on my scar made me feel cherished.

Opening my eyes, I shifted to look up at him, the last of my distress ebbing away. Samael was looking down at me as if I was the end and the beginning of his world. There was a desperate fire within his gaze.

"You've survived worse," he said. "You're strong."

"I'm tired of being strong," I admitted.

His brows knitted together and his nostrils flared. "I know."

The devil set me down, took me by the hand and led me away from the carnival. The sounds of joy and frivolity faded behind us until we stood on the outskirts looking in. The shadows surrounded us, and suddenly, I felt cold. He pulled me back against his side, looking positively gleeful as I melted against him.

I rested my head on his chest, closing my eyes, but couldn't hear his heartbeat. His chest was as silent as the grave, and it made my heart squeeze tight in response.

"Octavia, do something for me," Samael whispered, his forked tongue brushing my cheek. I looked up at him from beneath my lashes, wondering if there were a few things I wouldn't do for the indulgently sinful smile he gave me.

"What sort of something?" I asked, breathless, and this time not from fear. "I'll do anything."

He held me close. I relaxed and felt immensely grateful to have him here in front of me. It had been so long since someone had hugged me. His fanged teeth nipped at the fleshy part of my ear, causing a sting of pain. I gasped, shocked, and he chuckled darkly.

"I want you to wake up, Octavia."

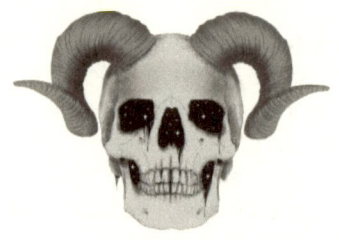

Chapter Sixteen

'*Wake up, Octavia,*' Samael's voice echoed in my ears. I pulled in a deep, gasping breath.

Slowly, I opened my eyes. I felt disoriented and my head spun violently, bile creeping up the back of my throat. Crusty sleep itched in the corner of my eyes, and everything was blurry to begin with. When my vision finally focused, my heart squeezed tight in my chest with fear.

Less than an inch from the end of my nose hovered a person. A small, pale, and unfamiliar face. Her lips tinged blue and puckered with curiosity, while her pale straw-coloured brows were drawn together. It took me a minute to realise the child had her hands planted on my chest. The full weight of her body pressed down against me. Igniting a heavy pain in my sternum. Suddenly, I was suffocating beneath her slight weight, and panic was tightening my airway.

"Get off," I wheezed. Just barely swallowing down a scream

of stress. I wrapped my hands tight around her wrists and shoved her back. "Get off me. Right fucking now."

The girl was quick to scramble backwards. She swept her matted hair from her face and raised her palms placatingly. Giving me the space I desperately desired. I watched her closely as I sat up.

"Okay," she said, her voice hoarse and husky as if she hadn't used it in a long time. "It's okay. I do not mean to scare you. It just looked like you were waking, and I wanted to be sure you were okay."

She sounded strange.

Not in the tone or pitch of her voice, but in the way she put her words together despite the round child-like features she possessed. She spoke the way Prudence Heira always had. In full sentences, with an all too formal and aged inflection. As if she were a wizened old woman instead of a tiny young girl. A shudder rolled through me, the hair on the back of my arms standing on end. She was creepy.

I tried to put more space between us. Shifting back, I gazed around the room to take stock of where I was, inching backwards as I did so. Every slight movement left me battling dizziness and fatigue. My mouth had dried out, and my tongue felt uncomfortable.

When I ran into another body, warm and soft behind me, I flinched. Glancing over my shoulder, I found Max grumbling in his sleep, eyes moving rapidly behind his lids. The bulging, shifting movement made my stomach turn. White webs were weaving around his legs. Just like the people upstairs. The webs were wrapping slowly up his body, weaving a soft cocoon to encase him.

Beneath my outstretched fingers, the strands were as soft as human hair, but I didn't like the look of it and quickly tore it away from his legs. It shredded with ease, disintegrating in my grip. He was now free, yet he barely moved.

223

"He has been asleep too long..." the child's soft voice rang out from behind me, startling me. I'd been so focused on Max that I'd almost forgotten the threat at my back. She sounded serious. "Wake him soon, or else he won't wake at all. Not until the end of the cycle."

Glancing back, I studied her with building suspicion. The tension in my shoulders increased, my muscles aching with pain. I could have sworn there had been nobody else awake in the house when we bunked down for the night. There hadn't even been a whisper of someone else moving around.

"Who are you?" I asked.

"My name is Lorena," she said, her pale features scrunching with soft concern. She waved her hand at Maksymilian, who muttered in his sleep, rolling until he curled up in a ball. "You must wake him up, now."

Some part of me still thought it might be a trap. Some part of me still didn't trust the girl who had appeared out of nowhere. With one hand pressed to Max's arm, I swallowed and tried to figure which was the biggest risk. The girl, or losing Max.

"I..." I faltered for a second. "Why should I do what you say?"

Her lips pursed. Her pale eyes flicked up, annoyed by my question, but her quick response was urgent. "Because if not, he will not wake for a good half a decade, at least. He will be stuck in our cycle. You will not get your friend back. Is that what you want?"

"What's the cycle?" I asked, my heart beginning to pound in my chest. I glanced at Max again. The soft, white webbing had regrown, creeping up his body. Beyond that, there didn't look to be anything wrong with the way he slept. In fact, it was a blessing that he wasn't snoring. Normally, he could make the room shake.

The girl's lips quirked into half a smile, an expression far too old for a child. She raised a single, pale brow and tilted her head at me. "Wake him up and I will tell you."

Huffing at the manipulative statement, I narrowed my eyes at her, before raising a finger to point in her direction. My words, a warning and a threat: "Don't move. Don't you dare come any closer!"

I wasn't certain that she was human, not a lingering spectre of a dream. Or one of Samael's many demons, intent on making my life harder. I wasn't certain I could actually follow through on any threats of hard. Not when my body ached with relentless fatigue.

I hesitated but eventually knelt by Maksymilian's side. The urgency in her voice had spurred me into action. Threading my fingers into his shirt and pressing myself against his chest, I shook him as hard as I could.

"Max?" I called his name. He tucked his chin towards his chest and snuffled, the shift in position causing him to snore. The soft hairs of his coppery beard brushed against his hand, tickling me. But no matter how hard I shook him, he didn't wake up. "Maksymilian?"

When my hand brushed against the hard item in the chest pocket of his shirt, I swallowed roughly. Biting down on my lip. I'd had a lot of stupid ideas in my life, but this one I knew might top them all.

Seeing the girl and Lorena's serious face, I felt a wave of dread. My fingers fisted in his shirt, nails scraping against his skin, but he barely moved. His chest rose and fell so slowly, his breathing paced.

"Maksymilian! Wake up!" I tried one last time.

When he didn't respond, I plucked the lighter from his pocket and weighed it in my hand. My teeth pinched my lip again, indecision causing hesitation. I reached for his wrist, holding it tight as I lifted his arm and cradled it in my lap. He really was dead weight when he was sleeping. The man snored gently as I sucked in a deep breath and rolled my thumb against the lighter. It lit up. Holding my breath, I held the single dancing flame to the

225

tender skin of his wrist.

Fire was a pain I knew intimately. After my ordeal at Pride Palace, I knew he couldn't sleep through the sizzling of his flesh. I could only hope that Maksymilian would forgive me.

He woke with a yelp of pain. "Fuck!"

Max bolted upright, completely dislodging me and shoving me from the couch to the floor. My tail bone smarted from the impact and unwanted tears brimmed in my eyes. Max's attention settled on me, his gaze still bright with pain as he gripped his wrist. His eyes narrowed to slits when he noticed the cylinder clutched in my palm.

When he spoke, it was through gritted teeth, his voice still husky with the remnants of sleep. "What are you doing, Octavia?!"

Guilt flooded through me, and I realised that stupid, impulsive thoughts shouldn't always be acted on — even if they worked. I blushed. Swallowing roughly, I floundered for the right explanation. "I couldn't… I couldn't get you to wake. And she said you needed to right now, or you wouldn't wake up again. I thought you'd rather…"

He glanced at the blonde girl. There was a pregnant pause as he looked between us, his lips flattening into an unimpressed line. "A child said to wake me, so you burned me?! Give that back to me!" Max snatched the lighter out of my grip. I didn't fight him on it. His grip white-knuckled around it as he inspected the angry red mark on his skin.

"I'm sorry," I whispered.

Max's attention snapped back to me. "If you were sorry, you wouldn't have done it."

I couldn't argue with that.

He scrubbed his hand across his face before fisting his free hand into the long locks of his hair, holding it by the scalp and tugging gently. "Devils, my head is killing me. And my arm. Jeez, Octavia." The dark look he offered me assured me he thought it was all my fault.

"That would be the sleep hangover," Lorena said from behind me. "It is from waking up too early in the cycle. It feels rather like someone split your skull open with an axe, doesn't it? Sloth nearly had you, it seems."

"What do you mean too early?!" I gasped. Betrayal surged through me, even though I'd been worried about trusting her. This girl didn't seem like the adversaries I'd faced in other challenges, but she still made the hair on the back of my neck stand on end. "You told me he had to be woken! I knew I shouldn't have listened."

She laughed, a soft, childish sound that made me shudder. Her blue eyes brightened with a strange delight. Maybe she was just a demon in disguise, here to steal away a little piece of our souls.

"Who are you, again?" I asked, trying to ignore the fact that Max was still glaring a hole through the side of my head.

"I told you." She sounded exasperated now. She rolled her eyes towards the ceiling and her thin arms folded over her chest. The disgruntled look softened by her childish features. Her nightgown swished as she padded closer to me. "I am Lorena."

"Okay. What's the cycle, Lorena?" I pushed, pressing my lips together and hoping that I looked stern enough to demand an answer. The chancellor in Suain had mentioned the cycle more than once and never gave us any good information. We'd left the town just as uninformed as when we'd arrived. Now that multiple villages mentioned it, it struck me as more important. As something I really should know and understand.

Her head tilted, the matted braid of honey hair falling over her shoulder. She toyed with the ends of it, tugging at individual strands. Finally, she relented. "It is the period in which Lady Sloth keeps us asleep. The villages, and even the city, run through a cycle. We sleep for nine years at a time, never aging, rarely waking. Then, for one year, we may wake up. We live, and at the

227

end of that year, on the night of no moon, Sloth draws us back to quiet slumber. Back to the peace of her dreamscape."

She may as well have struck me, for how dumbfounded I felt. Silence stretched between us as I tried to process what she was saying. I spluttered, "What?"

"Which part of it confuses you?" Lorena asked, flashing that sweet but obviously fake smile once again. The question felt condescending. I had to bite down on my irritation as she continued, "I will try my best to clarify. I am sorry if it's not making sense. I am very sleepy still."

Twisting the sleeve of my shirt, I glanced over at Max, but he looked just as bewildered as I felt. He had his head cradled in his palms, eyes half closed. Turning back to Lorena, I cleared my throat. "You only get to be awake for one year in every ten?"

"That is right," she said, swaying on the spot.

Something didn't seem right. Lorena looked to be younger than ten years old. How could she sleep for that long and then look so young? I didn't understand. "And you don't age while you sleep?"

Her soft smile widened, and she nodded. "That is also true, yes."

Max leaned forward, his fiery locks of hair brushing my shoulder and tickling my neck as he shifted. He moved closer, his body heat radiating behind me. "How do you not die? If you're sleeping for nine years without food or water?" he asked. "It doesn't make a lick of sense. You'd starve. Your body should age, and wither, and *die*."

Lorena merely blinked, another bright giggle escaping from her thin chest. "It is the magic of sin. What else? Haven't you ever heard of the angels managing the impossible? If Sloth can control your dreams, why can't she sustain your life too?"

Max looked like he'd bitten on something sour. His entire face scrunched up. "But…"

"Do you not believe in magic?" Lorena cut across him. She

glanced down at me, more specifically at the cuff around my wrist. "Strange, as you are in The Devil's Trials. There's a lot of magic surrounding those events. Everyone knows it."

"It's not that." Max huffed. One of his hands landed on my shoulder, a heavy but reassuring weight. He gave it a soft squeeze, as if to silently tell me he was on my side. "I just don't understand why you wouldn't leave when you wake up. Why go back to sleep when you could leave and stay awake and live your life?"

"Well…" Lorena took a moment to think about it, smoothing her small hands down the front of her nightdress. "Sloth gifts us with both dreams and nightmares. They say that the emotions of a nightmare fulfil her, and the paralysing fear within them is satisfying. But dreams… Dreams mean we can be anything we want, despite our normal limitations. Dreams give us what we want when we want it. They are what tempts us to stay with her. You see it as being stuck in a slow cycle of never really living, we see it as living our best lives."

Max didn't let it go. "But don't you want to live your actual life?"

"Why would I want to live here? It is bitter in Kyama. The realms of the other sins aren't much better, from what I've heard. No matter where we live, we would be oppressed. But I've lived full and fantastic lives in my dreams. I've grown into an adult and had children. Lived out many of my desires. I've been happy, I've been sad. I've experienced almost everything I could ever dream of," she spoke in a rush, her chin lifted with defiance. "Why should I want to come back into this child's body and struggle in this world?"

Max and I exchanged a look. His thick auburn brows knitted together, his nose scrunched up.

"…Oh," I whispered, filling the silence with a single word, because I didn't know how to respond. I'd wanted to stay in my dreams before, when the world had been easy or happy, or just plain intriguing. I wished I could return to that dream after waking up. But I'd never wanted it so much that I'd give up years of my existence to stay.

"A stasis is a small price to pay for true happiness, don't you think?" she asked. Neither of us had an answer. I had no idea what a stasis was, and Max looked downright pained.

Caught up by my curiosity, I reached towards the girl. Only to think better of it and hesitate, drawing my hand away. "How old are you, Lorena?" I asked.

"Hmm." She tapped one finger against her chin while she considered it. "This body must be all of ten years old now, so I suppose I have been through ten cycles. If I had not dreamed with Sloth, this would be the hundredth year since my birth."

"You're one hundred years old?!" I gasped. "That can't be right."

"Do not look so shocked. My mother is much older than I," Lorena said. She yawned so widely that I could see the back of her throat. Her fisted palms rubbed against her eyes. "I think I must be going back to bed soon."

"How did you wake up?" I asked Lorena. I couldn't stop the questions now, wanting as much information as I could get from this girl. Demon, spectre or even a dream of my own; she was telling me more than anyone else. The first to freely answer my questions since the trial had begun.

"I had a nightmare where I went through the mirror, of course. If it is violent, sometimes it can pull us from even the deepest of sleep." She yawned, offering a flash of pink tonsils, quickly obscured by her palm. "I am going to go back to bed, but... You should leave. Kyama is only mid-cycle, and if you stay too long, you will find yourself a part of it."

Without saying goodbye, Lorena abruptly left the room, her steps echoing down the hall. I blinked after her, unsure of how to take that ominous final warning.

Max rubbed his eyes. "...I'm pretty sure that was a dream. I'm still asleep and dreaming of the pale-faced people sleeping upstairs."

Craning my neck to get a good look at him, I scoffed. "You think you slept through that burn on your arm?"

"Good point, well made." He grumbled, glaring down at the small wound as if it were the worst injury, he'd ever received. My guilt had ebbed away. He had no room to complain when he could have been asleep for a decade. "You could have woken me gently."

"You say that like I didn't try. Burning you wasn't my first thought."

"It's going to scar," he said.

My throat tightened, voice thickening, and I stared down at my hands. A flush of heat creeped up my neck. "I said I was sorry. You know I wouldn't want you to have scars."

Max said nothing at first. I could feel his attention, and the way he studied the scarred side of my body. The ripples that the flames had left on me. When he finally answered, it was to change the subject. "Do you think she's right and we should get out of here?"

"I don't know," I admitted, pinching my lip between my teeth. "But I think there's something creepy about this place. Maybe it wouldn't hurt to leave. I'm still so tired, though."

There was a big part of me that wanted to stay in the warmth of this room. Even with the strange inhabitants of the house asleep above us. I wanted to close my eyes again and delve back into the dreams of Samael. To sleep until I finally woke up rested, although that seemed less and less possible each day.

"I wonder how long we were asleep." Standing up, Max stretched his arms with a soft groan. I blinked, captivated by his exposed skin and toned muscle. I shivered gently as heat fused through the rest of my body. Quickly, I looked away. "I'm still completely beat."

'One week,' Samael answered, growling softly in my ear. It startled me. I'd wondered why he hadn't spoken sooner. *'You're*

running out of time, Octavia. Do as the child said and leave the village.'

Inhaling a sharp breath, I rubbed my eyes and tried to work out if a week could have really passed us by while we slept. It felt like it had been all of an hour. No matter what Samael said, it hadn't been long enough to fuse my body with energy. I was sure I would never feel rested again.

"Maybe we can chance a quick nap?" he asked. Max glanced over his shoulder, not at me, but to eye the pillow longingly. "Just a short one. For some extra energy."

'No!' Samael all but roared in my head. *'Do not go to sleep, Octavia.'*

I felt a sharp spike of pain behind my eye. I groaned softly, dropping my head to my hands. My entire body was heavy, but the devil continued his litany of unhappy grumbles. His voice preventing me from succumbing to the desire to sleep. Eventually, I sighed, forcing myself to move.

"She's right," I said, finally, but mostly just to get the devil to shut up. He huffed and I realised he knew it was the only reason I agreed with him. "We should leave."

Max looked devastatingly disappointed. He heaved a sigh, and it almost sounded like I'd broken his heart.

"Alright," He agreed. He fished a rumpled piece of paper out of the depths of his pockets and smoothed it out. He squinted at it, meandering towards the door. "Let's keep on at it, then. We're going to Cottle Creek next."

Despite feeling like my limbs were filled with sludge, I managed to get myself upright. Following him to where he stood. He stood bracketed in the front doorway, with a straight spine and tense shoulders, muttering angrily beneath his breath. Something had fully woken Max up.

"What's wrong?" I asked warily.

When he didn't respond, still cursing under his breath, I reached out to tug at a lock of his hair. He twisted, glaring over his shoulder at me, but I held my ground, repeating, "What's wrong?"

He turned to face me, his jaw tense and gaze wild. "The horse is gone."

"What?" I pushed him to the side, peering around him. "Where'd it go?"

"How should I know?" he scoffed. "Do I look like a two-bit side of the road psychic?"

"Sure, you do." Turning, I squinted at him, cocking my head to one side. I pressed my fingers to my temples and closed my eyes. "Go on. Tell me what I'm thinking, Max."

"Octavia," he warned, his expression flattening. "You're not funny."

I couldn't help my smile. I winked at him as I pushed past and sauntered out into the snow. "It's all in the eyes. You've got that charlatan gaze, Maksymilian."

His scoff of disbelief followed me all the way to the road. For the next two hours, every time Max spoke, I gasped with exaggerated surprise. I stared at him wide-eyed. Pretending that I'd been thinking that same thing. Every time. It was amusing, or so I thought, until he pushed me into a tide of waist deep snow.

Max needed a better sense of humour.

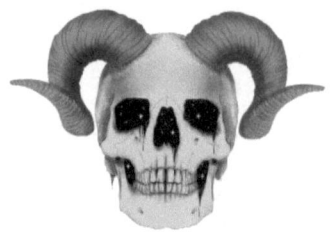

Chapter Seventeen

Cruel beasts of the night came out to play. I heard them while lying on my back, staring at the sky during our travel break. The shrieking sound may as well have turned my bones to liquid for fear, my comfort evaporating. My heart sunk from my chest and now beat in my boots.

Rolling onto my front, I scrambled up onto my hands and knees, craning my neck to catch sight of them. High above me, half-camouflaged by the grey clouds and ever-present misting rain, I could just make them out. Creatures with the bodies reminiscent of the human women they had once been. Their skin was grey and gaunt, their sharp wings black and leathery. Once women, they were now weapons, sharp and powerful and looking to feast on us.

They circled above. Looking to pick the meat from our bones. Fear overwhelmed me as I anticipated their attack. My memory of Monika's entrails after their claws had shredded through her was as clear as day. It was a sight I'd never forget. Moving as slowly and quietly as I could, I crawled across the grass to Maksymilian. I could have sworn he'd been right beside me a minute ago. In fact, I was sure of it, but now he felt a world away.

"Max," I whispered, dreading the risk of catching their attention., but I needed to find him. "Where are you?"

"What's happening, Octavia?" he asked, slowly sitting up on my left. I jerked away from him in surprise, acutely feeling the weight of his attention. Uncomfortable with the worry that caused the muscles in his brow to tense. He looked me over, as if quietly assessing that I was okay, which caused a lump to grow in my throat. I didn't dare actually ask if he cared. Or why.

"We need to get moving," I told him, softly. I tilted my chin, indicating the sky. "There are harpies here. I don't know about you, but I don't want them to eat me."

"Harpies?!" Max yelped, his head jerking as he stared up into the clouds. The wind picked up, blowing strands of hair across his face. A crack of lightning flashed through the sky, a jagged strobe that lit up the deadly creatures. Max paled, his face pinching. For a flickering second, I saw genuine fear in his eyes before he exhaled heavily. "Fuck. I've never seen one before. I thought... I thought they were stories."

"Shh!" I reached for him, cupping my hand over his mouth to cut off anything else he had to say. He spoke too loudly, and I was terrified of anything that might draw their attention. Max's eyes widened, and his throat bobbed as he swallowed. I tried to ignore the way his gaze darkened, the entirety of his attention focused on me. Instead, I breathed, "You need to be as quiet as you can. They're blind, they're hunting us by listening for us."

It still haunted me, the memory of their milky white gazes as they'd hunted Monika and me through the rain. There were moments in my life that I would never forget, etched into my very soul. Sitting by her side so that she didn't die alone was one of them.

Mostly, I was determined to remember it as one of the few good things I'd ever done. A moment of selflessness. More of a kindness than killing the girl in Envy's basement. Some bitter part of my soul recognised that I would most likely die alone. With nobody to sit by my side and hold my hand, nobody left to care that I was gone. I'd wanted, briefly, to save her from that same fate.

"Where should we go?" Max whispered. He took my hand and held tight, our fingers lacing together.

The feeling of his warm palm anchored me, settling some of the ever-whirling thoughts in my mind. I looked up at the circling beasts, sure that if they dove on us, we wouldn't survive it. The only way I'd lived through it before was through sheer, stupid luck.

"I don't know," I whispered back, biting down on my lip. "We need to find somewhere to hide."

When I looked around, though, we were stuck in an awful span of open space. Long, overgrown grass all around us and little else. I felt like I could see halfway across the world. There was nothing ahead of us. Nothing but barren lands and immediate danger. We were completely vulnerable, and now I couldn't remember why we'd chosen to stop here.

Max's thumb stroked along the back of my hand in small, comforting movements. He rose into a crouch, squeezed my hand, and pulled me to one side. "This way…"

It was easy to let him take the lead. I watched the circling creatures, prepared to run if necessary. Especially when the way we moved now, taking cautious and quiet steps, felt slow and dangerous in its own right. Max led me deeper into the thick grass, the dried stems catching on my arms and hair, creating barriers that seemed to hold me back. It made my skin itch until I wanted to crawl right out of it.

A harpy screeched loudly. My pulse bounded, deafening as it echoed in my ears. When the beast dove for the earth, it was far enough away from us that I could relax. Just incrementally. Max's grip on my hand tightened and he pulled me forward faster now. Too fast. The toe of my boot caught on a stick and I staggered, slamming into his back to catch myself.

Max was too slow to mute his reaction, though, a loud yelp of surprise spilling from his lips. It echoed in the air, followed by a single second of stunned silence. My heart sank as Max and I exchanged a nervous glance.

The beasts shrieked in response. Answering his call, and swooping on the earth with their claws outstretched, again. This time, they were on the mark. Headed straight for us. We crashed into the ground, grass cutting my face, sticks and stones biting my palms.

Black talons just barely grazed the back of my jacket, and the sheer power of their wings whipped my hair around my face. In my peripheral vision, I could see the dark stain of the harpy's lips, and the glint of their fangs. Ready to feast.

"Run!" Max cried.

Pure panic choked out any response, but I agreed, scrambling to my feet. I was unashamedly aware that I only needed to stay one step ahead of Max to save my life. The harpies would take whomever they caught onto first. If they took Max, I'd be safe. I felt guilty but tried to reassure myself that he would do the same. Max was a member of the Wastelands Rebellion. He couldn't really be trusted.

We fled. Struggling to run through the thick foliage, the beasts screamed and swooped behind us. They very narrowly missed once more, and I just knew our luck couldn't hold out a third time.

If they struck again, one of us would die.

A soft, white fog rolled around our feet. Max cried my name, a loud plea. He turned unexpectedly, his warm, hard chest slamming into my body and sending me off kilter. His face was a picture of distress, his expression twisted as if I'd harmed him. He lunged for me and missed.

I plummeted to the ground and the miasma swallowed me whole.

Pain lanced up my spine as I landed hard against a cold and unforgiving surface. The impact must have addled me, though, because when I looked up, I was seeing triple. I rubbed my eyes twice, but they didn't go away.

Three, slender men with pale skin and dark hair that flopped across their foreheads smiled at me in unison. Flashing too-perfect sets of white teeth. One of them loped towards me. He was surprisingly graceful in his movements, for someone with such long limbs. The other two stayed back, leaning against either side of the door frame with their arms folded across their chests.

The daring one, the one who approached, dropped to rest one knee in front of me. His eyes were milky, sightless, and they sparked a memory within me. Three cursed men, captured as part of a glittering collection of humans. Identical triplets. His name, however, stayed just out of reach in my memory. I knew I knew it, only I couldn't call it forwards.

"You're back!" The man cried. It sounded like they'd been waiting for me, although I couldn't remember ever promising to come back. The cheer in his voice ignited a strange uncertainty that bubbled in my gut. Glancing over his shoulder at the other two, unmoving — but still smiling — I bit down on my lip.

The realisation that I was back in Envy's castle came too late and hit me hard. My entire body tensed as I closed my eyes and counted softly to three. Willing the cursed triplets to disappear. Invidia was one of the last places I ever wanted to be stuck again. Too much had happened here. Lady Luck didn't favour me, however, because all three were still there when I opened my eyes.

"Um," I muttered, leaning back from him slightly. "Yeah. I guess I am."

He laughed. The sound of it grated against my nerves, and I glared at him, fisting my hands by my sides. He glanced over his shoulder at his silent clones. "I don't think she remembers us, boys."

I scoffed. "I remember you. The cursed triplets."

Surprise lit across his features, and the man stood. He took my hand and hoisted me to my feet in one smooth move. Tall and scrawny, he didn't look like he should have had enough muscle to help me. I'd underestimated him. He folded his arms across his chest. Blowing a lock of hair from his face, he demanded, "Who are we, then?"

Trying desperately to relax, despite the tension building across my shoulders, I lifted my chin. Faking confidence that I didn't feel. Something about his expression felt like a trap. "You're Envy's cursed triplets."

He snorted, looking amused. "You don't remember our names, huh?"

Grimacing, I shrugged. As if it didn't matter and their names weren't important. "Not really."

I wouldn't apologise for it. I'd met so many people in the trials and lost a majority of them. I remembered the men who protected me from the angel, but the small details had faded away. Details like their names.

"I'm Zeres." He stabbed his thumb at his own chest, and then tilted his head back slightly to gesture at his brothers, offering me a crooked grin. "Ciris and Eros are back there. You'll work out which is which, eventually."

Both of them stared at me silently, and for long enough that I looked away.

"Where's Max?" I asked. He'd been with me a moment ago. I desperately needed his quiet reassurance that things were going to work out. He'd never doubted the path we were taking.

Zeres's face smoothed out as he gave me a blank look. "That's the wrong question to ask, really."

"Max," I repeated. "He was right with me. We're..."

"You're what?" he asked, tucking his hands in his pockets and tilting his head. He pushed himself onto the balls of his feet and bounced as he waited for my answer.

"I can't remember what I was doing," I admitted, scrubbing my hands across my face. The skin of my jaw was puckered and strange beneath my fingertips. It reminds me to let my dark hair swing forward and shield my face. I tried a different question. "How did I get here?"

Zeres blinked, shrugged and glanced over his shoulder at the other two. "That's still not the right question."

"Don't know," one of them added.

Recognition felt like a sharp slap to the face. I narrowed my eyes at him. "You're Eros. The two word man. Good to see you haven't changed."

It was his turn to flash that crooked smile, nodding. The look he shot his brothers was supremely smug. "Remembers me."

The blind man looked put out, his nose scrunching, lower lip dropping. "It doesn't matter who you remember or not, anyway. You need to go, Octavia." He waved his hands at me, as if he could shoo me away and I'd disappear.

Stepping out of the way of his waving hands, I blinked at him. "Go where?"

"Down the hall," He gestured flippantly behind me. "Go. Run and hide. It's all part of the game."

My entire body became tense, every hair standing on end, putting me on high alert. Nothing good could come of Envy and a game. I quietly asked. "What sort of game?"

"Ah!" Zeres smiled widely. He leaning in close enough that I could smell the hint of an orange boiled sweet on his breath. "Now that's the right question, Octavia. We're playing hide and seek. Envy's on the hunt to catch one of his treasures. You've got two minutes. Find somewhere to hide."

"But I'm not one of his treasures!" I protested.

My blood had turned cold. When I glanced over his shoulder, both of his brothers had disappeared. Zeres put his hands on my shoulder and pushed me lightly. Encouraging me to move. "Doesn't matter. You're here, so you have to play. Tick-tock, tick-tock. Time's running out."

I turned and bolted up the stairs to my left. Somewhere along the way I'd lost my shoes. The soft carpet runners kept my feet from freezing. Some halls in the castle were familiar, but mostly, I had no idea where I was going. Or where I'd come from. I stumbled into an unfamiliar library.

The carpet beneath my feet was thicker and plusher. I wriggled my toes, luxuriating in the soft feeling of it. Towering bookshelves lined the walls, each one crammed full of thick tomes that I couldn't read.

Quickly, I scanned the room for any sort of hiding spot. Momentarily, I hoped the heavy curtains could hide me, but the open window left the thick, green drapes billowing. It would give me away in a second. I debated climbing the shelves to check for space above. It would take too long, I decided. My two minutes had to be up. I needed to find something quickly. I spied a space between two of the shelves and decided I'd force my body between them. No matter what it took.

A man peered back at me through the gap when I came close. He had already wedged his thin frame into the tight hiding space. His crooked grin was haunting. "My spot," Eros said, in his blunt tone of voice. He reached out, shoving my shoulder until I stepped back. Obviously, he wasn't willing to share. "Go away!"

"Shit," I swore.

Turning on my heel, I fled for the hall again. It felt like my time had well and truly expired. I could imagine that Envy was already sauntering down the halls of his castle. His crown sitting crooked on his head as he hunted us down. Last time I'd been

STEPHANIE GLUCK

within these walls, I'd learned a lot about what Envy did to those he favoured. I knew the way he pleasured and broke them simultaneously. Treating his people like toys, he could pull apart and put back together again. He didn't care if they were missing pieces when he finished with them. There was no way I could lose this game and subject myself to that.

His shadow flashed on the wall ahead of me. A flicker of his dark wings. I tried to move faster, running down a hallway that never ended, my feet slipping on the carpet. I threw myself into the next available room, dropping to my knees and wriggling beneath the bed. Another of the triplets was there with me, his long body taking up most of the space.

Ciris, I realised, when he didn't speak but shook his head at me, eyes wide and panicked. He waved urgently for me to go, so I had to quickly backtrack to avoid getting hit.

It appeared nobody was saving anyone else tonight. It was every person for themselves. Dread was pooling in my veins. My mouth dried out as a noise echoed down the hall. What would happen if Envy caught me and recognised me as a person who had helped Margot escape? Would he torture me within an inch of my life? Would he draw it out, so that I spent a thousand days and nights wishing I were dead?

Worse still, he might make me replace her in his locked chest of treasures.

I realised I was frozen, vulnerable by the bed. Scrambling for the door, I threw it open to find a sharp turn and another set of stairs. I staggered down them as if my life depended on it — and maybe it did.

"Where are you?" Envy called out, his voice bouncing off the walls. His laugh was petulant and cruel. A shiver ran through me at the sound of it. "Come out, come out wherever you are…"

Careening into the next room, I closed the door behind me, and stood with my back to the wooden surface. I willed my heart to beat quieter, afraid of the angel hearing it.

Bundles of drying plants filled the room I had entered, along with an old chair placed to one side and a small table with a chipped teacup abandoned on top of it. Most of the liquid had drained dry in the cup, and the leaves inside formed a pattern that vaguely resembled a hellhound. It looked familiar.

I'd been here before.

"Eadlin?" I whispered her name. Almost certain that I was back inside her office, even if it looked a little different to how I remembered. Knowing her temperament, and the fact she believed I'd won the envy trial through nothing more than her own good graces, I wasn't certain she wouldn't kick me right back into the hall. "Are you there?"

Nobody replied. Not the crone. Not Envy. Not Samael. I was alone.

Tentatively, I shuffled further into the room. There were books splayed open, bundles of dried leaves set within the pages. A large stone bowl sat on a workbench. Edging closer, I peered inside. The contents within were blood-red and mashed beyond recognition; a jar of dead scorpions was beside it, the lid missing. Crouching, I looked beneath the bench, but somehow the space looked too impossibly small for me to fit. There wasn't anywhere good to hide.

The sound of footsteps in the distance left me nauseous, my stomach roiling with nerves. On the far side of the room, beneath the window, a large cast-iron pot bubbled. A sweet scent filled the air and mist spilled over the edges onto the floor. More books, a large, ornate mirror, several flickering black candles surrounded it, dripping with wax, and a plant that grew round little purple berries.

I hesitated, considering risking Eadlin's concoction to escape Envy. There was no knowing what it would do — but was it worth the risk? Even if it was harmless, I could end up cooked within it. I looked back and quickened my pace upon hearing Envy's wings.

Trying to swallow over the lump in my throat, I moved closer and closer to the cauldron. Certain that if it was a bad idea, Samael would persuade me otherwise. Trusting that he would gently turn me to the right path. Another step forward, but he said nothing. I closed my eyes, trying to ignore the panicked cry from my instincts that told me to just hide — to try to escape the oncoming threat if it was the last thing I did — and searched for any sign of the devil. Any brush of his presence, or discomforting twist of his magic against my mind, body, or soul.

But I was, in fact, truly and utterly alone.

The realisation was startling, so uncomfortable, that my breath caught in my throat. Samael had only ever left me alone when I was dreaming. Even then, sometimes, he was present there too. But his growling voice, impatient instructions, and smart remarks hadn't faltered since the day he'd started speaking to me.

Which meant... "I'm dreaming," I whispered.

Acknowledging the truth shattered the tension but increased the commotion in the hall. Someone screamed shrilly, and I heard Envy's cruel laugh of delight.

The door flew open behind me, slamming into the wall hard enough that it made me jump. Spinning, I turned to face the source of my terror.

Lord Envy looked exactly as I remembered him. Impossibly young to be an angel of sin, but still brimming with power. Desiring everything that others possessed, everything unique. He pushed up his sleeves to his elbows, showing off his muscled forearms. A live, thin black snake curled around his wrist like a decoration. Atop his head, he wore his diadem of silver snakes that kissed in the middle of his temple. His most terrifying feature was the victorious smirk that stretched wide across his mouth and set his green gaze blazing.

"Ha! I found you!" His dark wings rustled as he sauntered closer. "I win, little human."

"But... I'm dreaming," I whispered to myself more than him, clutching to that lifeline. Samael had been telling me all along that

I was dreaming. That I just needed to wake up. "I'm dreaming. This isn't real."

When Envy stepped further into the room, it didn't feel like a dream. It felt real enough that I stepped back, desperately trying to preserve the space between us. My body reacted as if he were a real threat, even if he was just a figment of my imagination.

The angel's dark smile turned malicious, and he advanced again. I stumbled backwards, my thighs hitting the cauldron. The heavy white mist swirled around my ankles.

"Come on. Wake up, Octavia. Wake up." I pinched at my skin, hoping the sharp flare of pain would help me wake. Instead, it only left an irritated welt behind. My nails bit into my skin, but it didn't help.

Envy sauntered closer, his hand outstretched, reaching for my throat. A memory of Pride holding me in the air by my wind pipe caused a sweat to break out on the back of my neck. It felt like I might spit up my heart. I was sure it was lodged that high in my throat.

My pleas became desperate. "Wake up. Wake up. Wake up."

Dimly, I remembered a small girl, with straw coloured hair in a matted plait. I'd asked her how she'd woken from her own nightmares. I'd not understood her response. She said she'd gone through the mirror. An impossible answer.

My entire body flushed hot, then turned cold. Desperate to get away from Envy, I staggered to one side. His fingertips grazed the column of my throat, and I knew — just instinctively — that he'd let me slide past him. That he was toying with me already, making this into an even bigger game.

Envy's wings shot out, closing me in so I couldn't get around him. It didn't matter. I didn't need to get past him because I wasn't heading for the door. I remembered the large round mirror and the black wax candles.

"Through the mirror," I said out loud to myself, not the angel. Mostly so that I could mentally prepare myself for what I was about to do. I twisted before Envy could reach for me again and launched myself towards the mirror. It didn't show my reflection, just a scene of the Slothland woods, and softly falling snow.

The fog grew thicker around us, curling around my legs. Envy growled with displeasure. Fragments of the mirror shattered everywhere.

Everything disappeared.

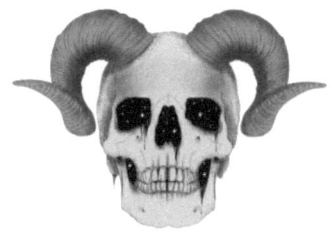

Chapter Eighteen

Waking was a slow and cold process, especially now that it was snowing again. Maksymilian loosely threw his arm over my waist, but he barely shifted. I stared absently at the freckles that dotted along his collarbone. He was mumbling softly. Did his dreams feel as real as mine? I needed to learn how to identify them quicker and get out of them faster. Or one day I couldn't wake up. Sloth would not kill me with merciful speed. They would keep me as prey. Never returning to reality.

I peeled Max's heavy arm off my waist and sat up. I knew I should have woken him, but I gave him a few more minutes — or selfishly, give myself a few minutes of peace. There was nothing inherently wrong with this man, but I found myself constantly aware of his presence.

Climbing out from beneath the tree, I stretched. The snow had been beautiful when I'd first seen it. Tiny little crystallised flakes that Max told me were unique. It seemed impossible, since there were so many falling at once, but I took his word for it. Before long, though, I realised that the snow, albeit beautiful, just made everything slippery and wet. It meant I was always cold and damp. I could never be comfortable.

When I arrived back at the tree, Max was sitting upright, rubbing sleep from his eyes. He yawned widely and raked his fingers through his hair, wincing when he pulled at tangles. His beard had grown again, thick and wiry around his chin.

"Morning," he greeted when he spotted me. His dark eyes lit up and I bit down on my responding smile. "Colder than the devil's balls today, isn't it?"

I snorted, rubbing my stiff, chilled fingers together. "Even colder than that, I think."

Max pulled a small paper-wrapped package from the bag and tossed it in my direction. I was so tired, still, that I fumbled as I tried to catch it. It dropped into the snow at my feet, the wrap quickly turning soggy. Groaning, I scooped it up and brushed off the snow to unwrap it.

There was no way of suppressing my delight at the sight of a hunk of hard cheese inside. Max beamed back even wider. So, I crawled back into the tree trunk to sit beside him and eat it quickly. It was crumbly and sharp, but after days of walking, and nights filled with nightmares… It was a luxury.

Not as good as a hot meal, of course, but without a horse, we were walking long days. The possibility of hot food sounded like a dream, as that would be only place I'd be getting some, in Sloth's manipulated dreamscape.

Max began braiding his long auburn hair. Scraping it back and quickly twisting the strands around each other with practiced ease. He took a strip of cloth and secured it all off the back of his neck. He absentmindedly toyed with the coin on his necklace, finding comfort in its presence.

"Stop watching me," he said, as he opened his own breakfast, chewing loudly. It was one of his more annoying habits, the way he smacked his lips as he ate. If we were together during the Gluttony trial, I would have pushed him into the sweet river. "Someone might think you're obsessed."

"With you?" I scoffed. "Never!"

With my knees drawn to my chest, I watched the snow fall, trying — and failing — to find the motivation to keep walking. The cold was bitter, and every night my feet froze through. I didn't really appreciate the horse until she was gone. Now, I felt like it would almost be easier to keep hiding away.

"Tell me something about you," I asked, both to fill in the awful silence and to procrastinate our leaving. "Or about your home."

"See!" Max smacked his lips. "You're obsessed."

Shooting him a droll look, I flicked a piece of snow in his direction. It splattered against his nose, and he poked his tongue out in response. He had become more relaxed since leaving the rebellion camps. However, when he reached in his pocket for his dwindling supply of chuckleweed, I wondered how long that would last. If his chilled edge wasn't drug-fuelled rather than distance from the stressors of the rebellion.

Every morning since we had left the last town, I asked him to tell me something. About three days in, he'd started throwing random and potentially incorrect facts into the mix. Loudly arguing that I hadn't been specific enough when I'd asked.

The day before, he'd told me the moon was round. Which I knew was wrong, because sometimes the moon wasn't even in the sky. Even then, half the time it looked like a sinister smile. There was no way the moon was round, and how would he have even known?

Max scratched his chin, tearing off a strip of thin rolling paper and setting about making his smoke. Finally, he nodded, deciding he'd give into me today. "We start working in the Kyanite mines when we're six and three-quarters years."

He was glancing at me out of the corner of his eye. Waiting

for a reaction, I'd bet, so I carefully schooled my face into what I hoped was a bored expression — even though I felt shocked. I could remember my little sisters at that age. They were still thin and giggly, and unbelievably stupid. There was no way they would have gone to work.

"Why do they make you start so young?" I asked, when I realised, I'd paused too long.

Max shrugged. He fidgeted for his lighter in his pocket. The one he'd not let me touch since I'd burned him. "That's when they think our spindly arms are strong enough to hold a pick axe. Put us to work young and we can only get stronger quicker. Or die trying."

"A pickaxe?" I asked, I'd never heard of one before. He lit the smoke, the sweet smell of weed floating around us. Like usual, he offered it to me, and I shook my head, gesturing impatiently for him to answer.

"Yeah," he said, shrugging. "It's this tool we slam against the rock. It chips away at the surface until you find bits of jewel underneath. It's normally pretty rough, the jewels not the axe, but when they've been cut and polished up, it's... Worth it."

There was a hint of adoration to his voice when he said that, a breathlessness that made me wonder if he missed it — the jewels, not the work — but he snapped out of it pretty quick. He climbed out into the snow and stretching his arms above his head. He inhaled again and nodded at me. "There's your *Maksymilian's Factoid of The Day*." He laughed. "Let's get moving."

Grumbling, I trudged out after him.

No number of facts, or singing, or banter could make up for the long walk in the snow. It was so deep I had to attempt to raise my knees and step forward. Praying with each step that I wouldn't fall into a ditch I couldn't see. The long travel made for a hard day, with burning thighs and numb feet by lunchtime.

We sat on a log at the edge of a frozen lake. We both knew and didn't comment on the fact that we were running out of food because there are no animals to hunt in the snow like this, and fish couldn't be caught when the lake was iced over. We hadn't seen a house to raid in days. The only solution was to get to Cottle Creek fast.

"So," Max began as he was packing snow into the water canteens. Nothing good ever came when a conversation started with that word. I raised a brow at him, almost daring him to continue. "You and Heira..."

My stomach soured around the piece of stale bread we'd eaten.

"I don't want to talk about Nik," I snapped. "Change the topic, Max."

He raised both hands placatingly. "Hear me out, Octavia."

Scrunching my face to him, I wanted to say no. I wanted to reject the idea and stick to silly topics like the moon and whether the sky was grey here because it reflected the dirty snow. Tackling serious topics sounded exhausting.

"Go on..." I said begrudgingly, allowing it only because he'd indulged my request for a fact earlier.

"I just want to know if I have competition," he said simply. Max packed up and gestured for me to hurry without looking at me.

"Competition for what?" I asked, frowning.

He glanced back over his shoulder, lips quirking in a cheeky grin. A dimple flashed in his cheek. "You."

"Oh." I didn't give him a proper answer. That one word preoccupied me for the rest of the day, and right into the nightfall. Rattling around in my brain like it wanted to stick — why would Max want me?

"Tell me something?" I asked, again, the next day. We were battling through the endless monotony of the snow.

Max took a moment to think. He walked in front, stomping down on the snow to make it easier for me to follow. We hadn't discussed his flippant comment at all the night before, too exhausted at the end of the previous day. But that didn't mean I could stop obsessing over it. I wanted to ask him what he'd meant. I wanted to press him for more details. I couldn't bring myself to make a fool out of myself.

"Deer have purple tongues," he said.

I paused mid-step, glaring at the back of his head. When I thought about it, I'd never seen a deer before. I thought I had eaten one, maybe in Gula, but I'd never seen one in the wild.

"Really?" I asked slowly, frowning. Sometimes, I really couldn't tell if he was teasing me.

He burst out laughing. The sort of bright, rambunctious laughter that's usually so contagious that you can't help but chuckle along too. But my cheeks fused with heat. I should have known the moment I'd asked that it wouldn't have been true. That today was the day for an impossible fact.

"I thought you didn't lie." I sniffed, feeling stupid and more than a little embarrassed. "Give me a different factoid of the day. A truth!"

"Why should I?" he said, still wheezing with amusement. His laughter involved his entire body, head thrown back, squinted eyes, bent knees, and wrapped arms. He felt it with every fibre of his being.

Smacking my lips, I floundered for a good reason, ending up with, "Because you like me? Because you *want* me?"

Max stopped walking, and predictably, I slammed right into his back.

When I bounced back, he twisted, wrapping his arms around my waist and crushing me against his chest. He was warm and solid, his beard tickling my face. Thrown off by my teasing at our sudden proximity, I swallowed and looked up at him.

His chest rumbled with a suppressed chuckle. "So, what if I do?"

He closed the space between us. His lips hovered a fraction from mine, and my entire mouth dried out. He was going to kiss me. I knew it with more certainty than I'd known anything before. I could feel his breath on my lips. Smell the smoke that lingered in his beard. He just had to lean in and kiss me.

Instead, he stuck out his tongue, boldly licking up the scarred side of my face. He held tight when I recoiled, thrashing backwards to try to put space between us. Max was strong enough to keep me pinned. "No two people have the same tongue print," he said, watching me intently.

"What?" I screeched, floundering to get away from him. Desperate to wipe at the side of my face and hide my scars from his scrutiny.

"Factoid of the day," he said, relaxing his arms. "You asked for it."

We staggered apart.

Grimacing, I wiped my sleeve down my face, trying to remove any trace of his spit from my skin. "Devils, you're an idiot, Max."

I lurched forward, shoving him sideways. He indulged me, pretending to stumble. I sniffed, willing the heat that crawled up my neck to calm down. I couldn't believe I'd thought he was about to kiss me. I overtook him and I didn't speak for the rest of the morning.

After a long walk, we trudged into a clearing that surrounded a vast lake. Snow piled high on the edges and the surface glistened with a thick sheen of ice. Hesitating by the edge, I folded my arms across my chest and bit down on my lip.

"I feel like we've been here before…" I muttered. I glanced back over my shoulder at our footprints in the snow. Wondering if we'd turned the wrong way when we woke that morning, and just trudged back the way we came. I could have sworn we'd had lunch at a lake yesterday.

Max snorted. He moved too close to me again, his breath hot against the back of my neck, and I cringed away. "That's unlikely," he said. "We've been walking in one direction the entire time. It's just that all these frozen lakes look the same."

Glancing out at the water, I supposed he had a point. Yesterday was the first time I'd seen a large body of water frozen over in testament to the bitter cold. I ignored the nagging feeling in the pit of my belly and nodded. "Yeah, I think you're right. Everything looks the same when it's covered in a layer of snow."

"I like that." Max grinned. "You agreeing that I'm right? It's about time you acknowledged it."

The next day, his factoid was that some lizards could lose their tails. Another useless tidbit of information that did nothing to satisfy the desire I had to know more about him. But unless I asked for it specifically, it seemed like he wouldn't tell me. But I didn't want to play into his hands and be specific in my request. I didn't want him to know I was thinking about him at all.

That same day, we walked by the shores of another lake. The soft mid-morning light filtering off the frozen surface. I frowned, staring out at it. A chill worked across my scalp and slid down my spine.

"Max," I said, swept up in the chilling feeling that everything was the same as it had been once before. That I was walking through my own footprints. "I swear, I'm telling you, we've been here before…"

His thick brows knitted together, and he rubbed his chin

through his beard. "I don't think so."

"It is!" I protested, waving my hands through the air in exasperation. It frustrated me that he wouldn't listen. "This is the same lake that we walked around yesterday, and I bet the day before, too! We're walking in giant circles."

"That's impossible," he said gruffly, dismissing the idea. "I'm a better navigator than that, and we've been walking in a dead straight line."

"Now you're definitely lying!"

His cheeks reddened, his dark eyes gleaming with indignant fury. "I don't lie, Octavia."

"Well, it could never be a dead straight line because you walk like a drunk," I said. Mocking his movements. His fury had ignited mine, as easily as sparking his lighter. I disliked his quick dismissal, but I had a feeling I had been at the lake before. More than once.

Max spluttered. "I do not!"

He spun on his heel, stalking away from me and pulling his lighter from his pocket. He paced the edge of the lake the same way we had yesterday, and the day before. The utter familiarity of it had me shuddering, and I fidgeted with discomfort. He was about to slip and fall, just like he did yesterday and the day before.

Max swore loudly as his foot went out from under him. His boot lost all grip on the ice, and his arms cartwheeled to keep his balance. He just barely kept his grip on his prized lighter, but his smoke slipped from between his lips. The soft orange glow dying as it hit the snow. He landed hard next to it.

That proved it, at least to me. I knew I wasn't imagining things now. I'd re-walked the same path three times over. Battled through the same monotonous mounds of snow to make no progress. Suddenly flushed with anger at how easily he'd dismissed me when I was right, I marched up behind Max, folding my arms and leaning over him.

"Do you trust me?"

Max tipped his head. "What?"

"I said…" My pitch raised an octave. "Do you trust me?"

His eyes narrowed, and his throat bobbed. I sucked in a sharp breath, mentally preparing myself for his rejection.

"Actually, yes," Max said. "Are you surprised by that?"

Truth be told, his admission took me back, but I didn't want to admit it out loud. Instead, I held his eye and willed him to take me seriously. "Then believe me," I said. "Believe me, when I tell you, either we're walking in circles or we're dreaming because we've been here twice before. Which one's more likely, Mr. Navigator?"

I'd expected him to admit that we'd been traipsing the same path. Maybe even to say he'd led us in a circle deliberately. But he didn't. Instead, Max's lips parted on a harsh inhale, and something flickered in his gaze. They glowed with a dark and more violent light. It didn't match the man I knew, even after travelling together for days. It was enough for me to recoil in shock. Realisation crashed over me, and I felt incredibly stupid for not catching on sooner.

"This is a dream, isn't it?" I asked, through the fingers pressed to my lips. My head throbbed with a sharp pain I couldn't ignore. I thread my fingers through my hair, tugging at the strands sharply, although pain had never worked before.

"Octavia…" He said, my name spoken like a warning.

"I thought I'd woken up from the dream about Envy. I thought…" A flush of mortification ran hot through my body, because I should have known better. I rarely remembered my dreams, but Envy's smirk stayed vivid in my mind. I shouldn't have trusted the reality around me.

"Come on, Octavia." Max, or this dream version of him, had acted like I hadn't spoken. He lumbered to his feet, dusted snow off his coat and turned his back on me to continue on. "We'll never make it to Desidia if you don't keep walking. You're getting lazy."

There was no way I could make myself move. I was trapped in the snow due to the overwhelming horror. With my cold fingers still pressed to my lips, I watched him leave me behind. "How could I not have known?" I whispered, even though I knew Sloth could make dreams feel so real. "How…"

Now that I'd realised, I was dreaming, it was easy to look for the signs. Tiny details that could never be changed in reality that were different here. Including the shining tattoos that lined my wrist beneath the cuff. They'd transformed into four thick black phases of the moon, a pattern I'd never seen before. I rubbed my thumb against them, wondering if they'd smudge.

They didn't.

I buried my face in my hands, unnerved because I'd thought I was awake when I wasn't. I'd believed that this was my reality — and what an idiot that made me. Going through the mirror failed, pushing me from one dream to another instead of waking me.

The biggest clue that this wasn't real should have been Max's announcement that he wanted me. His flirtatious looks and proximity made my heart skip a beat. It's unlikely that someone like Max, with his fiery red hair and blunt honesty, would desire someone like me. I should never have believed it.

In comparison, I was nothing. A woman full of struggles, anger, and doubt with no real way to conquer them. Where he was an infinite possibility, I was a passing moment, a speck of time destined to be left behind. I should have realised it the moment he said it — nobody would want me. Not even a rebel like Maksymilian Tate.

My chest hollowed out as devastation settled in. I tightly held myself, digging my nails into my arms, feeling the sharp pain.

"Please, please wake up. Wake up," I begged. It didn't work. When I looked up, Max was still traipsing away from me, and he hadn't paused once to look back.

Staring after him blankly, I shivered. The snow had fallen

again. The dusting, though potentially beautiful, felt hopeless. I pressed my cold palms to my cheeks and took a deep breath.

"Come on, Octavia," I rallied myself. Trying to remind myself that I survived worse than a monotonous dream. "There has to be a way to wake up."

Physical pain wasn't working, no matter how deep I raked my nails into my skin or pulled at my hair. If emotional pain worked, I would have already woken up. My breath came in short pants, my chest turning tight, bound by the invisible strings of my anxiety. I wracked my brain for the answer. Trying to remember how I'd woken up from any other dream throughout my life. I'd slept, day after day, for my entire existence, and never had a problem waking. So surely sleeping, dreaming and waking should have been some of my best, well-practiced skills.

Slight fragments of old dreams came back to me. The memory of falling through holes and tripping down stairs. The jolt of fear that followed, the catch of my breath in the back of my throat. Each tumble had always sent me reeling, straight back into consciousness, woken with a start.

My teeth worried against my bottom lip until it stung. In the absence of a solid plan, courage wavered; failure would mean no future chances. It felt like a risk. Some of my riskiest plans had worked through the trials. If this was only a dream — a way for Sloth to tap into my energy — then surely, I couldn't actually hurt myself.

Despite Max's intent to abandon me, I overcame my fear of injury and moved forward.

The frozen lake was glossy beneath my boots, the surface too slippery to find any grip. It didn't take long to find and then lose my footing. My breath caught as my feet slid out from beneath me. Gravity laid claim to my body and pulled me down fast. Hard. My knees seared as I crashed into the ice, my entire body jolting. The fall, and the impact, failed to jolt me from sleep to consciousness.

Instead, I curled forward, pressing my pounding head to the ice and tried not to cry. Gasping to balance my emotions and combat the wave of my pain. It felt like I'd splintered my kneecaps down in the middle.

Dream or not, the pain, the fear — all of it — felt all too real.

"I just want to wake up," I whispered into the frozen surface, my fingers turning numb from the proximity. "Please. Please."

The girl in Suain had said that I needed to go through the mirror. Which I thought I had, fleeing from Envy's hunt, straight through an actual representation of a mirror. I'd smashed through glass and wound up in yet another sin controlled moment. A dream not a nightmare, this time, but a never-ending loop of monotony.

There were no mirrors here. Nothing but snow, ice, myself and Max. Who had reappeared behind me. His reflection in the icy surface appeared distorted as a flash of orange. A single flame in this cold landscape. Holding back my tears, I studied his face through the ice.

He put a hand on my shoulder. The weight of it softly reassuring, and I sat back on my heels.

"Are you okay?" Max asked. "That was some fall."

"There are no mirrors here," I whispered. Something had occurred to me, but I wasn't sure I wanted to believe it. If the fall had hurt me, this idea would have been even more dangerous. Biting down on my lip, searching for the courage to try two risky plans in quick succession.

Max's face on the ice shifted, and his grip on my shoulder tightened. I didn't turn to look at him, just in case the sight of him meant I wouldn't follow through. He could convince me to stop.

"What do you mean?" he asked, voice husky and low. "Come on, Octavia, we need to get off the lake."

The suggestion sounded reasonable, but everything in the dream seemed reasonable and real enough — even though it wasn't.

"There are no mirrors, but plenty of reflections," I said, fisting my left hand. I glanced once at the strange and unfamiliar tattoos on my wrist — too wrong to be my reality — and slammed my fist against the ice. Pain fissured up to my elbow. It should have been impossible, but cracks appeared beneath my clenched fist.

"Stop it, Octavia." Max reached for my wrist.

I pulled away from him, slipping from his grasp and beat down against the ice again. "We're going through the mirror, Max. Right now."

The cracks spider-webbed out from my fist, racing in every direction. They grew bigger and deeper. The ice beneath us let out an almighty groan. Without hesitation, I slammed my hand into the ice again.

It broke beneath me — us — shattering and falling into the icy depths of the water. Max shouted a protest and called my name, both lost to the whip of the wind as the ice gave way. He slammed into my back, pushing me forward, and I plummeted through the ice.

Plunging deep into the chilling depths of the lake. Instinctively, I tried to kick, swim, but water had rushed into my ears, nose, and mouth. Instantly, a powerful force sucked me to the side, pressing my body against a thick layer of ice. I could never get back through it or find my way back to the opening.

Finally, I closed my eyes. Swallowing my panic, I succumbed to the bone deep cold. Praying to the devil that I'd been right, and had sacrificed myself to waking, not death itself.

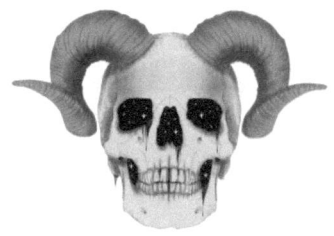

Chapter Nineteen

Max had his face pressed against my chest when I woke, his ear pressed above my heart. One of his hands roughly gripped my jaw, and he let out a groan of pure relief. He sagged against my body, almost like I had stolen every ounce of his energy.

Dazed, I blinked at the snow-covered trees, the soft brightness of the day beyond them. The sky here was blue, not grey, and the snow had stopped falling. Max's body was warm against mine, but his weight was too much to bear. I groaned softly in protest. My throat ached with the sound, my head spinning as I moved a fraction. He stiffened and pushed himself up onto his arms, his face swimming into view. Each of his features scrunched with soft concern, then blurred as my head spun.

"Octavia," Max breathed my name with such wonder that my heart stuttered. A sweat broke out across my brow. "I swear your heart had stopped. Devils, I thought you were dead."

"Why…" My voice sounded rough, gravelly, like I hadn't spoken for months. I had to ask him, despite the pain and panic in my veins, to see if I was dreaming. "Why would you care if I died?"

His full lips flattened, his eyes narrowing on my face. Although some of the relief in his expression remained, as if it were too great for him to hide it completely. "Because you're my ticket into Eternis," he said. "Why else?"

Suspicion made it difficult to distinguish him from the other Max. The one that had laughed and walked with me for days on end, traipsing through the snow. Dreams and reality had intertwined so closely that I no longer knew which one was which. I didn't know if I could trust him, or myself, I didn't know if I was awake.

A lump formed in my throat, and I struggled to sit up, my vision blurring and swaying in protest. My mouth felt dry, my throat still scratchy, but I ignored it in favour of asking. "Is this a dream, Max?"

He scoffed, scooping up a handful of snow and holding it to my mouth. I let him push it past my lips, the snow melting as it met the warm heat of my mouth. The fluid was a relief for my dry tongue. I closed my eyes, swallowed, and grabbed more snow.

"Unlikely," Max said, finally answering me. With tension between his brows, he gestured for me to keep drinking. "In my dreams, I'm usually on a beach in the sunshine without a care in the world."

"Prove it," I said, fisting my hands in my lap as I tried to find my equilibrium. There was a part of me that wanted to scramble back from him, give myself space, in case it was the same Max who had been intent on letting me rot inside that dream. Dooming us to walk that same path forever. But the rest of me couldn't move. My limbs ached with fatigue, and my stomach rumbled in demand. A sharp pain piercing through my skull. I almost felt hungover, like I'd spent too much time drinking Gulan wine instead of sleeping.

Max scrunched his nose, rubbing absently at his chin. "You want me to prove that I dream of beaches?" he clarified. He reached for me, but when I flinched, his hand dropped away. Instead, he reached into his pocket for his lighter. He turned it around and around, as if testing the weight of the familiar object. "Did that faltering heart of yours do something to your brain?"

His comment might have been funny in any other situation, but it felt flippant. Adding another crack to my hastily built emotional shield because I didn't know what was true or false. I didn't know whether I believed he was here, that I was here. I grasped at his face, tilting his chin to look him in the eye. I wet my lips, and almost begged, "Prove to me I'm awake. That this isn't just another dream. Please, Max."

His face contorted at those two words. Max looked pained. His grip white knuckled around the lighter. He rested his forearms on his knees, crouched in front of me, and asked softly, "How am I supposed to do that, exactly? I don't know what you want from me."

Fear turned my blood hot enough that I expected the snow to melt around me. If this wasn't the real Max, if I couldn't trust him. I needed to get as far away from him as I could. I drew my knees slowly to my chest. "That sounds like something evil dream Max would say…"

He dropped the lighter and raised his hands, indicating he meant no harm. Strain pinching at his lips as he watched my pathetic attempts to shuffle backwards. "Don't move, Octavia. You need to rest a moment." When I continued my botched crawl, he closed his eyes and shook his head. "I really don't know what you expect me to do. Except this…"

He reached out and flicked me hard between the eyes.

"Ow!" I cried, the sharp pain bouncing through my skull.

His face tilted to one side as the world spun. I clutched at my forehead.

"You're a dick!"

A grin crept across his face, lighting in his eyes, as he tried not to laugh at me. "Was that not proof enough for you? I doubt I'm going around flicking you in my dreams. At least..." He cleared his throat, his cheeks reddening. "Not that sort of flicking."

"No," I bit out the word. My heart was fluttering in my chest faster than a candied butterflies' wings, the need to flee making me want to crawl out of my skin. "This could still be a dream."

This time, he chuckled. A soft and sensual sound. Max reached out and grasped my chin, forcing me to look at him when I'd desperately tried to keep my focus anywhere else.

He leaned close. "Are you saying you dream of me a lot, Octavia?"

"You wish!" My scoffed response was automatic, and I glanced away because I couldn't move past the distrust that had settled in my bones. "I don't know what to do. Tell me something."

The moment I asked it, I flinched. I should have asked for something, anything, else. Maksymilian's Factoids of the Day stuck in my memory. I couldn't tell if they were real or a figment of my dreams.

"What sort of something?" he asked, just like he had before. My stomach dropped.

"Something about me," I whispered, asking for something different this time. Something I'd never asked in the dream. "Tell me something you know about me."

The strength returned to my voice as I asked, because I was certain that there was very little Max — the man of my dreams or reality — could tell me. We weren't friends, not really, and while we'd travelled together for weeks on end, he didn't really know me.

He frowned but nodded. Standing tall, he stretched and

folded his arms across his chest, staring down at me. "Your name is Octavia-Something-Nox. You're from somewhere in the Pridelands, the same place as Heira, from my reckoning. You've beaten Gluttony, Envy, Wrath, and Pride, and we're currently trying to take you to face Sloth. What else can I tell you? You don't smoke, but you complain a lot. You talk in your sleep, but mostly it's too mumbled to make out. I'm surprised you've survived this long because I swear you trip over your own feet every hundred steps and even after riding on her for days, you were still scared that the horse would bite you. You keep coins tucked in your boots, even though that must hurt your toes. You chew on your bottom lip when you're worried and eat the best bits of your food first, which is painful to watch, because it's like you're suffering at the end of each meal when you get to the part you don't like. Which, incidentally, is any bit of meat that touches a bone."

While he spoke, I'd gone still, eyes wide and chest aching. I knew he'd been paying attention to me, but I didn't think he'd noticed that much. It was easier to think of him as a stranger and to be a stranger in return. Easier than getting close and letting him know me, because all the people I dared to let close had died. A selfish part of me didn't want Maksymilian, with his cheeky smile and dry honesty, to become another name on the list of souls I had to remember and honour. Just another death that helped me succeed.

I huffed, turned my head, and stared into the snow. "These are all things dream Max would know, too."

Max shook his head, his hands curling into fists. "Dream me wouldn't know everything I know, because it's made up from your brain. You don't know everything I know."

Wrapping my arms around my waist and gritting my teeth, I tried to process what he was saying. "That's... confusing."

"But true," he insisted, crouching down and leaning too close to me again. "And Octavia?"

265

"What?" I bit out, tired of this conversation and of this dream — if it was one. I was ready to wake up now.

He waited for me to turn back to him, to face him properly.

"I think you talk to the devil," Max said with quiet confidence. "Even though I can't hear him, you can. I think he whispers in your ear to give you a bit of courage and confidence. I think that's who you talk to in your sleep, and when you mumble beneath your breath. When you think I'm not listening." He paused, pursing his lips. "I don't think you're just talking to yourself, like Heira said. Someone's responding."

His reminder of overhearing my fight with Niklaus bothered me and his accusation of me talking to myself, trying to pray to the devil. Even if he was right. Samael's presence in my mind had been a guarded secret for so long that I couldn't help the fear that crept through me.

"Excuse you?" I asked, hoarsely. A seed of hope sprouted amidst the fright, longing for someone to know and for me to stop pretending. I wasn't sure that I trusted him. I still wasn't sure that he was real. This could all be my subconscious, a dream, formed from desperation to share the burden of the devil. "You're speaking in tongues, Maksymilian."

"The devil has magic," Max said, not backing down. "More than any of the seven sins. What's to say he couldn't visit any of our subconsciousness, whisper in any of our ears. He'd have to be that powerful to have reigned over Kaida without the sins stealing his crown right off his head."

Threading my fingers together and pressing my knuckles to my lips, I thought it over. Lifting my gaze to hold Max's eye, I inhaled deeply and lay it all out there. "That would mean the devil knows your plans. That he knows you're coming for him."

"So?" Max asked, a smile pulling at his lips. He held out his hand, and when I took it, he pulled me to my feet. "His awareness will make my win all that more satisfying. It'll mean he's waiting for me, and it'll be a real challenge."

"Oh." I swayed on the spot, needing a long moment to find my balance.

"Also…"

"Yeah?" I glanced at him.

"Next time you speak to him, tell the devil I said hello," He murmured, on the cusp of a laugh. "And ask him if there's a shortcut to Desidia that we're missing."

'I can appreciate his foolish confidence,' Samael said, his voice so unexpected that I shuddered. Max placed a hand beneath my elbow, easily holding me up. *'It'll make it all that much easier to kill him, but I can appreciate it.'*

"You're back!" I cried, and at the confusion flitting across the red-head's face, I added, "Max says hello…"

Max's eyes widened incrementally. His gaze flaring with understanding, before he slid his grip from my elbow to my hand, holding on tight. He pretended not to hear me while I attempted to talk to Samael.

'I was never gone, Little One.' Samael said. *'You just couldn't hear me. I admit I'm getting frustrated of Sloth shutting me out of your mind while you sleep.'* There was a tinge of annoyance in his tone, present enough that my stomach turned queasy.

"How am I supposed to know if I'm sleeping or awake? My dreams feel so real," I asked, wondering if I'd have to rely on whether Samael deigned to speak to me. His presence was an easy sign of reality, but he wasn't always willing to chat. He could have spoken to me the moment I woke but had refrained until now.

The devil's sigh suggested he had other important matters to deal with. *'You need to look for the cracks in your dreams. The moments that don't align with the truth of reality…'*

"Like the tattoos…" I whispered, turning my wrist over and looking at the inked designs. The pig, snake, lion, and peacock were back. Glittering permanent reminders of what I'd endured.

'Exactly like those, Sloth can't recreate the magic of the

other sins, and their magic is imbued in the ink representing their challenges. That is why they change in your dreams, Octavia. Find these things and use them to anchor yourself in reality,' he said it as if it were the simplest answer, the easiest thing to do. *'You were asleep for too long this time. You're running out of time. You need to wake up quicker.'*

Biting down on my lip, I dared to consider the other possibility: the dreams where Samael stood in front of me, entirely present, entirely mine. "Why not stay?" I asked. "If the dream is good…"

'Do you want to pass this trial?' he asked sharply. *'Do you wish to meet me in Eternis or are you tired of trying, Octavia, like many of your fellow competitors? Sloth always claims the weak of soul.'*

"Of course, I want to keep going, but…" I couldn't deny the bone-deep ache of exhaustion I felt, and the mental scarring that had come from always trying so hard only to find another, more difficult challenge ahead of me. Things had not been easy for a long time, and I wanted so badly for something to go well, for my luck to turn.

'But sometimes your dreams are easier to suffer than reality.' Samael murmured, finishing the sentence for me. His words punctuated with a soft hiss that made me think of his delicately forked tongue. *'You must remember why it is you want to live. What you want from this life… You need to find a reason to persevere. It needs to be something that drives you Octavia, something more than just the promise of the future.'*

"But what if I don't have something like that?" I asked him, my grip on Max's hand tightening as fear shot through me. The feeling so sharp I could have sworn I'd been stabbed.

'Then, this may be your final trial, Octavia.' Samael sounded sad, but much like Max, he'd never shied from telling me the truth. *'You need to decide what you truly want and if you are willing to suffer for it.'*

268

"Are you finished?" Max said, suddenly. He waved a hand in front of my face. "I'm right here. You could answer me."

"Huh?" I asked, looking up at him and feeling disoriented as I was pulled from one conversation to the other. With my free hand, I brushed my hair from my eyes, trying to reorient myself.

"Devils, no wonder Heira called you spacey." He laughed. "Stop focusing on the devil and focus on me. One conversation at a time." He stabbed his thumb against his chest. "Right here. Right now."

"Alright." I conceded mostly because Samael had turned quiet, and I couldn't feel the reassuring soft brush of him against my mind. Once, that would have been worrying, but I was just relieved to have spoken to him. More so, to know that I was truly awake. "What's the plan for today? I'm freezing."

"We need to make it the rest of the way to Cottle Creek," he announced, tugging me forward a step. "Which brings me to what I've been meaning to tell you... I've got bad news."

There should have been no way for things to get worse than travelling by foot across frozen plains with little sign of life around us, but I knew it could be. I sighed. "...Go on. Tell me."

"Something, or someone, has eaten all our food while we were asleep." Max looked glum. His entire face had fallen. "Including all my weed."

Losing his smokes seemed to be the worst blow for him. I was sure he could survive for days on snow and chuckleweed alone. Groaning softly, I rubbed my hand down my face. "Does anything ever go right for us?"

"We're alive, aren't we?" Max summoned optimism from devils knew where, a forced smile flashing across his features. "Mostly in one piece."

"What do you mean mostly?" I asked, the knot in my belly intensifying.

"Your distrust of me after I tried to get your heart going has created a hole in my own." Max pressed his hand to his heart

269

dramatically, staggering as if he might faint. Then he paused long enough to grin at me. "Do you get it?"

It was tempting to slap him, because for a split second I'd truly thought something else was wrong. "Devils, you're over-dramatic today."

"Don't complain when I'm entertaining you, baby." He consulted a crumpled paper in his pocket before lifting our pack and guiding me down the road. "Just accept it."

"Don't call me that," I grumbled.

"There you go," He laughed. "Complaining again."

"Stay awake, Octavia," Max said sharply. He was just as close to falling asleep as me, but he squeezed my hand tightly. "We're almost there."

"How do you know?" I asked. We'd been walking for hours. I cautiously walked through the night, on edge at the thought of danger. My feet had gone numb hours ago, and my steps had dragged, slowing our pace further. Max was too tired to carry me, and I was too stubborn to stop. We had to reach the next town.

"There was a sign. How else?" he said, as if it were the most obvious answer. Which I supposed it was, but I barely noticed the signs. Half of them were knocked down and covered in snow, and all the signs, whether standing or not, made no sense to me.

"Great." I sounded as miserable as I felt.

"Come here." Max tugged me close, settling his arm around my waist and crushing me against his chest. He slowed his pace, keeping step with me, even though it would take us longer. The warmth of his body was dangerous. My chin dropped against my chest, the jerking motion startling me awake again. "Not far now. We can't sleep. Not yet."

"Eventually, we're going to have to rest," I whispered.

A pained look crossed his face. "I know. But last time we

slept too long. The snow's thinning now and it doesn't fall as much. I think we're running out of time to make it to Desidia."

I nodded, concentrating on putting one foot in front of the other. "Let's sleep one at a time, so there's someone to make sure we wake up."

Max nodded silently, as I worried about whether the plan would work.

Cottle Creek, it turned out, was an old, barren creek bed. The creek had muddied, slushed snow but no flow of water. It wrapped itself around a small village filled with wooden walls and silent chimneys. The absence of life was unmistakable.

"It looks just like Suain," I said. I had a bad feeling about this place.

"It's another ghost town." Max was quick to agree. "We need to break into the houses, Octavia. We'll find food, and then one of us can sleep."

We split up, and I dragged myself up a set of stairs. I heard Max kicking at a door in the distance, but I couldn't do the same. Instead, I tried the handle. Locked. I pushed on the door as hard as I could, but it wouldn't budge. I managed to dislodge the hastily nailed wooden panels at a small side window, finding a way in. Straining, I pulled the first panel off, then the second, dropping them haphazardly by my feet.

Stepping on top of them, I stared through the dirty window and into the dark, abandoned house. I shattered the glass with my elbow and used my coat for protection as I searched for the window latch. As soon as I undid it, the wind caught the window, blowing it open until it smashed against the house. Heaving a breath and trying to ignore any thought that was a bad omen, I crawled inside the house.

It was dusty and forgotten. Knowing now what I did of Sloth

and her people, it wasn't unexpected. It was unlikely anyone had been in the house for years. I scurried around like a mouse, trying to find anything edible to take with me. Three homes later, I had a small stash bundled in my arms. Dried meats preserved cheeses and a bitter flagon of wine.

Max waited for me in the middle of the village. He was just illuminated by the soft glow inside the chancellor's home. I couldn't bring myself to approach it this time, even though it was probably our best bet for food. I wouldn't risk waking the sleeping inhabitants. He leaned against a tree, food bundled under one arm, his expression grim.

"What is it?" I asked, feeling a sense of dread at the sight of his expression.

"There's other trial competitors here," he said, gesturing off to his left.

"Who?" I asked. Instantly filled hoping I'd find Nash. I didn't know if he survived the massacre in Glorae, but I remained hopeful he was alive. Optimistic that he was working his hardest to defeat the next trial. The thrill of that possibility, and the hope of seeing him chased off the heavy edge of my fatigue. I almost dropped the wine in my rush to push it into Max's arms. "Where are they?"

"Over there." He jerked his head towards a large towering tree. Dangling vines and fragile red leaves covered it. I raced towards it, slowing only when the web-wrapped bodies came into view.

Seven webbed cocoons lay at the base of the tree. Max's boot prints littered the thin layer of melting snow around them, but otherwise, they were silent and unmoving.

"They're sleeping," Max said. When I twisted to look back at him, he was drinking from the wine. "I checked. They're all alive, just asleep. I couldn't get them to wake."

That didn't matter. If it was Nash, I'd make him wake up. I'd force him to come with us. He was the one man I wouldn't leave behind.

While Max dug into the food, I dropped to my knees beside the first body. He was right. Their chests rose and fell with very slow, spaced breaths. I tore the webs from their faces, peeling them back from frigidly cold skin. Leaning close, I inspected their faces closely for anyone I recognised. There were some hints of familiarity, people I'd seen in each trial over again, people I'd walked beside silently, not bothering to get to know them. But there was no sign of Nash or Finley. No sign of anyone who mattered.

Rocking back onto my heels and tipping my head to stare sightlessly into the sky, I heaved a sigh. It was difficult not to be disappointed. Even though not finding them could mean they were alive and pushing forward in the trial.

"Samael?" I called, not bothering to whisper now Max knew the truth of it. Behind me, he grumbled but didn't protest. "Samael?!"

'Yes, Little One?' Samael answered suddenly. The brush of his presence filled me with relief and a renewed energy. I sighed heavily, dropping my chin to my chest.

"I need you to tell me something."

The devil made a disapproving sound. *'You do know, I'm not at your beck and call, right?'*

"I know." I bit down on my lip. "But I just need to know if Nash Wickham is alive."

'How should I know?' Samael asked, and I faltered. Only for a second, and I looked at the iridescent cuff on my wrist. It was the sign of the trials I could never hide.

"I think you always keep track of us and know which players are left in your game," I said.

The devil laughed. *'You are, sometimes, more perceptive than I give you credit for, Octavia.'* He sounded pleased. *'For that reason alone, I'll give you what you desire. Yes. Nash Wickham currently lives.'*

Sagging forward with relief, I nodded. Of course, he'd made it out of Glorae safe and sound. He was resilient and determined, and I shouldn't have doubted him. Nash was one of the few people that deserved to win the trials. We would walk through the gates to Eternis together.

"Has Sloth claimed him?" I asked, studying the bodies in front of me, lost to sleep. Was that what would happen to me if I stayed in the dreams too long? Would I be quiet, peaceful but unmoving, or lost to a never-ending nightmare?

Samael growled. *'If I tell you, will you keep moving?'*

"Sure," I sighed, weighed down by my own swirling worry. "We won't stay here long."

'Not yet,' Samael conceded. *'Your friend still fights her influence.'*

Max cleared his throat behind me, drawing my attention. It seemed there was only so much time he'd give me to talk to the devil. He began eating, then handed me the wine when I approached. I raised it to my lips and took a swig, an immediate bitterness burning my throat.

"I'll sleep first while you eat," Max said. I wanted to cry at his words. The buzz of energy from finding other competitors had faded, leaving me with a hollow emptiness in my chest. I wanted to be the first one to sleep. I wanted to get some energy back. Max didn't allow me to protest, tucking cheese into my hand and leaning against the tree. He tucked his chin against his chest and closed his eyes. "Wake me when the sun comes up fully."

He was snoring before I'd swallowed my first mouthful. I ate slowly and drank tart wine to stay awake. Even when there were only crumbs left, it felt like the time had dragged. Morning was approaching, the winter sunrise staining the sky, but a fully risen sun was hours away.

Pacing through the small town, I dwelled on everything Samael had said. I was trying to sort my thoughts out and find a reason to keep going, a reason to pull myself from Sloth's tempting dreams, but it wasn't as easy as he made out. The trial instructions were unclear, leaving me without a firm plan and feeling untethered.

What would happen when I finally met Sloth?

What if she failed me anyway and I've given up my chance to stay in the right dream?

I returned to where Max was sleeping after the sun had risen and the snow had started to melt. He snored loudly, his chin tucked against his chest. Exhaustion overwhelmed me as I knelt beside him.

"Wakey, wakey, rise and shine," I murmured, shaking his shoulder. When he didn't rouse, I moved straight to pain because, devils, I needed to sleep. I didn't have time to waste in waking him slowly. My fingers wrapped around one of the braided pieces of his fiery hair, and I tugged hard.

Max woke with a gasp, his hand flying up to cover mine at his scalp. His eyes had snapped open, pain shining in his gaze as he looked up from beneath his dark lashes.

"Octavia..." he said cautiously, battling a wide yawn. "What the—"

"You said to wake you," I interrupted, curled into his side. Seeking the warmth of his body and breathing out a sigh that relaxed every muscle in my body. "My turn. Goodnight."

Exhaustion overcame me, and sleep claimed me quickly. The last thing I remembered was the feeling of being lifted from the ground and bundled against a hard, warm chest. I wanted to cry out because the feeling of being stolen away from Pride's palace was so reminiscent, but my protests were lost as Sloth claimed me.

Pulling me deep into a dream.

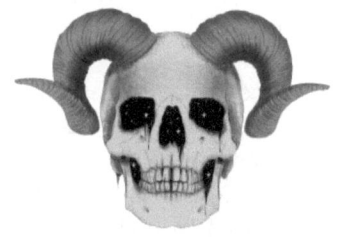

Chapter Twenty

I knew it was a dream the moment I opened my eyes. Not through any intrinsic gut feeling or heightened awareness, but because Samael leaned against a pillar in the distance. His pristine white wings folded tight against his back, and his arms folded across his chest. As I focused on him, I saw the edge of his sly smile as he gazed into the distance.

"Hello," I whispered as I approached.

My words caught on the breeze, floating across the room. The devil turned to look at me slowly, his eyes rotating through the iridescent colours of an oil spill, his full lips twitching into a smirk. He looked me over, a quick, flicking assessment followed by a short, sharp nod.

I wish I knew what that nod meant, I wish I knew what he was thinking.

"You shouldn't be here, Little One," Samael said.

My own smile slipped away, and I twisted my fingers

anxiously into the fabric of my long skirt. I'd wanted him to light up at the sight of me. I wanted Samael to declare that he was going to keep me close. I wanted the devil to want me.

"But…" I whispered, dejected.

He reached for me, capturing my hand and lifting it above my head. He coaxed me to twirl. The long skirt flared around my ankles. My soft, gauzy top swishing to reveal the soft curve of my breasts. My scars were visible, but I didn't hide. Not from Samael, not when the devil looked at me like I was the meal he wanted for his last. Not when he gazed at me like I was the beginning and the end of the world.

It turned my blood hot, desire entwining with my pulse. I licked my lips and looked up at him. A blush spread high across my cheeks, making my face flame.

He watched the movement of my tongue over my lips and let out a small, throaty growl. His forked tongue flicked over his lips. "You look good in the clothes of my lands," he said, gruffly. "Beautiful, even."

My blush deepened, smile widening, and I glanced down at the outfit. Brushing my fingers over the gold stitching at the hem of the gauzy black material. It was light, almost like wearing nothing at all.

"It's… Very pretty." My compliment sounded stupid the moment it left my lips. I didn't see clothing the way others did. Ophelia would have adored this luxurious outfit and understood its cultural significance.

Samael seemed to understand, because he chuckled at my discomfort. "Welcome to Eternis, Octavia."

Wide-eyed, I blinked at him, jerking back a fraction and realising I'd paid little attention to my surroundings. Too consumed by the devil himself.

We stood in a room carved from polished black marble, which was cold and smooth beneath my bare feet. The veins of blue, red, and gold run through it, reminiscent of the coffin from

Avarice.

Samael stood by a tall pillar, gazing out at his lands. When I let go of him and crept forward, I could see that this place was carved into the very side of a mountain, and beneath us, water rushed down into a river, snaking out to meet a lake in the distance. It was noisy and peaceful, all at the same time.

The devil's lands were dynamic. Mountains rose and fell in the distance, and as the sun set little villages lit up. Soft lights twinkled in the distance, signalling that we were not so alone here.

Twisting back to face him, I asked. "Is this…?"

"My city?" Samael grinned. "My home?"

With bright eyes, he nodded, but then appeared tired, as if this ordeal had depleted his energy. "Yes. I thought, on the chance you fell asleep again, you might want a little more motivation as to why should keep going. I thought you should see where you're heading and what awaits you here."

I paced in a slow circle, taking in the wide windows, rich, dark curtains, and glittering decor. Samael stalked across the floors without so much as a sound, following me as if he were hunting prey. He gave me five minutes to look and then beckoned me further into his home.

Long corridors and large open doorways showed me glimpses of lavishly decorated rooms, of opulence worthy of the seven sins — proving that the devil embodied them all. Distantly, I wondered if he lived here alone, since there was no sign of life beyond us in these rooms. Or if it was just my dreams, providing the wistful illusion of privacy. Creating a moment that belonged to us, and us alone.

"Tell me then," I said, keeping close to him. "What waits for me here?"

We descended a steep set of stairs, carved into the side of the mountain. They opened up into a large solarium with a glass roof, which offered a spectacular view of the setting sun. Colours marred the sky. Bright greenery surrounded us. When I inhaled, the air was crisp. Surprisingly, Eternis felt full of colour and life.

The devil led me to a plush lounge and let me sit. I sunk into the cushions and looked up at him.

He smirked wickedly, spreading his arms in offering and tilting his head. A lock of hair fell over his forehead.

"Me," he said, full of arrogance.

"You…" I confirmed softly, trying to hold in my nervous laugh. "The devil?"

"Yesss," the word hissed off the edge of his forked tongue. "Does that surprise you, Little One?"

Swallowing roughly, I was reminded of Max asking me the same question. I watched as he turned away, reaching for an ornate silver teapot and two tall glasses rimmed with gold. It felt strange to behold the devil pouring me a cup of tea.

When he passed it to me, my fingers shook, the liquid sloshing over the edge. Slowly, I raised it to my lips. The tea was hot and had a spiced, nutty taste. It warmed my bones, relaxing my muscles, and I exhaled softly.

"That you'd offer yourself up to me? Yes. It surprises me a lot." I admitted, feeling bold enough to be truthful. "Tell me… why me?"

His devilish smirk widened, although his eyes narrowed in slight rebuke. "Don't lower yourself to fishing for compliments, Octavia." He sipped at his own tea, settling in a large backless chair, his white wings ruffling. "You intrigue me, and that's all you need to know."

I studied him. He wasn't hiding himself from me this time. There were no alterations to his image. His eyes glowed with an edge that could be nothing short of magic and power. His wings were soft, glossy, perfect, and his horns twisted from his crown. He was unmistakably powerful.

"Is this a trap?" I asked, gripping the cup tightly.

"Would you like it to be?" Samael answered my question with one of his own. He flashed a grin that was pure predator, and my skin prickled with warning. He leaned forward, sipping again at his spiced milky drink and asked, "What do I get if I capture you? What's my reward, Little One?"

"Uhh," I hesitated, my mouth had gone dry. Words fled my head before they could make it off the end of my tongue. My heart thumped. Was he flirting with me? "Well…" I floundered for an answer, suddenly unsure of every coherent thought I'd ever had. Hyperaware of his attention on me.

Samael only smiled wider, his eyes glimmering, as if he'd won a game. I didn't even know we were playing. I wondered vaguely if life with the devil would always be like that — straggling two steps behind him, trying to find the wit to keep up.

"Will you give me anything I want?" The devil asked. His voice was a soft, husky murmur that lit me on fire. I squirmed in the seat, suddenly glad we weren't sitting on the same couch. "Would you give me your body, mind, and soul?"

It felt difficult to breathe.

"Oh, so you just want my soul?" I finally murmured, struggling to keep my composure. The way he was looking at me made me feel like I was the only soul in existence. It threatened to light me on fire. "I — I should have known."

He rested his arms on his thighs, watching me so closely that I had to look away. Tipping my chin and staring through the glass ceiling, wishing that I was better at collecting myself. The orange sky had faded, consumed by the night, and stars twinkled above us. It did nothing to offer me a reprieve; I was all too aware of the intensity of his gaze.

When I peeked back, he was still staring at me. My heart thumped dangerously, and I looked away again.

"What are you doing?" I asked.

"Waiting for you to wake up, Octavia," he said, quite simply.

"What if…" I wet my lips, swallowing roughly and feeling like I was about to disappoint him. "What if I don't want to wake up yet? What if I want to stay here with you?"

Samael looked devastatingly grim. He set down his cup, tapping his slender fingers against his stubble-covered jaw. "Then, perhaps I've failed."

"Failed me or failed you?" I asked, unsure of which was better or worse.

"Both."

The solemnly spoken word hung between us, and suddenly, I wanted to cry. I wished I could open my mouth and force the question back in so that he would go back to looking at me adoringly, instead of as if I'd ruined everything.

The devil's next breath released as a hiss on the tip of his forked tongue, shaking himself lightly. Samael rose from his seat. He whistled, a sharp sound. In the distance, a beast howled in answer and moments later padded into the room.

A shaggy hellhound — as white as Samael's wings — stretched out beside the devil, who absently stretched behind its ears. Hungry yellow eyes settled on me, tracking every twitch I made. It was the biggest hellhound I'd ever seen, but strangely I wasn't scared, instead, I felt a bone-deep sadness at the loss of the floppy-eared pup in Glorae. I hadn't had her long, but she hadn't deserved to die at the hands of the rebels. Closing my eyes for a brief second, I reminded myself that she could have found her way free.

"Come on, Octavia." Samael held out a hand, face bright, expecting I'd do as he said.

He was right. I didn't hesitate to let him pull me to my feet.

"Where are we going?" I asked.

"I cannot force you to wake up," Samael said. "So, I won't waste my breath to convince you. We both know if stubbornness were a sin, you'd never win the trials. I'm going to selfishly indulge myself and show you around my realm."

"Oh." I liked that he called spending time with me, even in a dream, an indulgence.

Samael's mouth quirked with a hint of wry amusement. "Oh,

indeed."

His city glittered in the night, set along the banks of the river that had flowed from the mountain. It threw light across the river, the glassy surface reflecting it back, and in the dark sky there were more stars than I'd ever seen.

Samael had held me tight and flown us down, an experience that didn't give me half as much anxiety as flying with Pride. He'd moved slowly, drifting lazily on the wind, allowing me to soak in Eternis in all of its glory. Much like the realm he'd shown me before, from the old word, everything was built from tiny polished stones, creeping with ivy and tiny flowers that glowed beneath the starlight.

The wide windows showed they had nothing to hide. Many of them sat outside on tables and chairs, smoking lazily, cups in hand and smiles twisted onto their lips. There was a blatant peace within them I'd never seen amongst the humans. Their small quirks proved them to be more demon than human - horns, a second set of eyes, strange skin colour, talons, and wings.

Decadent scents wafted across the streets until my mouth watered, stomach rumbling loud enough to make Samael laugh. We strolled down the streets slowly. Samael had his fingers entwined in mine, his strong palm warm, and his pace deliberately slowed to keep in step with me instead of ushering me forward. His people smiled at him and greeted him, but also quickly moved out of his way.

Demons, as well as half-demons, old and young, filled the streets, chattering and shrieking.

"Eternis," the devil murmured. "Home to the misfits of magic that humans might otherwise condemn."

A complicated knot twisted in my stomach. I'd have liked to think that humans wouldn't condemn the small children running across the path, chasing bubbles and giggling brightly. Or the woman who looked mostly human except the hypnotic swirl of her eyes, which once I met them, entranced me until Samael shook me out of it.

I recognised how humans greeted Cyn with stiffness. People tolerated them but did not accept them. The rebellion would have used these people to make a point. A grand display that humanity wouldn't accept magic. They showed no compassion for those affected by sin or magic.

I felt numbingly sad, because I had been one of those people, once — who felt neglected and abused by the world of magic, forgotten and left to rot in the squalor of our small village. I'd resented the idea of the sins, and the magic they possessed. It had never helped me or mine.

Without the devil's presence and magic, I would have joined these people. Amid my dream, my shame burned bright.

Studying his people from the corner of my eye, I decided I could never fit in here; I would never smile so widely or feel so free.

"Why do you want me to succeed so badly, Samael?" I stopped walking, tugging his hand for his attention, and the devil glanced back over his shoulder. Despite his rebuke about fishing for compliments earlier, I wanted to know. "Why me?"

His dark brows sunk into a frown, his forehead creasing, accentuating the scar through his left brow. His jaw tightened and his lips pinched with obvious confusion. "Should I not want you to win?"

"But why me?" I repeated, gripping his hand tighter, in case he tried to slip away. "I'm not besting all the sins. I've had a lot of help to pass. And I'm not... like these people."

"This again!" Samael groaned, the confusion smoothing from his face. His dark wavy hair fell in front of his eyes as he narrowed them at me. "Don't you tire of being insecure, Little One? Are you not exhausted by your imposter syndrome?"

"I'm not insecure!" I objected quickly. I didn't know what imposter syndrome was, but I doubted he was offering it up as a compliment.

"Yes, you are, Octavia. Incredibly so."

Samael twisted on the spot, turning back to me and using our entwined hands to tug me forward. I stumbled on the cobblestones, and then he crushed me against his chest. He forcefully turned my head to face him, his wings rustling in annoyance. My hair fell, exposing my perceived imperfections. The parts of me that I wanted to hide.

The devil studied me closely, the shape of my face. He lingered on my scar and looked into my eyes. No matter how hard I tried to jerk my face from his grip, he didn't let me go. "Pride was mistaken, when he said you would pass his trial even without him granting you a passage through the final judgment. You have more pride than you think. You would cut off your nose in spite of your face."

The bridge of my nose prickled, and I inhaled sharply, trying to form the mess of my thoughts into words. Trying to think of something sharp and barbed to say back at him. Because his words hurt me, even if I didn't truly understand them. I knew he was telling me I should have failed that trial, and although it was something I'd always known, that I should have failed in front of Envy and again to Pride, it hurt more to come from the devil himself — from the one I'd always thought wanted me to win.

His tongue flicked, emitting a hiss of soft displeasure. "Insecurity is not the same thing as humility, but Pride's ego can make it hard for him to differentiate. Many have passed his challenges across the decades who the like should not have, yourself included. Let go of self-doubt and have faith in your capacity to succeed, Little One. It is the only way you will win." He was still staring into my eyes intently, the greens, gold, and pinks of his gaze distracting me from the point he was trying to breathe. "You should be confident. Think of all you have survived, before the trials and during."

"But…"

Samael's grip on my jaw tightened so hard that I was sure I'd bruise. "Do you know the purpose of the devil's trials? Do you know why I make you face each of the sins? I assure you it is not purely for entertainment."

"…No."

His lips thinned, his features flashing with indignant fury. "Then how do you presume to know what I seek in my competitors, and more, in the people I desire to see win? How do you presume to know what I want in my immortal companions?"

I was dancing along a precarious line. From the tension in his jaw, the colour staining across the dark hue of his skin, it was easy to tell that the devil didn't like anyone to think they knew what or why he did things.

"I…" I murmured, dropping my gaze. "I don't know, I guess."

"Exactly." Samael nodded, and when he let me go, I sagged with unexpected exhaustion. His arms wrapped around me, holding me tight against his strangely silent chest. A small reassurance after his pointed rebuke. I embraced the hug, craving affection like a touch-deprived woman.

Shifting, I glanced up at him. "What is it?"

"Hmm?" He blinked down at me. A muscle in his jaw still thrumming.

"The purpose of the devil's trials," I asked. "What is it?"

"Ha!" A chuckle rumbled in his chest, his familiar deep, husky amusement lightening some of the strain on my soul. When he laughed, I wanted to smile. "That's for me to know, and you to find out, Little One. Now, what do you want to do with a night in Eternis?"

Typical. I should have known he'd still refuse to tell me anything of use. Frowning at him, I studied some of his citizens from the corner of my eye. "Won't everyone be going to sleep soon?"

"Hardly!" The devil scoffed. "We are a nocturnal city. And this is all but a dream. Who sleeps in a dream, Octavia?"

Pulling back from him slightly, I considered what I wanted to do. Since this was a dream, and it surely was with the roguish angel beside me, I could do anything at all. The opportunities were endless.

"Can I meet someone who's won the trials?" I asked, as he re-threaded our hands together and led me further along the riverbank.

Samael stilled for half a step as if I'd surprised him. It took him a moment to recover, and I wondered why it had startled him.

"No," he said, finally. "It would not be the same. This is only a dream, Octavia. A poorly shaped mirage of the places you could go. I assure you my actual city is even better. If you want to meet an immortal soul, you must come to Eternis yourself."

I should have known he'd say that. He'd spoken before about tempting me to keep going. I bit down on my lip and glanced at the smooth surface of the river, the reflection of the stars. "What is there to do, then?"

"Plenty. We could have a meal? Explore the city." He paused again, and this time when he turned to look at me, he was smirking. "Or perhaps you'd like to play a game?"

"What sort of game?" I asked. Cautionary tales warned against playing games with the devil. The same very foolish thing I'd done by entering his trials. Every story had the same warning. You couldn't win against the devil.

"Cards," Samael said, wrapping a hand around my waist. His fingers brushed across my skin, tickling the underside of my breast, but smoothing pointedly over the tattoo Cyn had given me in the first trial. My lucky dice. "Isn't that your thing?"

Biting my lip, I shrugged.

It felt like forever since I played cards or held my lucky die. I took advantage of idle moments during the war to fleece soldiers of their money, and upon returning to Ilrea, I stole a moment to play. Since then, I'd barely thought about it. Hardly wanted it. I wasn't turning cards to survive any more, I didn't need the high of the win to convince myself that living through another day was worth it.

"I don't know…" I said, feeling slightly sick. In the past, I always knew what I wanted - to play and win.

"Are you telling me you don't want to play?" he asked, his full lips twisting into a wide smile. He paused in a doorway, and the splash of light from within crowned him, almost resembling a halo.

"I never said that," I snapped so quickly that it surprised me. My pulse raced at the idea of missing out. "But I want you to play too," I insisted, squeezing his hand and daring to look him in the eye. "I want to beat the devil at a game."

"That's unlikely, Octavia." He laughed. "But as you wish."

We sat in a small living room, on an assortment of large, decorated cushions. It was a room of about six players, and when Samael had entered, they'd all greeted him with soft deference. Shuffling to make room for the both of us. A man to my left smoked from a pipe, exhaling soft yellow smoke every now and again. It smelled sickly sweet, like the spun sugar I'd tried in Gula.

"The name of the game is Demon War," Samael told me. Everyone else held their own softly murmured conversations, watching us from the corner of their eyes. "You've played a variant before, I believe, they called it Tavern Wars?"

Shock jolted through me, and I jerked back from him, frowning. "You were listening back then?"

"Of course," he said with a wicked smile.

The trials had barely begun when I'd played that game. Samael had ignored me until I was knee-deep in mud at the Feast of Samael. When a woman across the room set down a stack of coins, I swallowed roughly. "I have nothing to bet with."

"I have been following you since the moment you signed your name and pledged yourself to me," Samael answered, as if watching the world from behind my eyes was inconsequential. "Check your pockets, Octavia."

When I did as he said, I found five thick, gold devil's coins in my left pocket. The coins were shiny, as if no one had ever touched or spent them before, with the devil's curled horns imprinted on the back.

Holding them in my hand, I wondered if I hadn't changed at all. I felt exhilarated holding the coins and anticipating the game. I wanted to keep it; I wanted to risk it; I wanted more. I bet I could turn five into twenty with ease. All I needed was a little luck.

Eying everyone else's bets, I licked my lips and leaned close to him. His wings brushed against the back of my neck, his body warm when he touched. "Refresh my memory on how to play, Samael."

"So bossy," he said, but he sounded amused. "In Eternis, they call it Demon War. It's much the same as the games you've played before. Easy to win, easy to lose. Favoured towards the dealer. The dealer deals a card to everyone, and if your card is higher than the dealer's, you win. Lower and you lose. If you match, we play a second card." He paused before asking, "Understood?"

I nodded. "Sir, yes, sir."

He smirked like he was the one who'd won, his eyes darkening with promise. "I like the sound of that."

My breath caught in my chest at the implication in his voice, my lips parting to force my next breath.

The devil laughed, flicking his fingers at the host who hovered in the corner of the room. "Bring us another drink."

The man scurried out of view and returned a moment later with more decorated glasses. He poured the same spicy milk concoction we had in his home into them, filling them to the brim.

The man passed out glasses to everyone in the room. I struggled not to spill it as I placed a coin in front of me, like the other players.

Glancing at Samael out of the corner of my eye, I asked. "Are you going to place your bet?"

"Oh, Octavia. I'm the dealer." He grinned, looking positively devilish. "You're in my city. My home and house always win."

Samael leaned into the centre of the game and retrieved the pack of cards. He shuffled them deftly, cut the deck and dealt. I should have known Samael would never enter a game as a normal player. He entered to win.

With the cards dealt, the players flipped them over, starting from Samael's left. I watched with interest what everyone did. I traced my fingers over the card's black back decorated with a golden-horned skull, similar to the coins we wagered.

I flipped the card. "Seven."

Samael gave me a wolfish grin. "King," he said before he'd even turned his card over. He snagged my coin, along with all the others.

"Deal again," I demanded softly, tossing a coin forward. I hid behind a sip of tea as he gave me a reprimanding look.

The next round flew by. He shuffled quickly and tossed down the cards.

"Four," I huffed, filled with the heavy dread of knowing that I'd lost this round already.

"King," he said, again.

"How lucky," I said, and laughter rippled around the circle. The man on my right offered me his pipe, and I shook my head. He shrugged, as if it didn't matter, and inhaled deeply. The soft cloud of yellow swirled around our heads. It made my eyes burn.

Samael dealt again after stealing away all our coins.

"Ha!" I cried when I flipped over my next hand, looking down at the letter inscribed on the side. I knew what that meant. "Jack."

Samael's eyes glittered with unconcealed mirth. He tapped his hand on the back of his card and didn't bother to turn it over. "King."

I frowned. "How do you keep drawing kings?"

Again, everyone laughed. This time, it felt like they were laughing at me, not with me. My cheeks heated, embarrassment flushing across the bridge of my nose.

Samael stroked his chin, rubbing at the shadow of stubble beneath his fingers, indulging me as he turned a coin between his slender fingers and said, "What can I say… I'm magic."

"You're a cheater," I accused. Across the room, a woman sucked in a sharp, shocked breath.

Samael twisted, leaning so close to me I felt overwhelmed by the spicy scent of him. He was instantly intimidating.

"Those are almost treasonous words, Little One, but I am the devil, and I *always* win." His forked tongue flicked out, brushing against my cheek. I blushed. "You're lucky I like you."

"Do you like me?" I asked. Lifting my chin as if I had all the confidence in Kaida, I challenged him, "Prove it."

The host set down a silver teapot in the middle of the circle, with a loud clatter. I ignored him, even as it began to tremble and bubble, a thick white mist spilling from the spout. It bubbled across the floor, rolling towards us. I'd seen that mist before, Sloth's miasma. My time was running out.

The woman who had gasped, with her locks of gold-spun hair, was there one minute and gone the next. The host, too. Samael turned closer to me, and if his tongue darted out, it'd land on my lips, not on my cheek.

He was mesmerising.

The man behind me disappeared, but I barely noticed, reaching for Samael, sliding my hands up his arms. A soft growl rolled from the back of his throat, and his head ducked closer to mine. I tipped my chin, well aware we were sharing breaths. He looked at me like I was everything, like it would cause him pain to lose me. His look conveyed everything I desired in life and dreams.

"Wake up…" Samael said.

"What?" I shuddered, overwhelmed by the sudden and harsh slap of rejection. "I thought you were going to kiss me."

He reached for me, cupping my face between his hands. They were warm against my skin. He compelled me to look at him, fixating on his full lips. Wishing that he'd kiss me goodbye.

"Octavia, listen to me, you need to wake up before…"

The miasma bubbled up around our waists, and just like everyone else, Samael disappeared.

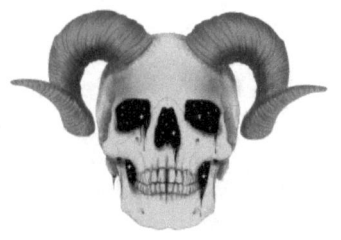

Chapter Twenty-One

The mist took over, flowing into my nose and mouth, paralysing my limbs as the world around me turned white. Endless, worse than heavy snowfall, it comprised nothing but infinite space and lost time. When Samael disappeared, I had thought I would too, but I had fallen prey to the miasma. Curling around my limbs, it trapped me, leaving me lost within a world of white.

Samael had told me to wake, but I struggled with the concept. Unable to work out how, or why I would pull myself out of this moment. Especially when nothing moved, not even me. I lay on the floor, trapped in the mist, lost in a moment of nothingness.

I saw grey wings and felt feathers against my spine. Distantly, I could hear the soft scuffle of movement, feet dragging against marble, ever so slowly. They took their time to approach.

I fought to breathe, move or do anything. Fought to wake, as the devil had ordered. My brain spun with a million thoughts, each coming and then slipping away, but my body remained useless.

The flash of grey wings again. If I could have, I would have tensed. Reminded of Pride and the hue of his feathers.

"No. Don't do that." Words spoken in a childlike voice. At the soft rebuke, my muscles relaxed, following the command. The footsteps grew closer, feathers flashed in my vision again, and lightheaded spinning took over. Not that anything could truly move when the world was blank, nothing but white mist and suspension. I felt untethered though, lost and drifting. A slow, cold voice drawled a clear demand. "Stay with me, Octavia. You'll like your next dream. I promise I'll give him back to you. That's what you want, isn't it? The devil... Samael... Lucifer... You'll take any of his forms."

Humming, a soft agreement, I closed my eyes and stopped fighting the miasma. I relaxed and gave in. I didn't need to wake yet. I would stay a little longer.

He swore. A blunt, low curse in an unfamiliar language. His hands wrapped around my body as my legs gave way and I crumpled to the floor. Voluminous skirts engulfed my body as I pressed my hands against the cold stone, struggling to breathe.

The devil hissed in his strange language, soothing me with his touch. Rubbing circles between my shoulder blades.

"Samael." His name spilled from my lips the moment I found my voice. I chanced a look up, to make sure I wasn't imagining it.

He was there, by my side, his wings tucked in tight, his horns polished and curling back towards his ears. His dark shadow of a beard accentuated his tense, sharp jaw. His thin nose flared, bright eyes narrowed, the only sign of his distress. There was something slightly different about him this time. He'd lost the ease and relaxation he'd had in Eternis.

Samael looked like... well, like he'd walked out of a dream. He wore a black shirt, the top buttons opened, exposing his collarbones and a small golden wishbone. His sleeves were rolled up to his elbows and his black leather pants hugged him like a second skin. He left his hair loose, allowing it to fall to his shoulders in a slight wave. His dark locks were kept in place by the thorned gold crown he wore. I noticed it matched the rings on his fingers and the earring in his left ear. He wasn't just dressed up for a special moment; he was decorated, adorned.

"Octavia," he said my name with a sigh, as if it were a prayer or a curse. "I thought I'd lost you to a dream without me. You should have woken before the miasma took you."

"I'm here," I whispered back, unable to look away from the thorny crown. He'd worn nothing like it before, and there was something about it that changed his face. His skin appeared darker against the gold, with pronounced shadows in his eyes and sharp cheekbones. His lips had a haughty turn, and he radiated a power that I had always known existed but never seen. This version of Samael was sharp.

"What happened?" he asked, his hand moving from my back to lift my chin, but he didn't hold my eye. Instead, he looked me over, as if checking for invisible scars. But as far as I knew, I was in one piece.

My mouth felt dry. I licked my lips, but it did nothing to help. "... I don't know. I don't remember."

Samael looked grave, but he nodded. He guided me by holding my shoulders and demonstrating deep breaths. Until I was breathing in time with him — because I'd never noticed him deliberately breathing before. I supposed, along with his non-beating heart, he might not need to do it.

"You need to stand," he told me, pulling me up with him as he rose. "Quickly now."

"Why?" I asked, feeling dizzy. The heavy skirts of my dress brushed around my ankles, and I glanced down, not entirely shocked to find myself in a different outfit. It was a different dream, but somehow, I missed the comfortable clothing of Eternis. The dress was a picture of the middle of the night. It could loosely be called black, if not for the hues of violet and navy woven through. It was generously opaque, a shimmering fabric that clung to my body. The corset enhanced my curves and flowed into a skirt. Technically, it covered me. It proudly displayed every scar on my skin, visible above and beneath the fabric.

Staring down at my body in horror, I felt my eyes prickle and tried not to cry. A lump grew in my throat as I self-consciously wrapped an arm across my chest and placed a hand over my scars to hide them.

Samael let out a hiss. "Don't. You look stunning, Octavia."

"No, I don't," I whispered, unable to look at him. "I look broken."

His fingers caressed my face, the scarred side. He always touched that side of my jaw, as if he preferred it to my unblemished skin. He tucked my hair behind my ear. He slid his fingers down my neck, the soft touch making my thighs clench in answer, before he pulled away. "Perhaps your strength, despite being broken, is what makes you particularly stunning. The world has no time for perfection, not anymore."

"You're just saying that."

"Believe what you will," Samael said, after a pause. "But I know what I know."

He took my hand, squeezing it gently, and waited with more patience than I deserved for me to look up at him. I pulled in an unsteady breath and tried to piece myself back together. "What are we doing?"

His lips thinned into a grim line. "Sloth has dropped you into an active dream, Octavia. One not born of your imagination, but of a collective," Samael said. "We must let it play out."

I frowned, shifting my weight and realising I was barefoot. The stone floors chilled the soles of my feet. "Can't you change the dream? Can't you pick what we do, like you did before?"

The other dreams felt like his creations, not Sloth's, especially when he let me choose what to do.

"No. This dream is partly mine. In reality, I am also sleeping," he said, shaking his head. His grim expression didn't fade. "Octavia, look up and look alive. We're in the old world again. We're in my second home, the realm of death and today... Well, today is a grand celebration."

"What's wrong with that?" I asked, his discomfort left me wary. "You look unhappy, Samael."

He glanced away, but only for a moment. "This is not a celebration for the living to bear witness, whether they are dreaming or not. This is dangerous for you, Octavia."

He took my hand, and I stared down at our entwined fingers, at the gold rings he wore, one thick one with an emblem stamped on it dug into the side of my finger uncomfortably. "I don't understand."

"Of course you don't, and how could you? This is beyond the expanse of human imagination. Even in your wildest dreams, you would not have come here."

"Why do I feel like you're insulting me..." Inhaling deeply, I tried my hardest not to feel hurt at the tone of his voice, at the fury still etched into every feature. He kept looking past me, and I twisted, trying to see what had caught his attention.

Samael caught my face before I could focus, drawing me back to him. His hands were icy against my skin and one of his rings grazed my cheek. "Octavia, I'm not insulting you. Look at me. You must focus," he spoke with so much authority, that I obeyed automatically, looking into his eyes, listening carefully. "You must stay close to me all night long, do you understand? You must not eat anything you are offered. You must not drink, no matter how parched you feel. Most importantly, you must not let any of them touch you, and I promise they will try."

"What?" I was beyond confused.

His wings rustled, and I supposed I should have said yes sir again. But I didn't understand, my head spinning with the gravity of his tone. I twisted to look over my shoulder again, but we were alone in the quiet hall, and I didn't know what dangers he was alluding to.

"Your human soul is a bright spark in a sea of darkness. The creatures at this celebration... They will be attracted to you. But you must not let them touch you. Promise me," Samael said, voice urgent, eyes blazing when I looked back at him. "Sloth is playing a dangerous game, throwing you into a dream where old magic still exists. A dream used for the meeting of souls. This is not just a dream, it's a level of reality. A dimension you never should have been able to access."

"What happens if they touch me, Samael?" I dared to ask, even though I had the creeping feeling that I didn't want to know the answer.

He went still, too still. His face smoothed out and the light in his eyes shuttered. "You die, Octavia."

"What?" I asked, my lip curling with disbelief. "No. You said it yourself, I'm sleeping. It's only a dream."

The devil's expression turned sad, almost pitying. That look rocked me to my core. "Plenty of humans die in their sleep, do they not? You would join them. You need to trust what I'm saying. Promise me you will avoid their touch?"

"Samael," I said, wanting him to take it back, or explain it better. "I promise. But..."

"Hush," he said, pressing a long finger against my lips. The thorned ring prickled against my skin, drawing a bead of blood that he quickly wiped away. "We need to enter the ballroom now."

"Why?" I asked, filled with anxious jitters and suddenly unable to stand still. I fisted my hands in my skirt. "Why can't we just leave? Let's do something else."

"Because I am the devil, Octavia," Samael said. "While that might only mean oppression and suffering to humanity, I have existed for longer than your world has been a spark in the universe. The sins were virtues in the old world, but I have always been the devil. Long have I ruled over the dead, and death-adjacent, and some rituals must always be attended. Including this one."

"Samael…" I breathed his name again, a second plea. His warnings left me antsy. I didn't want to do this, not now, not ever.

"Hold your head high, Octavia. Lift your chin." He took my hand, gripping it tightly, and this time we walked briskly, at his pace instead of mine. We approached the dark doors, and they flew open ahead of us, anticipating his presence. Samael led me forward with one last instruction, "Walk in like you own the world."

It was easier said than done… To strut at Samael's side as if I belonged there, to stop myself from pausing and staring, because I thought with his demons, I'd seen everything. But not yet. Here I found the creatures of horror and nightmares, and everything in between. The ballroom was a large platform suspended among the clouds and stars.

Soft, sensual music played as creatures stood together, some dancing, others chatting, all pausing to watch us enter. My skin burned, I was all too aware of their attention.

"My prince," a skeleton greeted Samael, stepping forward. His bones were old, yellowed, and his eyes were nothing more than dark hollows. The sight of him stole my breath, but he paid me no mind. Instead, he bowed low and scuttled out of the way.

"Welcome, Lucifer," rasped a woman in a dark cloak. She had a long-handled, sinister blade held loosely by her side. She drew close, too close, a thin, greyed hand reaching for my arm.

I recoiled into Samael's side and out of her reach. He hissed at her, a sharp warning, and the woman backed away.

Samael led me forward, his constant movement propelling me until we reached a giant throne. Just like his seven sins, it seemed Samael could not resist one. He threw himself into it, while I stood awkwardly next to him, his hand holding mine, thumb gently stroking my hand. A small, comforting movement that did wonders for my nerves.

"Do continue your celebrations," he boomed with a wave of his free hand. His command echoed across the stone platform, and instantly, the creatures turned back to their companions. It didn't take long, though, for the first of them to brave approaching the throne.

A decaying man, with flesh peeling away from his face to reveal the bones beneath, approached us. He held out two glasses. Samael took one without a word. He pressed another towards me, and suddenly my mouth felt bone dry. I licked my lips, swaying on the spot. The soft bubbling liquid looked so tempting. But before I could reach for it, Samael waved him off.

I licked my lips again, conscious of how dry my mouth felt. How badly I wanted a drink.

"Don't smile, but smirk," Samael instructed, not looking at me. I stared at him as if he had grown three heads, certain that nobody knew how to smirk on command. "Imagine you are above them all — and you are, Octavia. Remember that. You are the devil's companion tonight. If they could touch you, they should kiss your feet."

"Who are they?" I asked, whispering to him. Conscious of who might hear us. Some creatures drifted in our direction, but thought better of it, turning back to the crowd, again.

"The dead and the dying. The goddesses of death. The judges of the afterlife. Specters, and reapers alike. Death is a magic that crosses time, and worlds itself. In the past, people celebrated the Day of the Dead on a regular basis, but now it serves as a time when those who symbolize the afterlife come together. Twice a year, we cross dimensions and time to meet in a dream."

"And you?" I almost didn't want to ask. Not when he sat on a throne of skulls with a crown of thorns. Not when creatures had bowed their heads as he passed. "If that's who they are, who are you?"

"Oh, Octavia." His rasping laugh drew their attention, again. I shuddered as he answered. "I'm the king of the dead."

Before long, two bold, reedy, thin creatures approached. They had pointed features, dark eyes, and dark lips. Their hair, one silver and the other black, was piled on top of their head to showcase their necks.

They were as decorated as Samael, and the one with the silver hair adorned herself with a necklace of bones in varying lengths, pulling it tight around her throat as if it might choke her and fanning it across her cleavage. Her darker counterpart wore a stack of bracelets on each arm. When she drew closer, I realised she had adorned herself with tiny human teeth.

"Lucifer, you're here! Better late than never," the dark-haired one crooned. She leaned over Samael, placing her hands on his shoulders and kissing his cheek. My body flushed hot at the sight of it, proving I'd never really defeated my envy. Despite the way Samael squeezed my hand so tight that my knuckles cracked, I looked away.

The woman leaned towards me, as if to kiss me too. Samael wrenched my arm back, hard. Pulling me pointedly from her reach.

She clucked her tongue and raised a thin brow. "I've never known someone to be continuously tardy to parties in his own honour."

"Ker." The devil greeted her with a lazy smirk, offering a slow dip of his chin to acknowledge them. He glanced at her counterpart briefly before averting his gaze, appearing bored.

"Moros. Good to see you both."

"Who's this?" Ker asked, seizing me up. Her attention made my skin crawl, as if little spiders had burrowed beneath it and scuttled around. I couldn't bring myself to meet her eyes, suddenly filled with fear about what I might find there, about the small intimacy she just shared with Samael.

The devil's tone turned icy. "She's all mine, I'm afraid. You know I don't like to share."

"Why she's positively glowing…" Moros called from a step behind Ker. When she smiled, it was a flash of sharp, black teeth and elongated fangs. "Lucifer, did you bring a live one for us to play with?"

Ker laughed, a deadly sound that chilled me to the bone. "Mmm, are we passing judgment on the humans tonight? Want a little help in your rag-tag realm?"

"Not at all." Samael uncrossed his ankle from his knee and stood from his throne, placing himself between me and the women. He stared down his nose at them with a chilling look of command. "You will leave her be. She's here as my guest."

"Where's the fun in that?" the dark-haired one murmured. She moved into my line of sight again. "Come out from behind the big bad devil, Little One." She raised a bony finger and beckoned.

Her use of the nickname Samael had given me sent a shudder down my spine. Samael turned rigid, a low growl rumbling in his chest when she came too close.

She continued, undeterred. "Ker, my sister, is the goddess of brutal deaths and I'm Moros, the goddess of impending doom. I'm sure you've felt my influence before. I see there's trauma behind those eyes. You know how it feels to be on the brink of death. Who are you, child?"

"I'm Octavia," I said, feeling compelled to answer.

Samael flashed his fangs in warning, shifting to slide between us again. His grip on my hand was so tight that his ring had pierced my skin. Blood dripped down my fingers, and Moros watched it fall against my skirts.

"Don't speak to them," he hissed. I blinked and felt chastised, dropping my attention to my feet.

"Pay no mind to him. He is so terribly rude." Moros dismissed the devil as a minor inconvenience. She was nothing if not persistent. "Come with me, us ladies shall chat. You can leave the devil to his brooding."

"Actually," Samael said, his tone icy, grip so tight that I thought he might break my hand. "I think it's time to dance. Shall we, Octavia?"

He swept me onto the floor before I could agree or protest. Ker reached after me as we moved. My breath caught in my throat, and sickeningly I wondered if I truly would die should she touch me. Her fingers narrowly missed my cheek.

Samael led me into the crowd of dancers, who parted for him, her laughter trailing behind us. It took every ounce of strength I had not to look back. I thought that if I looked at her, she would come for me again, and this time Ker would be unavoidable.

"My heart's racing," I told Samael. He placed my hand on his shoulder, sliding one of his hands up my back. He caressed my exposed skin, his touch forcing me to straighten. He took my other hand in his, holding it tight, and when he moved, I followed.

"I know," he said, pressing his lips into a thin line. "We can all hear it."

"What do you mean?" I asked.

Dancing with Samael was different to dancing with Pride. When he'd first suggested it, before pulling me away from the throne, my entire stomach had dropped, because I'd long since learned that dancing with an angel was a spectacularly bad idea. I felt safer in his arms than I ever had with Pride, though. The dance felt smoother.

Samael's head tilted, and a lock of dark hair fell across his eyes. "Octavia, this is the realm of the dead. Nobody here has a beating heart, nobody but you."

"I…" It shocked me to hear, although I didn't know why. I'd had my head laid on his chest in more than one dream and realised how quiet his chest was, but it hadn't occurred to me that I was the only living being here. Somehow, this dream now felt a little more real, and a lot more dangerous. My palms turned sweaty, and my throat turned dry.

"Can't you feel it?" he asked, twirling me through the room, our pace increasing slightly. "The way the music rises and falls. The tempo keeping to the beat of your ricocheting pulse. The dancers are falling into step with every subtle change in pace, swirling to the soft hum of your life. We're not dancing to music, Little One, we're dancing to the beat of your life."

He was spitting these words through clenched teeth, tension corded in his neck. He glared around the room, ensuring nobody came close, and the circling couples all shifted away.

"Samael…" I said his name a third time since I woke in his dream. Another soft plea. The fury in his eyes scared me. "Are you angry with me?"

"I *am* angry," he snarled the words. "Not at you. I'm furious that Sloth has put you in this position at all."

"You don't have to protect me, not if you don't want to." I bit my lip, swallowing hard and forcing the words out. My entire body was aching with dismay because I wanted him to stand between me and these creatures. A powerful, indisputable shield. But I'd walk across the platform alone if he didn't want to deal with me. "I won't be a burden to you."

"Octavia," He growled. His eyes flared with light, narrowing on my face so intently that I couldn't look away. "Am I wasting my breath convincing you to continue to live? Begging you to find me in the heart of Kaida? Do you actually want to die? If you do, just tell me."

He spun me around and around the room. Now that I knew the music was following my pulse, I couldn't ignore the thump,

thump, thump within me.

"No," I whispered, finally. "I promise you, I want to live."

His nostrils flared. "Then why would you say such stupid things."

Frustration welled up inside of me, along with a wave of emotion that pushed me to the cusp of tears. "I'm not trying to be stupid. Samael, I don't want…" I faltered.

"You don't want what?" he snapped. "Do you think it is a risk for me to stand between you and the many faces of death, despair, and decay? Do you think they can hurt me?" He allowed a pause for contemplation. "If so, you think very little of me, Octavia. I tire of your underestimations. You must understand who I really am."

"You said their magic could reach me," I protested, although not with much conviction. "You said that it could kill me."

"You, Octavia. Not me." He dipped his chin, offering me a long, pointed look. "They cannot steal what does not beat. The devil doesn't die." He spun me quickly, his hand sliding down my back and he lowered me into a dip. I saw the crowd's hungry look as I glanced around the room.

He pulled me back up, pulled me close, in a bold, swirling movement, until I was pressed tight against his chest, breathless. "I will stand as the shield between you and death for as long as I need Octavia. I promise you, that for as long as you desire life, for as long as there is a possibility of you reaching me, then I will stand between death and your soul."

Inhaling sharply, I lifted my chin to look at him, lips parted with a question.

"Uh-uh!" Samael admonished me before I could speak. "Do not ask me why. If you don't know by now, then I won't answer."

"But…"

He cut my protest off with a sharp look. My pulse still thumped, nerves jittery as unanswered questions filled me. If he wouldn't answer, then I wouldn't ask, and I simply let him twirl me around the room.

We couldn't dance forever, especially not as the crowd drifted closer, again. Each of our turns became dangerous, some of his people reaching out in attempts to touch me. Samael growled whenever they approached, causing them to retreat, unapologetic. I understood that the temptation of claiming my soul might be worth the consequence for them.

"What do I do, now, Samael?" I asked him, feeling claustrophobic, unsure of where this dream could go next. Would there be any other end to this than death, any other way to escape?

"Now?" he asked, turning the full force of his attention back to me. His eyes glowed, his fangs flashing. "Do explain what you mean by that."

"If you're shielding me from death…" He twisted, putting himself between my body and a reaper. "What do you need me to do?"

He frowned at me. He tapped two of his fingers against my back, a slight reprimand.

"I've told you, Octavia." Samael didn't sound annoyed, but the crease in his brow deepened. "You must wake up."

"I don't know how to wake. I would, if I could."

"Yes, you do." He gathered me close, hooking his arm around my waist and crushing me against him. I closed my eyes for a second, my forehead pressed against his chest. "You can wake up at any time. It's only a dream."

"A deadly dream."

"Albeit that," he said. I had the distinct impression that if the consequences weren't so dire, he'd find this funny. "Wake yourself, Octavia. Come find me in reality."

"Are you waiting for me, Samael?" I asked, desperate for his validation.

"Always."

We spun, one last time and he dipped his head, brushing his lips against mine. When he pulled back, I could see my reflection shining in his eyes. He let me go, and reached for my face, holding me tight. His transformed into sorrow. A reaper approached from the left, his scythe outstretched.

"Now, Octavia. Do it now. Wake."

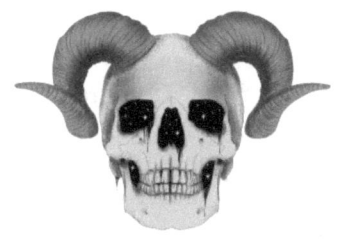

Chapter Twenty-Two

"Thank the devil!" Maksymilian cried. His flaming red hair swam in and out of my blurred vision. I focused hard on his face, which was pale, freckled and full of concern. "You're awake. *Finally*."

"Max?" I croaked. The mattress beneath me was one of the softest I'd ever felt. It shifted beneath my body as Max crawled closer, the springs sinking beneath his added weight.

"You've been asleep for weeks," he said. He slumped down onto the pillow beside me and curled close to my body, smelling distinctly of sweat and chuckleweed. "I had to keep checking to make sure you weren't dead. There were a couple of close calls."

"Never. I'm hard to kill," I said, rubbing at my head, a familiar headache setting in above my left eye. I felt hungover, completely parched. My head had not adjusted to reality. Closing my eyes, I can still see Samael twirling me around the ballroom.

"I feel like death," I groaned, fighting a yawn.

"I can imagine," Max chuckled. He sat up, reaching for a glass on the nightstand.

"Here." He helped me put it to my lips. "Drink something."

It was water, cold and wildly refreshing, but I'd half been expecting the spiced tea from my dreams. For a flickering moment, I felt sad, missing something I'd never truly tried. Mostly I missed the devil, though, craving a few more moments between his pure intensity and magnetic power.

"What happened while I was out?" I asked.

While most of the time, my dreams and nightmares had slipped away from me when I woke. This time, I remembered every little detail and mourned leaving it behind. I wondered if the world had moved on while I slept for what felt like a lifetime.

"The snow has finally stopped falling, which feels like a dangerous sign. But beyond that, nothing has changed." He shrugged, setting down the glass and flopping back against the pillow. "I've been carrying you each day. Did you know you're damn heavy when you're sleeping? I think I'm the fittest I've ever been now."

He flexed one of his arms, showing off his muscles, and I rolled my eyes.

"What about sleeping?" I asked, frowning. "You, I mean. Not me."

"What about it?" He turned his head, blinking at me, and I could tell he really had no idea what I meant.

"How have you managed to wake up?" I asked. I'd had to wake him up before, and I doubted he was immune to Sloth's power. Max was a lot of things, but he was definitely only human.

"What do you mean?" he asked. "I go to sleep, snooze for a while. Then I wake up and keep going."

Staring at the roof, I considered it and shook my head. "It's got to have been longer than two weeks then, Max."

"Definitely not," He protested, sounding utterly offended. He scrubbed his hands across his face. "I've been keeping track of how long you've been sleeping. I walked for thirteen days before we got here." He paused, huffing. "I don't lie, Octavia."

"I know you don't," I said, cringing at the placating edge in my tone. "And I know you think you're telling the truth. But there's no way that you've only slept a few hours at a time. It's just not possible with Sloth."

"Octavia Nox. I swear..." He was sitting up now, his face clouded over. He looked ready to argue. Reaching for him, I pressed my palm over his mouth to cut off his protests. I didn't have the energy to fight.

"Agree to disagree," I said, narrowing my eyes in warning that he better not lick me again. Peeling my hand away from his lips, I asked, "Where are we?"

"It's a town called Nuriv." Max shuffled back on the bed, and I followed suit, perched beside him. He looked conflicted. "The people here... They're awake, Octavia."

"What?" I snorted. "That's..."

"I know. Weird, right?" he agreed, nodding. After so many ghost towns and so many empty steps, it felt impossible to see another living, breathing human being. "They said their cycle ended five nights ago. They have a year to live their lives, and if I'm honest, they look utterly miserable about it. I've never seen a bigger collective of sour faces, and I lived with Chester for a long time."

That drew a throaty laugh from deep within my chest. "How long have we been here?"

"Three days," he admitted, pulling the components of a smoke from his pocket. "I'm glad you woke up, though. Besides the not being dead part, they told me you're running out of time."

"How would they know how much time I have left?" I asked, confused.

"They always wake up as the trial ends," Max said with so much confidence that I blinked. But then he shrugged. "Or so they said. I guess we have to trust them."

"Oh." I fidgeted with the blanket. I realised I hadn't confirmed if I was still dreaming, if I had truly woken up from the Day of the Dead. I traced my fingers over the four familiar tattoos, feeling relaxed. Closing my eyes, I searched for Samael, the soft brush of his presence against my awareness making my heart soar.

'Welcome back, Little One.'

"Don't call me that anymore," I murmured. "Not after Moros."

'As you wish.'

Max pointedly glared at me, reaching over to flick me on the side of the face. "Don't check out to talk to him while I'm talking to you! We've got to get moving, and you've slept long enough." He grumbled about the devil as he got off the bed and paused in the doorway, scowling at me. "Now get up and wash, because you stink."

"Oi!" I cried, picking up the pillow and flinging it at him, but it fell to one side.

He looked for a second like he was going to laugh at me.

Before he disappeared, I called out, "Hey Max?"

He reappeared, mouth puckered with soft concern. His gaze raked over me in quick assessment, and I fought back a smile.

"Thanks for looking after me while I was out," I said quietly, having decided he deserved my gratitude. For not leaving me in the snow. When he probably should have — my sleeping body couldn't have been an easy burden to bear.

He shrugged like it was nothing. "You'd have done it for me, right?"

Max disappeared before I could answer, but I thought about that long after I'd scrubbed my skin clean, long after the water had turned cold. He'd beat on the door, telling me to get out or he was coming to make sure I hadn't drowned. It was then that I decided he was right. I would have done it for him too, dragged him across the land to make sure he was safe.

I couldn't figure out when Maksymilian Tate became

important to me.

Despite their dishevelled appearance and mourning rituals, the people of Nuriv remained remarkably giving. They let us stay one final night and then plied us with more food than we could carry. As the chancellor escorted us to the boundary of their village, I clutched a bag of hot roasted chestnuts.

"It's less than a day's walk," he said gruffly. His smile lacked warmth, with only a faint movement of his lips. "That's it, and you'll be at Desidia. You can see Sloth and be free of this challenge at last."

"Thank you," Max said to him, sincere in every word. "For everything you've done for us."

The chancellor ducked his chin, already backing away from us. "It is the least we can do."

We walked in relative silence until we finished the nuts and I tucked crumpled paper in my pocket. We walked until Max couldn't handle the silence anymore.

"Maksymilian's factoid of the day," He announced suddenly.

I recoiled, staggering to a halt. "What did you say?"

He glanced over his shoulder, not slowing his pace. His calm smile betrayed nothing. "You heard me. I know your ears work, Octavia."

It had been a blow to the chest, so hard that I felt off-kilter. I'd convinced myself that every moment of that dream had been just that. Nothing more than a dream, but his grin told me otherwise. He twisted the lighter in his hand, spinning it around and around as he frowned, deep in thought. My heart thumped harder from within the confines of my ribs, and I wondered if I was truly awake. Or if Sloth didn't have a complete and unrelenting hold on me.

"Teeth are the only part of the body that doesn't heal," Max announced from ahead of me.

I didn't respond, not right away, as I tried to process what he was saying. There was a lump in my throat, and the threat of emotion prickling across the bridge of my nose. Finally, I scoffed. I trusted that this was my reality. I brought factoids into the dreams and the angel tricked me with threads of reality. I had a trust that this was the real Max.

Throwing my hands in the air, I said, "That one has to be a lie."

He slowed down, giving me a minute to catch back up to him. When I got close, Max nudged me. His expression turned serious. "I told you, I never lie. You need to believe that, Octavia. It's important to me."

Sucking in my lower lip, I nodded slowly. "I believe you."

I just didn't understand why it mattered to him that I believed it.

We walked without stopping until my legs ached and my head throbbed. The ice surrounding Desidia shimmered beneath the light, just as the people of Nuriv had described. A winding stream that once might have been water, but now only resembled layers of ice. Even though the snow had stopped falling days before, it still piled at the banks of the river.

It was then that the fear set in. Suddenly, I couldn't walk any further. Stuck on the cusp of the ice-covered bridge, staring into a city of spindly naked trees, smattered with snow. I was on the edge of the fifth trial, so close to the angel that my muscles locked with fear. Bile rose in the back of my throat, and I closed my eyes, trying to even out my breathing. It was an inevitable confrontation, but even after battling and facing angels for so long, the idea of confrontation still made me sick to my stomach.

Large wrought iron gates marked the entrance of Desidia. Set with pale blue stones, and iron snowflakes, they loomed in the distance. The city lay quiet beyond them. We were close enough that we should have been able to hear the bustle of people and life. But all I could hear was the chirping of birds in the trees, and the crackle of Max's smoke as he inhaled deeply.

It took him a moment to realise I'd stopped walking. He twisted to look back at me, his thick brows raised with questioning. "Are you coming? We're here."

My answer lodged in my throat, and so I shook my head. My hands had trembled, but I didn't want him to see, burying them in the pockets of my coat.

Max blinked. He looked thrown at my response. Snuffing out his smoke in the snow, he took a tentative step back towards me. He held out a hand, his fingers curling as they beckoned me forward. His blue eyes widened, and the idea struck me that he was treating me like a wild beast. Liable to attack or flee.

"Come on," Max coaxed. "You're almost done."

"But…" I wrapped my arms around my middle, squeezing tight. The pressure did nothing to help my building fear. "What if this isn't the end? The clue wasn't clear. What if there's more? I'm so tired Max."

"What do you mean?" he asked, frowning. He raked his fingers through his long hair. "The clue said you had to find Sloth. This is where she'll be…" He gestured towards the city,

"It's never this easy," I whispered, watching him wide-eyed and unwilling to step onto the bridge. "You don't understand."

Max scoffed, his entire face crumpling. His hands fisted, dropping to his side. "You think getting here has been easy? Have we been walking the same path?"

"You don't understand," I repeated. "Usually there's something we have to do. Don't eat the heart, find restraint. Steal the stone, show kindness. Wage war, have patience… Demonstrate humility… I'm not… This is different. I haven't

313

done anything."

"I don't have a clue what you mean." Max began patting at his pockets, searching for another smoke. He had found weed in Nuriv and it calmed him down. It stopped his hands from trembling and brought the over-confident drawl back to his voice. "You've done exactly what the card asked you to do. You made it to Desidia, almost. Come on, Octavia."

Shaking my head, I edged back a step. "What if she demands I do something horrible? What if…"

"Like what?" he asked, stepping forward. His face set, features filled with determination, as he crossed back over the ice bridge to follow me. "What could she possibly ask of you? You can't live your life wondering *'what if'*… That's not living. You'll never get out of your head. You'll never win, and I know you can win, Octavia. You and me, we're going to Eternis."

"Like anything… She could demand anything of me, and I'd have to do it. I'd be forced to obey or forfeit to her. These angels have complete control. They…" I twisted my fingers beneath the leather strap secured around my thigh, running my finger against the handle of the deadly blade.

My heart squeezed, haunted by past impossible orders that I still had to obey. Even now, I marched on Eternis to complete them, or risked feeling Pride breathe down the back of my neck. Pride was a trauma I hadn't overcome, and I feared being bound by Sloth. That I could win the Devil's Trials and still end up secured to these sins, stuck in their debt.

Aware of my obligations, I wondered if I could have fulfilled Pride's demands by stabbing Samael in my dreams. If I could have freed myself. I hated myself for not thinking of it sooner.

Max started towards me, pausing only long enough to light his smoke and take that first, long drag. "Tell me what you think she's going to ask of you, Octavia?"

"What if she asked me to kill you…" I whispered, cocking my head and meeting his eye.

"You wouldn't," he said. His step had faltered though, and Max almost slipped on the ice beneath us. He shook his head, more for himself than me, and fidgeted with the coin around his throat. He stopped in front of me. "Of course you wouldn't."

"You don't understand, Max," I said, reaching to untangle his grip, squeezing his hand tight. "I'd have to do it. If Sloth asked, I have to follow her orders."

"No, Octavia. You'd have a choice, there's always a choice. And you would choose not to kill me. We've walked this far with your nastily big knife strapped to your thigh and you haven't stabbed me in my sleep yet."

"But…"

Max inhaled, and exhaled, blowing the soft smoke between us. He was firm when he continued, "I trust you not to kill me. No matter what Sloth demands."

My teeth pinched against my lower lip. The idea of someone trusting me left me shivering. I didn't deserve that level of friendship. "Maybe you shouldn't put that much faith in me."

"Octavia Nox, listen to me." Max all but yelled at me. "I trust you."

"You're an idiot," I countered. "You're going to get yourself killed."

"I know," Max admitted. He shrugged, flippantly. "But you're stuck with me because you promised to take me to the end. A deal's a deal, Octavia."

"Max…" I said his name gently, ready to tell him he shouldn't believe my promises. Ready to admit that I didn't think I'd kept a single one in my entire life. He dropped the smoke, having inhaled it too quickly, crushing the red ember beneath the toe of his boot. He moved to cup my face with his hands. So similar to the way Samael had held me in my dream that my heart stuttered in my chest. "Max…"

"You'll do it, Octavia. Everything you promised me and more," Max said, looking as if he truly believed it. He stroked my cheeks with his thumbs and stared intently into my eyes. I could see myself reflected in his blue irises. "You might not have faith in yourself, but I have enough in you for the both of us."

A spluttering noise rolled from deep in my chest. He was being foolish. More than foolish, stupid. There was no reason for him to trust me, not really. There was nothing I'd done that earned it.

"That's ridiculous, why would you—"

He cut me off. "Because you have the devil in your corner." Max was calm and matter-of-fact about it. "He wouldn't be there if he didn't want you to win. Despite him whispering in your ear, Octavia, I believe you're still an inherently good person. You might be someone who's been told their whole life that they're not, but you're good enough for me."

My body turned hot and cold in quick succession. Anxiety became a noose around my neck, and it was suddenly too hard to breathe. I stared at him hard, trying to ignore the building tears that stung my eyes. "I don't think anyone's ever told me that before."

"Which part?" he asked, not backing down from the challenge or from my emotions. When the tears spilled over, more scared than grateful, he brushed them away. "Tell me."

"That I'm good enough."

"Pfft," Max scoffed, his warm brown eyes rolling. "Now, who's the one lying? I couldn't be the first one to have ever told you that." Straightening, he tapped his fingers against my scarred cheek and nodded. "Now, dig deep, get a pep talk from that monster in your mind, and let's enter that city. I've got my first Sin to meet."

He sounded strangely optimistic. As if he'd wanted nothing more than to meet one of the seven deadly sins, and I didn't know how to crush that joy. I wanted to remind him that the angels were dangerous creatures. His life was better lived without having met them, but the words wouldn't form.

'He's right, you know,' Samael said, startling me.

Heaving a sigh, I whispered, "I think he'd be ecstatic if he could hear you say that."

'He's not the first to tell you that you're enough,' the devil continued firmly. *'I was.'*

"Is it a competition?" I asked, thinking of the devil but staring at the redheaded man. Both of whom seemed to go out of their way to lift me up. Pushing me to continue through the trials. Both had their own reasons for wanting me to keep going. "Neither of you needs to be the first."

'For your affections?' Samael growled softly. *'I'm thinking it might be a competition, after all. Although it would be all too easy to remove him, and as I said in your dream. The devil always wins.'*

"It's not. He's not a threat, Samael," I said sharply, and a little too loudly. It drew Max's attention, and he studied my face intently. Ignoring him, I continued, "Max doesn't like me. He just needs me."

Samael snorted, brushing against my mind before his presence ebbed away. *'You're not stupid, Octavia, but sometimes, you're not very bright, either.'*

"Hey!" Max cried, reaching to tap me on the nose and demand my attention. His face had screwed up, his cheeks turning red as he scowled. "I heard that. Stop telling that bastard lies."

"It's not a lie," I told him. Folding my arms across my chest, I stared him down stubbornly. "I'm learning to tell the truth from you, remember? Honesty is the best policy, or whatever."

Max stared at me. "When did I ever say that I didn't like you?"

"Uh." I tried to think of an example. I was sure there'd been a time or two, but I couldn't recall them.

"Exactly" He sounded smug. Moving closer, he looked me dead in the eye — not looking to see me, but Samael. His stare hard. "It's my turn now, Devil. Leave her alone. Octavia and I have a bridge to cross." He gestured at it, the slope of pure ice that separated us from the gates of Desidia. "Literally."

He took my hand and held on tight. His jaw set with a stubborn edge, and without hesitation, Max led me towards the bridge. "Why are you both making this a competition?" I groaned.

Max ignored the comment. "Take it slow, stepping onto the bridge. It's going to be… Completely shit."

He wasn't wrong.

My feet slipped out from under me at least four times as we tried to cross the bridge. Each hard landing came with a crunch of bone and screaming ligaments. Twice, I knocked into him, bringing him down with me. The first time we fell, Max was full of curses, but the second time he laughed. He hauled me to my feet.

"Keep going, Octavia, we're almost there." Max shuffled forward to the top of the bridge and, much to my surprise, then he sat down.

"What are you doing?" I asked him, wondering if he'd hit his head on his last fall. "Get up."

He grinned at me, wide and carefree, proving that Max Tate didn't hold on to anything for very long. Not when there were the little moments of life to be lived.

"This…" He leaned forward and pushed his hands against the icy bridge and propelled him onto the descending half. In one swift, slippery move, he slid to the bottom of the bridge. Rolling into the piles of half-melted snow that waited for us below. White flakes smattered through his hair, his freckled skin pink from the cold.

"Come on, Octavia." Max beckoned me forward with a wave of his arms. "Don't be scared!"

His wording made me angry. Inexplicably angry. My hands fisted by my side and I glared at him from on top of the bridge. I'd faced more than he'd ever understand, and he thought I was scared of the ice? Suddenly I wasn't cold, a flash of fury heating me from the inside out.

Max was unaffected by my emotions. He met my glare with a lazy grin, folding his arms across his chest and lifting his chin. He waited expectantly until I'd calmed down and huffed out a breath. Until I sat on the peak of the bridge, the ice freezing me through thick woollen pants. I could just see inside the gates of Desidia from here. It looked as quiet and still as the outside.

Max didn't move in time. I slammed into him and sent him right back into the snow. My shriek turned into a nearly hysterical laugh. He deserved it.

"Okay." Max laughed too, struggling to stand and brushing himself off. "Standing in the way wasn't my brightest idea."

There were flakes of snow in his beard as he helped me to my feet. Gripping my shoulders, he turned me to face the large, black-iron gates of the city. Sloth's insignia of the snail unmistakable in the pattern. Max squeezed my shoulders, his breath hot against my ear, as his thumbs massaged the tension from my muscles. "You're not facing this alone, Octavia."

He pulled something from his pocket. The folded clue we'd been given in Kyama. He'd kept it through each long day of walking, and now he pressed it into my hand. The ink had faded from the worn paper. Gingerly, I unfolded it, staring down at the meaningless squiggles. Max had read it so many times, repeating it aloud at night, that I could almost recite it by heart. Even if I couldn't read it.

A grim weight settled over me. Even if he were by my side, whatever Sloth asked of me next wasn't something he could help with. The trial had to be faced alone. I'd lost the friends that could have endured it with me. But if I kept going, and won, I held firm to the hope that I'd find Nash and Finley again.

I didn't tell Max that. He held my hand tightly and guided me right up to the edge of the city. I quietly let myself believe in the hope and optimism he held. That everyone and everything would be okay — that we had completed the challenge by making it this far.

Desidia, the frozen city of Sloth. We'd made it, and we'd won.

I almost believed it.

Right until the moment we staggered through the gates of the city. It was vast and quiet that we dared to grin at each other, staring up at the giant building that was so grand it could only house an angel of sin. Built of glittering, thick ice that wouldn't melt. Even the weak rays of the sun had no effect except to make it glitter. It was astonishing, but by now I didn't expect anything less of the seven deadly sins.

Glancing at Max, he nodded at me. He let me go to move ahead of him. I wiped my hands on my thighs, inhaled deeply, and convinced myself that I could keep going. Despite the fear, and the fatigue.

Everything was fine for a split second. Quiet, beautiful, and surreal. Until I stepped forward and fell over a body lost to the snow.

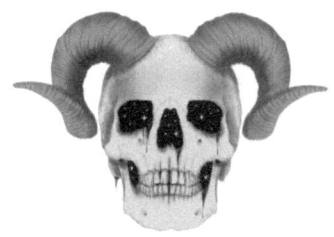

Chapter Twenty-Three

The body swept my legs from beneath me and I crashed into the snow. My breath caught in the back of my throat as, for a single second, I was weightless and infinite. Before gravity pulled me down, relentless in her claim of me. Forcing me to sink into the mound of flesh and snowflakes.

My body pressed against his, which lay cold and unmoving on the ground. Pale to the point of blue, his cheek was frozen beneath mine. Recognition sparked within me. A shudder worked down my spine, like the caress of a single fingertip.

I took a second look, pulling myself back fractionally to study the stillness of his face.

A scream caught in the back of my throat as my body shuddered again, and again. Bone-deep recognition, warring with desperate denial. I retch, but nothing comes up. Suddenly, I realise I'm touching him, his body, and I rear back, slipping on slush.

A thin layer of ice flaked across his skin. It crystallised on the end of his blonde lashes. His lips had turned a hue of blue that left me deeply uncomfortable. His hazel eyes were closed, mercifully so, but I still waited for a beat, hoping that he'd open them. Hoping he would transform and smile up at me.

"Nash?" I whispered his name, reaching to touch his face. It was freezing beneath my fingers. Anxiously, I rubbed my hand against his skin, deciding he needed to get warm.

He didn't move, rigid beneath my touch.

"Nash?" I said again. Somewhere in my chest, it felt like my heart had stopped beating. Like ribs are all cracking to form a path for it to fall out. Dread pooled through me, beneath my tongue, in my stomach, in my veins. It couldn't be Nash. It couldn't. It had to be someone that looked exactly like him. Samael had promised me that Nash was still alive, that Sloth had not laid claim to him. Because I was going to find him at the end of this trial, and we would continue together. It couldn't be Nash. Not my fiercely loyal and protective friend, the best friend I'd ever had. He couldn't be lying dead in the snow. It wasn't possible.

I retched again.

"Octavia?" Max called my name, but he felt so far away.

When I glanced up, he was staring at me, his expression a mixture of sadness and horror. He lifted both hands and edged back towards me, limping slightly. I took him down with me when I fell. Hard enough to hurt him.

I glanced away. Not wanting to see the pity in his eyes.

Numbly, I reached for Nash again. Brushing his hair from his forehead and then pressing my fingers against the side of his neck. Closing my eyes against the wind as I searched desperately for any feel of his pulse. I'd have taken even one slow throb of his heart.

"Octavia," Max repeated.

"We found him," I said. Relief married with sadness and complete, head-spinning disbelief. Nash was here, right in front of me. I just needed his heart to beat. I needed him to move and wake. I needed to hear his infectious laugh and know that everything was going to be okay. "Finally."

"Who?" Max asked. He crouched on the other side of the body. Pulling my band back from Nash's neck and replacing my fingers with his own. I watched his face, waiting for his expression to brighten as he found a pulse, but it didn't. He remained grim and impassive.

"This is Nash. I've told you all about him, remember?"

I had. I'd filled the long journey with stories of my friends. Nash had featured in many. Recounting their strengths, their weaknesses and their most annoying habits. Mostly, though, I'd talked about Nash, trying to describe his art in a way that did it justice. I glanced down at his still-pale face again and nodded sharply.

"There's no pulse," Max said.

"He's asleep," I argued. Ignoring the feeling of my chest cleaving in two. Tears rolled down my cheeks, and rain dripped from the sky. The universe, crying alongside me.

"Octavia." There was an edge of pity in Max's tone that I hated.

When he reached for me, I flinched back. Straddling Nash's hips, brushing locks of blonde hair from his eyes and dusting snow off his body. I sniffled, wiping at my tears, and frowning at his unmoving body.

I shook him gently, and then harder, but he didn't stir. "He's asleep," I repeated. "This whole trial is about sleeping."

"He's not asleep, Octavia."

Stubbornly, I ignored Max. Sloth must have had him entwined deep in a dream. Glancing up at the red-headed man, I frowned. "Help me wake him."

He clucked his tongue and crouched in front of me, filling my vision. He reached for my chin, gripping so tight that it hurt. He forced me to look away from Nash and up at him.

"Look at him," Max said firmly. "His chest isn't moving.

He's not breathing. His heart isn't beating. He's not asleep, Octavia."

"No!" I argued. My throat constricted as if Pride had his hand wrapped around it again, threatening to squeeze the life right out of me.

I shook my head, curling my fingers into the frigid, iced material of Nash's shirt and shaking him harder. My entire body trembled. It took me a moment to realise the sound of sobbing was coming from me.

"This is Sloth's entire plan. You don't understand. She's the one that makes us sleep until we don't want to wake up any more. She makes it difficult. We just need to help him wake up and he can come with us." I held out my hand, glaring at him demandingly. "Give me your lighter."

"No," he said, blunt as ever. He folded his arms across his chest, his gaze so full of bright pity I couldn't look at him. "Octavia, you need to get off him."

"Max," I sighed. I didn't have time for his shit, and neither did Nash. I needed to wake him up as soon as possible. "Give. Me. Your. Lighter."

It had worked to burn him and wake him up. It would work on Nash, too. The sooner we woke him, the sooner we could warm him up.

"Put your head on his chest, Octavia," Max said, his tone turning gentle now. "Listen for his heartbeat."

Dread had seized me, my heartbeat pounding in my ears, too slow as I stared down at Nash, feeling dizzy. His face was so still, so perfectly still. There was a part of me that knew. That hadn't felt his chest rise or fall beneath my hands. There was no flicker and twitch of dreams behind his closed lids. He hadn't mumbled for Alby in his sleep — as he often did.

Still, I didn't want to do it... Admit it.

When I glanced at Max, he was staring back at me. His lips pressed into a grim line, his eyes pinched with dismay. He nodded at Nash again, waiting for me to do as he said. Swallowing roughly, I leaned down, pressing my ear to his chest. His frozen body chilled the side of my wind-bitten cheeks. An ache flowed through me at the sudden idea that I'd never said goodbye.

His chest was as silent as Samael's; his heart was just as still.

"No," I whispered, squeezing my eyes closed. Screwing up my face to stop the onslaught of terror and despair that flooded through. My ears rang, my nose prickled and once the tears started, I couldn't stop them. A sob caught in my throat. Followed by another and another, until I was choking on them, struggling to breathe. "No. Nash. No."

"Octavia..." Max said. I flinched, clutching at Nash for dear life. I didn't want Max. I just wanted my friend to wake up.

"No. He has to be sleeping, Max! He has to be!" I sobbed, holding tight to him, willing his heart to beat beneath me. Praying for him to gasp in a delayed breath. Through tear-blurred eyes, I glared at Max because he was there. He was the easiest person to be angry with. "You don't understand. I haven't seen him since the attack on Glorae. I haven't..."

"I'm sorry," Max said.

He sounded like he meant it, too. That was the worst part. I didn't think I'd ever heard Max apologise for anything. He was always unapologetically himself. He'd whispered the words for the cavernous hole of hurt that had been buried in my chest.

"Nash was supposed to win," I told him, wailing the words. The rain chilled me through, as still the universe wept. "He was the only person to deserve it. The only person who never gave in to the shitty things we had to do to pass. The only person who remained optimistic. He was supposed to make it all the way to the end. He was supposed to win!"

"Can I help you up?" Max asked, reaching for my hand. I snatched it away from him, my tears still spilling onto Nash's throat. I could see tiny snowflakes on his eyelashes.

"No," I whispered. That hole in my chest widened into an

aching and impossible void. For all our troubles, Nash had been my best friend, the one person I could rely on through every trial. He'd kept me going, even when I didn't want to, even when he didn't realise he was helping me. Shaking my head, I choked on another sob, my lips trembling as I denied it, over and over. "I didn't even get to say goodbye. I didn't... He's asleep. He's just asleep."

"Octavia, listen to me." Max was infinitely patient with me, but there was a hint of stress in his tone, and he kept glancing at the too-quiet buildings around us, looking for trouble. He crept forward, gripping my hand tightly, warming my fingers as he massaged them. They tingled beneath his grip, having numbed in the cold. "You need to let go of him. We need to move. I know you love him, but I have a bad feeling about this..."

"I... No." I sobbed. "No, you can't make me."

I had loved him. Not romantically, but in every way that mattered. I would have thrown myself in front of all the sins again for Nash Wickham. And now I'd lost him, too. Just like everyone else.

Max's face fell and his strength fractured. He shook his head. "I'm not going to make you do anything you don't want to do, I promise."

"He deserves better than this. Dumped in the snow. Nash deserves proper rites," I protested, jerking my hand free of Max and carefully smoothing out Nash's shirt. I'd crumpled it, and I hadn't meant to force him into disarray.

I scrambled off his body, kneeling by his side, and desperately trying to straighten out every imperfection. "He deserves a burial stone and celebrations of his life. Devils, he deserves to live. More than anyone. More than me."

Max pursed his lips. "What's a burial stone? Maybe I can help."

"A burial stone," I repeated, my words marred by my sobbing. I tried not to show the infinite well of hopelessness that was filling the void in my heart. Tried not to blame Max for his ignorance. "You know, it sits in a field with the dead with his name on it. Something to remember him by."

Max rocked back on his heels. His neck craned as if he were looking for something suitable, but then he shook his head, shook himself. He scrubbed his hands across his face, looking pained.

"All I have is this," he said. He reached into his pocket and pulled out a fistful of coins. Sloth coppers, marked with the snail, he stacked them three high and then reached for Nash. I flinched, wanting to protest, wanting to stop him from touching my friend, but I couldn't bring myself to move.

Carefully, Max stacked the three coppers atop each of Nash's closed lids. "This is how we send people at home into their next life. With more wealth and fortune than they had in this one. Giving them a chance in death."

I knew that. I could remember the body in Pride's tower, with gold coins adorning its eyes. Coins I'd stolen, turned between my fingers, a body whose possible new wealth and fortune I'd taken with me. When I pictured the beautiful, jeweled casket of Greed, all I could see was Nash inside. Coppers sitting on his eyes. It made me sick.

"It's not enough," I told him miserably.

Wrapping my arms around my middle, I hugged myself tight. I wanted to knock the coins free and leave them there all at once. It was a beautiful gesture, given that Max didn't know him, but Nash should never have needed it. "Nothing will ever be enough. Not for Nash. Not right now. He's worth more than this, Max."

"It has to be enough," he said urgently. "We need to get you to Sloth."

"I can't just leave him here," I whispered. The thought of leaving Nash to the bitter cold and the everlasting quiet made my heart crack a little further. Lost to the snow and never seen again.

Max looked like he was in half a mind to drag me off Nash's body and pull me away. His fists clenched and relaxed, the tension in his brow smoothing out with concentrated effort before he started again. "Octavia… Please."

Samael brushed against my consciousness. A warm feeling buzzed through me, but even that couldn't settle that ice invading my bones. Tears rolled down my cheeks, dripping from my chin.

'He's right, Octavia. Again.' The devil didn't seem happy to admit it, either. *'You can't stay here. It's dangerous to be out in the open in Desidia.'*

Stubbornly, I shook my head, holding tight to Nash. "Yes, I can. I can stay. He needs me."

'Your friend is at peace now,' Samael continued. *'He was struggling for a very long time. You know that.'*

"I don't believe you," I spat.

Max might always tell me the truth, but Samael had lied for his own benefit. He was a cheater; he was the devil. Nash couldn't have been struggling, not for that long, or he would have said something, anything. We were closer than those sorts of secrets, or so I'd thought. He would have asked for help.

'I know death intimately, Octavia. I am a part of death itself,' Samael whispered in my ear. *'Trust me when I say he is with his lover now. Death is a better fate than the heartbreak he would have found at the end of the trials when he realised he was alone.'*

"Alby's dead, too?" I choked on the words, tears brimming fresh in my eyes. Snot bubbled in my nose, and Max looked disgusted at the sight of my distress. "He wouldn't have been alone. He would have had me."

Max's throat bobbed, his eyes closed, and he swore softly. "Devil's above, devil's below."

'Yes. His soul was claimed not one week after you met him,' Samael said. *'You know that wouldn't have been the same. Even the fiercest friend is not the same as a soul mate lost. He would have been irreparably fractured.'*

"Was it my fault?" I asked, unable to help myself. My hands trembled violently. I could remember the sickly man in the cold room, pleading for death with his eyes, as Nash embraced him. Even after I asked it, I knew it wasn't my fault that Alby had been waiting to die.

'Even you are not so arrogant to think you control death, Octavia,' Samael hissed. I could imagine his anger — the narrowing of his eyes, the flare of his nose, and the way his lips would thin and his feathers would ruffle — as he said it. *'Now do as your friend says and move. Sloth may be slow-moving, but she does not have infinite patience for stragglers. You are almost out of time.'*

Ignoring the devil, I leaned over Nash again, swiping at my cheeks so that tears didn't fall onto his face. The wind had swept his blonde hair into a tangled mess. I busied myself with brushing it back into place. He looked peaceful in death, and that hurt worst of all.

"May your spirit rest a lifetime in Eternis," I whispered, recalling the old prayer. I bent over him, my forehead pressed to his, almost able to count the snowflakes kissing against his lashes. "With your lover by your side. May you prosper, indulge and laugh in a sinner's paradise. I'll see you in the next life, Nash Wickham, I promise."

Max's arm wrapped around my shoulders and squeezed me gently. His body was warm, and I couldn't help but sag against him. The rain and wind had chilled me right through. "Are you ready, Octavia?" he asked. "Let me help you up."

"No," I whispered, closing my eyes and tipping my head up to face the skies. "No. I'm not going anywhere. I'm done."

Shrugging out of Max's grip again, I curled up by Nash Wickham's side and let myself cry deep, gut-wrenching sobs until the fatigue hit. It pulled at my body, weighing down my bones, and I gave in to it. Finally, relenting to the fatigue I'd felt for weeks now.

I relinquished myself to Sloth, to her dreams. Hoping she would transport me to a place where life wouldn't hurt as much. Not caring if I woke again.

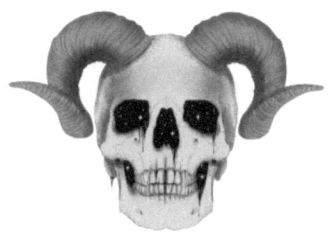

Chapter Twenty-Four

I lrea was dark and cold, but instantly recognizable as home. The memories of this place haunted my dreams and my waking moments. I'd never forget the alleyways, the broken stone underfoot, and the constant mirage of grey.

The wind whipped around me, battering my body. It was relentless, determined to howl in my ears and chill me through. I shivered, the hair on the back of my arms standing on end.

Standing in the dark alleyway, hugged my body and tried to process the aching hole in my heart. Even Sloth's dreamscape hadn't dulled the pain of seeing Nash's corpse. I'd seen many people die, even before I'd entered The Devil's Trials. My village was a place of poverty, and people often withered away before our eyes. Lost to nothing more than bone dust and memories.

Nothing had prepared me for losing Nash Wickham. I'd never even considered the idea that he could die on me. Although everyone else had felt so fleeting, and fallible. He was the one person who should have surpassed us all. There was no world in which my outliving him made any sense. Not with the threat of Pride still lingering over me. Especially not with the devil as my constant companion.

Swallowing my emotions, I closed my eyes against the fresh onslaught of tears. Trying to push my emotions into a tiny, imaginary black box. Pretending it was locked too tightly to open and created too strong for them to burst free. It was difficult. It took time to battle the overwhelm, as I gasped for air, trying to suck down a full breath. I was grateful for the shadows of Ilrea. I couldn't bear to have anyone watch me struggle.

Not these people. Not anymore. I was no longer interested in their pity.

"Octavia?" someone called from the mouth of the alley.

Shock rippled through my body at the sound of a familiar voice. I spun and stared down the alleyway. Peering into the depths of the shadows, my entire body tensed. Fresh tears brimming in my eyes, unable to be contained. I sobbed aloud.

"Dad?" I whispered.

He stepped into the sliver of early morning light, looking exactly as I'd always remembered. Short and worn out, his body was thick with muscle, fatigue, and hard work which pulled heavily at his skin, aging him beyond his years. Dark circles cupped his eyes, creases split his forehead, and callouses branded his hands. My dad opened his arms, beckoning me forward.

I was running before I could think better of it, sprinting towards him. Soft hope soared through me. I hadn't realised just how much I had missed my family until that very moment. Or how comforting it would be to see one of them. For all our differences, my scarred heart had loved them a little more than I'd admitted. "Dad!"

Our bodies collided, and he wrapped his arms around me, drawing me into a tight hug. He was familiar, secure. He was home. He squeezed me tight, and for the first time in a long time,

I relaxed.

"Hello, possum," he said, rubbing his palm between my shoulder blades. He murmured against my shoulder and rocked me side-to-side. Almost like I was still six years old and had scraped up my knees doing something silly. I trembled. He held me tighter, not pulling away until I was breathing steadily. My tears had soaked his shirt. Dad pulled back and looked at me. Concern creased across his face. "Not doing so well, huh, poss?"

"That's the understatement of a lifetime…" I said, laughing half-hysterically. His fingers stroked through my hair, brushing it away from my marred skin. He frowned but didn't comment on the changes in me. He just let me be. Let me feel.

He still smelled like the potato fields. Rough dirt that they ploughed vegetables from, and the soft edge of grease. It made me wish I'd never entered the trials and taken my chances at home. I could have stayed with him a little longer.

"Tell me what's happening, Possum," he said. I smiled sadly. He hadn't called me that in years. Not since my younger sisters had come along, and the stress in our household had increased. Not since I realised, he used the same endearment for them, too. When suddenly I hadn't felt as special as I had before.

"Dad…" I sighed.

He shook his head, rubbing a hand through his short-cropped dark locks. "Now, Octavia, let's see if your old man can't help? I know I'm not your mother, but I still know a thing or two."

I stared into the lines of his face, his too-serious eyes and studied the nose we shared. He'd never offered his advice to me before, but maybe I'd never wanted to listen, either. A hesitant smile twitched against his lips, and I nodded slowly.

"Okay…" I whispered, letting him bundle me out of the alley. We strolled through Ilrea as I let it all out. Once I started talking, I couldn't seem to stop. I told him about every death, every failure and how each of them made me feel. Each one had felt shocking, and sad, but this one was the worst. I tried to describe the way losing Nash had hit me the hardest. How I felt like I was about to crumble completely, but the words didn't feel like they came out right. Words couldn't encompass the source of strength that he had been through the horrors and hardships of the trials.

We stopped walking at the edge of a little park. It was one of the very few green and lively areas of Ilrea. Only because the chancellor's wife had once complained that there was nothing pretty to look at. In all my years skulking around the village, I'd rarely come here. It was usually full of shrieking children. But today, it was different. It took me a moment to realise that it was because the colour had faded from the world.

I saw everything in black and white, which made the grass seem lifeless. The park felt bare and colder without colour. There was still an old metal slide. A patch of mostly trampled, muddied grass, a single patch of white flowers and a lonely bench.

Usually, it was occupied by someone trying to sleep, but today, it was empty. We sunk down onto it, staring ahead as if the broken park reflected our broken lives. Or my broken life. My father, I remembered, was dead. Just like Nash. Just like everyone I cared about, really.

Misery welled in my gut. My dream had become a pity party.

"You're stronger than that, Octavia," he said. Dad gripped my hand, as if he were anchoring me in place, and keeping me present. Even though I wanted to check out, desperate to feel nothing. Telling him everything hadn't been a relief. It had only hurt more, spiking extra feelings that I wanted to bury away.

"How would you know?" I said, sniffling. "You barely know me, dad."

He chuckled and I bristled at the sound. "You've always been the strongest of my kids, possum. Never cared what anyone thought of you, did you? Never cared what anyone wanted you to do. You walked in your own line, even if it was crooked every now and again."

I flinched. His words didn't feel like a compliment, not really. It made no sense to me. All my life, it felt like I'd cared too much, not too little. He'd called me wildly independent, always saying that I never needed him. But maybe I'd needed him more than he'd thought. Maybe if I'd leaned on him, I wouldn't be in this mess. Maybe my life would have been safe, or normal. I wouldn't be choking on my own regrets,

I stared down into my lap, studying the dirt beneath my nails intently. I picked at the edge of one, procrastinating. A solid lump in my throat. My head pounded.

Finally, I admitted it. "I don't want to keep going, Dad. I'm tired."

He clucked his tongue, his face falling with blatant disappointment. "Why not? You could win."

"It's too hard," I said, my voice cracking as that hollow feeling inside of me intensified. "I'm tired of trying so hard and never getting ahead."

Exhaustion felt like a terrible excuse, and it was, but that didn't mean it wasn't true. I'd been tired before. Everyone had been at some point in their lives. It was nothing like I felt now, though. I'd slept and slept for weeks in this trial but never rested. My bones could turn to dust and I'd fade away at the slightest inconvenience. That was how little energy I had to hold myself together.

"It's okay to be tired." Dad surprised me, wrapping his arm around my shoulders and pulling me close again; I'd thought he'd push me to continue. Urge me to make something of myself and finish the trials. "It's okay if you want to rest, Octavia."

My head dropped onto his shoulder, and I sniffled. By now, I must have cried a river's worth of tears. I stared out at the empty park, saying nothing, feeling nothing. The morning fog crawled across the grass.

Finally, I sighed. "Will you still be here when I wake up?"

"Of course," he murmured, brushing my hair from my face.

335

I shifted, laying my head in his lap, taking a moment to memorise the shape of his face. Just in case this was the last time my mind could conjure him up. Just in case next time he wasn't so clear, or I forgot something important about him.

"Liar." It wasn't an accusation, just the truth, the harsh word bitter on the edge of my tongue. "Because this is just a dream, and you're dead, too. Everyone around me dies."

His soft chuckle did nothing to reassure me. The miasma fog rolled closer, creeping towards me. I blinked. I went from lying on his lap to having my cheek pressed against the icy surface of the bench.

A sob choked in my throat, unbidden, unwanted. It felt like I was losing everyone all over again. Dad, Nash, and even parts of myself. I was unrecognisable compared to the woman I'd once been. It felt like the last straw, carving a deep chasm of loneliness in my chest. It threatened to turn me inside out.

"There she is!" Someone cried from the far end of the park. "There's Octavia Nox!"

Bolting upright, I clutched at the bench, the world spinning as I fought for equilibrium. My chest tightened, ached, and I stared through wet lashes at the mob of people approaching. A mix of familiar and unfamiliar bodies.

They stormed towards me, their fists clenched by their sides, bodies tense with anger. Their faces blurred and I couldn't focus on them. They weren't recognisable, but familiarity still struck me. These were people I knew. People who belonged here, in Ilrea, when I didn't.

"I can't believe she came back!" There was a fierce anger in their voices, rage that built and burnt as rapidly as a wildfire.

Approaching quickly, one of the faceless men spat at my feet. The glob of his phlegm landed on the toe of my boot, and he hissed, "greedy bitch!"

My nails dug into the wooden bench, carving gouges into the surface. I tried to lean back and away from them, but my body wouldn't move. I was stuck in place. Cringing away from their hostility, but also desperate to rise and strike back. An anger I hadn't felt since my days with Wrath coursed through my veins. I despised them for not letting me wallow in peace.

A woman in the back let out a shrill laugh. She waved her hand at me flippantly, a swipe of long nails. "With the trail of bodies in her wake, I'm surprised she's not covered in blood," the woman sneered.

It was only then that I noticed their weapons. Mismatched blades with jagged edges and pitchforks with sharpened points. Tinted with rust, like nearly everything else in Ilrea, but they were still enough to do damage. One faceless man on the left had his hands wrapped tight around a wooden stick. The end sharpened into a point that could skewer me through. Wishing I could move, I realised that Sloth had conveniently left me without a weapon of my own.

Breathing shallowly, I tipped my chin, faking a confidence that I didn't entirely feel. My skin prickled, my body breaking out into a cold sweat as I stared them down. Unable to move, unable to flee the inevitable confrontation. I knew the alleyways of Ilrea better than the letters that made up my name. If I could just move, escape them, I would be free. If I had to fight them… Well, I wouldn't die easily. I'd lived through enough trauma and war to fight to the bitter end.

"What do you want?" I asked, hearing the thread of worry in my voice.

My body wouldn't budge. My legs felt too heavy, weighed down by my misery to move an inch. My dad would have said I was wearing concrete boots for all my ability to leap into action.

"We want you to die!" that same woman hissed the words at me.

I flinched. For the first time though, my heart didn't race in horror at the thought of my life ending. Dying had always been one of my greatest fears, fuelled by the idea that I'd never lived or achieved enough. Driven by the desperate desire to keep on. Instead, this time, the beat of my traitorous heart slowed down. Shifting into a steady thump, thump, thump that echoed in my ears.

Maybe I wanted to die, too. Just like Ophelia, Monika, Ngaire, Nash, Dad. So many others. Maybe I wanted to join everyone else in the peace of oblivion. It would be easier, surely, than living with the new hole carved into my chest. Instead of walking around like a part of me was missing, trying to pretend I was still whole.

Easier than living with the pain of outliving someone you loved. I had loved him, Nash Wickham. Two souls trapped in a platonic tangle, so deeply entwined that my life felt dull without him. Losing him had leeched the colour from the world. Now I even dreamed in black and white.

"What did I do to you?" I asked, trembling beneath their scrutiny.

The man with the sharpened stick levelled it at my heart. Narrowing my eyes, I stared into his blurred face, where his features should have been.

I wanted to dare him to do it.

I wanted to tell him I couldn't die, because the devil, the harbinger of death, was on my side.

It wouldn't work. Even if it did, I wouldn't care, because maybe I'd see the people I'd loved again in the next world. Just maybe, I'd have another chance. A second attempt at life.

It was a fanciful idea, but I didn't think it was how my death would go. There'd be no prayers in my name or safe passage to the next world. I thought of the cruel women at Samael's Day of the Dead celebration. They wouldn't give up on our souls. My bones would become another trinket in their jewellery collection.

"You took them! You killed them!" they screamed the words, unified and three times over until it rang in my ears. A chant of the damned. The miasma rolled around my ankles but didn't claim me, didn't climb any higher.

Slowly, I lifted my hands, raising them to show that I wasn't a threat. I was half-surprised I could do it, that my body had found the will to move. These people would have never believed I was a threat, anyway. Not Octavia Nox, more likely to be killed by her own lack of common sense than anything else.

"They're all gone!" a man said as he moved to the front of the group. Although I still couldn't make out the finer features of his sneering face, I knew who it was. Chancellor Heira. Behind the grey of the world, I was sure his eyes burned with a familiar shade of green fire. Just like his sons.

He was furious, each of his words cracked with grief. As he moved, the rest of the crowd all inched closer, spreading around me in a dangerous circle. They blocked any chance of fleeing. Chancellor Heira pulled himself to his full height. He stabbed a finger in my direction. "Mikhael. Your father. Prudence. Helina. Alby. Nash."

My bottom lip wobbled, fresh tears stinging in my eyes. I had more to shed, an infinite supply that I might as well drown in.

Licking my lips, I spoke over him, adding in the names of my own, "And Ophelia. Monika. Aieke. And probably even Margot. Don't forget about all those people who died without me knowing their names. All those soldiers cut down at the end of my sword. The ones that begged for mercy I couldn't give them. The ones that burned in a shattered glass palace. The ones who died wanting to see change in the world. The people I... I stepped over... Just to succeed."

My words trailed off into choked crying. I sobbed and sobbed, looking down at my hands and seeing blood slicked across them. Dripping from my fingertips.

Those deaths were all my fault. Even if I hadn't killed them myself. It was my fault because I survived. It was my fault good people had suffered the worst of fates, and impossibly, I still breathed. My heart still beat. Broken but alive.

"You deserve to die next!" The chancellor screamed in my face. Spittle flecked against my cheeks. I didn't disagree with him. "You're climbing over their dead bodies to get ahead!"

Suddenly, I could move more than just my arms. I jerked forward, staggering off the bench. All my pent-up desire to retaliate previously now propelled me towards Chancellor Heira. I slammed into his chest, gripping at the plush wool of his coat and using him to hold myself upright. I stared up at his blurred face and my heart beat louder in my ears.

"I'm already dead," I said, hissing the words. "I'm already dead and nobody noticed."

"Liar." The crowd roared back. The exact accusation I'd made to my father moments before. The pointed end of a pitchfork pressed against my shoulder, pain searing through my arm. It forced me to let the chancellor go until I stepped out of their way. The circle of angry faces tightened around me. They wanted me to move, but they didn't want me out of their sights.

"My death has been slow," I said to the chancellor. "I've bled out in every trial, drop by drop, until there's nothing of me left any more. I died when they died. Chunks of my heart feel like they've ripped from my chest. But nobody noticed, nobody cared, because my body isn't the one left to rot."

There was a beat of lingering silence.

"You're despicable." A woman swung her shovel at me. For a second, I thought my end was coming from its blunt edge. I recoiled, expecting the collision, and prepared for pain. She missed by a hair's width, and the force of my flinch knocked me off balance. I staggered into the men behind me.

"It's not about you!" the woman cried. "Living but hurt is still alive. So selfish. You've always only thought about yourself. You think the sun rises and sets at your desire."

The men behind me grabbed at me. It was useless to struggle, as they grunted and held me in place. Chancellor Heira reached into the inner pocket of his luxurious coat and withdrew a blade.

It was Pride's blade. Pitch black and drawing in the light. Emanating shadows and pulsing with unknown power. A blade gifted by an angel, designed to harm the devil. A blade that he turned on me.

The chancellor pressed the sharp edge of it against my throat.

Without warning, my apathy disappeared. I'd thought I was past the fear of death, but chilling fear flooded through me. The back of my neck prickled, and my hands shook.

"Don't." I caught myself begging him. Tears dripped off my nose and acrid spit pooled in my mouth. Too scared to swallow it, in case the movement sliced my throat through. "Please don't kill me, Chancellor Heira."

"Devils, you don't even know the meaning of the word '*please*'," a man behind me hissed. His breath felt hot against my skin. I didn't dare cringe away from him and closer to the blade. He continued, "Everyone else paved the way for your success. You walked all over them, without a please or thank you. Why should we listen to you when you say it now?"

"You don't deserve our mercy!" someone else roared, and the rest of the crowd cried out in agreement. "You deserve to die!"

A fist flew into my stomach. It knocked the wind right out of me. I doubled over, feeling pain in my throat as the blade drew blood. The man behind me shoved me roughly to the ground. The knife skimmed my throat, not slicing deeply, but still enough to make me shriek. Small rocks embedded in my skin as I slammed into the ground. I clutched at my neck, feeling my blood slip over my fingers.

A vicious kick to the ribs forced a cry from my throat and I crumpled into the lingering miasma. Pain lanced through my body. Once they started attacking me, it turned into a frenzy. Fists, feet, and weapons slammed into my body. Beating me until all I knew was pain.

I curled into a tight ball, the rising mist caressing my body. Finally, I ran out of tears. Maybe I deserved to die.

341

The miasma claimed me before I could find out.

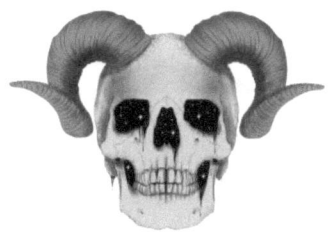

Chapter Twenty-Five

His tattooed knuckles cracked. His jaw tensed, the muscles in his neck corded. I didn't know how they, too, didn't pop or crackle for release.

Anger rolled off his body in waves. The sort of tension that was catching and could sour the mood of anyone around him. I recoiled, but Nik wasn't glaring at me. Instead, he stood nose-to-nose with a familiar wiry bearded man. Two souls whose feud had nothing to do with me, but somehow affected me all the same. The entanglement of their anger effectively trapped me.

I was still dreaming in black and white. But even in a world still devoid of colour, both of them were instantly recognisable. Both of them made my heart ache in strange ways, my stomach flopping with nerves.

"What's the matter, Silver-Spoon?" Max taunted softly. "Can't handle it?"

Niklaus scoffed, staking closer until they stood nose to nose.

He was the taller of the two. He towered over Max, but the bearded man was broader, stockier, and I thought more willing to fight dirty. I could see other people crowding in on us, a mixture of familiar and unfamiliar faces. I couldn't work out how I'd got in the middle of their fight.

"It's your responsibility now," Niklaus said, his eyes flashing with warning. "You wanted it. You wanted to steal what's mine. Now you have to deal with the consequences. Don't like it? Tough shit, Tate."

Max fisted his lighter, his hand twitching like he wanted to use it to break Niklaus' jaw. They circled each other again, with slow, paced movements. I debated whether it was worth getting in the middle of their altercation. Given the mocking edge to their tones, the fire in their eyes, and the tension building in the courtyard… Probably not.

I didn't even know what they were fighting about.

"She was your problem first. You wanted to make a daring rescue. Said we just had to have her for the cause…" Max snarled. His eyes flicked in my direction and my stomach dropped so hard it may as well have turned to stone.

Oh. Maybe I knew what they were talking about. Me.

Heat crawled up the back of my neck, but I couldn't bring myself to look away from their fight. It was like watching a disaster unfold. Only I was about to be the casualty. The cries of the villagers in Ilrea still rang in my ears. Maybe they were right, maybe I thought I was too special. Maybe I was selfish. Especially if my dreams revolved around two strong men fighting over me.

Niklaus scoffed, drawing my attention back to them. He didn't look at me. I had a feeling he knew exactly where I was, anyway, hyper-aware that I was watching. "That didn't mean I wanted to be saddled with that burden forever. You swept in and offered her what she wanted. Prince-Fucking-Charming, you are. She's all yours now."

My head pounded with a pulsing dull ache that started in my

temple. I rubbed my eyes with the backs of my hands. His words sparked a wave of confusion within me. I stared down at my feet, suddenly wondering if he couldn't be talking about someone else. Doubting that I was the topic of conversation, after all.

Niklaus and I had a lot of shared experiences and trauma. Not enough that I would have called it a bond between us. I'd saved his life, and he'd saved mine, but that didn't make us connected — it just made us desperate. Maybe even just to hold on to a fraction of our pasts, of the people we knew.

I'd left that behind — him behind — though, or at least I thought I had when I'd fled the rebellion camps with Maksymilian. When I'd decided that my desires for my survival were more important than Niklaus' plans of revolution. When I put myself first.

Max laughed, coldly. "That's not how it works," he said. "You changed all her plans to get her by your side. You dragged her halfway across the Pridelands, unconscious, and now you're saying you don't want her?"

"Huh." Niklaus's expression turned snide. "Neither do you, it seems. Have you realised that she's a demon yet? That she looks human but sucks all your energy away. Nothing more than a leech."

All my doubts slipped away. Bile rose in my throat, and for a brief few seconds, I closed my eyes and wished them away. Not that it had ever worked in my dreams before. Reluctantly, I looked back at them.

Both men had stopped pacing around each other. They were still rigid with tension, but then they slowly turned to face me. I felt like I was shrinking, becoming tiny and worthless beneath the intensity of their gazes.

"No. I don't want her…" Max said. He grinned, in a creepy way, that caused my skin to pebble with discomfort. "It was funny to make her think I did, though. It's amazing what she'll do to feel wanted. Such a desperate woman."

I was going to be sick. Pursing my lips together, I pressed my clenched fist against my abdomen to abate the wave of nausea. It felt like I'd always known this truth, but that didn't make hearing it any easier.

"Me either," Niklaus said. "What will we do with her?"

They shared a look. They laughed. Bright sounds of shared amusement. As if they'd never been enemies at all — or at least, only ever been my enemies. I guessed they'd both been playing me all along. Everyone who watched laughed as well.

Heat crawled down my body, flushing from head to my toes, until I was suffocating on my embarrassment. My feet wouldn't move, though, just like the last dream. I couldn't get away from my mortification. I glanced between them, biting down hard on my lip, but it did nothing to wake me from this dream.

Ignoring Niklaus and his cruel amusement. I turned to Max, edging forward a step, my hands raised in supplication. "Max…"

"Didn't you hear me?" he asked, speaking louder. As if increasing the volume of his voice would make it easier to understand. Or make it hurt worse. The stocky man stalked forward, getting up in my face. The hard tension in his expression made him almost unrecognisable. He'd never looked at me like this before. This wasn't my Max - but maybe he was dead, too. "I don't want you. Nobody does."

Inhaling sharply, I rocked back on my heels. It felt like he'd physically struck me.

"Don't worry…" a nasty voice floated out from behind me. It was close. Too close for comfort. "I want you, Octavia."

Before I could move, his dirty hand clutched at my face. His fingers pinned against my lips and gagged the scream that rose within my chest. He smelled overwhelmingly of stale wine and grease. Chester pulled me back against his soft chest, his sweaty skin pressed flush against me. I struggled and he laughed. The sound gave me chills. My limbs felt heavy and uncooperative as I tried to break free of him. Chester's breath was hot and putrid against the side of my face.

I shuddered, staring at the two men in front of me, screaming silently for one of them to intervene.

They didn't.

Instead, their smirks grew wider. Niklaus folded his arms across his chest and watched. Max fiddled with his lighter, flicking it on and off, on and off.

"You're all mine now," Chester crowed, using his leverage on my face to tug me backwards.

Everything spun.

The world turned black.

The scene had disappeared in the blink of an eye, and when I refocused, the courtyard was gone. Niklaus and Max were nowhere to be seen. Chester wasn't touching me, even if I could still feel the ghost tickle of his hot breath.

I was alone. Thank the devil for small favours.

This new place was unfamiliar. A long hallway stretched out in front of me, a mix of shadows darkening the end. The walls were a simple, off-white and the paint was old and peeling back in places. Small pieces flaked away, drifting through the air in front of me and settling in the hall. Almost like snow.

There were no decorations, nothing except deep gouges of panic in the walls, the scrape of nails carved through paint. When I looked at them, I could almost feel the flakes sliding under my own fingernails. I imagined them cutting painfully into the tender flesh of my nail bed. Forcing my nails to snap as I clawed for purchase. Rendering my hands useless, leaving my fingers broken and bloody.

When I looked down, my fingers were aching. They bled as if the gouges in the wall were mine. I just didn't remember creating them. I twisted to flee the hall, but a solid wall trapped me in. There was only one path ahead. Only one way to move. My heart pounded, as holding onto traces of the adrenaline and fear.

The hall ahead of me was lit with a soft yellow light. It flickered intermittently, and every other second darkness smothered the hall. My heart stuttered, gearing up for a threat that I didn't understand.

My saliva turned bitter and my jaw ached from the clench of my teeth. I tried to relax, parting my lips, rolling my shoulders, peeling my tongue from the roof of my mouth. But it was useless. Tension coiled through me, winding me tight.

There was a door at the end of the hallway. The obvious exit, too obvious, really. A poisonous sense of dread had filled my veins. Filling me with the deep and intimate knowledge that I wouldn't enjoy going through that door. Combined with the grim realisation that I needed to go through it, too. I couldn't stay here.

One step forward. That's all I took.

A man appeared in front of the door.

A familiar man.

Chester.

Despite his blurred features, I knew who it was. As if I'd built from a hazy memory instead of knowledge, but his sick, wide grin was unmistakable. The pungent rot of his teeth carried down the hall. He sat in a rocking chair, the same one I'd seen on his front porch.

He rocked on it now. It creaked loudly beneath his weight, the joints groaning in protest.

The sound made me shudder, drawing in a deep and ragged breath. I didn't move. I couldn't move. A beat of sweat dripped down my spine, unexpectedly cold.

Chester didn't have any issue moving. He rocked in his chair and appeared an inch closer. Although he still sat close to the door, the space between us felt shorter. It took a moment to catch on. I hadn't moved, and neither had he. The corridor had shrunk. It felt thinner, shorter now. Inevitably pushing us together.

The creaking sound of his next rock was like cold water dropping across my scalp and sliding down my neck. My mouth dried out. I blinked, and then he was closer still. There was nothing I wanted less than to be close to Chester, locked in this tiny hall with him. I pressed myself back against the solid wall, wishing I had another escape.

"Stay there," I told him. There was no use trying to inject my words with confidence, not when my fear was clear in every syllable. "Don't you move."

Chester didn't reply, but he grinned wider. Smug as he stared me down.

His chair rocked. The gap between us closed.

I was going to be sick. The room spun. I felt like I was going to pass out. Devils, I wished I could've.

The light flickered. My fingers ached. When I looked down, blood oozed from my palms, my nails having sliced through my skin. The blood slipped down my wrists, dripping onto my bare feet.

The rocking chair creaked. My gut clenched uncomfortably. If it was possible to die of fear or pure apprehension, I was well on my way there. Although I didn't know what was coming, I didn't want to find out. There was no way I could let Chester get near me.

A high-pitched ringing sounded in my ears, creating a fog through my head. I could think straight, or about anything except the way his rocking chair was tipping forward. My lungs burned and the tremors in my limbs increased. Stress was tearing me to pieces, ripping me into tiny flakes, like the paint falling from the walls.

The corridor had thinned so much that I could feel the walls brushing against my arms. The rough surface scratched against my skin. It felt like I couldn't breathe. I was simultaneously breathing too fast, panting to get more oxygen. I closed my eyes, wishing I'd pass out. When I opened them, he was still there.

Chester grinned with vindictive promise. Confident he would win.

His chair rocked.

The lights flickered around us, plunging the hall into a split second of pure darkness.

He was close enough that I could smell him. The soft hint of deep smoke, the promise of explosions and fire. The scent was reminiscent of pain and death.

"What do you want with me?" I asked.

We inched again, with the creak of his chair. Now I could see the texture on his face, pocked against his skin and the way he sweated. Small beads gathered in his hairline and slipped down his ruddy face.

I tried to back up, but there was nowhere to go. The wall behind me was cold, chilling me through my shirt. There was nowhere to go, nowhere except the door behind him. The only exit. The only way to escape him.

Chester was constantly in my way. I'd have liked to have never met him again after his first recruitment speech in the village. Frustratingly, our paths kept crossing. Even in my dreams. I'd have to get past him, in order to get free. It was a sick reflection of reality, and for a beat, I resented Sloth for it. For not making these dreams easier on me, when I was already hurting so much. There was only so much one woman could take.

The rocking chair creaked.

He laughed.

A sharp, sick feeling slid through my veins. My nails scratched against the wall behind me. My weapons and my wits had abandoned me. Chester was right in front of me, close enough to kick my shins. His boot knocked against me. Pain lanced up my leg. Gritting my teeth, I hissed at him. A warning.

If he rocked again, the chair would crush my feet beneath him.

He clutched the chair, his blackened fingertips drumming against the wood. He stared at me curiously. There was no reason this man should have ever taken an interest in me. Not unless he

350

knew about Samael. If he had, he would have never let Niklaus bring me into the heart of his operation.

Pulling at the frayed edge of my nerves, I lifted my chin. "What do you want, Chester?"

"I want to hurt the devil," he spat the words, his spittle landing down my front. I should have known. It was his one goal in life, his obsessive rhetoric. That humanity needed to rise against the supernatural. "I've worked out exactly how I'm going to do that."

I asked, "How?"

But I didn't want to know. Not really. Devils, I'd never wanted to know anything less. Ignorance was bliss and I prayed I'd remain an ignorant fool. His chair creaked, and I prayed to the devil himself that I'd die before he could touch me.

The rocking chair tipped forward, finding my toes and crushing. Pressure and pain built through my legs. A loud scream escaped my throat, sucking the air from my lungs. Oh, the pain was so staggering that black spots danced across my vision.

I didn't want to look at him, but I still took a peek, unable to stop myself. Chester was reaching for me. His broken, bitten nails were jagged and dirty. His face was lit with cruel glee. Devils, I didn't want him to touch me. There was no way around him. My feet seared with pain that I wasn't sure I could move.

His fingers brushed my cheek, skimmed against my jaw, and he wrapped his hand around my throat.

A pitiful sob rolled from my lips as it reminded me of Pride. Visions of the golden angel flashed before my eyes and I trembled. That golden god would haunt me forever.

Chester squeezed tight, the maniacal glint in his eye promising that he wouldn't let go as the angel had.

The lights flickered.

The pressure on my throat disappeared. In the blink of an eye, I was standing back at the end of the hall. Space stretched between Chester and me. The hall was long enough that I could draw in a deep, gasping breath. My fingers rubbed against my throat, feeling the ghost of his fingers.

The yellow light flickered overhead. Chester still sat in the rocking chair ahead of me, tapping his fingers against the wood. Sitting in wait. The dark door still loomed behind him.

A quick glance over my shoulder confirmed it was still the only exit.

Dragging in my next breath, I rubbed at my shoulders. Trying to pull myself together and relieve the tension coiled in my muscles. It was useless, like cupping water in my hands and expecting it not to seep through my fingers.

Shuffling forward a single step, pain seared through my feet, stopping me dead in my tracks. When I looked down, black and blue bruises covered my feet. Each one was shaped suspiciously like the base of his rocking chair.

I hesitated, wondering if I'd dreamed it all up. But the pain I felt was undeniable. It hurt too much to move.

Chester rocked forward again.

My entire body broke out in chills when I realised everything was repeating itself. He was drawing closer, and I'd have to face him again. My thoughts felt heavy, shrouded with a dull fog. I was unsure how many times we'd been through it already. It would explain why my fingers numbed, and my nails snapped off, left in jagged pieces. Or why my knees seared as the air kissed against open abrasions. Each step forward caused a sharp inhale of pain. I felt battered, broken, and I suspected it was all his fault.

The familiar pattern appeared. A rock, creak, and the corridor shortened.

The light flickered, and his expression never changed. It turned my stomach, the vindictive glee shining in his eyes. I imagined he found pleasure in seeing me break into pieces before him. That the sound of my pain left him giddy.

My gaze flicked to the door. I tried not to look directly at Chester. It was the best way to stave off my growing fear. But a lightheaded sensation was overtaking me, making it more and more difficult to breathe.

He was approaching faster now. The gap between us disappeared too quickly.

I sucked in a breath, gathering my wits, forcing myself to stagger forward on broken feet. Even as pain through me, radiating up my shins. My knees wobbled, but I grit my teeth and swallowed against the pain, forcing myself forward. It was hard to gain speed, but I ran as hard and as fast as I could.

I'd barrel right through him. If I could, I just needed to make it to the door. To make it out.

Chester caught me around the middle. His fingers scrabbled against my skin. A wail pierced through the air, transforming into a half-wild, high-pitched scream. My ears rang, my chest heaved, and I realised I was making the feral sound. I was screaming and thrashing against Chester, but he easily overpowered me. My tired, broken body didn't have the energy to best him.

His raspy laugh echoed in my ears. Then, he threw me to the ground. My knees slammed against the floor, and something within them popped. A small flick in the back of my leg followed my excruciating pain. It was so bad that my screams dried up, turning into heaving, gasping pleas for relief. Prayers for the sweet relief of death, or for anything other than what I felt in the moment.

The lights shuddered. The last thing I saw before we were plunged into darkness again, was Chester's foul, smug smile.

When the hall lit up, I was on my hands and knees. Gifted the illusion of space between us. My knees still seared with pain, worsened by my position, and it felt like I couldn't move my foot. My weight pressed my limbs against the floor, adding to the strain. I slumped forward, landing on my stomach. For a single moment, I lay still and wallowed in my pain. Giving myself a second to feel and accept it. I knew I'd have to at least try to push through it. Even if it killed me. Slowly, I wriggled my toes to test out the movement of my feet again. Both my legs remained useless.

Everything hurt. I'd felt pain before — a lot of pain — but this was worse, compounded. It was relentless. It was enough that, as I lay there, I wished for death. I wished Samael would show me mercy. The king of death could come for my soul and take me away.

The rocking chair creaked.

Fear shot through me, a poison that lit a fire in my veins. The sound made me think of pain, and everything tensed. I tried to get to my feet, but my useless legs gave way. I crumpled. My chin slammed against the floor, sending my teeth sharply through my lip. Bitter blood pooled in my mouth. I spat it out, groaning.

My entire body trembled every time I tried to rise. Refusing to hold me.

The rocking chair creaked again. He was approaching.

My body flushed hot and cold. There was no pretending that I wasn't scared. I wasn't a woman who was determinedly unafraid, standing tall before things that made my knees knock. Normally, embracing my fear kept me alive, but in this dream… It was a thick sludge that I choked on.

I had to move; I had to get past him. And even though I didn't know much, unable to reason through the haze of never-ending pain, instinctively I knew if I didn't move it would get worse. There was no telling how, but this wouldn't be the end. I couldn't stand it much more.

With my legs dragging behind me, I pulled myself forward with my arms. My fingers scrabbled against the floor for purchase. I heaved my body further down the hall. He drew closer. So did I. I met him halfway without the wall herding me forward.

When Chester looked down at me, there was unmistakable amusement in his expression. He was enjoying my suffering. I'd never seen him so happy before. He sickened me.

We came to a crossroads in front of the door. When I looked

up, I finally noticed the thick square lock hanging from the handle. It needed a key. Of course, it needed a key.

My heart withered and sunk to my stomach. I wanted to wake up, but no matter how much I thought about it. It never happened. I closed my eyes and counted to three. No luck. I was still on the floor, and he was still there.

I leaned into the pain, thinking the blistering edge of it would wake me, but it did nothing. A moment later, I realised I didn't actually want to wake up. I didn't want to face Nash's cold, dead body, and the deep ache in my chest. I just wanted out of this dream.

A soft white mist poured out from the crack beneath the door. My muscles relaxed, relief sweeping through me at the sight of Sloth's miasma. It drifted over me. Reaching Chester's chair, I forced myself towards it. I gave in to the mist, but it didn't take me quickly enough.

"Fuck you, Chester," I whispered, as his rocking chair shifted, curving down across my already broken hands. Propelled by the slight kick of his legs, by his weight tipping forward. My hands cracked and shattered. I screamed and screamed and screamed.

The light flicked, and the room turned mercifully dark. My last thought was that, just maybe, this was what I deserved.

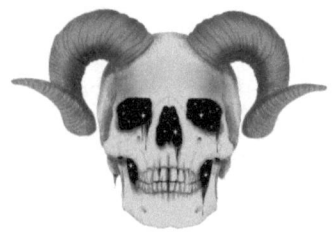

Chapter Twenty-Six

There was a faint sound in the darkness. A soft scratching that I ignored at first. More intent on feeling my way through the darkness, inching through my newfound blindness. The lights hadn't turned back on, and I was on my feet, so I assumed that I'd finally escaped Chester. That Sloth had granted me a new dream.

My heart still raced from the last dream, though, the beat of it clamouring in my ears. The edge of pain is still sharp in the back of my throat. I ran my hands down my arms and wriggled my toes. The ghostly feel of broken bones lingered, but as far as I could tell, I was completely unharmed. Almost back to normal, which was to say, some level of fractured whole because I'd never be complete again.

It took a moment – maybe too long – to find my bearings in the darkness. My entire body felt coiled tight on the precipice of running away. There was no telling what Sloth had brought into this next dream. I didn't know if I could handle more pain or torment. I'd expected that relinquishing myself to this sin would have meant soft dreams, happy dreams. Moments that were easier to bear than the heartache of losing a close friend. I thought the angel would have curated a world I wanted to go back into. Except here, nothing more than my own overwhelming feelings surrounded me.

The same things I hadn't wanted to experience.

The scratching noise in the distance grew louder. Swallowing against my sharp sense of lingering fear, I lifted my hands and shuffled through the dark. Tiny steps, with my hands splayed out, as I waited to bump into the next danger. It was too dark for me to be comfortable. I kept imagining that the Erlkangs would seep from the shadows and come for my throat if I stayed still. It kept me moving, following the sound.

I stepped into daylight. The soft rays of the sun were so unexpected, so bright, that I cringed back. The shadows had disappeared behind me, no longer providing a place to hide. I stood in an open courtyard of grey stone. It was vaguely familiar, and yet I couldn't pinpoint where exactly I was. The stone was cold beneath my naked feet. Inhaling deeply, I fisted my hands by my side and stared around the yard.

But I was not alone.

The person in the distance was heart-falteringly familiar. I hesitated, but only for a second, long enough to confirm it was him. Then, I ran. Uncaring of the tiny rocks that dug into the soles of my feet. Unconcerned by the distance between us.

I just needed to see him.

The closer I got, the louder the scratching grew. He was creating the noise, and it beckoned me forward. But he barely noticed me approaching. He was on his hands and knees, leaning over the stone. His hair fell across his forehead, obscuring his face. But I could see the familiar pinch of his lips and the concentrated furrow of his brow. Nash Wickham was deeply focused on his task. Pieces of chalk fisted in his left hand, and his right dragged across the stone. Beneath his fingertips… Art.

"Don't step on that, Tav," he said as I neared. Proving he had seen me coming. "You'll smudge it."

My heart squeezed at the sound of his voice, my breath catching in the back of my throat. "Hey, Nash."

He glanced at me, barely a flicker of his eyes, before his attention turned back to his drawing. It was just enough to hurt, just enough to realise the blue smudge on his face was full of colour.

The only colour to have crossed into multiple dreams. Glancing at his fingertips, my spirits lifted to see a dusting of purple and green staining his skin. Nash was the source of colour in the world, my source of colour. I didn't know what I was going to do without him.

"Don't do it, Tav!" he said sharply when I stepped forward again. His eyes narrowed, but he still focused on the mural. "I mean it. I'll be really cross if you ruin it."

I wanted to laugh. Not because it was funny, but with the relief that rose through my body. It was just like Nash to tell me he'd be cross instead of angry. To barely acknowledge me because he was so focused on rubbing the different shades of chalk together. I wished he would look at me. Just so I could be sure that he was okay.

Careful not to move, not to disrupt the splashes of colour all around me, I crouched down to his level. Studying the side of his face intently. He looked like the man I knew, but something didn't feel right. I just couldn't quite pinpoint what had felt off.

"Nash…" I reached for him.

He shifted away from me, lips quirking as he muttered my name in return. "Octavia."

"What are you drawing?" I asked, changing tactics and trying not to feel hurt by the way he'd dodged me. It was hard to get a good look at his artwork. Now that I could see the colour in each stroke of chalk, I could tell that the picture expanded right across the courtyard. Widespread, detailed and beautiful. Nash had to have been drawing for a very long time.

"All seven of the sins. As we've known them. Although I guess I don't know Lust and Greed, not really, since I won't get to meet them." He didn't stop drawing as he explained. He dropped the blue chalk and reached for a grey piece instead.

He continued to sketch, speaking quicker now. "See, I drew the potion we drank in Gula that makes you never feel hungry. Surrounded by food that looks more like art than energy. It's all a little bit poisonous. The sides of the apples are rotting away, and the mushrooms are the spotted sort that would kill you.

Next, I drew the rain in Invidia. The way the city turned slick beneath it. The lights shone off the cobblestones and reflected the leathery wings of the harpies. I even hid pieces of akelda in that one, because they were so hard to find. And I drew the crone. I think it's a pretty good likeness."

Nash glanced at me but didn't pause long. "The sunsets over the barren mountains from Wrath, red-brown dirt, the bones of the dead baking beneath them. One of those skulls is Niklaus, do you think you'll be able to pick him out?"

My stomach twisted then, as I remembered that I'd never told Nash what had happened after he left the battlefields. That Niklaus still lived.

"Then," Nash said, sweeping his arm to show his left. "I tried my hand at the stained-glass windows of Pride's palace. Each one shattered into a thousand tiny pieces. Flecked red with the blood of the dead and left to settle below the big glass bell. There's a peacock somewhere in there, too. White, of course."

"Oh," I whispered. There was nothing else to say. When I stood and craned my neck, I could see more of his mural. I could see the thread of death and decay that he drew into each part, threading them together. It was surprisingly morbid for a man who had always been so hopeful.

"Nash… Aren't you sick of drawing?" I asked. "Or sick of dreaming?"

He turned towards me, shooing me back a step, filling the space that I'd stood within with colour. "I'm not dreaming, Octavia. You are."

"This is a dream," I told him, as firmly as I could. A quick glance at my wrist showed smudges of chalk in various colours. Beneath them, the tattoos of the sins were unrecognizable. It was definitely a dream. The images were too skewed, and the whisper of Samael was absent from my mind.

"I'm drawing a dream now. Can't you see it?" he asked and paused in his frenetic movements. His face collapsed with a frown, a piece of white chalk rolling between his fingers. "There are mirrors within each one, decorated with moons and stars, the same mirrors Sloth hid in my dreams. Also, a giant snail. Did you notice they're everywhere in the Slothlands? Not giant snails, but regular-sized ones. They have tiny little blue veins in their shells. Snow-snails, I called them."

He paused, wetting his lips, and a shudder rolled through his lanky body. "It snowed in all my dreams. I hated it. Could never escape it. Whether I was awake or asleep, I was always so cold."

A shiver rolled down my spine, a memory of the bone-deep chill of the Slothlands. The icy terrain was haunting, but it sounded as though Nash had found it miserable. I didn't doubt it, either. He'd always sought the sun.

"What will you draw for Lust?" I asked him, determined to turn the conversation back towards something brighter. Nash turned back to his art. The crease between his brows smoothed away as he started on the swirling shell of another blue snail.

"Alby, and the pink cherries he liked from the markets. Finley Nightingale's crooked smile and wild curls. The white sand beaches and seashell jewellery that he told me about. The painted boats of their dead." It was a simple answer, but I couldn't imagine it panning out. Not when Nash, like me, had never even seen sand and the seashores.

I nodded slowly, daring to ask, "And Greed?"

Swivelling his attention, Nash Wickham looked at me. Properly. His head snapped up and his eyes settled on my face, his scrutiny so intense that I felt self-conscious. He wet his lips, tipped his chin and shrugged. "I'll draw you."

"Me?" I gasped, slack-jawed and blinking.

"Don't you think you're greedy, Octavia?" Nash asked, his head cocked to one side.

It felt like a loaded question. A pointed question. Like we both knew the answer, but only one of us had the gall to tell the truth. I shifted from foot to foot, beginning to worry about the answer.

"I… What?" I spluttered. "No. I'm not greedy."

"I think you are," he said, simply. He reached for the blue chalk again, nudging me back another step. "You don't mean to be. At least I don't think you do. *But you are*. You take from other people all the time. You need all their attention and their energy. You need their support and their help. You're sort of like Sloth in that regard, stealing the core energy from other people to survive. The problem is: you rarely think about anyone else, only yourself. You keep taking more and more. Tav, that's what makes you greedy."

My blood had turned hot and then went ice cold. My skin prickled with discomfort. Nash barely looked at me as he spoke his truth, still focused so intently on his art. He barely seemed to care that it hurt me to hear what he thought. Or that it might not be true.

I knew I was selfish and thoughtless at times, but I'd never considered myself greedy. I'd never had enough wealth or materialistic possessions to think it applied to me. Greedy people were… Obsessed with wealth and coin. A flicker of dread in my gut made me wonder if that was me.

Nash seemed to think that greed wasn't just about what you

had, but how you acted. The impact you had on other people. Greed might not have been as limited as I'd thought.

He dusted the blue chalk from his fingers, stood, stretched and wiped his hands against his thighs. It left a streak of colour behind. Brightening the black-and-white world, as he always did. Nash picked out more pieces of chalk and shuffled past me. He set to work on another clean patch of stone. I followed him like a lost child. It was hard not to beg for an ounce of his attention, especially after what he'd just said. I so desperately wanted him to look at me, smile, laugh and tell me he hadn't meant it.

"Nash," I said, crouching in front of him again, trying to capture his attention. There was a lump of discomfort developing in my throat. "What does it matter if I'm greedy or not? This is just a dream."

He barely acknowledged my words. "No, it's not just a dream."

"It is… We're dreaming, and you can wake up with me." I reached for him, but he shuffled out of my reach again. Nash turned his back on me, and I shook my head.

"Nash, I need you to wake up with me." This was begging and I knew it. I wasn't above it. I'd beg Nash Wickham to crawl from the depths of his grave. It that made me greedy, demanding his return, so be it. "Please, Nash."

"Octavia, I can't do that." The statement, and his repeated use of my entire name, was so blunt that I flinched. Rocking back on my heels. He was here. Right in front of me and I wouldn't let him go now. Nash could wake up and we'd keep going, we'd finish the trials.

"You're right Nash. I am greedy," I said. "I need you. Please, I need you to wake up with me. Don't stay here without me. We have things to do, we have a trial to win. Come on, Nash."

"I'm not asleep, Tav." His head snapped up and he glared at me. Even without colour, his eyes burned bright with the intensity of his anger. "You know that. I know that. So, accept it."

My throat tightened, and my eyes burned. "You have to be asleep. You're right here, stuck in Sloth's dreamscape. You're—"

"Dead."

I gasped, "Nash…"

His hazel eyes narrowed, his grip on the chalk tightening. He stood, and even though I'd been trying to reach for him, when Nash moved forward, I stepped back. His chin dipped, expression serious.

"I'm dead," he repeated.

"No!" It was so easy to deny it. I didn't want him to die. I didn't want to do these trials without him. Nash had patched up so many holes in my soul, and he didn't even know it. He'd helped me knit myself back together, time and time again. Sometimes, he'd been the only reason that I smiled. There was no way I'd survive without him. Not now, not anymore.

Continuing with reality felt impossible as I mourned him. I'd be alone in my grief, and that was something I was unwilling to face. The pain wasn't worth it.

Nash was relentless in his denial, staying firm. "I'm dead, Octavia. We both know it."

"But…" I gestured at him. "You're here."

"Look me in the eye and tell me you haven't dreamed of dead people before." His nose flared, locks of hair falling across his face. "I did. I dreamed of Alby every single time I closed my eyes. Octavia… Even if I hadn't died, I would have given into Sloth. You don't know what it felt like to exist with him, away from the worries of life, in a place where he wasn't sick. Given the choice, I would have stayed here, with him."

"You can't mean that." My stomach churned with discomfort. "Nash, you know you would keep going.

"No, you just want to believe I would have kept on." He turned away. His attention drifted back to his drawing, and he picked up the black chalk, adding shadows down one side.

"What's the point of winning if he wasn't waiting for me in the end?"

"But…" I faltered. There was no good argument for his word. No way to convince him it would have been worth it.

Nash clucked his tongue. "Living isn't everything, Tav. Not if you're not happy. Why would I want to stay in a world where I was cold and miserable?"

"And dying is better…?" I asked, biting out the words. His logic was wrong. "That's your answer to unhappiness, Nash?"

"How long has it been?" Nash asked, and now he sounded tired. He glanced over his shoulder, but only for the briefest of moments. "How long since you remember being really, properly happy, Tav?"

"I…" It was difficult not to flinch again. Difficult to admit that I couldn't remember the last time I'd been truly happy. The light buoyant feeling of joy felt like a myth these days. It paled in the face of relief, which I'd felt a thousand times over in the last few months. Stress and worry crushed my happiness. They were emotions I felt all the time. I sighed heavily, admitting, "It's been a while."

Nash jerked his chin. He didn't look unsympathetic. It almost looked like he understood. "I would have been happy in my dreams with him. You have no idea how much I wanted to go right back to sleep whenever I woke up. How much I missed him when I woke. Sometimes, it felt like we lived years together in one dream. It was gutting to wake up and find out it had never really happened. To know that I didn't have him close and might never see him again."

My lips pinched. Sudden fury blazed hot in my veins. I hated that he preferred to wither away in his sleep for a mirage of his partner, rather than continue through the trials with me. Crossing my arms over my chest, I huffed at him. "What about in death then? Will you be happy with him there?"

Nash blinked at me. There was a flicker of sadness in his

eyes. "I guess I don't feel anything there. I wouldn't know. My feelings are artificial. This is your dream, not mine. You don't dream when you're dead."

I turned away from him, trying to control the onslaught of emotion. The way the bridge of my nose prickled. Threatening a fresh wave of tears. The mural of the Invidian streets gleamed before me. He'd captured the shimmer of streetlights in the slew of rain perfectly. That, too, made me want to cry.

"This is cruel," I said. Seeing him, only for him to refuse to wake felt like just another knife sliding between my ribs intending to injure my heart.

He shrugged. This version of Nash was too flippant and too uncaring for my liking, tainted by the toxicity of the dreamscape. "Take it up with Sloth."

My body felt like it had turned numb, caught in a wave of despair. "What?"

"The content of your dreams," Nash said. "Take it up with Sloth. She's the one who chooses what you experience." He changed colours and then stood to squint down at his work. "Or don't. Just stay here and rot. Doesn't matter to me…"

"You don't care because you're dead," I said, scowling.

"Yeah." His mouth quirked into the soft edge of a grin. For one lingering moment, he looked like the man I knew. "I am."

There was a wry amusement in his tone. So alike his usual self that it felt like a punch to the gut. I stood, completely winded, and watched him work. He moved as if I weren't there, concentrating on his sketch as he added colour to the world. I'd never see Nash draw again, I realised. If he was dead – I'd long since missed the chance to see him create anything beautiful. Or to see him smile. This was my last chance to speak with him.

It wasn't the same, though. This mirage from my imagination paled compared to the man I'd known. He could never compare. Misery welled in my gut, and I hugged my waist tightly.

"There," he said. Nash stood, wiped his hands together and

then beckoned me over to his side. I followed, not sure what he wanted. Just as unsure of whether I trusted him – this version of Nash who told hard truths and didn't let me touch him. "Greed."

When I looked down at the stone surface, my heart jolted in my chest like a strike of lightning. True to his words, it was a picture of me. Those were my eyes, my strong nose and the mottled, textured skin of my cheek, jaw, and throat. I looked... Haunted and profoundly sad. A soft whimper rolled over my lips. Nash could have always seen me like this, pitiful, or maybe — given that it was my dream — maybe this was how I saw myself.

"Nash..." I whispered.

He turned to me this time, and instead of twisting out of reach, he stayed close. Both his hands lifted and pressed against my cheeks. His fingers were so ice-cold that I could truly believe that he was dead. He looked me in the eye, but the spark was missing. There was no life within him. "Yes, Octavia?"

"Why are you here?"

"I think it's because you wanted to see me," he said. "You missed me enough that Sloth re-created me."

That sounded like the truth. "I don't want to do it without you."

"I know." He sounded sad, although it didn't reflect in his features. "But you need to... Or you don't."

"What do you mean?" I asked, although I had a feeling that I already knew.

"I think you should keep going. Or at least that's what I would have said in life," Nash said. "Sloth would want me to convince you to stay, I suppose. That's why I'm here, too. You're hurting, and you wanted to see me. Maybe Sloth thinks you'll want to stay here with me like I wanted to with Alby. We always want to stick around for the people we miss most."

"All my dreams turn to nightmares, though," I told him. "Why would I want to stay in a nightmare?"

"Because a nightmare is pain that can't actually hurt you. It ends. It's not real. It's suffering that goes away…" Nash shook his head. His thumbs stroked against my cheeks, brushing away tears. "It still hurts less than the pain you'll feel in life. It's just dulled enough that you'll stay here instead."

"Hmm." I made a non-committal sound. "So, I should stay?"

"If you want," Nash shrugged, as if it didn't really matter. "The thing is, Octavia, for all your many faults, you never quit. Do you?"

He let go of me. Nash stepped back, smudging his mural underfoot as he put distance between us. I went to follow him, but I couldn't make my legs move. Once again, I was stuck, locked in front of his rendition of myself.

Nash walked away from me without looking back. Drifting into the far side of the courtyard. I tried not to scream.

"Don't leave me!" I yelled after him.

His hand waved. Still, he didn't turn. "Make a choice, Octavia. Quickly."

"You didn't let me say goodbye!" The words burned my throat, torn from deep inside my chest. Filled with building rage and grief, a whirlwind of emotion that I couldn't contain. It wasn't fair to be robbed of the chance to say goodbye. Not to this half-rate version of him, but to the man before he died. I couldn't even remember what the last words I'd said to him were. Fear that they weren't something pleasant was eating me from the inside out.

"Nash Aaron Wickham, get back here!" I yelled.

His laugh floated back to me, although I couldn't see him anymore. "Goodbye, Tav."

It wasn't enough. Nowhere near enough.

I fell to my knees, pain searing through them, and pressed my hands to his artwork. The chalk residue was grainy against my skin. In a fit of rage, I rubbed my hands over the picture of myself. Ruining it. Colour seeped against my skin.

I screamed and screamed, letting violent emotion manifest in noise, but Nash never answered.

He never returned.

A sob burst from my lips, and I found I could move. I ruined the next drawing, dragging my feet through it, and the next. A soft white fog rolled around me, drifting over the chalk-covered surfaces.

I collapsed again, drained of energy. Unwilling to deal with any of it. My body pressed to the cold stone, and I stared up at the grey sky. The fog washed over me, claiming me for the next dream. I realised it was the way Sloth washed away one dreamscape to create another.

Which meant Nash wasn't coming back.

It meant I couldn't stay here and wait for him.

The flippant call over his shoulder wasn't enough of a goodbye. I'd never be able to say it to him. He'd never know the imprint that he'd left on my life. I trembled with sadness as the miasma claimed me.

Nash Wickham had changed me, shaped me into a better person. I'd never be able to thank him for it.

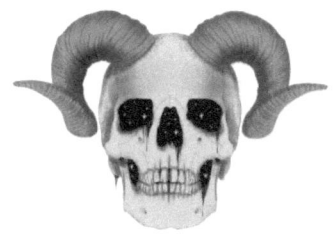

Chapter Twenty-Seven

I floated in a pool of dark water. It was cold, almost icy. It turned my skin frigid and lowered my body temperature until my breath misted in the air.

The sky above me was as dark as the water below. It glittered with the light of tiny, soft stars. It was almost as peaceful as the sky had been in Samael's purgatory. Everything was blissfully silent, even the thoughts in my head. There was no whirring worry, or predictions tracking of what might happen in the future.

My brain didn't remind me of all the times I'd failed or embarrassed myself in the past. My head was blissfully empty.

Alone in the cold, with nothing but dark space stretching out beyond me, I was unafraid. My heart rate slowed for the first time since I'd relinquished myself to Sloth. Driven myself into the supposed safety of these dreams. Instead of racing in fear, or pumping through an adrenaline spike, it had relaxed.

A thump, thump, thump became a background melody as I

drifted through the water. Floating in a lazy circle. I did nothing but stare into the sky and count the stars.

"Hello?" I called out, moments, minutes, or hours later when the drag of time had become too much. When the novelty of idleness had worn thin.

Nobody answered.

Except for my voice echoing back at me, drifting into the space around me.

There was nothing to do except float. Except wait for something, anything, to happen. I didn't think I'd had this much time to myself, to think, since even before the trials had begun. Now, I had nothing but time. The thoughts in my head came back, but slower than normal, as I considered each of them. Giving them the time they deserved.

It was strange how many regrets a human being could have if there was time enough to reflect. I stopped counting the stars, or even paying attention to the moment they winked out of existence. Instead, I considered my life.

If I had tried harder as a younger woman, I might have turned out a far better person. Hard-working or intelligent, maybe even just skilled enough to survive without risking my life. If I'd cared more about anything other than the fleeting high of a win, I might have been able to turn one coin into two and then three. Without relying on luck. That soft, momentary feeling of accomplishment may have become a more frequent, natural feeling. If I'd tried harder.

A different version of myself would have been more palatable. Easier to digest than the woman I was now. My parents might even have been proud of me. The way that Chancellor Heira and his wife always had been of their twin boys. Beaming at their accomplishments, boasting about them whenever they could. I couldn't remember a single time that my mother had spoken about me with pride. I was not a woman to brag about.

It became difficult then to remember the soft lines of my

father's face. Or even my mother's stronger features. No matter how hard I focused and tried to picture them, something was always missing. Trying and failing made my heart beat a little harder, still slowed, with a deeper chest ache accompanying each beat.

I was losing them.

Although I could remember the dirt that never quite scrubbed out of the creases in my father's knuckles. The soft grey shirt he'd worn on every one of his rare days off. Or the way my mother always hugged me around the middle. So tight that my ribs felt like they were going to crack. There was never anywhere to go until she released the tension in her surprisingly strong arms. She'd always hugged me like that each morning, so tight, as if she'd never see me again.

Maybe my mother had known that one day she wouldn't. I didn't think I'd ever see her again.

Even if I stood right in front of her, I imagined I'd be unrecognisable.

Drifting through the water in slow circles, I sighed heavily. No matter who I tried to recall. Everyone's faces felt blurry at the edges now, features lost to obscurity. There was only a glimpse of Ophelia's soft plaited hair woven with tiny flowers. The flash of Niklaus' tattoos, brightly coloured and disappearing beneath his clothes. The tiny red marks on the bridge of Helina's freckled nose from where her spectacles pinched against her skin. The smudge of colour on Nash's sharp cheekbones, after he'd wiped his hands on his face as he painted.

Each lost as we'd faced different sins. Ophelia, the glutton, wrathful Niklaus, Helina lost to her stubborn pride. On reflection, I could admit that the devil's trials hadn't been at all what I expected.

It was laughable now, to realise that what I'd imagined in the beginning was so far from the truth. I'd thought we'd be facing the sins outright. That I would have had to stand in front of

Gluttony, knees knocking, and best him in a duel. The devil wanted more introspection than action. He wanted us to evolve beyond the people we had been in the beginning. We hadn't been good enough for him, or Eternis, in the beginning. I wasn't sure I'd be good enough in the end, either.

It was easy to feel like I'd failed Samael. With the sins, or their supposed allies, giving me aid or free passes through the trials. I didn't deserve their help. Maybe instead, I'd deserved to die in Ilrea, at the end of Boyd's rusted blade. Or in the place of anyone else that I'd grown to care about.

The people who truly deserved to succeed.

Tears pooled in my eyes, dripping free and sliding down my cheeks to mix with the water. Fuck, I was so sick of crying. It was a useless waste of my precious energy, and it didn't make me feel better. I kicked out but still moved at the same slow pace. My chest squeezed tight, and my heart felt like it was growing heavy.

Too heavy, like it might turn into my own personal anchor and drag me down into the bottomless depths below.

"Hello?" I called again. My voice echoed uselessly into the abyss. "Is there anyone out there?"

This time, I didn't expect an answer.

I was so devastatingly lonely. The cavern of loss in my chest couldn't be filled. I'd lost so many people. Too many of them had stamped themselves into my soul. Attaching themselves to me with such vigour that their deaths had ripped pieces free.

That might be why I drifted now, untethered from the woman I'd once been. They'd taken too much of me with them. Wilful ignorance and false cheer wouldn't repair the damage they'd left behind. They were a pain that demanded to be felt.

Devils, did I feel it. I cried and cried and cried. Until my eyes stung and my head throbbed. But it changed nothing, not the lazily circular course of my floating, not the way my limbs were weighed down. Not even the soft twinkling of the stars above me.

"Please…" I sobbed the words now, a soft cry for anyone to

answer me. "Please…"

"Oh, hello," someone answered. Their voice was soft and childlike, floating across the water as if the speaker were a great distance away. So far away that I might never reach them. That didn't matter, though. I latched onto the sound and the hope it represented. Any tension I felt melted away to make room for pure relief.

"You're here!" I cried out. "Oh devils, you're here. I'm not alone."

"You're never alone," they said. Their voices were soothing, and it made me want to close my eyes and drift off to sleep. "I've always been here with you."

"Who are you?" I asked. "Where are you?"

They giggled. A soft sound and although I couldn't see her, I envisioned a child. "I'm everywhere. In each drop of water and each twinkling star. I am, in essence, everything around you."

"What…" I was kicked out, struggling to move. There was nowhere to go except around in circles. The push of my legs only spun me in the other direction.

"Do you understand?" she asked.

"No." I sighed. "But I never do, and that doesn't stop the world from turning around me."

A moment of silence lingered between us, and for a beat, I thought she'd left. I thought I was alone again. Instead, grey wings swept through my peripheral vision, along with the flash of ice-white hair. The water around me rippled, gently swaying, as if there were something else in here with me. The temperature dropped another degree. It was freezing around me, a thin sheen of ice rippling out from where I lay.

"You can get out of the water now, Octavia," she said.

I blinked at the stars. "Get out?"

Another giggle, light enough that it coaxed me to smile. "You can simply stand up."

"Oh." It felt like I'd been floating forever, drifting in

untethered circles. Not once had I thought of just standing up. I pushed my legs down. They sunk deeper. It was icy around, the movement creating cracks in the surface. Thin fragments of ice slipped below the surface of the water and disappeared.

My feet hit the ground. I jolted, faltered, and then stood. The pool of water ended at my waist, my hair dripping over both shoulders. Tentatively, I wrung it out, shivering against the chill of the night.

"Could I have done that all along?" I asked.

Another giggle, and this time I knew they were laughing at me, not with me. "Yes."

"Who are you?" I asked, again. They'd never told me. The light, childish edge to their voice made me think of a little girl. Not unlike the one who had woken in the outer villages. Creeping intuition told me I was dealing with something a lot more dangerous, though. So many of my other dreams had left me wound tight with stress. I had no reason to believe this one would be any different.

"You already know who I am," she said. Her voice echoed across the water. "I am Lady Sloth."

My heart may as well have plunged to the bottom of the lake. I stared into the glassy surface of the water, searching for any hint of the angel. It felt like she was right there, in my peripheral vision, but kept just out of reach. No matter how many times I turned, Sloth was nowhere to be found. Swallowing, I gathered my courage, asking, "Why are all my dreams nightmares?"

Sloth hummed. "Not all of them were."

"You know what I mean," I snapped.

My frustration had welled through me so quickly that there'd been no time to temper my reaction. It felt like the angel had been slowly torturing me, keeping me trapped in my mind, suppressed by the anxious pressure in my chest.

"Most of them were horrible. You couldn't call them dreams. I didn't get a lost lover like Nash or a life I didn't want to leave.

You've just given me death and trauma. You've made me hurt. I get enough of that when I'm awake. I'm tired of it! I'm tired of everything!"

My tantrum wouldn't win me any favours. Still, it felt good to release the pent-up emotion and get it off my chest. It was far more cathartic than crying about it. I pouted at the sky and the stars because there was still nobody to direct my anger towards. The angel hadn't faced me directly.

"Climb out of the lake, Octavia," Sloth said

"And go where? There's nothing here. Nothing but me…" I complained and as soon as I spoke, the landscape shifted before my eyes.

Where there had been nothing but darkness, there was now the soft rise of a snowy bank in the distance. The water pushed back at me, resisting my departure as I waded towards the shore. For a split second, I considered lying back down in the water and succumbing to the quiet again. It wasn't enough. I kept moving.

An icy wind bit into my skin, whipping against my cheeks as I scrambled up into the snow. The snow slipped beneath my hands and knees, and I collapsed into it.

My teeth chattered, and my body shook. I'd been cold before, but not dripping with water and left-in-a-frozen-wasteland cold. This was beyond anything I'd felt before. Succumbing to the ice, I lay still, focused only on the slow pace of my breathing. A piece of my hair fell in front of my face. I could see tiny icicles on the frozen strands.

I considered closing my eyes and letting go. Freezing to death couldn't be the worst way I could die. It seemed relatively painless.

"Did you not want to have this conversation face-to-face?" Sloth coaxed me into movement as she spoke. I opened my eyes. "Many of your competitors did."

"Where are you?" I asked, curling my hands in the snow and drawing in a deep breath. A moment of procrastination so I could

375

find the gall to force myself to move. I clambered up onto my hands and knees, wobbling back onto my feet.

When I sighed, it misted in front of my face. Fell to the snow and rolled around my feet, as if my every breath was part of her miasma.

"Over here," Sloth called. I turned, following her voice. "Keep walking, Octavia. Not long now."

The landscape changed as I walked. The bland snow remained, but the mist in the distance faded, revealing trees covered in ice. Long, sharp icicles dropped from each branch, looming above me as I crept beneath them. I had a violently clear vision of one breaking free and plummeting straight through my heart, so I shook my head to control my breathing as I inched past them.

My steps led me to a wide clearing covered with a blanket of snow. A large tree rose from the depths of the earth. The branches were decorated with crisp red leaves and lethal drops of ice. The angel I sought crouched at the base of the tree. Her head tipped forward, pale hands buried in the snow. Her soft grey wings were shielded from the falling snow.

The leaves crunched underfoot. At the sound of my approach, the angel stilled. She stood and turned to face me. Lifting her hand and beckoned me forward with a lazy curl of her fingers. My heart beat slowly but thundered in my ears, and I did as silently commanded, closing the space between us.

Standing before the otherworldly angel of sin, I realised she sounded like a child because she was one. There was a youthful roundness to her face and body, a plump edge to her lips and her wind-kissed cheeks. Ice frosted across her skin. Her hair was long, flowing to her waist. A sheet of blue-white hung straight and still as if it had frozen in place. There was snow beneath her nails and snowflakes crystallised on the end of her long eyelashes.

Sloth smiled at me, offering a slow, shy expression.

"Tell me," I whispered, forcing myself to ask. Her childish

appearance wouldn't fool me. She was — no doubt — every bit as dangerous as the rest of her brethren. Perhaps even worse. The angels of sin couldn't be trusted, no matter how soft they presented themselves. "Why did you give me nightmares and not dreams?"

"It's just as easy to keep someone amid their trauma as it is in their desires." It sounded like such a simple answer. Sloth continued, waving her delicate hand through the air, "Humans are so… grievously prone to wallowing. I get such a yummy taste of emotion from a nightmare, from fear and fury, tears and worry. Dreams are nice, but often humans dream of such mundane things."

I frowned, scrunching up my face. I hated the way these sins spoke, expecting that I could understand the underlying meaning of their words. It implied that I would be stupid if I didn't. It reminded me of Pride. I shivered, speaking through grit teeth, "I don't know what that means… Prone to wallowing."

Sloth blinked slowly. Her head tilted, and her pale blue eyes narrowed on my face.

"It means you like to suffer, Octavia." She reached for my hand, her fingers frozen as they laced through mine. The tiny flakes of ice irritated my skin.

My entire body tensed. I didn't like the angel touching me. She kept talking before I could object, tugging on my hand to lead me on another walk.

"But you do not like to carry your pain with you. In a dream, you can let it go. For someone like you, that means you're likely to stay. It hurts less in the web of my magic than it does to stay alive."

"Am I going to die here, then?" I asked.

Once, dying felt like my greatest fear. I couldn't imagine anything worse than my life cut short before my next win. I had so many monsters hiding in the shadows, so much pain to bear, that death almost looked like a sweet relief.

I continued before she could answer, "If the alternative is being alive and in pain... If I am dying, just tell me. I'd rather know and be ready."

"Do you want that?" Lady Sloth paused. She tilted her soft face towards me, her white brows knitted with curiosity.

Pressing my lips together, I considered the question and countered with one of my own. "Pain, life, or death?"

"Any of them. All of them." Sloth smiled, and this time, it threw me off. She flashed her teeth. Pointed like tiny little icicles, dangerously sharp. Just like Samael, she had fangs. "Or none. If you stay with me, Octavia. I could give you all three. If you chose life... Well, nobody can guarantee what you would feel there."

It was difficult not to consider it. There was a certain peace to the world we walked through. We turned away from the tree and entered tiny villages, the cobblestone walkways smattered with melting snow.

It could be easier to stay here with Sloth. But then I thought of Ophelia, biting into the flesh of her own bloody heart. Of Nash, telling me I was greedy. I flinched, suddenly feeling raw and exposed.

"Will all the dreams be so hard on my soul?" I asked. "I'm tired of being afraid. I'm tired of being hurt."

"It won't be easy," Sloth said. "While not as gluttonous as my brother, I do need sustenance, and the pain of your feelings is delightfully addictive. I can promise you many things though, little human. Many things that you so desperately want. You will see the people you miss dearly. I will reunite you with the people you lost. The pain you feel will always pass quicker than it would if you woke. You don't have to carry it from one dream to another."

"Would I die here?" I asked.

Lady Sloth had said she would give me life, pain, and death. While my body lay preserved like the rest of her society.

"Eventually, yes, you are only human, after all. It takes time, as many things do in the Slothlands." She giggled again. I didn't understand what was so funny about it. "But you would pass in reality much faster. This will give you a longer life. It would be close to the immortality the devil promised you but without the hardship of the next two sins."

Glancing away from her, glaring at the tiny, perfect houses around us. It felt like she was underestimating me. I'd faced four sins before her. Surely, I could face the two after her as well. I was stronger than anyone gave me credit for, even if it was at the expense of other people.

"I could face Greed and Lust," I said, my tone sharp. "If I wanted to."

"Could you?" Sloth asked. It was an innocent question. Her tone pitched just enough that I could tell she thought my claim was false. "My brothers are more than you could ever imagine. You will suffer if you face them. I'm certain of it."

Disentangling my fingers from hers, and pulling my hand from her grip, I folded my arms across my chest. Two big paces put some space between us. Enough for me to take a full breath.

"What do you want with me?" I asked, daring to face the angel again. I hadn't fought my way through the ordeal that had been Pride, stolen away from the rebellion camps just to have an angel declare I wouldn't make it.

If Samael thought I could win, then this sin had no business implying otherwise.

Sloth dipped her pointed chin and flashed her sharp teeth. Tiny snowflakes had settled in her hair, their unique patterns surprisingly clear. It formed a crown. "Take a guess, Octavia."

"You want me to stay…"

"No." Sloth brushed a strand of hair from her face, looking disinterested in whether I stayed.

"No?" I asked, surprised. I'd thought her entire trial was trapping us in her web of dreams. I'd thought she would have wanted to claim as many of us as she could. Finding out that my assumptions were wrong was jarring. It unsettled me to think that maybe now I didn't know how to win. "But…"

"I want you to decide what you truly want," Lady Sloth told me. She reached up, pressing her icy hand to the smooth skin of my unburned cheek. Her hands were still icy, and I struggled not to jerk away. Instead, I stayed as still as I could.

The angel looked grave. "Life or dreams, Octavia? You have entered Desidia and met the sin of Sloth, and so it is time to make a choice."

"Right now?" My mouth dried out, throat tightening with anxiety. A moment ago, I'd been floating in a lake, with more time than I knew what to do with. Now a hard and life-altering decision was thrust upon me, and I had no time to truly consider it. Surely there were more dreams to come, more days to wander across her city and gather my thoughts.

I'd thought I'd face Sloth in person, not in an impossible dream. The snow fell harder, turning into a flurry around us both.

"Stay here or wake through the mirror," I said. "That's my choice?"

Lady Sloth giggled. Her icicle crown was growing beneath the fall of the snow. "The mirror itself does not exist. It's just a representation that's easy for humans to conceptualise. The simple idea of being able to move through something to pass from dreams to waking. Clever, no?"

I said nothing and she clicked her tongue.

"Chose now, Octavia," Sloth demanded.

"Um," I faltered, fisting my hands by my side. Worried I'd make the wrong choice. A choice I couldn't take back and would regret. "I don't know."

The angel looked up, turning her face to the snowflakes, and she smiled at them. Relishing the joy of their arrival. It was as if I didn't exist, as if she weren't asking me to make a hard decision. The flaking ice on her skin grew more intense, some of it falling away, before more crusted over.

"There's no time like the present," she murmured. "Choose dreams, Octavia, and I vow that your next one will be pleasant. You will not regret staying with me."

There was a small part of me, as tiny as the snails that had appeared in the snow — their shells veined blue like Nash had said — that believed she might be right. That I could exist in the dreamscape with a little pain but no regrets, and it could be a lifetime of relief compared to the constant struggle of living.

"What do you want, Octavia?" she asked again.

"I…" I fumbled, unsure of the right path.

There was nobody to ask. I couldn't rely on the judgement of others. There was just me and Sloth. I missed the voice inside my head, my dark, possessive, guiding devil. My heart pounded, thumping against my ribs so hard it was a wonder it didn't break free.

"I want to see Samael."

"Done." Sloth smiled, all pointed teeth and icy breath. She stood on her toes, rising up slightly, and brushed her lips against my scarred cheek. It was a frozen feeling, and when she dropped back down, the world dropped away. Disappeared.

I screamed as I fell through the frozen earth.

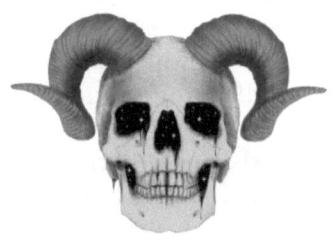

Chapter Twenty-Eight

"Octavia!"

So often, I'd murmured Samael's name as a reverent prayer. Wishing and praying that he would save me, that his magic would carry me safely through.

This time… This time my name was the prayer. I could hear the weight of his relief in every syllable of my name. The devil's strong arms wrapped around me, holding me so tightly that I groaned with pain. He didn't release me, bowing his horned head and pressing his face to the side of my neck.

His mouth brushed against the tender spot where my neck and my shoulder met. Coaxing another soft groan from deep inside my chest. I'd missed him. Missed seeing Samael as more than a whisper in my mind. Sloth had been cruelly manipulative in these dreams. She offered me a taste of the devil as a being I could touch, hold and lean on. His own influence on the dreams was so reminiscent of the being I knew I couldn't help but trust the dream form of him. I couldn't help but miss him whenever I woke.

White wings encircled us both, blocking out the world. Samael shifted his weight from foot to foot, rocking me with the movement. Soft, soothing noises flowed from the end of his forked tongue, and I relaxed against him. Turning boneless as even more tears welled in my eyes and dripped down my cheeks. The release of energy had me sagging against him, and his fingers massaged along my spine.

"You're alive," the devil murmured against my neck. The rough stubble on his chin prickled against my skin as he buried his head against me, inhaling deeply. His entire body shuddered, and I let out a hiccuping sob. "Thank the mother. I couldn't reach you in life or in dreams. I thought you had died with your friend."

Nobody had ever sounded so aggressively relieved to see me. I'd never felt as wanted as I had in that moment. The devil didn't let me go. He held me tight until I pressed my palms to his chest, pushing back in a plea for a full breath of air.

He relaxed, incrementally, giving me the space to move. Although his ominous eyes studied me intently, as if he were searching for cracks and imperfections.

"Would that have been the worst thing?" I asked. "It's strange that a god of death would worry about that."

When I looked around, we were back in his solarium in Eternis. The glass ceiling above us reflected the same starry sky I had stared at for so long in the lake. They twinkled, winking out of existence as I watched on.

"Octavia," Samael said my name like a warning this time. His cherished prayer was long gone. His scarred brows sunk to knit together, as he reached for my chin and tipped my attention back towards him. "Are you here to say goodbye to me? Is that why we're in this dream?"

"Maybe," I said, hedging.

Confrontation had never been my strong point. Although I'd

improved a lot over the past four trials, confronting Samael was something else, entirely. He let go of me, and I staggered backwards. His wings pulled close to his body and allowed me room to move. I bumped into the plush couch and sank to sit on the velvet cushions, picking nervously at the button.

"Do elaborate," Samael said, folding his arms across his chest.

"There's nothing waiting for me in reality," I said. "I could stay with Sloth and be happy."

Samael loomed in front of me. His wings rustled with irritation, his forked tongue flicking at the air. "Do you think that's the key to happiness, Octavia? Avoiding your pain won't lighten your soul."

"What does it matter? Nobody wants me out there, anyway!" I cried. "I'm a blight on society!"

My sudden anger was overwhelming. Samael didn't understand — and how could he? We were nothing alike. I was human and he was a demon from another world. He was powerful where I was lacking. He'd never struggled in the ways I had. He would never know my pain.

Samael's lips twitched with a hint of amusement. I glared at him. Daring him to actually laugh. It took him a minute, but the devil schooled his face into a more impassive expression, murmuring. "That's a big proclamation for you, isn't it? Do you know what a blight is?"

"People have literally said it to my face before." I sniffed, looking away. Not willing to admit that I didn't know what it meant. It had hurt when they'd said it, so I'd thought it would be effective now.

His big, white hellhound padded into the room. It leaned heavily against the angel's side. A yawn flashed its thick fangs. Samael scratched the beast behind the ear and asked, "Would you like me to tell you what it means?"

My jaw set, and I fisted my hands in my lap. I could feel the heat rising in my cheeks and flushing along my neck. "No. I didn't say that I didn't understand it."

"Fair," he said, his forked tongue flicking into the air. He moved a step closer to me. "Well, what about me, then?"

"What about you?" I bit out, trying to relax my white-knuckled grip on the cushions. Samael looked unimpressed with the snappy edge to my tone, but I couldn't take it back. I didn't want to take it back. I wanted him to understand the force of my conflicted feelings and brewing frustration.

"I'm waiting for you out in the real world," he said through grit teeth. Samael looked down at me fiercely, his words blunt as he continued, "Do you really think I would have supported you — *protected you* — if I didn't want to see you arrive in Eternis, Octavia?"

There was a lump growing in my throat. I swallowed roughly, still doubting every word he said. The devil was a liar. Everyone knew that. But a part of me wanted to believe him.

I raised my chin, defiantly meeting his eye. "You've always told me not to trust you."

Samael looked nonplussed by the comment. Instead, he took a step closer, tilting his head at me. He was so close that his scent had become suffocating. Spicy and alluring, it was at once distracting.

"Do you trust Maksymilian Tate?" The devil asked.

My heart dropped and my stomach soured. I hadn't thought he'd go too far to threaten someone else to convince me to wake. My teeth pinched against my lower lip, a sharp enough pain to help me collect myself. "Why?" I asked. "What have you done to him?"

"Nothing." Samael looked momentarily triumphant. "But while you remain in these dreams, avoiding your very human pain. He's kneeling in the cold snow with his hands pressed to your chest. He's breaking your ribs and forcing your heart to keep beating. That man is the only one keeping you alive. If he tires or stops, I will take your soul. You will die."

"Why would he do that?" I asked, breaking eye contact with the devil. My stomach churned. It had twisted into a complicated knot. I didn't like the idea that my life was literally in his hands.

"Consider that maybe I'm not the only one waiting for you out there," Samael said. "You might call yourself a blight, Octavia, but there are people who care whether you wake up in the morning. You're just wallowing in your pity too much to acknowledge it."

I tipped my head back and stared determinedly at the stars as I considered his words. It was easier to speak when I wasn't looking at him. Easier to throw accusations. Samael intimidated me, and standing up to him was difficult.

"You're lying," I said. "You're just trying to manipulate me."

"I am dishonest about many things, yes, but not about this, Little One." Samael stalked forward.

He sat on the seat beside me, the force of his weight tipping me sideways. It pressed me against him, against his cold chest, where I could listen to his still heart.

"Prove it."

"I cannot. Not here. This is not my realm." Samael brushed a lock of hair from my face. "That man promised he would take you to Eternis, and he will die trying to keep your heart beating. If you do not wake, death will claim you both."

"You're just…" I spluttered, trying to put space between us, as I repeated my claim, "Samael, you're manipulating me."

"Yes, I am. I'm the devil, Octavia. You should expect nothing else."

When a grin split across his features, it was pure devilish chaos. His opalescent eyes glowed brightly. They swirled with bright colours. The longer I looked, the more I felt like I was tumbling into a black hole. Lost to infinity, with nothing to hold on to.

"It doesn't change facts, though," Samael continued. "You have many reasons to live, but you're stubbornly ignoring them all."

He broke eye contact, and I drew my first full breath in minutes. Clamouring to hold on to my wits. "But Nash—"

Samael turned back and reached out for my face. I flinched as his black, claw-like nails brushed over my jaw. My discomfort didn't stop him. He forced me to look at him again. "Do you really think your friend would want you to die just because he did?"

I grit my teeth, letting the hurt I'd carried since seeing Nash again spill out. "He called me greedy. I don't think he'd care at all."

"When?" Samael asked. His thick brows rose, and he scrunched his nose in a curiously human expression. "I don't recall him ever doing that. In fact, I remember him asking you what's not to love about you. Nash Wickham cared about you, and you shouldn't forget that just because he's gone."

Nash Wickham had become my best friend. It hurt too much. Now that he was dead, to think he'd cared about me as much as I had him. That I'd lost him before I could let him know he meant everything to me. That he helped me feel human and stopped me from feeling alone. He'd been one of the first, and few, people who had ever accepted unconditionally. Now the only way I'd see him, or be able to tell him everything, was in these dreams. I could have him, and everyone else I'd ever cared about, back in my life. Sloth had made it all so tempting.

I sucked in a sharp breath. "He told me in—"

"In a dream?" Samael cut me off. He waved his hand, scoffing and dismissive. "That's the thing, Octavia. These experiences Sloth gives you, they're not real. They're not the truth. You call me manipulative, but Sloth is playing with your psyche and emotions. Sloth is weaving you into a web of despair, with just enough hope injected so that you stay. That was not your friend calling you greedy. That was yourself. Your mind designs these beings, prompted by Sloth. He did not think of you as greedy. You believe you are."

My mouth had turned dry. My lips curled with a frown. I twisted my fingers together, fretting, and Samael reached for my hand. He stilled the movement, stroking his fingers over the back of my knuckles.

"You don't know that," I said. "You're not all-knowing and all-powerful, Samael."

He shook his head and squeezed my fingers, none too gently. "The immortal souls call her a vampire," Samael explained. "After your human stories of folk with pale skin and pointed teeth who drain their victims dry of everything they have — but Sloth isn't coming for your blood, Octavia. She's feeding like a glutton on your vulnerability."

"I…" Pulling from his grip, I wrapped my arms around my waist and squeezed tight. A futile attempt to keep myself whole. I didn't know what to tell him. I didn't want to disappoint Samael, but I didn't want to leave my loved ones behind either. Sloth had promised I'd see them. That I could be happy with them.

My breathing turned shallow with distress, and I glanced at the devil from the corner of my eye. He didn't look unsympathetic. His long fingers thread together, and he shifted, crossing one knee over the other.

"It's a difficult decision," Samael nodded. He leaned back and shifted closer to me. "It's not designed to be easy."

"Why not?" I huffed.

This time, Samael tipped his head back and laughed. The rough, growling sound of it was familiar and warmed my heart. "How else would you grow, Octavia? If not through difficult situations. Simple tasks are for the weak."

"I'm sick of growing," I told him, stubbornly. "I'm sick of being strong, and tired of becoming a better person."

The devil nodded. "You're allowed to be tired. Nobody blames you for that."

"What do I do, Samael?" I asked him, shifting on the couch to face him properly. "If I wake up... I'm going to miss him so much. I'm so done with everyone dying. So many people who were better than me and look where it got them. Each one of them has stolen something from me. I'll never get it back. I'll never be whole again."

Samael pressed his hand to his stubble-shadowed chin. He tapped a single finger against his full lips and asked, "How do you judge who's better than you, Octavia?"

"Isn't it obvious?" I asked sarcastically, and then instantly wished I could take it back.

Samael had seen me at my worst. But I still didn't want to look like an idiot in front of him. A growl rolled from the back of his throat, a gentle admonishment, and he gestured for me to continue.

I hurried to explain, "People like Nash and Phee... They're light and laughter and they were everything. The world loses something big when they die. People cry and mourn them. I cry over their deaths. They made an impact."

"And what about you?" he prompted.

I couldn't look at him again. I stared down at my bitten nails. "When I die, nobody will cry."

Samael scoffed. "Now who's lying?"

Raking my hands through my hair, I twisted strands around my fingers and pulled until I felt pinpricks of pain. It should have grounded me, but it didn't help with a thing. "I don't know what to do, Samael."

"I know you don't," he said. He didn't reach for me again, didn't offer a touch of comfort. "Else, you would have made your choice in the last dream, instead of coming here to me."

"Why doesn't Sloth order me to stay?" I asked, thinking of the thousand times Pride had wielded that rule of the trials to his advantage. "Surely, she could do that."

"She could. Any of the sins could order you to forfeit if they wanted," he conceded after a small pause. "But where's the fun in that? They want you to lose of your own volition."

He may as well have slapped me. My jaw dropped and I stared at him with wide-eyed shock. "Fun?!"

The idea of the sins seeing our suffering as a means of amusement angered me. It was chilling to think they could consider this fun. That the complete and utter soul-destroying conflict that warred through me might entertain to Sloth. Her childish laugh echoed in my ears.

Samael's face crumpled into a frown. He studied me closely, as if my reaction had surprised him. As if he wished he could delve back inside my mind and sift through my thoughts for the answers he wanted. He raised his hands, placatingly, and explained, "The thing with power and immortality, Octavia, is that it loses its shine very quickly. If she forced everyone to stay, she'd be bored. Sloth would rather sway you with her creations, and create pure temptation that you cannot resist. That is power. Much the same way that Wrath made you kill even after you had already won her trial. It proved she held all the power."

"I don't know what to do," I repeated. Standing, I wrung my hands together and paced away from him. The hellhound regarded me with narrowed, yellow eyes, so I gave it a wide berth. When I twisted back to Samael, who had also risen. I pleaded from the depths of my chest. "Tell me what to do."

He shook his head, looking pained. Closing the space between us, Samael drew me into another bone-crushing hug. His strong arms caged around me, his lips pressed to the top of my head. "It has to be your choice, Octavia. That's how this trial works. I cannot decide for you."

"What do you want me to do?" I asked, the words mumbled into his chest. It felt like I was at an impossible crossroads. I didn't want to let go of my people, my loved ones, my best friends.

"You already know what I want, Octavia," Samael released me. He took a step back and dropped to his knees. He tipped his head back to look at me, soft, black curls falling away from his face. The light made his polished horns shine, and the serious edge to his expression made my heart skip a beat.

He looked like he was about to beg for my forgiveness, but that was a fool's thought. The devil wouldn't beg for a thing. He wet his lips, and my eyes followed the path of his flickering tongue. I waited with growing anticipation to see what he would do next.

"I would not be here, kneeling before you, if I didn't want you to persevere. These dreams are *nice*," — he said 'nice,' like it was a dirty word — "and you might see me here from time to time, but it would not be the same. I want to see you in the flesh, Octavia. I want to know how you really feel in my arms, to inspect every one of your beautiful scars for myself. I want to know exactly how you fit against my chest, perfectly, despite the ragged edges you claim to possess. I want you to find me in this solarium and bring me to my knees again."

For a second, I might have stopped breathing, staring down at the devil.

"You do?" I whispered, my voice wavering. "But..."

"No buts and no questions," he reprimanded. Samael stood so quickly that I thought I might have imagined him on his knees before me. He trailed his fingers down the side of my neck, drawing a shiver from my body. "I want what's mine."

"I'm not yours," I told him, my spine stiffening despite his tender touches. "I don't belong to anyone!"

"I'm the devil, darling." Samael's smirk was positively lethal, and my knees felt weak. "Everyone's soul belongs to me in the end."

"What if I wanted to stay here?" I asked him, suddenly worried about his answer, when he claimed to want me. It felt like I was testing him just to ask. The devil's face clouded with anger, his jaw sharpening with tension. "I could decide to stay here."

"Then I won't stop you," Samael said.

It hurt to hear him say it. I flinched back. I'd expected he would have claimed to fight for me. Even though some small part of me knew that was what he was already doing. It was the entire reason he was here. Fighting for me to continue. Implying that he might heal the holes in my heart.

Samael's nostrils flared, belying his turn in mood despite the way he smoothed out his features into a passive expression. "But I also won't continue to manipulate the dreams Sloth creates for you any longer. I'll become another softly blurred face on the edge of your imagination. You might choose to stay here, but I will not stay with you. You can have me in reality, Octavia, or not at all."

"It's going to hurt," I said, bowing my head. "To wake up, I mean, and keep going."

"Are you afraid of a little pain?"

"Yes!" I exclaimed, with my entire chest. Turning from cold and sad, to hot and furious in the blink of an eye, again. "I am, actually. It's never just a little bit of pain. It's my skin knitting back together or splicing open and bleeding everywhere. It's fractured bones and flames blistering my skin. It's losing people who mean the most, and then never wanting to get close to another person again. Those things aren't a small painful moment in time, Samael. They're cracks in my heart. In my soul. They alter who I am as an entire person."

"Your soul will be just fine," Samael said, soft and soothing. "I promise you."

I glared at him. "I'm tired."

"So, you've said." Samael glanced over my shoulder. His throat bobbed and then he looked down at me. He reached for my cheek but stopped himself short of touching me. His arms fell back to his side and the space left between us felt cold. That almost hurt more than his words. "You need to make a decision, Octavia."

"He's right," said a soft, childish voice from behind me.

392

"You're out of time now. You must make a choice to stay with me."

I startled, watching as the child-like angel skipped into the room. Her movements were light, and a soft smattering of snow followed her every step. Ice crusted over her skin, as it had been before, even without her frozen terrain. Sloth advanced on us quickly, smiling widely in a flash of pointed teeth.

Samael swept into a low, respectful bow. "Lady Sloth."

It surprised me, his smooth deference to a sin. Before I remembered, we were on her land and in her dreamscape. There would be a thousand unspoken political rules between them. It was confirmed when Sloth only dropped her chin in a nod, instead of bowing back to him.

"Lucie…" She giggled brightly. "Fancy seeing you here. None of the others like to visit. I even pulled Envy's likeness to one of her dreams, and you know, he refused to play with me."

"Well," Samael said wryly. "We all know Envy doesn't play well with others. He breaks the toys."

Sloth nodded. She picked a snowflake from her hair and flicked it to one side. Looking past me as if I didn't exist. She appeared more taken with the presence of the devil than with the idea of claiming me in forfeit.

"Are you finished trying to sway her away from me, Lucie?" Sloth asked, flashing her fangs at him.

"What happens if I don't make a decision?" I asked, suddenly. Cutting through their conversation. Looking between the two of them, Sloth felt like the opposite of Samael. With her icy blue hair and softly rounded features, compared to his sharp jaw and dark demeanour.

"If you don't choose?" Sloth clarified.

"I could refuse to choose," I said. "Then which one of you will take me?"

"I will," Samael confirmed. "But not in the way you're thinking. I won't force you to wake. You'll stay here a while

393

longer, within the dreamscape but without dreaming, and then you'll die, Octavia."

"I'm not scared of death," I told him, lifting my chin. "Not anymore."

His eyes narrowed on me. His lips thinned. I had the distinct feeling that he was unhappy with me, but I tried not to let it sway me. "You're not going to fight, Octavia? That's one of the things I liked best about you."

"Who am I fighting for?" I asked, challenging him.

His upper lip curled in a snarl, a growl vibrating in his chest. His white wings rustled. "For me? For Maksymilian? For everyone who died before you? Take your pick." He grew louder with each claim. His expression darkened, before he shouted at me, "For fuck's sake, Octavia, fight for yourself!"

It set my teeth on edge, to have the devil shout at me. To have him look at me with eyes full of disappointment. I wanted to scream back. I wanted to rage at him. Ignoring Sloth, I advanced on him, my hands fisted by my sides.

"I am fighting! I have fought!" I yelled, matching his volume, spitting the words at him with everything I had. "Fuck you, Samael. You said this wasn't easy. Don't pretend like I haven't tried!"

"You're right," Samael scoffed. "You're not afraid of death. You're afraid of living."

He had the audacity to roll those luminous eyes at me. I seethed, my heartbeat pounding in my head. My hands trembling with a rage so great I could taste it. I closed the distance between us, drew back my palm, and swung with every bit of might I could muster.

Samael caught my wrist before it could land. His cold fingers pinched against my skin. He held me tight, my open palm hovering an inch from his face. The devil's eyes flashed, his fangs bared in a hiss. "Uh-uh. You want to slap me, Octavia? Then come to Eternis and do it properly."

I stared at him, my chest heaving with ragged breaths. He didn't let go of my wrist, even when I pulled back. "It's going to hurt," I said.

He frowned. "You already said that."

Baring my teeth at him, I scoffed, "I meant when I show up on your doorstep and break your nose."

A slow smile curled at the edge of his lips. It brightened in his gaze. It was enough to ease my fury.

"Good girl," Samael purred, and my entire body flushed at his praise. He tipped his chin, staring down at me with fierce intensity. "Now, put your money where your mouth is."

He let me go. I staggered back and nodded.

The weight on my shoulders, increased by my worry, had eased now that I'd decided. I turned to face Sloth. Her lower lip dropped and quivered. Her blue eyes filled with glistening tears. It didn't sway me to see her upset. I kept my distance, and lifted my chin, drawing on the confidence that had come with Samael's praises.

"I choose life," I told the sin. "Let me wake up, now."

Glumly, Sloth waved a hand. Her entire face screwed up in childish, petulant disappointment. Snow sprinkled around the three of us, her miasma pouring into the room through the open balcony. It swirled around my feet.

"Enjoy your life, Octavia Nox."

Before I could say another word, Samael, and Sloth disappeared.

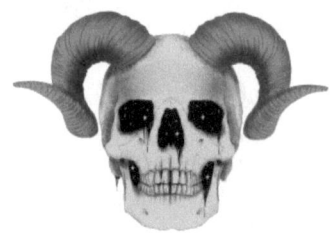

Chapter Twenty-Nine

Inhaling sparked a painful pressure in my chest as if my heart were seizing. I bolted upright, moving so quickly that my head smashed into someone else's hard skull. Pain lanced through my face. I sagged back onto the ground, letting the world tip around me. My entire chest ached, and now my forehead felt like it was splitting in half. It felt difficult to breathe.

'Sloth won't take you back, Octavia. You're awake,' Samael murmured in my ear. *'Take a moment to relax.'*

I struggled to breathe evenly, realising that I was still lying next to a dead body. The corpse of my friend. Suddenly, I was so aware of Nash's still and frozen form beside me. When I turned my head, just slightly, I could a dusting of snow covering him. Left undisturbed, while Max had been dealing with me.

"Devils…" Max groaned, holding his head with his palm. When it dropped away, there was a small lump forming on his forehead. His expression pinched with worry and pain, his gaze warming as he looked me over. Quickly assessing whether I was in one piece.

Gritting my teeth against the pain in my torso, I slowly sat up again. My ribs splintered with pain, and I held my side, sucking in a shocked breath.

Max smacked me on the hard arm with the back of his hand. "Never do that, again. Damn, you have a thick skull."

"Do what?" I asked, running my hands down my arms. I felt groggy as if I'd woken from the deepest sleep of my life too early. My brain hadn't caught back up to the here and now.

"Stop breathing for a start," he hissed. His entire face tightened with wild anger. He scrubbed his hands across his eyes, and when they fell away, he looked haunted. "Your heart stopped beating, Octavia. I did heart thrusts until my arms went numb. I wasn't sure how much longer I could go on."

"Heart thrusts?" I asked, blinking.

It felt like his words were turning into sludge in my brain. I couldn't keep up with what he was saying. Although Samael had told me that Max was keeping me alive, I hadn't really believed it. Or understood it.

"It's where you push on someone's heart to keep it beating," Max explained. His hands were trembling. His pupils had blown side, and he was breathing too fast. Noticing my attention, Max tucked his shaking limbs between his thighs as he spoke, keeping the tremor from my view. "It keeps your blood moving around. Keeps you alive."

"You can do that?" I asked, feeling as stupid as I sounded. Obviously, he could. He just had. Swallowing, I corrected myself, "I mean... You did that for me?"

"The surprise in your voice is actually very offensive," Max said. He glared out into the falling snow. "I'm not a bad person, Octavia. I'm not going to just let you die out here without trying to help you."

For the first time, without the risk of catching his gaze, I studied him properly. He'd never been particularly tanned or golden-skinned, but he looked paler than usual. The colour that had leeched from his face made his freckles stand out even more. There were heavy, dark circles beneath his eyes and his lips tinged blue. He was a wreck, and I had a feeling that it was mostly my fault.

"Are you okay, Max?" I asked, almost afraid to hear his answer.

"Devils, no." He was nothing, if not always honest. "I felt your ribs crack under my hands. That's the first time I've ever had to do something like that to someone before. I'd seen it but… I didn't even know if I was doing it right."

Max paused, tipping his head back. His throat bobbed as he swallowed roughly. He reached for the coin around his neck, swinging it back and forth. "So, tell you what, if you decide to try to die on me again, I'm not getting you back. I'm following you to wherever's next to kick your ass." He turned back to me, glaring fiercely. "Got it, Octavia?"

Emotion choked me up, and I nodded. "Understood."

Max nodded along with me. He patted his pockets, fiddled with the coin around his neck and stood. His body loomed over me, one strong hand held out in offering. "Get up," he said. "It's time to see Sloth."

Glancing away from his offered hand, I looked at Nash again. Reluctant as ever to leave him behind. He was truly gone. His body was still, cold and lost to the next world. I'd never see him again, never speak to him again. Maybe not even in the rest of my dreams. I'd never get to say I was sorry for worrying him, or to say goodbye. I'd never get to do anything except try to make him proud.

Just in case, somehow, he was watching on from the next world.

"Octavia." Max closed his eyes, his lips moving softly as if he were counting to three. "We need to go."

"Let's at least move him out of the walkway," I begged. I took Max's hand, pulling myself up and ending flush against his chest. Excruciating pain jolted through my ribs and pulled a sharp cry from my throat. "He deserves to be out of the snow."

"I don't think we have time," Max said. "You don't understand how long you've been out."

"I'm not leaving before I do this," I said, stubborn as ever. "It's important, Max. You didn't know him, but I did. Nash Wickham was one of the brightest souls in Kaida. He doesn't deserve to be left where people can trample on his body. He deserves some peace."

A groan of pain slipped past my grit teeth as I leaned over to reach for Nash's legs. His body was stiff, unmoving, and too heavy for me to lift for long. Not without wishing I'd pass out to escape the splintering pain in my chest.

"Octavia…" Max said, again.

Glaring at him, I grit my teeth. "I'd do it for you, too."

His blue eyes flashed, a muscle in his jaw beginning to thrum. Max grunted behind me. His aggravated huffing increased as he watched me struggle, increasing whines of pain slipping from my lips. Everything hurt, but I was determined to do it.

"Fine!" Max cried, throwing his hands up. "For devil's sake, put him down and don't hurt yourself, Octavia. I can't afford to carry you the rest of the way. Not again."

My cheeks, neck, and chest flushed hot as I remembered he'd carried me for a good part of this journey. It felt like he'd been keeping me safe for a lot longer than I'd realised. Bundling me out of his way and despite his fatigue, Max lifted Nash's body from the ground. His muscles strained as he hauled Nash's body to one side of the courtyard, setting him down beneath the trees.

The same trees from my dream were filled with crisp red leaves that dislodged and drifted into the snow.

I stared in horror at the bed of snow my friend landed in. His body was too stiff to land comfortably. I flinched at the sound it made on impact.

Max had the decency to look guilty. He stooped and tried to arrange Nash's body in a way that looked peaceful. I shuffled over and crouched by my friend's head, gently reaching to brush locks of blonde hair off his cold face. Out of his eyes, because in even death, I was sure he would hate to have it in the way.

"I'm sorry, Nash," I said, my throat tight with discomfort. "That I never told you how much you meant to me. How much your friendship kept me going? I'm sorry I wasn't there to help. That I couldn't stop death from coming for you. I would have stood between you and the rest of the world, if I could have…"

It was a bold thought, because I never could have stood between Nash and the slow cough. The infection he'd likely had before we'd even known one another, infected by his lover, and always doomed to die at an unhurried pace.

He had been doomed from the very start, and for that reason alone, I was immensely grateful for the time I'd been given to get to know him. For the beauty of his friendship.

Max's hand landed on my shoulder, and he squeezed. I was startled.

When I turned away from the body, his expression was grim.

"Octavia, it's time," he said. There was a weary edge to his tone, a regret and swallowing thickly, I nodded in agreement. He was right in everything that he didn't say aloud. It was time to go. I had to pick up my feet and leave Nash Wickham behind. Once and for all.

It was the hardest thing I'd ever done.

Harder than standing before any of the seven deadly sins.

We crossed a second bridge of ice. It was dangerously slippery, and Max and I clung to one another to keep our balance. My boots slipped and slid, finding no grip on the unforgiving landscape. It was only his strength that kept me upright. Each twist and lurch sent pain through my ribs, a never-ending torture that reminded me I was alive. In pain, but breathing, in pain, but blessed with a beating heart.

That I was lucky to be alive.

I had not been killed by Gluttony, Envy, Wrath, or Pride. Not even now by Sloth. I'd avoided the slow death she'd offered me, too. There was no choice now, except to keep going, to forge ahead in memory of everyone I'd left behind. I had faced five sins, and there were only two more left to go.

I didn't share my thoughts, my worries, with Max — but he still glanced at me, again and again, as if he knew I was fighting a battle he couldn't see. Concern pulled at his thick red brows and pinched at the corner of his lips.

"Stop looking at me like that," I said when he glanced back again.

"Like what?" Max asked.

"Like I'm about to drop dead," I answered, clutching my side. "I'm alive. I'm right here."

"I don't trust that you aren't just going to die on me," he admitted. "So, get off my case. After breaking all your ribs, I've earned the right to check on you as much as I want."

"Fine," I snapped.

"Fine," He mocked me, but he was smiling.

We walked through the quiet city in silence after that.

"We're almost there," Max rasped. He held out a hand for me, not to lead me ahead, but to allow me to walk with him. "Devils, I hope Sloth has some heating in there. I've never been this cold in my life."

I doubted it. Much like everything else in her icy realm, Sloth's home was an ice palace. A large building of ice bricks and frosted panes of glass. Her miasma drifted in soft tendrils across the front steps. It made my stomach turn to look at it. Reminded of how it had claimed me before, pulling me from one dream to another.

Turning over my hand, I checked the tattoos on my wrist three times to make sure I wasn't still dreaming. That I wasn't amid the dreamscapes, with no real way of getting free. Some part of me wouldn't have been surprised to find out that the sin had trapped me after all.

'You're awake,' Samael reassured me, not unsympathetically.

Max had no preoccupations about the fog. He kicked through it as if nothing stood in his way. He didn't hold the same fears that I did. I watched as he marched up the steps to Sloth's residence like he owned it. His warm grip on my hand pulled me after him. Clutching me tightly to ensure I didn't fall behind. I couldn't help but laugh for the first time since I'd woken.

"What do you think Sloth will be like, then?" Max asked, clearing his throat. "This is my first angel. You need to prepare me, you know. Since you're the one with all the experience."

I licked it at my wind-chapped lips and wondered if Sloth could be exactly as she had been in my dreams. Tiny, fragile and childlike, but as draining as Samael had said, too. Or would she be bigger in real life, large beyond the dreams she had been captured in before? The wind howled through the halls of the ice palace, the intensity of its bite making my eyes water.

"She's going to be…" I couldn't quite put it into words. It was difficult to describe the way Sloth had made me feel in those dreams. Or the overwhelming intensity of the sins who had come before. The way they'd made my knees tremble and my courage falter. They were beyond anything else I'd ever encountered. Truly otherworldly. "Completely unforgettable."

"Unforgettable, huh?" Max asked, laughing without a care in the world. As if he didn't believe she was actually a threat. "That's big praise."

"I don't mean it as praise," I admitted wryly. "More like she's going to scar you forever."

His brown eyes widened, a grin quirking across his lips. "That's even better."

We pushed through an open door, and the depths of the palace were as quiet as the rest of the Slothlands had been. A draught carried a chill past us, and I shivered. Thankfully, the icy walls had blocked most of the cutting wind.

Max tugged me closer to him, wrapping one of his arms around my shoulders. I leaned into his body, but there was no heat to draw from him. He felt as cold as I did. He squeezed my hand gently to capture my attention, and I blinked at him. The dazed feeling of apprehension in my gut was rapidly growing.

"Which way do we go?" he asked.

Shrugging, I wasn't sure how he thought I'd know. A moment later, I realised he didn't think I knew the answer. He was gently prodding me to take the lead. This wasn't Max's challenge; it wasn't his trial to face and he wasn't here to stand before Sloth. I'd have to go ahead of him and face her first.

We staggered down one or two wrong turns before I found the right way. The fog inside the house seemed to thicken as we drew closer, the biggest hint that the sin wouldn't be far away.

We wound through the halls, but the closer we came to the main chambers, the more my heart rate sped up. A thunderous beat that I was surprised Max couldn't hear. My palms pressed against a large set of doors with frosted panels. I pushed them open, wincing with pain as I stumbled into Sloth's den.

The large room was mostly empty, with wide open space and a thick, rolling white fog.

There was a bed made of ice and atop it lay an angel. Unmoving, except for the slow rise and fall of her chest. She was a child in the waking world, just as she had been in my dreams. Sloth's soft, round face was peaceful in her slumber. Her lips parted as she breathed through her mouth and her snowflake-flecked lashes pressed against her cheeks, the skin beneath them almost blue from the cold.

Sloth looked the most vulnerable I'd ever seen one of the seven deadly sins; her grey wings were even pinned beneath her back. The blade at my thigh felt like it weighed me down, heavy and tempting. Daringly I wondered if I couldn't just kill her while she slept. Curious whether it would free the sleeping humans from one of their oppressors. I doubted she would be any the wiser.

Max had been circling the room, but now he moved to stand by my side. His nose scrunched as he stared down at the angel, clearly unimpressed by what he saw. There was tension in his arms, as if he were waiting for her to snap into sudden awareness and attack us.

A half-delirious laugh rolled from my lips, and I tapped the handle of my knife. Still considering the dangerous move. "She's sleeping pretty heavily."

"That's fitting," Max said. He leaned into me, and I felt the shiver that ran through his body. "What are you supposed to do? Wake her up?"

"Or…" I couldn't bring myself to actually say the words. To tell him I was thinking of killing the angel. The last time I'd tried swinging the blade at Pride, I'd failed. Expressing the idea aloud felt like setting myself up to fail again.

"Or what?" Max pressed.

"Nothing," I said. My scalp prickled, and I suddenly considered that the angel could be pretending to sleep. That we had walked into a very effective trap. Tentatively, I reached as if to drag my fingers down the side of her ice-scabbed face.

"I wouldn't do that if I were you," someone called from across the room. "She bites, even in her sleep."

"Shit!" The familiar voice startled me. Twisting, I caught sight of the speaker instantly. They lounged on the far side of the room, leaning against one of the icy pylons as if they'd materialised from the miasma itself. "Cyn?"

Sharp teeth flashed in a wild smile. "Did you miss me?"

They pushed off the wall and loped towards us. Moving with unhurried steps and only a passing glance at the sleeping angel. Cyn reached for me, brushing flakes of snow off my shoulders, and ignored Maksymilian entirely.

"I thought you weren't coming into the Slothlands?" I asked. "I'm surprised to see you."

"Some evils must be faced," they said dryly, glancing towards the child-like angel. Cyn's entire face turned tight for a moment, blatant displeasure. "Samael has given me his express word that Sloth won't claim me while I do the work of the trials. But I'm not staying any longer than I need. You're the last of the living to come through the palace."

"Oh," I said. "And is Samael's word worth a lot to you?"

Obviously, I wasn't as subtle as I could have been because Max nudged me in the ribs. He lifted a brow when I looked in his direction. Cyn's swirling gaze raked over him. I wondered if Cyn had thought he wouldn't make it through with me. Or if I wouldn't have abandoned him along the way.

Their upper lip curled, flashing those pointed teeth. I realised how similar they were to Sloths, made for tearing into flesh. My gaze flickered between them, and Cyn let out a bitter laugh. Not for the first time, I wondered if they could read minds.

"What do I need to do to pass the trial, Cyn?" I asked, some of my tension slipping away. Cyn always provided direction and hadn't yet led me astray. I didn't know what they got out of doing Samael's dirty work in the trials, but it was none of my business. "I'm ready to finish this trial."

"Nothing," Cyn said. "You've already done everything you needed to do."

Max snorted. "What? But she's done nothing."

Cyn's forehead creased, their lips thinning, utterly unimpressed. "Just because you couldn't see her battles, boy, doesn't mean they didn't exist. Some of the hardest feats are overcome through self-reflection and self-determination."

Max's jaw tightened, and his chin dipped. He glanced at me, his brows knitting, but he said nothing.

"I don't understand," I muttered. It was a familiar claim. Some things never changed, it seemed.

"You do nothing now, because you did everything before," Cyn said, as if that solved my confusion. It didn't. "You persevered, Octavia. You kept living, to keep making active choices and experiencing life. That is how you overcome Sloth. You don't give in to the slow temptation of stasis."

"That sounds…" I drew in a breath, hating what I was about to say. There had been nothing easy about the inner turmoil I'd felt in those dreams. The soul-crushing desire to give up and stay. The way Sloth had pulled at my heartstrings and then effectively strangled me with them. "Easier than the rest of the challenges?"

Cyn shook their head. "Not everyone can do it. That's why so many of us avoid the Slothlands. Why she can't let her citizens wake too often or age too much, because then she'd run out of energy to steal. A lot of your fellow competitors relinquished to her, you know."

Glancing at Sloth, I felt slightly on edge. I was waiting for her to rise from the glass bed. She hadn't moved beyond breathing. Not even a twitch of her little finger, but I couldn't trust that she wasn't still an imminent threat.

Cyn grasped my cuffed wrist and pulled my hand free of Max's grip.

He tensed, grunting his objection, but didn't intervene.

I swallowed roughly and stared down at where they held me. "What now?"

"Now, you receive your mark, Octavia." Cyn tugged me in the direction they'd come from, and I followed quickly.

Glancing over my shoulder, I tilted my head in a sign for Max to follow us. He didn't hesitate and kept comfortingly close.

"You should be over the moon," he murmured. "You've passed."

"At what cost?" I asked. "I don't feel like I've won."

We left the angel behind. Following Cyn as they traipsed down a winding corridor. The further we descended, the warmer it became.

Max muttered under his breath.

Cyn's shoulders tensed, and they asked, "What was that?"

"Nothing," I replied, nudging him.

Cyn pushed their way through one last door, leading us into a small kitchen. Fire blazed in the hearth, the only source of warmth in the entire building. Max drifted towards it, raising his palms and huddling close. Although I wanted to follow him, the sight of the flames was too much.

He sniffled, and my entire body jerked with alarm.

"You better not be sick," I told Max, my stomach souring. I'd missed the signs that Nash had been sick. They'd been there, with some reflection. His lack of energy despite all our training. The dark circles beneath his eyes. The way he'd been winded and coughing throughout the last trial. I couldn't handle it if I was doomed to lose a second person to the same disease.

Max scoffed at me, waving off my worries. "It's just a cold. I'll be glad when we're done here. I can't wait to see the fucking sun."

"Pay attention, Octavia," Cyn snapped. For the first time since I'd met them, their apathetic exterior seemed to crack, demanding my attention. "You need to receive your mark and move on."

Frustration fizzled through me. Encouraged by the crackling flames in the hearth and the first flickers of warmth I'd felt in weeks. "What's the hurry, Cyn?"

They stared me down. "You're almost out of time to get to the Lust Trial."

"What?" Max choked on the question. "There's a deadline to

get there?"

"The island gates close in three days, boy," Cyn said. Their swirling gaze flashed with irritation. "If she's not there, she fails. Give me your wrist, Octavia."

My teeth remained grit, but the anger ebbed away. I shuffled towards Cyn and held my hand out. They took a firm grasp on my wrist, wiping over the skin with the pungent disinfecting solution. Quickly pinning my arm to the table, Cyn reached for their tools. They leaned low over my arm. There was less care and more rush than some of my other marks.

The pain was sharp but fleeting. When they leaned back, wiping a clean scrap of cloth against my skin, I flinched. The mark was tender, my skin red and angry, stained with shining blue ink.

It took the form of a tiny, slow snail.

Stealing my wrist back, I cradled it against my chest. Fighting the overwhelming emotion that crested inside of me. I hadn't noticed the snails before the dream, when Nash had mentioned them. Now they were everywhere, sliding through the snow beside his body, and crawling along the windowsills in this place. Nestled against Sloth's shoulder, the veined blue shell was a stark contrast to her pale skin.

Max came to stand behind me. He pulled me back against his chest and stared at Cyn over my shoulder. "How do we get out of here?"

Cyn dropped their pointed chin, growling in a way that reminded me they weren't human. The noise was all demon. "The door behind me. If you travel four blocks past the back of Sloth's residence, you'll come to a train station. Charon only visits that station once every ten years. Miss it and you're done. You'll be left here to freeze."

I sighed. "Okay."

Cyn checked a non-existent watch on their wrist. "Tick-tick. Better get moving."

Where I hesitated, Max wasted no time hauling me towards

the door. "Let's go. You're done here."

I staggered beside him, clenching my jaw against the constant pain in my chest. Trying to remind myself that this was the best possible outcome, that I had to have made the right choice. Samael was waiting for me in Eternis, and so I had to keep moving.

"Octavia?" Cyn called as I barrelled towards the door.

I hesitated on the threshold, glancing back at them. "Yes?"

"Be careful," Cyn said, sounding ominously dire. "Be careful of Samael."

Their warning followed me into the cold.

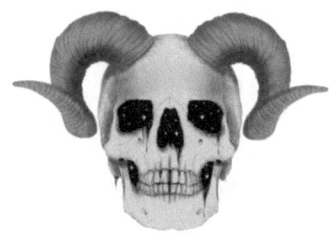

Chapter Thirty

We weren't the only ones waiting for the train. Fury ignited my veins. After running four blocks on low energy, both Max and I were out of breath. I marched across the platform, demanding the attention of…

"Finley Nightingale!"

He turned, his cheeks reddened from the slap of the wind, his curls mussed and wild. At the sight of me, his face fell. His features crumpled with a familiar devastation. The same one that echoed through the hole in my chest. That made every breath hurt, tinged with the weight of my grief.

Finley's shoulders slumped. "Octavia," he said as I approached, brushing past Kyra. "I'm sorry, Nash, he…"

My hand cracked against his cheek, as I packed every ounce of energy I had left into hitting him. His head swung to one side and my palm smarted. The ringing slap drew the attention of other competitors, but I ignored them. All of them. Instead, I advanced on Finley until there was nowhere he could go to avoid me. My pain had paled in comparison to my anger, and my hands trembled.

"You left him there!" I said words that started with quiet seething and escalated until I was screeching at him. "You left him on the ground! Forgotten! For people to walk all over him. You left him there! He deserved better than that. He deserved better than you!"

My hand reared back to slap him again or punch him. I didn't care, so long as it hurt. So long as he hurt the way I did. I felt like I was crumbling on the inside while I struggled to stay upright and moving.

Before I could swing, Max intervened. He caught my wrist and hauled me backwards, pulling me out of Finley's space and against his chest. "Easy now," he rumbled in my ear, holding me tight.

Instead of struggling against him to get free, I melted back against the security of his stock frame. Of the faint smell of chuckleweed that always lingered about him. The fight evaporated from my body and made way for nothing more than despair. I glared at Finley, tears brimming in my eyes, as I wished he'd fall apart too.

He hadn't bothered to cup his face, and his skin had turned red where I'd hit him. Instead, Finley stared back at me, looking as fractured as I felt.

"He deserved better!" I screamed at him again.

A few of the people around us shuffled away, disappearing from my peripheral vision. My chest heaved. It felt like I was curling in on myself. The fragment Nash's death had stolen from me had become a vacuum that could turn me inside out. A ragged sob rolled up in my throat. "You…"

"I know," Finley bowed his head, his voice soft, as he avoided my gaze. "I'm so sorry, Tav."

My entire body shook, trembling with a mixture of sadness

and rage. I'd felt desolation before, and bereft. I'd been haunted by deaths, but nothing hit me as hard as knowing Finley had abandoned our friend. The man had appeared to have a great relationship with him. They'd shared secrets and been close, but that hadn't seemed to matter in the end.

"You left him in the street," I sniffed, the volume of my voice rising again. "I fell over him, Finley."

His hands flapped in front of his body, as if he were looking for something to hold on to. But there was nothing to stabilise him. We were free falling through this together. "I didn't know what to do with him," Finley said, sounding distraught. "You don't understand, Octavia! He was so unwell, and then he just… He didn't even go to sleep or close his eyes. He just stopped everything."

Kyra drifted over to stand by his side, wrapping an arm around Finley's waist and squeezing gently. Her small comforts enraged me. He didn't deserve comfort, not after his choices. He deserved to feel the jagged edges of the world now that Nash wasn't in it. It felt to me like Finley had killed him. I needed someone to blame, and he was the easiest target.

"I really don't understand," I agreed. I tried to take a step closer to him, but Max held me firm. "So, please try your best to explain it to me. Because I would have done the right thing by him. I would have helped him. Right now, Finley, I want to kill you."

Finley's gaze dropped to the wicked blade strapped to the side of my leg. Even in the pale, sunless city of Desidia, it looked formidable, sucking in the surrounding light.

He paled and cleared his throat gently. His hands hovered by his mid-section, waving as he tried to explain. "He was so sick, Tav. By the village before Desidia he was coughing up giant chunks of thick, green spit, and he was barely conscious." Finley faltered for a moment, drew a ragged breath, and ploughed on. "We had to drag him into the city. I… When he died? It was a relief."

"A relief?" I repeated the word in a deadly whisper. It carried in the quiet of the station. My entire body turned hot with pure rage. In no reality was Nash dying a relief. I couldn't believe he'd said it.

"Fuck you, Finley!"

I lurched for him, moving so suddenly that I slipped free of Max's grip. I got three steps before the bearded man wrenched me around the middle and pulled me back. Max lifted me off my feet and physically hauled me away from Finley.

I screeched and kicked out. Fighting him this time.

His wiry beard tickled my skin as he grumbled in my ear, "Octavia, calm down."

"Calm down!?" I seethed, twisting in his grip and trying to knee him in the balls instead. It didn't matter who I hurt, now. He shifted, just out of the way, and I snarled, "I'll show you calm!"

"Hey! Hey!" Max grabbed both my wrists in his hands. He held me away from him, just far enough that I couldn't try another low blow unless I really kicked out. I struggled in his hold, but he stroked his thumbs against my skin slowly, soothingly. I flinched when his touch brushed over the new mark. I hated the feeling and relaxed into it all at once.

Max stared earnestly into my face. "It's not me you're mad at. Or that guy over there. Fighting everyone won't help you right now. Your friend is gone. You can't destroy yourself over that."

My knees wobbled and gave way. The air and anger rushed from my lungs as I realised he was right. Only his tight hold kept me upright. Tears dripped down my cheeks, and I fought to contain a rising sob. I wouldn't cry, not here, in front of everyone else.

Drawing a deep, ragged breath, I stopped struggling. Glancing over my shoulder at the bowed head of the curly-haired man, I called for him, "Hey Finley?"

His head lifted, a soft glimmer of hope shining in his dark

eyes. He took a tentative step forward. "Yeah, Tav?"

"Don't you ever speak to me again," I spat. "You're dead to me."

Finley's entire face fell, shuttering with emotion. Kyra glared at me accusingly, wrapping her arms around his shoulders and squeezing tight.

"He did his best," she hissed, but I ignored her. "Which is more than can be said for you. You abandoned Nash in Glorae."

The words were like a punch to the gut. I hadn't abandoned him, but nobody knew that. I glared at Kyra, wishing I could incinerate her with my mind. She would be on Finley's side. Always simpering for a second of his attention. She was a sucker for Finley Nightingale's smiles, and that made her untrustworthy too.

Max dragged me to the other side of the platform. He didn't say another word about my angry outburst and instead found his lighter, turning it in his hand. Repeatedly. The movement irritated me, but I couldn't bring myself to snap at him about it. He was right. I wasn't mad at him.

I was mad at everything.

The train arrived with a shrill whistle. It pierced through the air and disturbed the silence of the city. A grinding sound emanated from the tracks as the beast of a train screeched to a halt before us. Max had paled as he watched it approach. Steam billowed into the air.

The doors opened and a man slid out.

It amazed me that Charon was still so familiar, even though I'd only met him once or twice. His brown skin was supple and glistening, even in the dull morning light. My heart raced, as it had before, at the sight of the thick diamond glittering in his ear. His soft eyes rimmed with a thick, dark liner. Charon inspected us, a sorry lot of cold humans, before he bowed his head and gestured towards the train.

People rushed towards him from every direction, hurrying

for the safety of what they found familiar. We were a ragtag group, there looked to only be ten of us left now, and I couldn't help but wonder how many had opted to stay within their dreams. Tempted by the ease of existence that Sloth had presented. We all looked tired, and I couldn't help but wonder if it had been a hard decision for everyone else, too.

Max held me back until Finley and Kyra had disappeared into the train carriage. We approached the man slowly, and I found that this time I had more confidence. I looked him in the eye as I stood before him. Despite the sharp and shattered edges of my soul, I had more confidence these days. I would fake it until I made it.

"Charon," I greeted him, dipping my chin slightly.

His full lips twitched. "Hello."

"I don't have your fee," I told him, remembering that Ophelia had paid for one trip, and Nash the next. I'd never funded a ride on the train myself. I had the coins, somewhere, buried in my pockets, or in Max's coat - but I wanted to challenge the idea of paying for it.

"This ride is free," Charon said smoothly. He lifted his chin and stared past us into the foggy city, a shudder running through his body. "But don't get used to it. It's a one-time offer and only because I wouldn't want to see anyone stranded with this vampire. The sooner we leave the Slothlands, the better, and the exchange of coin will only slow us down."

"Oh." I blinked, recalling how Samael had said his demons called her a vampire. Narrowing my eyes at Charon, I wondered if he were a demon too, and I'd just never realised. There were no real hints, and I'd never know. It felt too personal to ask him, though, so resigned myself to accepting the mystery. I nodded, "Well, thanks I guess."

"Take this with you and find a comfy seat." Charon reached forward and tucked something into the depths of my pocket.

I tried not to flinch away from him, his breath cool against my skin. Max had turned still behind me, glaring at him over my shoulder.

Charon straightened as if he were suddenly bored with the both of us. He waved a hand flippantly towards the carriages. "I'll deliver the lot of you to the coast, and you can catch the ferry from there."

Stepping onto the train, I turned towards the closest door. When I opened it, I could see Nash and Kyra sharing a chair within the small confines of the carriage. My spine stiffened and I let go of the door handle. It banged as it closed, and I abruptly turned and headed towards the front of the train instead.

I couldn't handle an entire ride sitting that close to Finley. Not when I still wanted to hurt him.

Max and I found a carriage to ourselves. My entire body ached with bone-deep fatigue as I dropped into the seat stretching out to lie on my back.

I'd expected Max to take his own seat, given that there was so much room for just the two of us, but he lifted my legs and tucked himself to sit beneath them. Resting my calves against his lap, he placed his hand on my thigh. I swallowed roughly, staring at the ceiling, and decided not to comment on it.

The train shifted beneath us. A lurching movement, accompanied by another shrill whistle. Max reached out with his free hand, grasping the bars on the back of the seat in front of us. His knuckles turned white as he held on for dear life.

"I take it you've never been on a train before?" I asked, fighting a yawn.

Max snorted. His expression had tightened. When the train lurched again, he flinched. "Have you?"

"Course I have," I said, laughing roughly. Even though there was nothing funny about the conversation. "How do you think we get halfway across the world for each trial?"

If looks could kill, Max would have murdered me right then and there. "The rebellion wasn't exactly zipping around on the train network, no. You didn't notice we were all dead broke? Or that the warden to this thing is in the devil's pocket?"

To take his mind off it as the train gained speed, I sat up. I was practically in his lap, so I reached for the leather band around his neck. Sliding my fingers beneath the strap and against his warm, freckled skin. Max went still. I fidgeted with the token around his neck. "You've got this coin to spend."

He captured my hand, easing it away from his throat. His throat bobbed. "This coin isn't for spending."

A wry smile twisted onto my lips. He'd told me what that coin meant, but I wondered if it wasn't like his lighter, one of the precious mementos that soothed his anxieties so that he could keep himself from falling apart. It occurred to me I needed something like that so that I'd stop breaking down in front of witnesses. Once upon a time, I'd fidgeted with dice for the same reason, but they were long lost now.

"What about the three coins in your back pocket, the one in your chuckleweed bag and the coins you stitched into the collar of your jacket?" I asked.

Max flinched, his hand raised to the hidden coins. He gave me a narrow-eyed stare. "How did you know about those?"

"You're not the only one who coins them away," I said, shrugging. It was both an honest answer and not quite telling the entire truth. I'd kept coins in my boots for as long as I could remember, hidden away. I knew his were tucked into his collar because I'd felt them one of the times I'd tried to wake him. I'd debated if he'd notice if I cut them free.

He probably would've.

The train picked up speed, and we shot out of the city. The buildings of Desidia blurred around us and then opened into the snow-covered countryside. Max went back to holding onto the seat for dear life. His eyes squeezed closed tight.

"Devils," he wheezed. "I don't like this."

"It feels weird, huh." Surprisingly, I didn't mind the way the train raced across the earth, feeling faster than flight via an angel. The movement of it left my bones feeling heavy, all I wanted to do was lie down and have a nap.

"I think I'm going to be sick," Max groaned.

I peeked at him from the corner of my eye. His face had paled, freckles stark, and if I was honest — as liked me to be — he looked a little green.

"Please don't do that," I said, leaning away from him. "I will leave you here in your own mess if you vomit on me."

"You're a cruel woman, Octavia. Have you no sympathy for me at all?" Max followed my movements, slumping towards me, his arm wrapped around my legs securely. He was too heavy for me to wriggle free, and he had me pinned.

"It'll pass," I told him, shoving at his shoulder, praying that he didn't decide to tickle me again. "We should get some sleep."

"Thought you'd never want to sleep again." Max sounded surprised. He blinked at me, releasing the seat to scratch at his chin through his beard. "Feels like all we've done for weeks."

"It crossed my mind," I admitted. He was right. The idea of sleeping after enduring all that Sloth had offered me was stomach-turning. There was no guarantee of a blissful, heavy sleep. That the sin wouldn't still send her night terrors into our slumber as we raced away from her influence. I didn't think I had much choice, though. My entire body ached with fatigue, even though I'd slept for days and gained no energy. What little I'd reserved, we'd spent running for the train station. "But I'm so tired still. Sloth took everything she could from me. I'm going to need energy for the next trial."

Max nodded. He pulled himself upright, and I followed him. Instead of leaning against the cold window as I'd intended, I ended up with my head resting on his shoulder. His body was warm, and I was drawn to the comfort of his presence. Curled against him, my eyelids drooped. I yawed, fighting the last moments before sleep.

"Octavia?" Max whispered my name.

He prodded me, and I blinked with momentary disorientation. A sharp pain seared in my head, the beginning of a headache.

"Mmhnmn," I groaned, resenting the fact that he'd woken me before I could properly fall asleep.

"What did he give you?" Max asked.

"What?"

"The train guy," Max said. He pulled at the lapel of my jacket briefly. "He put something in your pocket. What was it?"

"Oh." I lifted myself off him, and reached into my pocket, withdrawing a folded flyer. "It's just a piece of paper."

"Give it here." Max waved his hand at me.

"Why?" I asked, holding it to one side, even though it was still easily within his reach.

He narrowed his eyes but looked amused at my question. "Are you going to read it?"

Huffing, I moved it closer. "Well, there's no need to be an asshole."

"I'm not. I'm just being honest. You can't read it, so give it here." Max snatched the flyer from my hands, and blearily, I watched as he unfolded it. Carefully, he smoothed out the creases and laid it flat in his lap.

It was strange, the way I always looked at the words — as if, magically, this time I'd be able to understand it. This time, maybe I'd understand. But it was always as foreign as ever. The unfamiliar shapes made my head pound harder when I squinted at them. My brain tried and failed to work it out, leaving me on the edge of irritability.

"Well," I prompted after Max had had time to read it through. "What's it say?"

"It's an advertisement…" he said, slowly.

I waited a moment, but he didn't elaborate. "Go on."

Max smoothed his fingers over the paper and cleared his

throat. Something on that paper made his cheeks turn red, a blush that connected all his freckles. He cleared his throat a second time, his brows knitting together. His reaction had me curious, more than I'd been about anything before. I wanted to know what it said. I prodded him in the ribs, watching expectantly.

"For the *Festival of Hearts*," he announced, a grin flaring on his lips and then disappearing as his blush deepened. "An annual celebration on Cupiditas Eylandt."

"Ah," I said.

He wasn't telling me everything, but he didn't have to if there was a celebration, a task, or a competition in any of the lands. That was usually the sort of mess we had to endure, and I'd begun to assume them, anyway. I curled back against him, stealing the warmth of his body and closing my eyes. "That'll be the Lust trial, then. Prepare yourself."

"How?" Max asked.

Instead of answering, I closed my eyes and went back to sleep.

The Festival of Hearts. I didn't have a clue what to expect.

Acknowledgements

Oh man, acknowledgements time. I never know exactly what to write in this space. Here goes...

As always, thank you to my husband Rhys who supports every word and every wild plot point. He listens to every ramble, tells me to have a hot shower when I whinge about my writers block, and comes up with bizarre new plot points that would never work because he's never read the books. I appreciate it all the same. Ira and Zia for snuggles, as always, pets are more than we ever deserve.

AJ... Yes, I know the book is dedicated to you, but you also get a spot here. This book was hard. Mostly because the concept of dreamscape is something I've been toying with for 16 years, and so getting it onto paper feels so surreal. I've had so much imposter syndrome over this book, and you've patiently talked me through it every single time. You've alpha read, you've listened to me rant, you've been the best freaking friend anyone could ever ask to have. You're amazing, and I won't let you ever forget it.

Krystal... My editor, you have been absolutely invaluable and I am so, so grateful that we ended up working together. I've learned more from your patient comments about my writing style and improvements than I have in years. I cannot express how your balance of constructive feedback and support hit me. I could take a step back and really see what you meant and I think this book is so much better for it.

Taylor M… You don't know it, but you're the first person who have popped into my inbox and asked to buy a copy of one of my books from me directly. Hopefully, I'm going to sort it so you're the first person to get a copy of this book. When you emailed me, telling me you enjoyed the series, it really helped boost me through the rest of my editing! Thank you!

Heather Mitchell… Heather is, was, and always will be one of the most extraordinary women in my life. She was my godmother. She was one of the biggest supporters of every endeavour in my life. No matter how big or small. If something happened worth celebrating, I'd get a handwritten card in the mail. She supported and celebrated every win. She was, in my humble opinion, one of the kindest, best souls on the earth. Just before Christmas, Heather lost her battle with cancer. There is a hole in my heart that will never be filled now that she's gone. I didn't get to say goodbye properly. I guess, in the same way that Octavia never said goodbye to Nash. Grief is overwhelming, and it can't be avoided. This is as close to goodbye as I'll get. Thank you, Heather, for every moment, every smile, and every minute of your life that you shared with me. I will never be able to repay you for it. I hope you have peace, and that your cat, Mack, was waiting for a cuddle.

Finally, thank you to everyone taking a chance and reading this far – you guys are the real heroes in my story.

If you, not unlike Octavia or myself, have recently lost someone dear to you – I am very sorry for your loss. If you are not doing okay, please consider seeking support wherever you can. Grief demands to be felt, and there is a strength in admitting you can't do it alone.

About the Author

Stephanie Gluck writes across the traditional lands of the Dunghutti people and pays her respects to Elders past, present and emerging.

Stephanie is a neurodivergent fantasy author who likes to imagine worlds beyond her own. When not writing, she avidly feeds her coffee addiction and adds to her ever-growing collection of books.
    She is a registered nurse and lives in New South Wales, Australia with her partner Rhys, and Great Dane, Ira, and her brother's German Shepherd, Zia (who has kindly contributed three dogs worth of fur to the writing process).

You can keep up to date with what Stephanie is writing next via her website: www.stephaniegluck.com or any of her social media.

 hello@stephaniegluck.com

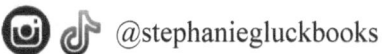 @stephaniegluckbooks